Praise for Da

THE PRISONER

"Extraordinary. . . . A brilliant, gorgeously written story of hope, betrayal and innocence lost. . . . The opening chapter of the spy novel for the twenty-first century." —*The Globe and Mail* (Toronto)

"Compelling. . . . Penetrates the camp, laying bare its daily workings. . . . A fascinating tour." —*Daily News*

"A taut thriller full of sharp observations. . . . Tensions rise to an explosive level." —*U.S. News & World Report*

"Masterful. . . . Here is the human cost of the war on terror, subtly delineated." —*The Economist*

"*Guantánamo* has a real impact. . . . Fesperman achieves a fascinating picture of a miniature security state thriving, like some anaerobic organism, in airless insulation from the inhibitions of a larger civil society." —*Los Angeles Times Book Review*

"Riveting. . . . [Set in] a pressure-cooker world. . . . One of the few novels to properly exploit the tensions inherent in the war on terror." —*The Buffalo News*

"[A] rich thriller. . . . [Fesperman] breathes real life into his fascinating characters." —*St. Louis Post-Dispatch*

"With a journalist's eye for telling detail, Fesperman captures the hothouse atmosphere of the tiny patch of land that is Gitmo. . . . The strength of *The Prisoner of Guantánamo* [is that] it seems more like fact than fiction." —*The Oregonian*

"[Fesperman] is one of the best writers of intelligent thrillers based on contemporary events working today. . . . Observant, thoughtful, witty and concerned, [Fesperman] has robustly adapted the thriller to the age of the global war on terror." —*The Baltimore Sun*

ALSO BY DAN FESPERMAN

Lie in the Dark

The Small Boat of Great Sorrows

The Warlord's Son

DAN FESPERMAN

THE PRISONER OF GUANTÁNAMO

Dan Fesperman is a reporter for *The Baltimore Sun* and worked in its Berlin bureau during the years of civil war in the former Yugoslavia, as well as in Afghanistan during the recent conflict. *Lie in the Dark* won the Crime Writers' Association of Britain's John Creasey Memorial Dagger Award for best first crime novel, and *The Small Boat of Great Sorrows* won their Ian Fleming Steel Dagger Award for best thriller.

THE PRISONER OF GUANTÁNAMO

DAN FESPERMAN

Vintage Crime/Black Lizard
Vintage Books
A Division of Random House, Inc.
New York

FIRST VINTAGE CRIME/BLACK LIZARD EDITION, JULY 2007

This is a work of fiction. Names, characters, places, and incidents either are the product of the author's imagination or are used fictitiously. Any resemblance to actual persons, living or dead, events, or locales is entirely coincidental.

The Library of Congress has cataloged the Knopf edition as follows:
Fesperman, Dan. [date]
The prisoner of Guantánamo / Dan Fesperman. — 1st ed.
p. cm.
1. Guantánamo Bay Naval Base (Cuba)—Fiction. 2. Prisoners of war—Fiction. 3. Military interrogation—Fiction. 4. Yemenites—Fiction. 5. Intelligence service—Fiction. 6. War on terrorism, 2001—Fiction. I. Title.
PS3556.E778P75 2006
813'.54—dc22
2006003197

Vintage ISBN: 978-1-4000-9614-5

Book design by Virginia Tan
Map by Mapping Specialists

www.vintagebooks.com

Printed in the United States of America
10 9 8 7

GUANTÁNAMO GLOSSARY

Biscuit	Behavioral Science Consultation Team. Doctors who offered interrogators advice on the background and psychological makeup of detainees.
Camp Delta	Main U.S. prison facility at Guantánamo Bay, with four separate camps. Camps 1–3 are maximum security, with Camp 3 being the most stringent. Camp 4, the newest wing, is medium security, offering greater privileges and barracks-style cellblocks, a status that has earned it the nickname "the Haj."
Camp Echo	A small CIA-run prison that is part of the Camp Delta complex.
Camp Iguana	A former officer's cottage on a seaside bluff that houses three juvenile detainees, located about a mile from Camp Delta.
Camp X-Ray	The abandoned cage-like facility that housed the first several hundred detainees, who arrived at Guantánamo before Camp Delta was constructed.
DI	The Directorate of Intelligence, Cuba's equivalent of the CIA.
DIA	The U.S. Defense Intelligence Agency.
DOD	The U.S. Department of Defense.
The Fenceline	The seventeen-mile boundary of the U.S. Navy Base at Guantánamo Bay, Cuba.
Ghost	A detainee, usually housed at Camp Echo, who has not been officially registered and whose identity is

	presumably unknown to the International Committee of the Red Cross.
Gitmo, the Rock, GTMO	Nicknames and the military acronym for the U.S. Navy Base at Guantánamo Bay, Cuba.
GWOT	The Pentagon's acronym for the Global War on Terrorism.
JAX	The U.S. Navy Base and Naval Air Station at Jacksonville, Florida.
J-DOG	The Joint Detention Operations Group, which provides the management and military police who run Camp Delta.
JIG	The Joint Intelligence Group, which coordinates interrogation operations at Camp Delta.
JTF-GTMO	Joint Task Force Guantánamo, the command structure for Camp Delta and all its security and interrogation operations.
MP	Military Police.
MREs	Meals Ready to Eat, the standard military food ration.
NCOIC	Noncommissioned Officer in Charge, usually used to describe an MP shift commander inside Camp Delta.
NEX	Naval Exchange store, equivalent to an Army PX.
OGA	Other Government Agency, Gitmo shorthand for the Central Intelligence Agency.
OPSEC	Operational Security.
OSD	Office of the Secretary of Defense.
RPG	Rocket-propelled grenade, a handheld anti-armor weapon.
SIB	"Manipulative self-injurious behavior," a military term for some suicide attempts by Camp Delta detainees.
The Wire	Slang for the razor-wire enclosure of Camp Delta; also the name of JTF-GTMO's weekly newspaper.

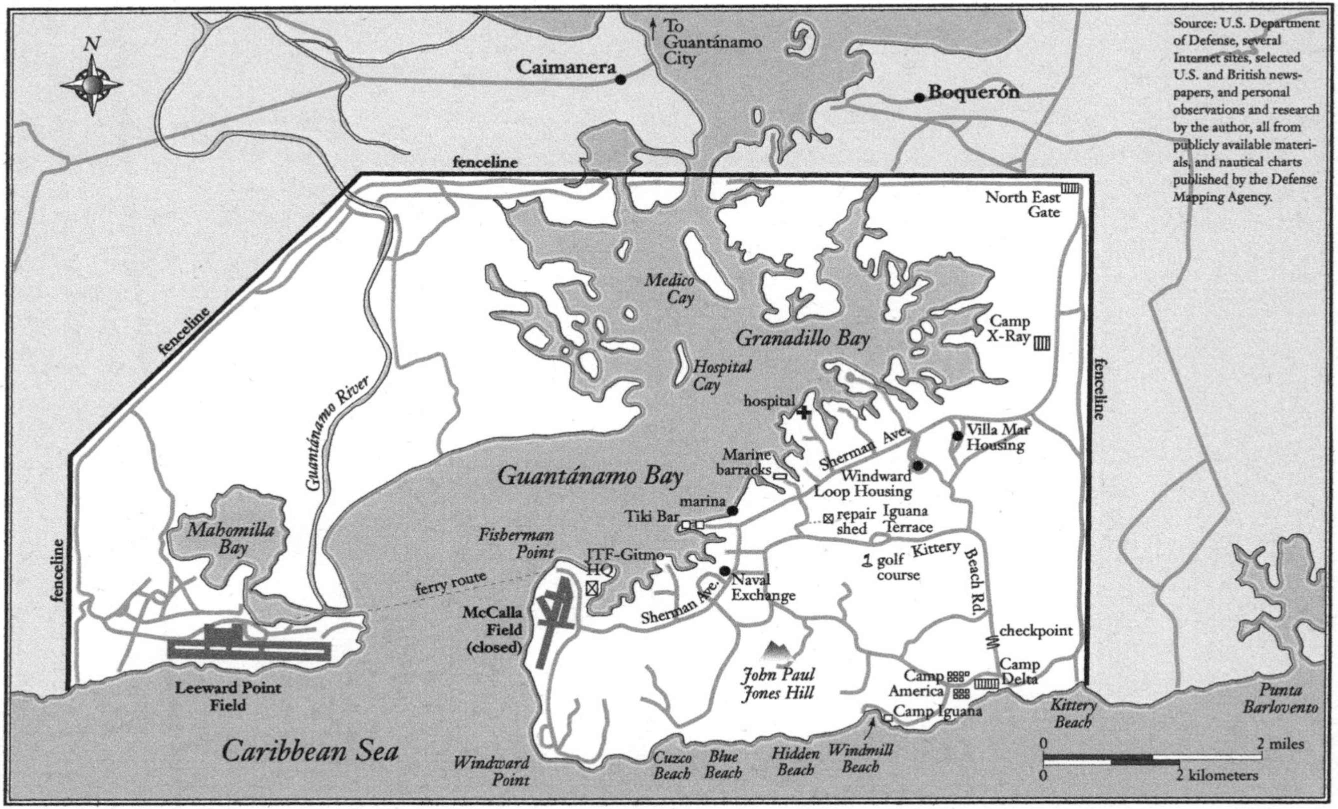
N
To Guantánamo City
Caimanera
Boquerón
Source: U.S. Department of Defense, several Internet sites, selected U.S. and British newspapers, and personal observations and research by the author, all from publicly available materials, and nautical charts published by the Defense Mapping Agency.
fenceline
fenceline
fenceline
fenceline
North East Gate
Medico Cay
Granadillo Bay
Camp X-Ray
Hospital Cay
hospital
Guantánamo River
Guantánamo Bay
Marine barracks
Sherman Ave.
Villa Mar Housing
Windward Loop Housing
marina
Tiki Bar
repair shed
Iguana Terrace
Mahomilla Bay
Fisherman Point
JTF-Gitmo HQ
Kittery Beach Rd.
golf course
ferry route
Naval Exchange
Sherman Ave.
McCalla Field (closed)
checkpoint
Camp Delta
Camp America
Camp Iguana
John Paul Jones Hill
Leeward Point Field
Kittery Beach
Punta Barlovento
Caribbean Sea
Windward Point
Cuzco Beach
Blue Beach
Hidden Beach
Windmill Beach
0
2 miles
0
2 kilometers

THE PRISONER OF GUANTÁNAMO

PROLOGUE

The American in camouflage came ashore overnight, and for hours he lay on the darkened beach as still as a spy, an infiltrator behind enemy lines.

A three-foot iguana spotted him first, nosing into soggy pockets at the water's edge just as the eastern horizon was turning pink. The soldier didn't budge.

Sunlight found him next, and as the tide receded the sand grew warm. Still he held his ground, even as a Cuban *soldado* named Vargas approached along the hillside above the dunes, boots crunching on a coral path.

For Vargas, still groggy at this hour, the morning patrol had been as uneventful as always. Downhill and to his left lay the glittering turquoise of the Caribbean, close enough that he could hear waves hissing upon the sand, although his view was blocked by an underbrush of scrub oak and spidery cactus. Uphill and to the right was his daily objective: a wooden watchtower on stilts, perched in the dawn like a heron waiting to strike. It was what passed for his office. Years ago, two soldiers would have been watching his approach—the overnight shift, awaiting relief. Now, budgets being trimmer, there was no staffing after dark, and the tower was empty and silent. It meant that Vargas's partner, Rodriguez, hadn't yet arrived with either the radio or the coffee. The radio, a gift from an aunt in Hialeah, was a massive silver box forever blaring with congas and brass. Much too loud for the breakfast hour, but Vargas endured it as long as the supply of caffeine held steady. Rodriguez always brought a full thermos of a brew that was thick, black and sweet, served by the thimbleful in sips to last out the morning.

Just beyond the tower was the sight that made this place remarkable, and that kept Vargas and his comrades in the Brigada de la Frontera employed. It was an American naval base, its eastern boundary marked by a long line of chain-link fencing. In some sections the fence was insanely high—three times the height of a basketball goal—and crowned by coils of razor wire. Its seventeen-mile perimeter enclosed the lower bowl of Guantánamo Bay.

Vargas had grown up in Havana, a world removed from this rustic outpost, and when he first arrived on the job a year ago he had been affronted by the presence of the Americans, taking it personally. Every day he heaved stones across the fence in anger, albeit while maintaining a careful distance, lest he step on a mine. Whenever he spotted a foot patrol of U.S. Marines beetling through the brush on the other side he got even angrier and shouted slogans of the Revolution, thinking that might taunt them into trying something foolish.

Rodriguez, six years his senior, never joined in. He only laughed, or told stories of the old days, when the Cubans used to train a spotlight on the nearest Marine barracks, morning, noon, and night, to disrupt the enemy's sleep.

But as months passed the routine grew boring, and Vargas's zeal cooled. He came to regard the intruders as part of the scenery, and now watched their doings as a naturalist might observe the mating habits of an exotic but invasive species. With binoculars you could peer into their small bayside village, with its stores and schools, its ball fields and drive-in movie theater, its golf course and fast-food joints.

The newest attraction was a sprawling prison they'd built during the past year—fencelines within the fenceline, concentric circles of captivity. The inmates wore orange jumpsuits, and through the binoculars they stood out like radioactive particles moving across the slide of a microscope. Now it was the Americans who kept the lights on at all hours, and in the winter months when Vargas's patrol began before sunrise the prison's forest of tall vapor lamps smudged the sky like a false dawn.

In recent months there had been more construction, as they built barracks for the troops guarding the prisoners. If Vargas hadn't known what they were up to, it might have made him nervous seeing so many new arrivals. They now outnumbered his own garrison in Boquerón—

a town that had been renamed Mártires de la Frontera, even though everyone still used the old name—by more than two to one. In the old days, Rodriguez told him, it would have been a provocation.

When Vargas thought about it long enough, his earlier resentment rekindled. Sure, the Yankee base had been there for more than a hundred years. But it was sheer effrontery the way the Americans still wore out their welcome more than four decades after the Revolution. For the Cubans, it was sort of like divorcing a flamboyant wife only to have her stern and forbidding mother refuse to leave the house, immovable from her perch at the end of the couch. Doing as she pleased even though you never chatted, and never exchanged pleasantries, even if sometimes you couldn't help but recall how much you had once loved her daughter, especially when the two of you had gambled and danced in Havana like there was no tomorrow.

But these little flare-ups of Vargas's temper always faded quickly. In fact, there was only one aspect of Guantánamo that he had yet to grow accustomed to, and that was the alarming presence of the iguanas. Big, green, and deceptively fast, they gave him the creeps, especially the way they brazenly approached to practically beg for handouts. Rodriguez only made it worse by feeding them, stooping low to offer bites of bread or banana. They ran toward him like pets, tongues flicking and tails swishing in an awkward gait. Vargas had watched Americans feed them, too—candy bars, potato chips, and other prepackaged junk. The lizards got so accustomed to freeloading that he couldn't hold out a hand without worrying that one of them would take a quick nip, mistaking his finger for something from a vending machine. Rodriguez always said not to worry, that they were herbivores. Vargas had his doubts.

The sun was creeping higher now, and Vargas was nearing the end of his patrol. Soon he would turn uphill, angling toward the fenceline that led to his tower. But first he had to make a brief reconnaissance of the shoreline, from the point where the trail skirted the back side of the dunes. When the weather was pleasant he sometimes detoured onto the beach. If it was hot enough he might even take off his boots to wade briefly in the shallows, watching for flashing schools of baitfish that rode in on the breakers. Today felt like just such a day, especially since no music was yet issuing from the tower.

His boots sank in the sand as he climbed the dune. Then the strand came into view, and Vargas froze. There was a man down there, a soldier in camouflage. Vargas knew right away from the uniform that it was an American, and he instinctively dropped into a crouch with his gun at the ready, fingering the trigger as tall grass brushed his cheek. He chambered a round of ammunition and was alarmed by the loud noise. His grogginess was gone. He was as alert as if he had gulped three cups of Rodriguez's coffee, and his palms sweated onto the gun's stock.

Was the enemy coming ashore? Was this only the first of many? Or had others already arrived and gone into hiding? He glanced behind him, heart beating rapidly. Perhaps someone was about to rise up and slit his throat. But all was quiet, and as he looked back toward the beach he realized that the soldier wasn't moving a muscle. He saw as well that the man's uniform was soaked, darkened by the sea from head to toe.

Vargas rose slowly to his feet. Then a sudden movement nearly made him cry out in astonishment. It was an iguana, a huge one, raising its head next to the soldier's waist. It had been poking around down there, probing the man's pockets, and its reptilian eyes swiveled like turrets toward Vargas. He wasn't sure what was more disturbing, the body or the way that the lizard had laid claim to it, but he was now certain he was viewing either a corpse or a drunk. Nothing else could explain letting that beast put its snout down your pockets.

He stepped toward the beach, and for a moment the iguana lingered, staring back. A ridge of toothlike scales stiffened along its arching spine, and it slowly opened its mouth to unfurl a long tongue in a yawning pink tunnel that, for all Vargas knew, led all the way back to the Age of Reptiles. In this pose it was the very portrait of B-grade menace from some horror matinee, and Vargas fought down a shudder.

Deciding that enough was enough, he shouted—an animal cry of rage and disgust. Then he raced down the dunes, a soldier on the attack, gun outstretched as his boots tossed sand in his wake.

The iguana fled in an instant, covering twenty yards before pausing to check its flanks. By then Vargas had reached the soldier and was no longer in pursuit. Now it was his turn to poke around the body.

Things didn't look promising. Seaweed was plastered darkly to the soldier's pale, bristly cheek, and his skin looked waterlogged, puffy, like sodden bread. Worst of all, the man's eye sockets were empty, hollowed out by creatures far hungrier than the iguana.

Vargas turned away, doubling over, then retching violently. His empty stomach creased, and he coughed up a glistening string of mucus. Wiping a sleeve across his mouth, he collected himself for another glance, then gazed uphill toward the tower. Somehow it seemed wrong to leave the soldier behind, untended. The scavenging iguana would doubtless return, and soon enough seagulls and turkey vultures would join in.

But for now his duty was to reach the tower and call in his discovery. Rodriguez would scarcely believe it, much less their officers in Boquerón. This was news, a real sensation. It would create a stir with repercussions all the way to Havana.

Dead or alive, the enemy had come ashore at Guantánamo, and that was cause for alarm.

CHAPTER ONE

ON THE FIRST DAY of his transition from captor to captive, Revere Falk stood barefoot on a starlit lawn at 4 a.m., still naively confident of his place among those who asked the questions and hoarded the secrets.

Falk was an old hand at concealment, trained from birth. The skill came in handy when you were an FBI interrogator. Who better to pry loose the artifacts of other lives than someone who knew all the hiding places? Better still, he spoke Arabic.

Not that he was putting his talents to much use at Guantánamo. And at the moment he was furious, having just returned from a botched session that summed up everything he hated about this place: too few detainees of real value, too many agencies tussling over the scraps, and too much heat—in every sense of the word.

Even at this hour, beads of sweat crawled across his scalp. By the time the sun was up it would be another day for the black flag, which the Army hoisted whenever the temperature rose beyond reason. An apt symbol, Falk thought, like some rectangular hole in the sky that you might fall into, never to reappear. A national banner for Camp Delta's Republic of Nobody, populated by 640 prisoners from forty countries, none of whom had the slightest idea how long they would be here. Then there were the 2,400 other new arrivals in the prison security force, mostly Reservists and Guardsmen who would rather be elsewhere. Throw in Falk's little subculture—120 or so interrogators, translators, and analysts from the military and half the branches of the federal government—and you had the makings of a massive psychological experiment on performing under stress at close quarters.

Falk was from Maine, a lobsterman's son, and what he craved most right now was dew and coolness, moss and fern, the balm of fogbound spruce. Failing that, he would have preferred to be nuzzled against the perfumed neck of Pam Cobb, an Army captain who was anything but stern once she agreed to terms of mutual surrender.

He sighed and gazed skyward, a mariner counting stars, then pressed a beer bottle to his forehead. Already warm, even though he had grabbed it from the fridge only moments earlier, as soon as he reached the house. The air conditioner was broken, so he had stripped off socks and shoes and sought refuge on the lawn. But when he wiggled his toes the grass felt toasted, crunchy. Like walking on burned coconut.

If he thought it would do any good, he would pray for rain. Almost every afternoon big thunderheads boiled up along the green line of Castro's mountains to the west, only to melt into the sunset without a drop. From up on this scorched hillside you couldn't even hear the soothing whisper of the Caribbean. Yet the sea was out there, he knew, just beyond the blackness of the southern horizon. Falk sensed it as a submerged phosphorescence pooling beneath coral bluffs, aglow like a candle in a locked closet. Or maybe his mind was playing tricks on him, a garden-variety case of *Guantánamo loco.*

It wasn't his first outbreak. Twelve years ago he had been posted here as a Marine, serving a three-year hitch. But he had almost forgotten how the perimeter of the base could seem to shrink by the hour, its noose of fencelines and humidity tightening by degrees. A Pentagon fact sheet for newcomers said that Gitmo—the military's favorite slang for this outpost—covered forty-five square miles. Like a lot of what the brass said, it was misleading. Much of the acreage was water or swamp. Habitable territory was mostly confined to a flinty wedge of six square miles. The plot marked out for Camp Delta and the barracks of the security forces was smaller still, pushed against the sea on fewer than a hundred acres.

Falk stood a few miles north of the camp. By daylight from his vantage point, with a good pair of binoculars, you could pick out Cuban watchtowers in almost every direction. They crouched along a no-man's-land of fences, minefields, wet tangles of mangrove, and scrubby hills of gnarled cactus. The fauna was straight out of a Charles Addams cartoon—vultures, boas, banana rats, scorpions, and giant iguanas. Magazines and newspapers for sale at the Naval Exchange were weeks old. Your cell phone was no good here, every landline was suspect, and e-mail traffic was monitored. Anyone who stayed for long learned to operate under the assumption that whatever you did could be seen or heard by their side or yours. Even on the free soil of a civilian's billet such as Falk's you never knew who might be eavesdropping, especially now that OPSEC—Operational Security—had become the mantra for Camp Delta's cult of secrecy. It was all enough to make Falk wish that Gitmo still went by its old Marine nickname—the Rock. Like Alcatraz.

He took another swallow of warm beer, still trying to calm down. Then the phone rang in the kitchen. He ran to answer in hopes of not waking his roomie, special agent Cal Whitaker, only to be greeted by the voice of Mitch Tyndall. Tyndall worked for the OGA, or Other Government Agency, which even the lowliest buck private could tell you was Gitmo-speak for the CIA.

"Hope I didn't wake you," Tyndall said.

"No way I'd be sleeping after that."

"That's what I figured. I was hoping to mend fences."

"The ones you just tore down?" Falk's anger returned in a hurry.

"Guilty as charged."

Tyndall sounded sheepish, new ground for him, although for the most part he wasn't a bad guy. A tall Midwesterner with a long fuse, he generally aimed to please as long as no sharing was required. Falk tended to get more out of him than others if only because they were part of the same five-member "tiger team," the organizational equivalent of a platoon in Gitmo's intelligence operation. There were some twenty-five tiger teams in all, little study groups of interrogators and analysts that divvied their turf by language and home country of the detainees. Falk's team was one of several that specialized in Saudis and Yemenis.

"Look, I spaced out," Tyndall continued. "Just blundered in there like a bull in a china shop. I wasn't thinking."

Occupational hazard with you Agency guys, Falk thought but didn't say. Unthinking arrogance came naturally, he supposed, when you were at the top of the food chain, rarely answerable to anyone, the Pentagon included. Teammates or not, there were plenty of places Tyndall could go that Falk couldn't. The CIA sometimes used a different set of interrogation rooms, and recently the Agency had even built its own jail, Camp Echo. It was Gitmo's prison within a prison, and its handful of high-priority inmates were identified by number instead of by name.

"Yeah, well, there seems to be a lot of mindlessness going around," Falk said.

"Agreed. So consider this a peace offering. Or an apology, at any rate. We might as well kiss and make up, considering where things are headed."

"The rumors, you mean? Spies in our midst? Arab linguists on a secret jihad?"

"It's not just rumor, not by a long shot."

Coming from Tyndall, that was significant, so Falk tried to goad him into saying more.

"Oh, I wouldn't believe everything you hear, Mitch."

Tyndall seemed on the verge of rising to the bait, then checked himself with a sigh.

"Whatever. In any case. No hard feelings?"

"None you couldn't fix with a favor or two. And maybe a few beers at the Tiki Bar. It's Adnan's feelings you should be worried about. I'll be lucky to get two words out of him after that little explosion. It's all about trust, Mitch. Trust is everything with these guys." He should have quit there, but his memory flashed on a slide they always showed at the FBI Academy in Quantico, a screen full of big letters saying, "Interrogation is overcoming resistance through compassion." So he pushed onward, a sentence too far: "Maybe if you guys would stop stripping 'em naked with the room at forty degrees you'd figure that out."

"I wouldn't believe everything you hear," Tyndall snapped.

"Whatever. Just stay away from Adnan. He's damaged goods as it is."

"No argument there. Tomorrow, then."

"Bright and early. And remember, you owe me."

Falk stared at the phone after hanging up, wondering if anyone bothered to tune in at this hour. Whitaker was no longer snoring down the hall.

"Sorry," Falk offered, just in case. "It was Tyndall. From the god-damn Agency."

No reply, which was just as well. The fewer people who knew about their little dustup, the better. People who ran afoul of Mitch Tyndall soon found themselves being shunned. It wasn't the man's winning personality that turned everyone against you, it was the perception that he was privy to the big picture, while all you had was a few fuzzy snapshots. So if you were on the outs with Tyndall, there must be an important reason, even if no one but him knew what it was. Falk had long ago concluded that Tyndall wasn't fully aware of his mysterious powers, and it probably would be unwise to clue him in.

The subject of their dispute this evening was a nineteen-year-old Yemeni, Adnan al-Hamdi, a pet project of Falk's if only because he would talk to no one else. Adnan had been captured in Afghanistan nearly two years earlier, during a skirmish just west of Jalalabad. He and sixty other misfit jihadists from Pakistan, Chechnya, and the Gulf States had been rounded up by Tadjik fighters of the Northern Alliance in the wake of the Taliban's mad-dash retreat to the south. They wound up rotting in a provincial prison for six weeks until discovered by the Americans. Adnan attracted special interest mostly on the word of a fellow traveler, an excitable old Pakistani who swore that Adnan was a ringleader. Adnan, in his usual monosyllabic way, said little to confirm or deny it, so into the net he fell, joining one of Guantánamo's earliest batches of imports. He arrived blindfolded and jumpsuited in the belly of a roaring cargo plane, back when the detention facility had been a rudimentary collection of monkey cages known as Camp X-Ray.

By the time Falk came aboard more than a year later, Adnan had been deemed a lost cause by Gitmo's resident shrinks, the Behavioral Science Consultation Team, known as Biscuit. He was a mute head case who regularly threw his own shit at the MPs, sometimes after mixing it with toothpaste or mashed potatoes.

So he was unloaded on Falk, whose linguistic specialty was the dialect of Adnan's hometown of Sana, only because Falk had visited the place during the Bureau's investigation of the bombing of the USS *Cole*, back in 2000.

Falk set about taming the young man with gossip and lies, tales embellished by bits of color recalled from Sana's dusty narrow streets. Before long Adnan at least was listening instead of shouting back or clamping hands over his ears. Occasionally he even spoke, if only to correct details that Falk got wrong. Progress was slow, but Falk knew from experience that hardness at such an early age didn't mean there were no remaining soft spots. Unlike most detainees, Adnan couldn't even grow a full beard, and to Falk the scruff on his chin was almost poignant, like an undernourished bloom in an abandoned garden.

Perhaps Falk also recognized a fellow loner. At age thirty-three he, too, was nominally alone in the world. He had no wife, no kids, no dog, and no fiancée waiting back in Washington. The Bureau's personnel file listed him as an orphan, a conclusion left over from a lie Falk had told a Marine Corps recruiter fifteen years ago in Bangor, half out of spite and half out of a runaway's yearning for a complete break. The recruiting sergeant could have easily flushed out the truth with a little more digging. But with a monthly enlistment quota to meet and a bonus of a week's leave hanging in the balance, he hadn't been inclined to question his good fortune once Falk walked through the door.

Besides, it had almost been true. Falk's mother left when he was ten. Shortly afterward his father began a love affair with the bottle. By now, for all Falk knew, the man really was dead, drowned by either alcohol or seawater.

His earliest memories of home weren't all that bad—a white clapboard farmhouse along a buckled road on Deer Isle, birch trees out back with leaves that flashed like silver dollars. There were five Falks in those days—an older brother, an older sister, his parents, and him. To stay warm in winter they slept head to toe in bedrolls around an ancient woodstove, arranged like dominoes on a creaking pine floor. At bath time they hauled in an aluminum washtub and poured hot water straight from the kettle, his mom scrubbing his skin pink while his sister laughed and covered her mouth.

When spring arrived his dad rode daily into Stonington, where the lobster boat was moored. He awakened at four, revving the Ford pickup until it rumbled like a B-17 on takeoff, its muffler shot from the salt air. After age twelve Falk accompanied him on summer mornings, although he remembered little of those harsh working days on the water apart from the chill of the wind in early June and the bitter cold of the sea, and the way his hands and feet never quite recovered until late September. Or maybe he didn't want to remember more, because by that time his father was drinking and his mother was gone.

Within a year they lost the house and moved to the woods, onto a stony lot of goldenrod and thistle where home was a sagging green trailer, the walls lined with flattened cereal boxes for insulation. In storms it heaved and moaned like a ship at sea. There were no more community sleeps. Everyone scattered to separate corners, and his brother and sister escaped as soon as they were old enough.

Falk sought refuge where he could find it—in the woods, on a cove, or at libraries, the tiny clapboard ones you came across in every community on the island. He took a particular liking to the one in the island's namesake town of Deer Isle, not only because it was closest but because it was the realm of steely-eyed Miss Clarkson. She demanded silence—exactly what Falk needed—and brooked neither nonsense nor intrusion, especially not from drunken males who came raging up the steps in search of wayward sons. In recalling her now, Falk realized she was the kind of woman he would always be attracted to—one who could glean the most from minimal conversation, as if she had an extra language skill. It was a little bit like being a good interrogator.

On his eighteenth birthday, a month after graduating from high school, he hitchhiked to Bangor, where he moved into a flophouse just long enough to get a new driver's license with a local address to show to the local recruiter. After basic training he arrived at Gitmo with the requisite shaved head and sunburned face. He had never been back to Maine, nor sent word of his whereabouts.

Falk owed plenty to the Corps—his balance, his patience, enough money from the GI Bill to put him through college. He made friends with a few good men who even now he would trust with his life. But having endured his harshest trials well before basic, Falk was resistant to the Corps' deeper strains of indoctrination. Not even three years of Semper Fi convinced him to wear a tattoo or post a bumper sticker. He still retreated when necessary.

It was that independent outlook, as well as his progress with Adnan, that soon earned Falk a reputation as having just the right touch for detainees adrift in Camp Delta's lower-to-middle reaches. This meant he almost never got a look at the few dozen detainees considered to be Gitmo's prized possessions, the "worst of the worst."

Instead he often held court with lonely and grizzled old men, or disturbed fellows in their early twenties—bricklayers, cabdrivers, cobblers, and farmers who had enlisted as foot soldiers of the jihad—subjects of dubious intelligence value whom the skeptics sometimes referred to as "dirt farmers."

In the course of these sessions he discovered the taming power of food—sweets in particular—and lately he had turned that weapon on

Adnan. Just last week a dripping wedge of baklava had elicited a lengthy discussion of explosives techniques, plus a better-than-average description of Adnan's weapons trainer, which ending up matching that of another detainee who actually remembered a name. Somewhere out there, presumably, others were now acting on this tip.

"Meat to the lions" was how one Army psychologist on the Biscuit team described the technique of swapping food for information. In Adnan's case it was more like cookies and milk after a long day at school, a treat to soothe the soul and get him busy on his homework. Falk had once even fetched a Happy Meal from the base McDonald's.

"You deserve a break today," he said, handing over the bright red box. The Madison Avenue joke whizzed over Adnan's head, but the young man wolfed down the tiny burger in gratitude, mustard smearing the corner of sun-chapped lips as he chewed. The only awkward moment came at the end, when Falk had to reclaim the plastic toy. It was a tiny Buzz Lightyear—even Happy Meals were out of date at Gitmo—and Adnan wouldn't let go until an MP stepped forward with a truncheon.

There was a brief sulk, a few muttered imprecations.

"Sorry, Adnan. It's contraband," Falk crooned in good-cop Arabic.

The plastic Buzz Lightyear now stood on the sill above Falk's kitchen sink, his resolute partner in the search for Truth.

Others were predictably skeptical of Falk's progress with Adnan.

"Why bother?" Tyndall had said a few weeks ago at lunch, speaking through a mouthful of Army fries. "He's out of his freakin' mind. The one time I had him we had to sedate him. Then he was like some nut talking in his sleep. Probably chewed too many qaat leaves as a boy. Fought one too many battles."

"Hell, Mitch, he's nineteen."

"Exactly. Too far gone, but not old enough to really know what he's seen—who trained him, or who made a difference in his network. Not worth the effort."

"Then let him go. Send him home if he's so goddamn worthless."

"Fine with me. Not my call, though. Draft a telegram to the SOD and I'll sign it."

That would be the secretary of defense, who had the final word on all such decisions.

Falk was foolish enough to take the idea to heart, but in the course of his inquiries on Adnan's behalf the brass learned of their rapport, which only doomed Adnan to further detention.

"Work with him," a visiting desk jockey from the Defense Intelligence Agency said. "Make him a personal project. Everybody else, hands off, and we'll see how it goes."

Translation: He'll go home only when he tells us what he knows, and it's up to you to deliver the goods. Leaving Falk, as it were, the master of the young man's fate. So earlier that week Falk had decided on a new course of action. He would rouse Adnan from his sleep in the wee hours—a technique the Pentagon liked to call "sleep adjustment"—in hopes of tapping into a different stream of consciousness from the one Adnan offered by day.

Falk had arrived at Camp Delta's front gate at 2:20 a.m. A bored and surly MP checked his ID against a list of scheduled visitors, then unlocked the gate to the first sally port. These transactions never involved an exchange of names. The interrogators signed in with numbers. The MPs, for their part, covered their names with strips of duct tape across their uniforms, lest their identities be passed along to a shadowy network back in the Middle East that might someday hunt down their families in Ypsilanti, Toledo, or Skokie.

Before opening the next gate, the MP relocked the one behind him, then repeated the process through two more portals. All of this chain-link jangling made it sound as if Falk were entering a suburban backyard and gave the place the feel of a kennel. It smelled like one, too, stinking of shit, sweat, and disinfectant. With showers strictly rationed, and no air-conditioning to counteract the Cuban heat, every cellblock stank like a locker room in need of hosing down.

By day the place could be unruly. Detainees didn't always take their punishment meekly, especially when you were moving them around. There were scuffles and staredowns, hunger strikes and shouting matches. When anyone got too unruly the MPs called in their version of an air strike—an IRF, or Initial Reaction Force. It was a sort of combat conga line of five guards decked out in helmets, thick pads, and black leather gloves, fronted by pepper spray and a riot shield. Whenever they trooped into action, rhythmically stamping their boots, the prisoners answered with the rallying cry of "*Allahu Akbar!*"—"God is great!"

Although you heard a lot about Delta's status as a sort of Babel Tower with its nineteen languages, the majority tongues by far were

Arabic and Pashto, and it was the Arabs who ruled the roost, sneering down upon the gaunt Pashtun tribesmen from the hills of Afghanistan and Pakistan. It was a viewpoint strangely in tune with that of the interrogators and analysts, who regarded most of the Pashtuns as dirt farmers.

A few of the Arabs had become jailhouse evangelists, and they could silence entire cellblocks with their sermons, calling down the wrath of God with fiery Quranic verse. It drove the MPs nuts, although Falk found the exhibitions oddly entertaining, maybe because it reminded him of listening to Sunday morning radio broadcasts as a boy, dire warnings of doom and damnation beaming through the static and whine of the AM dial.

But in the wee hours Camp Delta was quieter, calmer. It even smelled different. Sometimes you picked up a briny whiff of the sea. Falk figured it must be tantalizing for the inmates to be reminded that waves were breaking a mere hundred yards beyond the fence. Because if Gitmo was claustrophobic, Camp Delta was downright airless, a bell jar. A few hours inside the wire and his head was ready to explode.

In his first weeks here he had often visited Camp Delta after dark, mostly to check on his charges as they slept. Familiarize yourself with their nocturnal rhythms, he told himself, and maybe you'll discover a hidden point of entry to their memories. So he had strolled past their cells, glancing through the mesh and listening to their breathing, to their coughs and snores, vainly trying to crack their codes of silence in the dead hours before the dawn prayer.

In the higher-security blocks that he liked to patrol, each prisoner was curled on a narrow bunk, arm thrown across his face against the constant lighting. A few were always awake, an open eye watching from the pillow. Falk never acknowledged that he noticed, but as soon as he passed from sight he cleared his throat. It was partly to let them know they weren't dreaming, partly to plant the thought that—just maybe—he was always out there, lurking beyond the door.

Now and then he had come upon one of them writhing in some private passion, either masturbating or dreaming of a lover. Falk wondered what it must be like to emerge from that, journeying so far afield from this rocky edge of Cuba only to wake up back where you started, groggy from the heat, while some nineteen-year-old Reservist from Ohio shouted in English that it was time to get up. First for prayer, then for breakfast, and then over to interrogation, which was where

Falk reentered their lives, the cellblock stalker now showered and shaved in the full light of day.

After signing up to see Adnan, Falk glanced over his notes while waiting at the interrogation booth. His place of business wasn't much to look at—twelve feet by twelve feet, with a white linoleum floor, pale gray paneling, and fluorescent lighting, just like the other seven booths in the trailer. No windows, just a two-way mirror along one wall for whoever was watching from the observation room, which was usually nobody. There were no adornments, and no knickknacks, although lately the Army had taped up posters depicting a grieving Arab mom with a caption saying how much she wanted her son to come home. Those were displayed on the wall facing the detainee, with the implicit message being, "If you talk, maybe Mom will get her wish." Falk had already earned a reprimand for taking one down before his last session with Adnan. He did the same thing now, rolling it into a tube and placing it by the door.

The subject always sat in a steel folding chair behind a folding table with a wood grain Formica top, just like the ones you saw at church suppers and youth soccer sign-ups. The interrogator got a cushy office chair that rolled and swiveled, making him the room's CEO. If not for the eyebolt in the floor—for attaching the detainee's leg irons—the room would have looked like a place where you filled out loan applications or insurance forms.

None of this blandness had stopped Falk from cooking up a more dashing vision of the place the first time he laid eyes on it. Like virtually every other interrogator who arrived at Gitmo, he had come ashore certain that he would make a difference. He vowed that this booth would become The Room Where Secrets Came To Die, with him, of course, as the model executioner, lopping the heads off troves of vital information while armed only with patience and guile, cunning and wit.

One of his FBI instructors had compared it to cutting gemstones. You didn't set out to "break" a subject; that was mere brutality, an act of force that rendered everything the subject said as unreliable. Instead it was all about preparation—studying the angles, then searching for the point of cleavage where a firm but precise tap would turn the rough stone into a thing of beauty, revealing its secrets. You established rapport, built trust, and sprinkled your questions like crumbs upon the path to revelation.

His confidence in these methods was based more on pragmatism than altruism. His techniques were not just cleaner, they were better. But by the time Falk had arrived, most of the prisoners had been there for months, many for more than a year. The most precious gems had been set aside for others, and the remaining few of value had been subjected to the same questions so many times, and via so many different approaches—including some that were downright bizarre—that they had turned silent, uncooperative or, worse, said virtually anything they thought you'd want to hear.

Adnan arrived sleepy, hair tousled, which only added to his aura of boyishness.

"Want me in or out, sir?" the MP asked, in a tone that said he couldn't care less.

The MPs weren't always surly, even this late in the day, but they reserved a special scorn for those who spoke Arabic, as if it was a mild form of betrayal. If you spoke the language of the terrorists, then maybe you'd imbibed in other ways from their cups of poison.

"Out. And, soldier, unlock his handcuffs, please."

"Your funeral," he said, complying sullenly. Falk wondered if he talked like that to interrogators in uniform. Doubtful.

"So why did you get me up so early?" Adnan began, more annoyed than angry.

"I thought it might do us both some good. We've been in sort of a rut lately, don't you think?"

Adnan shrugged, then yawned. Falk almost wished that he had brought along some food. A glass of milk for bedtime. Maybe this was a stupid idea.

But he had already noticed at least one promising sign. In their many conversations Falk had noted that Adnan displayed some fairly simple tics and tendencies, habits that at times made him an open book.

Whenever the young man looked upward and to his right, he was almost always lying, as if that was where he looked for inspiration while searching his brain for a cover story. Glancing up and to the left meant he was stalling, waiting for the subject to change. When he stared down at the table he was usually lost in thought, having drifted to some other part of his life. At those moments you could rely on his every word. It was when Adnan was at his best. During those interludes Falk could almost pretend that neither of them heard the leg irons sliding on the floor when he moved in his chair. They were just shooting the breeze in a bar, perhaps, or at least that was the preferred location for Falk's imagination. He wondered where Adnan would have placed them. Maybe in a market stall off the souk, sipping a cool yogurt on a warm day, with the mud-wall architecture of Sana all around, casting him in shadow. A strong Arab coffee at hand with its dark sludge and its bite of cardamom. They would be seated before a backgammon board, or a folded copy of the daily paper, while the lottery sellers and tea vendors shouted their prices as they passed.

Relaxed moments like those had led to the few times Adnan had offered genuine revelations. And as those moments progressed Adnan tended to gaze up from his reverie straight into Falk's eyes.

Yet, for whatever reason, Adnan had clung to the one piece of information Falk wanted most: the name of his sponsor from Sana's local al-Qaeda cell. Not the propagandist or imam who had sold him on the idea of jihad in Afghanistan, but his sugar daddy and bankroller. Because somewhere higher up in Falk's chain of command, either in Langley or Foggy Bottom or at the Pentagon, the high priests had concluded that Adnan's paymaster was someone important, a face card without a face in their well-thumbed deck. So they wanted the name, of course, and the sooner the better. Which meant that Adnan, despite the scoffing among Falk's peers, was still a regular customer, even if lately all they seemed to discuss was home, or growing up, or the special way that his mother cooked lamb for the holidays.

This morning, Falk saw to his pleasure, Adnan was already adrift, looking neither right nor left, but totally relaxed. Now if Falk could just get the young man to take the next step and look him in the eye. For a while he tried small talk, gradually working his way around to the question that always stumped them. It was shortly before 3:10 a.m. when Falk made his play.

"So who was your sponsor, Adnan?" he asked coolly during a pause. "Who was Mister Moneybags with the air tickets and the big talk? The man with the plan?"

Adnan, caught off guard, briefly looked up from the table, eyes expressing mild betrayal. Then he shrugged, looking down again. At least it was better than his usual reaction, which was to look upward to his right and say, "I don't remember."

On previous occasions Falk had tried coaxing him further with treats, but treats had only made him babble more about home. Perhaps Falk had become a pushover. Even when dealing with a sensitive case like Adnan, putting a little steel in your voice never hurt from time to time.

"Maybe we should ask your sisters, then. What do you think, Adnan? Shall we send someone to Sana to say hello? They'd probably know, wouldn't they?"

Adnan looked up at Falk, glaring. It wasn't as if Falk would actually go that route—security goons of the home government bashing down a door, grabbing the first young women they found. But Adnan didn't know that, and now he was glancing at the two-way mirror as if someone else might be the source of this new approach.

"No one back there tonight, Adnan. Just you and me and the bedbugs. But the time for snacks and laughs is over. You know me and I know you, and you know what I need to help get you safely out of here. So level with me. 'Cause you know what? I won't be here forever, and the moment you get a new boss then they really will start thinking about asking your family a few questions. And you know as well as I do that the Yemeni Interior Ministry won't be handing out any baklava. So what do you say, Adnan? Who's the man?"

Adnan stared back angrily, yet he also seemed on the verge of some other emotion. It was an expression unlike any Falk had yet seen. Adnan looked down at the table for a few seconds, as if marshaling his thoughts, and when he looked up he was calmer.

"All right, then. I will tell you." He paused, looking directly at Falk, who didn't dare reach for pen or notebook. "It is Hussein. His name is Hussein."

"Hussein?"

"Yes."

"And what else? Hussein *what*? His full name, Adnan."

"That is all you need."

"Which narrows it down to a few thousand Husseins."

Christ, he'd been had.

"Not Hus-*sein*. Hus-*SAY*."

Hussay? Now what the hell kind of name was that? Some Yemeni variant? If so, it was none Falk had ever come across, although he had already learned repeatedly how little he really knew about the country's various cultural tics. Perhaps the name was unusual enough that it would really help, so he'd better make sure he had it cold.

"Hu-*say*? Is that it? Or Hu-*sie*? Say it again, slower."

"Hussay!" Adnan shouted it, slapping a hand on the table. Then he scowled and shook his head, annoyed and upset. His leg irons clanked. "I have given you a great gift, and you are too stupid to see it," he said, his voice rising on every word. "A great gift! Because my secrets, they are just like yours!"

"Like mine?" It made no sense, yet it was oddly disconcerting.

"Do you not see it? Are you so stupid?"

Falk had never seen the like of it. Adnan was fairly spluttering with rage, a liveliness he had always hoped for but never expected.

It was at this point that Mitch Tyndall had waltzed through the door, smelling of a shower, a shave, and the humidity of the night, brisk as a game show host as he smiled and pointed to his watch, tapping the face of an oversized Rolex.

"Sorry to interrupt, buddy, but I left a notebook in here earlier. And I've got a big fish coming in from solitary in about five minutes. So if you don't mind . . ."

Obviously he hadn't been watching from next door, much less monitoring their conversation with an interpreter. He'd simply barged in, assuming as everyone always did that any conversation with Adnan was expendable.

Falk would have leaped to his feet cursing had he not been so desperate to salvage the moment. As it was, he clung tightly to his seat with both hands. But one glance at Adnan told him the cause was lost. The young man was staring at him, dumbfounded, with a crestfallen look of betrayal. Hadn't Falk just told him that only the two of them were here? That no one else would know? So Adnan had presented his "great gift," no matter how cryptic, only to be greeted by this smiling lout in a suit.

Falk snapped.

"Goddamn it, Mitch! Just five minutes, okay? Five fucking minutes and I'm out of your hair."

Tyndall backpedaled, the smile fading but not gone. No one was ever supposed to lose face in front of the detainees. This type of dressing-down was strictly verboten.

"Easy, fella." He glanced again at his watch. "It's right there in the back. I'll just pick it up and go. I'm outta here."

Falk didn't answer, didn't even nod. And when the door shut he looked imploringly back at Adnan, trying to convey outrage and apology in a single expression.

"I didn't know," he said. "I really didn't know. And I'm sure he didn't hear a word, or he never would have interrupted. He's an asshole in a hurry, that's all. A walking joke."

Adnan didn't see the humor, of course. And some of Falk's hasty vernacular probably hadn't translated into Arabic as smoothly as he would have liked. What, indeed, would the concept of a "walking joke" mean to a Yemeni?

Adnan wouldn't say another word, and when the MP returned to escort him back he placed his arms around himself in an unwitting imitation of a straitjacket, refusing to meet Falk's glance as he glared toward the open door.

Fabulous, Falk thought. Just great. Nothing like wasting weeks of work. He was sure that was what had just transpired. Adnan's "great gift" now lay in ruins upon the table, still a mystery beyond the single name of "Hussay."

He left the booth before Tyndall returned, not wanting to risk a confrontation if he saw the man's face again. His footsteps crunched angrily across the gravel, emotions sizzling as he waited for the MP to unlock each and every gate. And now, back at the house, having just hung up the phone on Tyndall's "peace offering," he grabbed a second beer and strode back onto the lawn, still trying to cool the heat of his anger.

But what was this now, coming toward him in the dark? Headlights were approaching from the direction of the camp. It was a Humvee, judging from the wide spacing of the lights, rolling past the golf course, then pausing before turning up his street, Iguana Terrace. It moved slowly, deliberately. A business call for sure.

The beams crossed him in a blinding flash as the vehicle swerved into the small driveway. Falk considered his appearance—khakis and black polo, hair damp from perspiration. A soldier stepped from the driver's seat and headed for the front door. Somehow he hadn't spotted Falk on the lawn, and now he was knocking briskly, big knuckles rattling the screen.

"Out here, soldier."

A gasp of surprise, the soldier turning quickly. Falk wondered if he was reaching for a sidearm, but couldn't tell in the darkness.

"Mr. Falk, sir?"

"That's me. At ease, soldier. And you don't have to call me sir."

"Yes, sir." Flat accent. Yet another Midwesterner.

Falk strolled closer, feet tingling on the grass. He pulled open the creaking screen and motioned the man to follow him indoors, where the air was thick enough to choke on. When Falk flipped on the ceiling fan it was like stirring a kettle of warm soup. He turned toward the door, but the soldier was still out on the porch.

"Well, come on in."

"Actually, sir, I'm here to pick you up."

"Trouble inside the wire?"

The soldier hesitated.

"Well?" Falk asked. Then a thought occurred to him that made him panic. "It's not Adnan, is it?"

"The Pakistani Adnan or the Saudi Adnan?"

"The *Yemeni* Adnan. He didn't try to . . . ?"

"No, sir. Not this time."

Suicide was the subject they were skirting. There had been five attempts inside the wire in the last two weeks, none successful, and more than thirty since the prisoners had first arrived. And those were just the official numbers, a total that had dropped dramatically once the Pentagon started classifying many of them as "SIBs," or "manipulative self-injurious behavior." By now more than a fifth of the detainees were on Prozac or other antidepressants.

Adnan had never tried suicide, and he had refused all pills. But after what had happened in the past hour nothing would have surprised Falk.

"So everything's fine, then. Nobody to hose down or sedate?"

"Yes, sir. The problem's on our side."

Falk was thankful he hadn't yet turned on a light, because for a fleeting moment he almost wobbled, as a tremor out of his past shot through him from head to toe. It reminded him of the way the surface of the water jolts and wavers when a stingray suddenly beats its wings to flee across the shallows. Would a second MP now emerge from the Humvee to arrest him?

"Our side?"

"There's a Sergeant Earl Ludwig missing. No one's seen him since dinner."

Falk sighed, half in relief and half in weariness.

"Go on."

"The men in his outfit thought he must have switched to another shift. When they found out he hadn't, they got worried. About an hour ago somebody found his stuff on Windmill Beach."

"His stuff?"

"His wallet and his hat."

"No uniform?"

"No, sir. And no boots."

"They tell the MPs?"

"Yes, sir. But they figured . . ."

"That I could help. Being from the Bureau."

"Yes, sir. Given all of the, well, sensitivity down here, sir."

A tactful way of saying paranoia. This one had a future.

"Sure. I understand." Falk's pulse began to calm. "Where to, then?"

"The beach, sir. They've left his things where they found 'em. Treating it like a crime scene, just in case."

"Good thinking." Especially for the Army. Or so the Marine in him thought.

But it was the idea of this Sergeant Ludwig that piqued his interest. Going missing at Guantánamo was a major accomplishment, practically unprecedented. He didn't know whether to applaud or worry. He did know that if the sergeant didn't turn up soon it would create a major stir, which would be worth watching, if only for the novelty value.

Life on the Rock was about to get interesting.

CHAPTER TWO

THEY FOLLOWED THE BEACH ROAD until reaching the switchback maze of barricades at the checkpoint for Camp Delta, where they flashed IDs to a bored MP while another watched them down the sights of a .50-caliber machine gun. As usual, the prison was lit up like the Super Bowl. From this distance the glare of the vapor lamps made it seem as if a pale orange steam was rising from the fences and guard towers. The long white rooftops and ventilator hoods of the cellblocks made the place look more like a chicken farm than a penitentiary.

The Humvee rolled by the front gate, then turned the corner toward Camp America, motoring slowly past the bunkhouses, trailers, and sea huts where more than two thousand troops were sleeping. Windmill Beach was nearly a mile farther along. The pavement ended in a thicket of cactus and bramble at the base of a small coral bluff, and the beach itself was a broad crescent of sand about a hundred yards across. Next to it was a grassy picnic area with tables and a small open-air pavilion with a sheltered concrete slab. Before Camp Delta was built the beach had been secluded and rarely used. Falk remembered a few passionate liaisons here from his Marine days. He'd shared one with an ensign's wife, playing out the beach scene from the movie *From Here to Eternity*, enjoying himself so much in the entwining tide that he had never considered how stupid it was to be screwing the spouse of a Navy officer.

Now the spot was a convenient getaway, the site of frequent cookouts and parties for blowing off steam. There was no moon out tonight, but the beach was alive with flashlights. Four MPs searched the sands in the manner of kids hunting ghost crabs on summer vacation.

At the sound of Falk's arrival the beams went still. The MPs probably thought he was an officer. He noticed with amusement that all four were working with their backs to the water. The night sea often had that effect—all that limitless blackness, slurping and crashing unseen, as if threatening to beckon you deeper into the unknown if you stared for too long. Or maybe they were spooked by the possibility that Sergeant Ludwig's body was out there, bobbing toward them on the tide.

Falk wasn't at all unsettled, mostly because he'd grown up around the ocean. The coastline of his memories was a cozy place with coves, islands, and green treelines, of stony reefs where gulls and cormorants clamored. To him the night sea was as comfortable as a familiar room in a darkened home. He knew he could always find his way to the door without stumbling.

The wind had picked up, and the peaks of pearling waves flared iridescently. Despite what the MP who had fetched him had said, it looked as if the scene had been disturbed pretty thoroughly. Hardly a surprise, since someone must have checked the wallet for identification. But he was disappointed to see boot prints covering nearly every square foot of sand.

An MP helpfully turned his beam on Ludwig's belongings, a forlorn little pile with a wallet, a camouflage cap, and a set of keys. Now what were the keys for, unless the man still carried his set from home? Falk doubted a mere sergeant would have access to his own car. Gitmo's small rental motor pool had long since been gobbled up by top officers and civilians like him. Everyone else made do in shared vans, or by shuttling around the island in a fleet of old school buses, Camp Delta's version of mass transit. A few soldiers bought decrepit "Gitmo specials"—used cars passed down from one hitch to the next—but that rarely happened with Reservists.

Ludwig's uniform was indeed missing. Unless the man had walked here in swimming trunks, he had either gone for a dip in boots and cammies or had hiked off into the nearby hills after inexplicably removing his hat and wallet. Both seemed unlikely, but if Falk had to pick one possibility it would be the latter.

"We had to move his stuff, sir," the nearest MP said. "The tide was coming in."

That meant any path of Ludwig's boot prints marching toward the sea was gone by now, and there was virtually no way to distinguish his other bootprints from everyone else's. For all the talk of Camp Delta being home to the world's most dangerous criminals, it was woefully ill-equipped for the processing of an actual crime scene. The Shore Patrol on the naval base was more likely to have the right equipment than anyone here. The biggest push among their officers for better equipment seemed to involve creature comforts for the restless natives—big-screen TVs for watching sports via satellite dish, Internet kiosks, a big new deck for Club Survivor, which was Camp America's beachfront version of the Tiki Bar. Dozens of new sea huts were still being built, and the outpost was starting to resemble one of those boomtowns that accompany gold rushes and military occupations. Just last week the Morale, Welfare, and Recreation folks had flown in a rock band from the States. Earlier Jimmy Buffett had landed in the bay in his seaplane. A stand-up comic was due over the weekend. There were golf tournaments, boat rentals, softball leagues, scuba lessons. The fun never stopped.

"Who saw him last?" Falk asked.

"Private Calhoun. He's up in the barracks."

"And your name, soldier?"

The MP glanced down at his uniform, realizing with embarrassment that he hadn't removed the duct tape from an earlier shift inside the wire. He tore it off.

"Belkin, sir. Corporal Belkin."

"Well, corporal, I'll need to speak to this Calhoun as soon as possible."

"Yes, sir."

"Do you know him?"

"Calhoun?"

"Ludwig."

"Yes, sir. From my unit. Mobilized out of Pontiac, Michigan."

"Know him well?"

Belkin shrugged. "Well enough, I guess."

"Does he drink?"

"He'll have a beer or two. Not much else."

"Does he like to swim?"

"I've seen him in the pool before. Never down here. But I don't come here much."

"Anyone alert the foot patrols? In case he took to the hills?"

Marines still walked the base perimeter at all hours, and in the winding paths around Camp Delta there were often Army patrols, four soldiers in single file decked out in grease paint and forty pounds of gear. Falk knew the routine all too well.

"Yes, sir. They've all been questioned. Not a sign."

Falk nodded, then looked Belkin in the eye, trying to read his face in the darkness.

"What about suicide? You think he's the type?"

"No way, sir."

"Why not? They try it." Falk nodded toward the blob of light above Camp Delta. "Why not us?"

"Then where's the note?" A hint of sass. Maybe Ludwig was a closer friend than Belkin had admitted.

"Not his style, huh?"

"No, sir. Wife and kids. Good job."

"Doing what?"

"Bank manager. He'd been promoted just before deployment."

So he was probably the careful type, good at following orders. But Falk wasn't ready to concede the point just because he might piss off a buddy.

"The note could have blown away. Maybe the bank's in trouble. You check his wallet?"

"Just for ID." The tone was surly now. Belkin was definitely peeved. "Figured you'd want to do the rest."

Falk stooped to pick it up. It was a folding wallet of dark brown leather, already so damp from the sea air that you had to pry the sides apart. There wasn't much inside. A few charge cards. A limp twenty. A couple of receipts from the Naval Exchange, a Michigan driver's license, and a wrinkled old deposit slip, probably from his own bank. No snapshots of the wife or kids, meaning there were probably some posted by his bunk.

Falk's inspection was interrupted by the arrival of another Humvee. He gently placed the wallet back on the sand, turning in time to see the headlights go out. In the dimness you could just make out a small banner with two stars. The brass was here.

Striding toward them was Major General Ellsworth Trabert—"E.T.," as he was sometimes called, although never to his face, mostly for his penchant of seeming to materialize from out of nowhere, as he had just done. He was spit-shined and freshly ironed, as if he always rose at this hour.

Trabert had been in command of Joint Task Force Guantánamo for six months now, presiding over all operations from an administrative building on the far side of the base known as the Pink Palace, for the color of its stucco. He was an old paratrooper from Alabama, and never tired of mentioning both, a wiry man who put his faith in the Airborne, the Bible, and Crimson Tide football. Slow to bestow the level of trust on subordinates that made the chain of command function smoothest, he was nonetheless a nuts-and-bolts perfectionist and insisted on doing everything by the book.

The problem was that no one had yet written the book on how to run a place like Camp Delta, and the general was having to make it up as he went along. So far, Falk's employers at the Bureau weren't exactly thrilled with the results.

Falk heard rumblings from other agents months before his own arrival—vivid accounts of shouting matches at the Pink Palace, Trabert going red in the face as he leaned across the desk to mete out deadlines and tactical suggestions to civilian interrogators.

"If your methods are so goddamn superior," one Bureau memo had quoted him as saying, "then you bring me some results by the end of the week. If you've still got nothing, then we'll do it my way."

His way had consisted largely of throwing legions of hastily trained but highly motivated military interrogators into the fray, with a minimum of preparation and an excess of dramatic props—strobe lights and loud stereos, hoods and short chains, snarling dogs and miniskirts. As if they'd all been watching the same bad movies where subjects spilled their guts at the first sign of either long-term discomfort or a hot babe with cleavage. It was the sort of stupid business Falk had alluded to in his earlier snit with Tyndall: Turn up the air conditioner, strip the detainee naked, then leave the room for a few hours while he squirms uncomfortably, bent double because he's shackled to the eyebolt by a two-foot chain. Strobe them for an hour or two while playing heavy metal at top volume, or maybe the theme song from *Barney*. Then return and demand answers at the top of your lungs while an interpreter dutifully translates every obscenity.

Not all the sessions proceeded that way, of course. But Falk had seen and heard enough to make him shake his head from time to time.

And like his predecessors, he had complained to headquarters and sought counsel on what he should do about it. Every reply from the Hoover building sounded the same note: "Bottom line is FBI personnel have not been involved in any methods that deviate from our policy. The specific guidance we have given has always been no reading of Miranda rights, otherwise, follow FBI/DOJ policy just as you would in your field office. Use common sense. Utilize our methods, which are proven."

The upshot was that Falk was now forbidden from accompanying or observing any Pentagon-run interrogation, for fear he'd be tainted for future testimony before any civilian jury back on the mainland. The banishment also pertained to interrogations run by the CIA—as if the Agency would have allowed him in the room anyway.

Falk's complaints inevitably made their way back to General Trabert. It was one reason he would never be convinced that the data lines for his laptop were secure, despite Pentagon assurances. So you might say that the two men weren't exactly predisposed to have a pleasant chat at 4:30 a.m. on the beach.

The MPs went still as the general crossed the sand. He looked like MacArthur at Corregidor, only coming by land instead of by sea. Two of the soldiers pointed flashlights to light his way, and salutes snapped from all around. Falk had to restrain himself from raising his own right hand.

"Honor bound," a couple of the MPs blurted.

"Defend freedom," the general answered as he returned the salutes. Trabert had ordered those phrases to be injected into the daily mix of salutes, borrowing them from the slogan that appeared on the omnipresent logo for Joint Task Force Guantánamo: "Honor Bound to Defend Freedom." Falk always enjoyed the irony of watching soldiers shout "defend freedom" within the walls of a prison, but otherwise found it too gimmicky for his tastes, although he had to admit that for some of the MPs it seemed to have actually boosted morale.

After a few seconds of awkward silence it was clear that no one above the rank of corporal had yet taken charge, the sort of lapse you would find only with a Reserve or Guard unit, so Falk took the initiative. In doing so he summoned up some old codes of behavior he had never quite shaken. He nodded sharply—the civvy version of a salute—then spoke up in a voice that was firm and crisp.

"Morning, General Trabert."

"Morning, Falk. They get you out of bed for this?" With a look that seemed to ask whose bed.

"No, sir. I was up and about."

"That's right. You're one of the night owls."

Some of the MPs had complained about Falk's nocturnal patrols, carping that it got the inmates unnecessarily agitated, making their jobs harder. Trabert, to his credit, had told them to buck up, although he probably hadn't liked it either.

"You been briefed on this yet?" Falk asked.

"I'm told we have an AWOL. A first down here, at least on my watch."

Trabert hadn't seen eye to eye with his predecessor, a brigadier from a California Guard unit. One of his first acts had been to put a stop to the huge block parties held in neighborhoods of base housing that had been taken over by Camp Delta's minions. He didn't like the idea of all those loose lips in one spot, with alcohol flowing and civilians mixing easily with soldiers. But his greater obsession was making the trains run on time, and all the trains carrying intelligence back to Washington were supposed to leave the station fully loaded with new findings.

"Had time to form any theories?" the general asked.

If someone from the Bureau had posed the question, Falk would have simply said no. For Trabert he did a little tap dancing.

"Same as anybody else's, I guess. If he drowned, then he's probably still in uniform, boots and all, which seems damned strange unless he was suicidal. I'm told by a buddy he wasn't. If he's off on a hike, the patrols missed him, and nothing's gone off in the old minefields tonight to my knowledge. If he's drunk, I guess he could be passed out under a bush somewhere, meaning he'll turn up after daybreak. But apparently that's not his style, either. I haven't had time to ask yet if he might be shacked up somewhere."

The general flinched, as if you didn't talk about that sort of thing in his Army, at least not in front of others.

"Well, I've been led to believe by people who should know that he's just gone. Plain and simple."

"By his CO?"

"By people who should know."

It was clear from the general's tone there would be no further elaboration. Falk wondered who had made the decision to wake up the general on this matter and who else had been notified. For almost everyone at Gitmo, military or civilian, there was always another level you weren't privy to, some point where you'd reach a line and know it couldn't be crossed without special permission. The alphabet soup here was a rich and complicated blend of flavors, and under Trabert it always seemed to be on the boil. It meant, among other things, that this little beach party was rife with opportunities for going astray.

"Well, for the time being, Falk, why don't you scale back on your regular workload and take charge of this investigation. Assuming you're comfortable with that responsibility. I gather that lately the Bureau has been employing you as more of what used to be called an Arabist than as any sort of gumshoe."

He said it with a curled lip, as if he'd plucked "Arabist" from some DOD watch list.

"Just because I'm doing Q and A in Arabic full-time here doesn't mean I've forgotten how to be a cop," Falk said. "I'm still a special agent, which means I'm at home either running an investigation or handling a crime scene."

"Assuming this is even a crime scene. In fact, I'm assuming otherwise until someone shows me evidence to the contrary."

"I'd be a lot more comfortable with that assumption if your men hadn't trampled the scene."

"MP training today is geared more toward security and force protection, Mr. Falk. In the Global War on Terrorism there's not much call for a soldier who can dust for fingerprints."

"Then I guess your men won't mind if I offer some friendly advice from time to time while looking into this."

Trabert nodded tersely.

"Whatever needs to be done. In the meantime . . ." He consulted the luminous dial of a huge wristwatch. "At first light, about half an hour from now, we'll launch a full search and rescue op. Air, land, and sea. The works."

He was obviously overlooking Guantánamo's peculiar limitations.

"That's liable to be a little restrictive, isn't it, sir?"

It took a second or two, but the point hit home.

"Cuban airspace, you mean."

"And territorial waters."

"I guess that could complicate things, him going into the water so close to their side. What are we, about a mile from the fenceline?"

"More like two. But from what I remember of the currents he should make landfall with us. Unless the sharks get him, of course."

"You grew up on the water, right? Some kind of fishing village?"

"Deer Isle, Maine. You guys at the Pink Palace must do a lot of reading for you to know that."

"Comes with the territory."

The general turned to leave, but stopped after only a few steps.

"There's something else you should know," he said. "By late tomorrow some reinforcements will be arriving. With any luck you'll be able to return to your regular duties. Washington is sending a team."

"A team?"

"Two or three people. For security purposes."

"Kind of early to call in the cavalry, isn't it?"

"Maybe anywhere else. Not here."

"They coming on a regular flight?"

Trabert shook his head.

"Charter. Gulfstream out of Washington."

Just like for the visiting bigwigs from Capitol Hill and the Pentagon. Which said more about the urgency of this matter than anything had yet. Gitmo charters were like gold. Sergeant Ludwig's little swim, if that was what it was, was already making some wide ripples.

CHAPTER THREE

We all work very hard in the Joint Task Force Guantánamo and we like to unwind just as hard. Unfortunately, we tend to divulge information that is best left unsaid when we're in the company of others. Being sociable and popular is fine; however, when applied in the midst of the wrong crowd, it can compromise operational information. There are many popular meeting places on this island and many people with which to discuss topics of the day. Ensure that when you meet your friends or coworkers for lunch, a movie, or just casual conversation you police and sanitize your topics and think before you speak. You never know who may be listening to your "casual" conversations. "Think OPSEC."

—From "OPSEC Corner," a regular feature of JTF-GTMO's weekly newspaper, *The Wire*

BY THE TIME Falk got to breakfast, everyone knew. Not just about Sergeant Ludwig's disappearance, but everything—the general's arrival on the predawn beach, the special charter due in from Washington, and the overall discomfiture of the powers that be. Even Falk's little crack about Ludwig's possibly being "shacked up" had made the rounds, already producing a few jokes over the scrambled eggs.

For a place so devoted to secrecy, Gitmo's inner workings leaked like a cracked engine block, dripping a dark slick of rumor onto the rank and file. And in case anyone needed a reminder that something extraordinary was afoot, a Coast Guard helicopter had buzzed the shoreline all morning, wheeling noisily across the bay and out over the

Atlantic, daintily tightening its arc whenever it approached Cuban airspace. Falk's new assignment was, as they say, the talk of the town.

Camp America's seaside galley looked like a glorified Quonset hut—two bubble-topped chambers of stretched white plastic with only the tiniest of windows, making it seem as if you were eating inside a giant lightbulb. Falk filled a Styrofoam cup with the worst coffee in the Caribbean and headed for his usual table, a collection of civilian and military interrogators, translators, analysts, and clerks.

Like any society, Gitmo's was stratified. The MP proletariat of J-DOG, or the Joint Detention Operations Group, tended to keep to itself, nurturing its mistrust of Falk's would-be elite in the JIG, or Joint Intelligence Group.

The hirelings of private contractors were also part of the mix, mostly to help make up for the shortage of Arabic speakers and other linguists in the military and U.S. law enforcement. The two biggest players, United Security Corp. and Global Networks, Inc., were also fierce competitors, and lately they had been at each other's throats. Lawyers were involved. Official complaints had been lodged. So now their foot soldiers tended to sit at their own tables. The rivalry was either hilarious or dismaying, depending on how closely you had to work with them. Falk, in no need of their services, enjoyed promoting the theory that someday two contractors would go to war with each other on some far-flung shore of U.S. occupation, with the winner declaring its own republic.

Tyndall, one of the few Agency regulars at Falk's table, beckoned from one end as Falk approached. His face betrayed no sign of their blowup the night before. But Falk wasn't in the mood. Besides, Pam was waving from the other end, where she'd saved him a seat.

His relationship with Pam Cobb was another of Gitmo's open secrets. It offered a reading on the local sexual climate, which was both repressed and abundant, a Peyton Place painted alternately in Army drab and the sensual colors of the tropics.

Falk would wager that there were more pent-up libidos per square mile on this scuffed little heel of Cuba than in any town in America. And why wouldn't there be? Cook up a steam-bath climate in confined isolation, add soldiers, then more soldiers, and presto. Ratcheting the tension higher, males vastly outnumbered females. The long odds turned some men into slavering hunter-gatherers, knuckles dragging the ground. Marital status seemed to have little to do with it. It was like those ads for Vegas. What happened at Gitmo stayed at Gitmo. Or so you hoped.

Even Falk found himself returning to some of his Marine tactics of old, equipping himself with the customary tools of Gitmo courtship on his first shopping trip to the Naval Exchange—a blender for margaritas, a shaker for martinis, a hibachi for the patio, and a packet of condoms for emergencies.

It was the one forbidden act for which the authorities had tacitly agreed to look the other way. As if they had a choice. Try keeping a lid on it and the whole place might blow, leaving 640 inmates running the asylum.

Gitmo's living arrangements only added to the intrigue. The few MPs who hadn't yet moved into the new barracks were stuffed into vacant apartments in base housing, up to eight to a unit in a five-room place. Interrogators and linguists had also been farmed out to empty quarters, which were numerous now that the local Navy population was near its all-time low.

The most popular neighborhoods were Villa Mar and Windward Loop, where the billeting was often four to a unit, and two to every bedroom. It was like going back to college, with all the same challenges to romantic privacy—sneak a girl up to the dorm, hold the roommates at bay, and keep your friends guessing, with everyone making it back to their separate bunks by dawn, undetected by the campus police.

Falk and Whitaker got lucky with their arrangements. At first they had shared a bedroom in Villa Mar, with two men from the Defense Intelligence Agency in a room down the hall. But when the roof leaked during the one and only downpour since their posting, the two of them were reassigned to a two-bedroom detached house that had just come open on Iguana Terrace, well off the beaten path. Their neighbors to either side were Navy families stationed at the base, with a pleasure boat in one driveway and a trampoline in the other.

Pam came to Gitmo the week after Falk. She arrived on a Thursday, and by Sunday night she had already been invited to a pool party, a beach bonfire, a movie at the outdoor theater, and an afternoon of sailing.

Professionally the reception was cooler. She was fluent in Arabic, but had only recently completed interrogation training. The resident males were skeptical. A *female* interrogating Muslim men? And not just any Muslims, but ones stitched from Islam's toughest fabric—acid-washed in vats of fifteenth-century thinking, then wrung dry by combat and the rigid isolation of Camp Delta. They'd laugh this gal from Oklahoma out of the room. Or worse, spit a great gob of pious anger onto her unholy and uncovered face.

It had already happened to other women, and when Pam's first subjects immediately lived up to this billing the knowing crowd from Langley, the Bureau, and the Pentagon nodded smugly. The accepted theory was that she was yet another ham-handed Washington stab at "social engineering."

Then a funny thing happened. One or two of the Arabs, then three or four, then a dozen—a veritable groundswell—began to open up to Pam's questions in ways they hadn't for the men's. In a calm and patient manner that endured and then asserted, she gradually morphed into their mothers, their sisters, their daughters, or even—from a respectful distance, and only in the minds of the subjects—their lovers. Out spilled thoughts and articulations that the grizzled old fighters had given up for dead. One of them fell so head over heels for her that he began spinning grandiose yarns that even the most gullible analysts were not prepared to believe. He had to be pried from her custody, sulking and lovelorn.

Not only was Pam accepted into the intelligence tribe, but her success enabled her to avoid recruitment into one of General Trabert's more infamous experiments—an attempt to get information from the detainees by sexually humiliating them. One of Pam's shapelier but less fortunate roommates ended up stripping to her bra and panties in one such attempt. The vamping backfired, of course. The subjects only retreated deeper into anger and silence. The interrogator didn't fare so well, either. She locked herself into a restroom for an hour, sobbing in shame.

Falk and Pam first met one morning inside the wire. He had already noticed her the night before at the Tiki Bar, but she had been accompanied by at least five surrounding males, and from his vantage point a few tables away she had seemed more than able to meet their challenge, parrying advances with wit and poise, so he had kept his distance. Besides, he didn't like taking a number to wait his turn.

They came face-to-face the next morning at the holding cage. Falk had an 11 a.m. appointment to interrogate a young Arab of indeterminate citizenship, possibly Saudi. Pam also wanted a session with the fellow but wasn't scheduled on his dance card until the following day.

The pecking order on these conflicts was well established. Civilian interrogators such as Falk almost always got priority over their military counterparts. More to the point, Falk had reserved the slot. But instead of getting territorial he calmly let Pam state her case, which turned out to be pretty compelling: Another detainee had just offered her team a lead on this one's likely identity and role, and she wanted to nail it down ASAP. Falk gallantly stepped aside, feeling a bit like Sir Walter Raleigh letting the queen cross the mud on his cape. He knew better than to make a big deal out of it. She'd know where to find him later.

That night at the Tiki Bar she detached herself from her circle of admirers long enough to say thanks and buy him a beer. He saw right away why she would be effective at her job. Engaging enough to draw you forward, and open enough to respond in kind. Falk found himself talking easily about things that he hadn't mentioned to anyone in years. He nearly even slipped up and told an old story about his father. The next morning he woke up thinking it must have been the beer, or the lure of her blue eyes, or the way she kept flipping a drooping curl off her left eyebrow, with an endearing grace that showed off the fine line of her neck, a seeming invitation to plant a tender kiss on the smooth skin beneath her ear. Right next to where she'd dabbed that spot of perfume he could still smell the next morning, even though his room was redolent of sweat and grime and old newspapers.

He sometimes wondered if he would have even noticed her in another setting—amid the rich pickings of Washington, for example. At times she could be a little rough around the edges, an affliction Falk had often observed in military women. It was a survival skill in their environment, particularly for the officers, the tough front that signaled they wouldn't easily be pushed around. Well and good, he supposed, although at unguarded moments he found himself testing this facade, as if to measure its hardness. When Pam burst out with a stream of profanities while discussing the subject of Nebraska football—as a Sooner, she hated Nebraska—Falk was curious enough to ask, "Did your dad teach you that language, or your drill sergeant?"

He could have sworn she blushed slightly, but then she forged ahead.

"My dad *was* my drill sergeant. My first one, anyway. Or might as well have been."

"He'd be proud."

"Oh, he would be, as long as he knew I was defending the Sooners."

Far more disconcerting to Falk was the idea of dating someone who actually gave a damn about the chain of command's approval.

Considering Gitmo's male competition, he sometimes wondered what she saw in him. He wasn't remarkable to look at. Plenty of people who met Falk were convinced they'd seen him before—at the office cafeteria, in the back pew at church, or on the sidelines at their kid's soccer game. He had that kind of face—pleasant enough, someone you didn't mind having around, yet well suited to hiding in plain sight. His eyes, a stonewashed blue, invited trust even as they politely requested distance, with webbed lines at the corners that could have come from either laughter or worry. Around thirty, most people guessed, falling short by only a few years. But by the time they thought to probe beyond his Everyman qualities he had usually moved on, leaving them to wonder whether he was a not-so-young man in a hurry or just a man who preferred not to be pinned down.

Whatever the case, the reality now was that he was hooked, and apparently she was, too, no matter how events might have transpired elsewhere. If context was the magic ingredient in their romance, he supposed they would both find out soon enough after returning to the mainland. But lately he found himself hoping that wouldn't be the case.

"Heard you took a little walk on the beach with the general," she said as he sat down.

"You and everyone else."

"Solve it yet?"

He shrugged.

"I still say he's drunk in some young lady's bunk, passed out with her panties around his head."

She smiled with a hint of a blush, which had been his objective.

"You're assuming he's like you."

"Or every other man at this table."

Which made her look up, self-conscious for a moment. Women could never go for long here without being reminded of the way they stood out, and when Falk saw the look in her eye he regretted the remark and changed the subject.

"It sure screws up my schedule, though. I was making some real progress last night with Adnan. Until Tyndall walked in on us."

"Tyndall interrupted your session?"

"Didn't even knock. Said he'd forgotten something."

"And with Adnan, no less. Like throwing a rattlesnake at a nervous colt."

Pam was one of the few who had always encouraged him to keep trying with Adnan. She, too, dealt with her share of lost souls.

"He was right on the verge of a breakthrough, too. Even gave me a name. Not a whole one, of course, or he wouldn't be Adnan. But he sure seemed to think it was worth something. He was pretty pissed off once he figured Mitch had been listening behind the glass."

"I had kind of a strange session, too, that way." She looked at him funny, as if he might have already heard.

"Yeah?"

She seemed reluctant to continue, so he waited, staring. It was her eyes that you wanted to win over the most, he decided. Deep blue and searching, almost yearning. You wanted to be what they yearned for. Maybe that was her secret with the Arabs.

"Yeah," she finally answered, glancing down at a bruised wedge of cantaloupe, then looking back up. Those eyes again. "Your name came up. It was weird."

"My *name*?" Just what you wanted to hear, that someone inside the wire had pierced your veil of anonymity. Maybe a pissed-off MP had cursed his name within earshot of a cell.

"Not your actual name. But a description that sounded an awful lot like you. Ex-Marine, formerly posted to Gitmo, now a government interrogator."

"That is weird. Who was the subject?"

"Niswar al-Halaby. Syrian nutcase. Says he heard it from the Yemenis. Camp Three grapevine. Have you told Adnan all that?"

"Adnan thinks I'm a cop from California. And I've never said word one about the Corps." They routinely lied about themselves to even the most cooperative subjects. No sense offering any tools for leverage. "But you know how it goes. Talk to them long enough and hints of the real you come out anyway. Adnan's a smart kid. Maybe he pieced some of it together, or he might have just made it all up and gotten lucky."

"Did you have any connection with him or any of the other Yemenis from before? From the *Cole* investigation, maybe?"

"I'd never laid eyes on him until two months ago. Same with the other Yemenis."

"I didn't ask if you'd met them. I asked if you were connected. Maybe through a file, or a witness. Through any of your previous work."

"What is this, Pam? Should we go to a booth?"

"You tell me."

They had lowered their heads and their voices. To the rest of the table it probably looked like an intimate argument, or the arranging of a tryst. Falk glanced toward the end of the table and saw Tyndall watching with the air of a connoisseur. Then Pam leaned forward, her hands nearly touching Falk's between their trays as she dropped her voice to a whisper.

"I just want to know what I should do with this, that's all. If the Bureau made any previous inquiries about any of the Yemenis, or put them on some kind of watch list even before they got here, whether through your work or not, then it would help to know. But you seem to be saying that didn't happen."

"Not to my knowledge." She gave him a sharp look. "That's not a dodge. I really don't know. But I'm told there's no file on him or any of the others I deal with. Not from the *Cole*, anyway. If anybody else has designated him as some kind of figure of interest, then it's above my security clearance. Maybe you should ask Tyndall."

"Not even from a Cuban angle?"

"Cuban? As in Gitmo?"

"I don't know."

"Well, this gets weirder all the time." Now it was his cheeks turning hot. He hoped he wasn't blushing.

"Yeah. I thought so, too."

"So what the hell did he say, exactly?"

"If I'm leaving it out of my report, then I probably shouldn't tell anyone else. Even you. Not until I can go over it with Niswar again."

Falk wasn't sure how he felt about that. Was she omitting the detail to spare him or to avoid heat from above? Both, perhaps. With the military interrogators, there were always extra considerations involving your superior officers, and how they might react.

But Falk was even more puzzled by where the information must have come from. In the course of his give-and-take with Adnan, he would have sworn he hadn't let slip any specifics about his past.

"So who else was in there?" he asked.

"No one, fortunately. Just the MP, who doesn't know a word of

Arabic. Don't worry, if it ever goes into a report you'll be the first to know."

"Thanks. I think."

She smiled, a bit grimly perhaps, but before she could say another word Tyndall interrupted, settling into a seat that had just opened up to Falk's left.

"Life gets sweeter by the day down here, doesn't it?" He gestured to a swirled mound of chocolate soft-serve ice cream. It was the mess hall's newest attraction, although Mitch was the only one among them who ate it for breakfast. "Next week they'll probably be throwing steaks on the grill."

When neither Falk nor Pam answered right away, Tyndall awakened to the possibility he was intruding.

"Sorry. Bad timing?"

"No more than usual," Falk said.

"Like I said last night, I'm really sorry about that. It's just that I only had two hours to try and get a whole network out of my man Muhammad."

"Whatever," Falk replied.

"Hey. Blame our team leader. Demanding son of a bitch, especially where trivia's concerned."

"Trivia?" A new voice approached from the service line. It was Falk's roomie, Whitaker, looking for a seat. "You're not questioning the value of the product again, are you, Mitch?"

"Take mine," Falk said, standing. The long hours without sleep seemed to catch up to him all at once as he rose. What he needed most was a shower and a nap. There would doubtless be paperwork to file, colleagues of Ludwig's to interview, plus other leads to pursue, and the general would want it all done by yesterday. But without some shuteye he'd never get any of it done.

"You're just the man I wanted to see," Whitaker said. "Especially if you're headed back to our château."

"You need something?"

"No. Just make sure you check the mail on the kitchen table. It's not every day that a perfumed envelope arrives from Puerto Rico. Nice handwriting, too. Laying the groundwork for your next leave, big guy?"

"Woo-hoo!" Tyndall offered, fanning the flame. No one turned toward Pam, but Falk knew they were dying for a glance. She obliged them by standing.

"Here, Whitaker. Take my seat. I'll leave you boys to the kiss-and-tell."

She kept it light, but not without a passing glance at Falk that was several degrees cooler than a moment ago. So much for shared trust.

But that was the least of Falk's worries. At the mention of a perfumed envelope—from Puerto Rico, no less—he could already guess at the fragrance, a bouquet now blooming in his senses despite the mess hall's stale funk of overcooked eggs and wet mops. It was an island scent, part hibiscus and part spice, and it called from deep in his past. The idea of that letter sitting out on the kitchen table where anyone might open it made him weak in the knees. He had best be on his way.

"See you later," he said, moving quickly with his tray. At least no one knew the real reason he was blushing.

CHAPTER FOUR

THE LETTER MIGHT as well have been booby-trapped from the way Falk approached it. It sat on the kitchen table, as promised, but he was still working up the nerve to touch it. Leaning forward for a closer look, he instantly recognized the handwriting. Then there was the fragrance, streaming like smoke from a campfire. Unmistakably hers, no matter how unlikely.

Up to now his plans for the day had been pretty straightforward. He would tend to the needs of the Ludwig case and try to squeeze in another session with Adnan. General Trabert had told him to put regular duties aside, but it wasn't the kind of work you shut down with the flip of a switch, particularly with subjects like Adnan. A breakthrough could be like a paper cut, clotting quickly unless you immediately dug deeper. Although Tyndall's interruption may have already acted as a suture.

But now there was the letter to deal with. Falk circled the table. He opted first for a delaying action, heading briskly down the hall, dripping sweat in a burst of nervous energy. The heat, his lack of sleep, and this new development had his engine on the verge of overload.

He stopped at his bedroom door for a wary inspection. Nothing had been disturbed as far as he could tell. Not that any change would be noticeable in this wreckage—bed unmade, drawers ajar, a T-shirt still damp with day-old sweat draped on a chair. Newspapers and magazines were splayed on the nightstand, along with a file folder he should have returned yesterday. An appraising eye might have detected any number of reasons for further curiosity here.

He continued this cautious survey room by room, as much to calm himself as to search for anything amiss. Whitaker's quarters were neat as a pin. A half-completed letter home sat on the bedside table next to a humming clock. Falk caught the words "boredom" and "my darling" before moving on, shamed. Whitaker had presumably left the house just before arriving at breakfast, and the letter must have come just beforehand—an early delivery, but the times often varied here. Falk hadn't been at the house since heading to Windmill Beach at 4 a.m. At Gitmo, even in private quarters your privacy wasn't guaranteed. Anyone might have come and gone in the meantime.

He returned to the kitchen and picked up the envelope. It was sealed with cellophane tape, perhaps as an extra precaution. Or had someone on the base done it after inspecting the contents? The postmark was three days old. Not bad for Gitmo. It must have arrived on yesterday's plane out of Roosevelt Roads Naval Air Station, in Puerto Rico. He pried open the flap, and the smell of hibiscus intensified. For all his momentary paranoia, plenty of pleasant memories stirred as well. He recalled their first dance, her cheek brushing his. Later the scent had filled the hotel room, the young Marine hardly believing his luck. Months later, even when he knew far more, he had never stopped believing in her devotion, at least at some level. She said as much herself, in letters that had looked just like this one, minus the tape. But that was another era, another age here on the Rock.

Two pages of pink stationery were folded inside. Before reading them Falk looked over his shoulder, then walked to the front screen, glancing down the street toward the golf course before shutting the door. He sat down on the big brown couch by the window. First he counted the paragraphs. Five. The real business was always transacted in the third, but out of nostalgia he started at the beginning:

Dear Revere,

I have miss you much and so greatly. It has been so many years, and still can I see you with me. Do you remember our nights so wonderful together? We are in my dreams dancing late into starlight.

Same as always, so far—the halting English, charming in its clumsy syntax. If she was a professional, shouldn't it be flawless? But how could anyone not fall for a line so perfectly misshapen as "dancing late into starlight."

Last month I hear you are in Cuba, doing work for the country. It is for you very good. I hope you will find the time there to think of me and write to me.

Now for the business at hand.

Do you remember Harry our friend who lives nearby? He is wanting to see you also, and will wait for it to be soon. That way when you visit you can see us all.

The summer has been not so bad, and I have sometimes a new job.

And so on, for another several sentences of little consequence, small talk that fell flat after such a promising beginning. Then the usual conclusion, with its flourish of schoolgirl confections.

Love,
Elena
XXXOOO

Hugs and kisses, like always. Only this time they seemed like regular X's and O's, game pieces waiting to be deployed, with the outcome uncertain.

He sighed, folding the delicate paper back into the envelope. Should he burn it? Shred it? *Eat it*, for Chrissakes? Every option seemed belated. By now its presence must have been noted somewhere on the base. So he stuffed it into his pants pocket, realizing too late that he would now be carrying the scent if he met Pam later.

The news, it seemed, was that their "old friend" Harry wanted a meeting. Well, it would have to wait. Perhaps Falk would even ignore the summons altogether. In any event, what he needed most right now was a little sleep, tortured or not.

He was good at resting under pressure, having learned at an early age to shut his eyes as all hell broke loose in the next room, pushing himself beneath the surface of the sheets as if swimming for deep water, a chill refuge where no one else would care to follow. At Gitmo the technique was doubly helpful, easing him away not just from his troubles but from the heat, which settled heavily onto his chest the moment he crawled into bed. Deeper now, he thought, his breathing steady and slow. The light faded as a strange pressure built in his ears, as if he were a diver, and soon enough he had reached the desired level.

In what seemed like only seconds he was fighting for the surface, drawn by a persistent noise that he could no longer ignore. He lurched upward, gasping, bathed in sweat. And there it was again, a banging at the screen. A voice called out, vaguely familiar.

"Sir? Mr. Falk?" Then another round of knocking. "Are you here, sir?"

It was his MP escort from this morning. He checked his watch, shocked to see that it was almost 2 p.m. He had slept for five hours.

"In here, soldier. I'm coming." He threw on a shirt, still fighting the grogginess. On his way to the door he couldn't resist a glance toward the kitchen table, and was alarmed to see that the letter had disappeared, but then he remembered he had stuffed it in his pocket.

"What is it?"

The MP stepped forward, cap in hand.

"It's Sergeant Ludwig, sir. They found him."

"Alive?"

"No, sir. Drowned."

Bad news, but a blessedly quick resolution. Easier for the family and certainly easier for Falk. He'd wager that a blood test would show alcohol, no matter what the man's buddies thought. Almost everybody succumbed to it eventually down here, if only for one night.

"Sorry to hear it. But thanks for letting me know. Guess I should get down there."

"Actually, sir, I'm supposed to take you to a meeting."

"A meeting?" Probably a damage-control session. Trabert's idea.

"With the Cubans, sir. At the North East Gate. He washed up on their side."

"No way." It was stunning. Downright impossible.

"Yes, sir. The general wants you to accompany Captain Lewis when he goes to retrieve the body. I gather they're a little upset over there."

Damn right they were. Unless centuries of wind and current patterns had suddenly reversed course, or Ludwig had gone on some sort of record endurance swim, it should have been impossible for him to have ended up on the Cuban side.

So much for quick resolutions.

"Lead the way, soldier. It'll be just like old times."

CHAPTER FIVE

> The North East Gate is a reminder of the intent and capability of our adversaries to gain our operational information. Those adversaries can see us easily and clearly, hear us through sophisticated signal devices, and continually attempt to manipulate and distort our true purpose at Joint Task Force Guantánamo.
>
> —From "OPSEC Corner," a regular feature of JTF-GTMO's weekly newspaper, *The Wire*

THE NORTH EAST GATE was tucked in a remote corner of the base. It was a backwater Checkpoint Charlie with palm trees, the biggest difference being that its confrontations occurred well out of public view.

During the Cold War both sides had booby-trapped the approaching roads and spiked the plains with mines. Sometimes they exchanged gunfire. More often the tension escalated into something resembling frat house pranks. The Cubans used to get their kicks by tossing stones at Marine Observation Post 31, a small concrete barracks and watchtower overlooking the gate from a facing hill. They especially liked to do it at night, figuring that a direct hit would awaken any soldier trying to sleep. The Marines answered by blocking the line of fire with a forty-foot fence, just like the ones that driving ranges put next to highways to keep golf balls from hitting cars. The Cubans counterattacked by climbing the new fence to mount coat hangers, which clanked and rang through the night like wind chimes. Then they lit up the barracks with a spotlight, which the Americans extinguished without firing a shot by unveiling a huge red-and-gold Marine Corps emblem on the illuminated hillside.

Falk had sometimes patrolled the area as a Marine, walking the nearby roads in the swelter of full combat gear—weapon, flares, radio, food rations, and eight clips of ammo. It was a strange little world that turned spooky after dark, glowing a phosphorescent green through the lenses of his night-vision goggles. Every banana rat stirring in the brush had sounded like the advent of a commando raid.

During the first year of his posting the Berlin Wall came down, and for a few weeks the fenceline was tense. The last known exchange of gunfire took place the following month. But by the end of his third year the crumbling Soviet Union had cut Cuba loose from its purse strings, which left the enemy with more important worries than a few jeering Marines. Cuban bodies had sometimes washed up on the American side in those days, but they were civilians, not soldiers—would-be refugees who had drowned or were shot while swimming for freedom. No one ever made a big deal about it as long as the Americans sent the bodies back, and every now and then someone made it through alive.

Today the atmosphere was calmer than ever. The Americans had dismantled the booby traps and cleared their mines, replacing them with noise sensors and motion detectors. And for all the talk about OPSEC and renewed vigilance, they no longer staffed the observation post 24/7, relying instead on motorized patrols. Recently General Trabert had ordered the removal of a few coils of razor wire.

The Cubans had never gotten around to clearing their own mines, and whenever there was a brush fire a couple dozen more cooked off, exploding like bullets tossed into a campfire. The few remaining coat hangers had rusted into place.

But the North East Gate was still the one point along the perimeter where the two old adversaries regularly came face-to-face. It was the turnstile for the few aging Cubans who still commuted to on-base jobs. In the early 1960s there had been three thousand of them, daily enduring the taunts and abuse of Castro's guards in exchange for dollar wages. Only nine remained, and the youngest was sixty-four. They arrived at 5:30 a.m. and departed at 4:30 p.m., and every two weeks they carried home pay envelopes stuffed with American cash for themselves and about a hundred pensioners.

The only other regular contact was a monthly meeting between the commander of Guantánamo's naval base, Captain Rodrick Lewis, and his Cuban counterpart from the Revolutionary Army's Brigada de la Frontera, General Jorge Cabral. Their meetings were friendly and low key. In order to avoid unpleasant surprises, they gave each other advance notice whenever one side or the other was about to build something new or engage in a military exercise. General Cabral had learned of the imminent arrival of hundreds of prisoners from Afghanistan well before most of the American public.

They took turns acting as host. Usually there was little official business to discuss, so they talked instead of baseball, or fishing, or of the meal that had been set before them. As if to affirm the informal nature of their relationship, they sometimes engaged in small barters of contraband—a box of Cuban cigars for a carton of Marlboros, a country-western CD for a homemade cassette of salsa. Any issue that arose between meetings was generally handled by e-mail, unless there was a wildfire to fight, in which case they convened like old generals at the front, marshaling their resources to defeat the common foe.

But the discovery of Sergeant Ludwig's body called for extraordinary measures. No American had ever turned up dead on the wrong side of the fence. For the moment, Cold War tension was back in vogue, and Falk was about to get a front-row seat.

He arrived at the observation post to find three Humvees already parked. One had the general's two-star flag. Trabert was inside, waiting to take care of the necessary introductions.

"Falk, this is Captain Lewis. I want you with him when the Cubans hand over the body."

The captain cut an impressive figure. He was a tall, trim African American with a calm demeanor. It would have to be. His job as base commander required the skills of a small-town mayor as much as those of a military leader. Base families got skittish in a hurry when they were this isolated. They hadn't been thrilled with the idea of an al-Qaeda prison being built in their backyard, but they'd been pleasantly surprised by the vigor it injected into base life. Lewis had even joked about reinstalling the town's one and only stoplight, which had been retired to the base museum. From everything Falk had heard, the captain had been quite content to stay out of Trabert's hair, and vice versa, which made this meeting seem all the more awkward.

"I'll be introducing you to General Cabral," Captain Lewis said.

"As what?"

Lewis turned toward the general.

"What was the agreed-upon terminology, sir?"

"Liaison from the civilian side, representing Sergeant Ludwig's family. There will be no mention of your employer. The captain will do all the talking, Falk, but keep your eyes open."

"For anything in particular?"

"Anything out of the ordinary."

"This whole thing's out of the ordinary."

"All the more reason for another set of eyes."

Falk wondered if Lewis was unhappy about his presence. Cluttering the usual one-on-one intimacy, especially with a civilian, seemed indelicate at best. He noticed that Lewis had brought along a recent copy of *Sports Illustrated* with a cover story on a Cuban-born pitcher, perhaps as a peace offering. Trabert's maneuvers would probably cramp his style. But Falk wasn't about to get in the middle of an Army-Navy dustup, if it should come to that.

"So how will this work?" he asked Lewis.

"Pretty much like always. We'll go down to the guardhouse on our side of the fence with a couple Marines in tow. The Cubans will send an escort to take us across. This one's their show, so we'll meet in what used to be the currency exchange hut, on their side."

"You going, too?" Falk asked the general.

Trabert shook his head.

"Don't want to make it bigger than it already is. But I wanted to be here in case there's a hitch."

"Any reason to think there will be?"

"With new ground and old enemies, you never know."

Falk noticed a slight frown from Lewis, but the captain held his tongue. Then, with a glance toward the window, Lewis said, "Looks like they're here. That's General Cabral's ride."

A green truck with a canvas canopy had just pulled up on the Cuban side beneath a big white sign with red and black lettering that said, "República de Cuba. Territorio Libre de America." It was a Cuban taunt: "Territory Free of America." Soldiers jumped from the open tailgate.

"Looks like they've brought a few more than usual," Lewis said, not sounding thrilled. Trabert nodded, as if his worst suspicions had been confirmed. Then he trained a pair of binoculars on the scene.

"C'mon," Lewis said. "Let's get this over with."

Two Marines led the way. Also accompanying the captain was a staff interpreter. As they emerged from the shade of the observation post the sunlight struck them like a blade. A big iguana, legs pedaling, scuttled out of the way as they strolled downhill across the red-and-gold globe of the Marine Corps emblem. It looked like someone had recently touched up the paint job. Overhead, a pair of turkey vultures circled in formation with four skinnier, scarier birds that looked straight out of a Gothic drawing. It would have seemed ominous if they weren't already such a common sight.

"Cuban air force," Lewis said.

"Yeah, nice escort."

"Anything you need me to ask?"

"We need the exact location of where they found the body—right down to GPS coordinates if possible, not that I'm expecting any. And the exact time of discovery, plus any medical observations they might have recorded about the body."

Lewis nodded. They'd passed a line of red-and-gold tank barriers painted with "USMC" and reached the American guardhouse, where a Marine in full gear opened a gate just wide enough to let them pass single file. Lewis hesitated at the head of their contingent, awaiting the two Cuban soldiers now crossing the paved strip in the middle of a twenty-yard no-man's-land. There was no sound but their footsteps.

"Our Marines would usually wait for us here," Lewis whispered. "But General Cabral's e-mail said to bring them along to transport the body."

"Is that how you heard about this? By e-mail?"

"Right before lunch. Great for digestion."

"He say anything else?"

Lewis shook his head. "He's usually pretty chatty. But we'll see."

The Cubans were already waiting inside the shade of the white plaster customs office. You could hear muffled conversation in Spanish through the open window, which stopped the moment they entered through a glass door.

The room was almost unbearably stuffy. An orderly was still opening windows while another plugged in an oscillating fan that looked like something out of a Sears catalog from the 1930s. The man at the head of a small table, presumably General Cabral, kept his seat, smoking a cigar. Judging from Captain Lewis's hesitancy, Falk guessed that the general was usually quicker to his feet. Finally the man stood, big and clean-shaven, hazel eyes brimming with questions. His uniform was olive drab, and nothing fancy except for the patch on each shoulder with a single star. Keep it simple, Falk supposed, just like the Big Boss in Havana. He took the cigar from his mouth but didn't offer his hand.

"Asiéntese, por favor."

The captain and his interpreter took seats in old wooden chairs, which creaked as if they'd been there since the Spanish-American War. There wasn't a seat for Falk, so he stood next to the Marines behind Lewis, scanning the somber faces on the other side. They, too, had brought a man in civilian clothes. Maybe a doctor, but more likely from the political side, either the Intelligence Directorate or some other part of the Interior Ministry.

There was no meal, but an orderly entered with a tray of demitasse cups filled to the brim with Cuban coffee. As with the chairs, there was only enough for the two principals and their interpreters.

General Cabral then opened the meeting, apparently having decided that an introduction of lesser players was unnecessary.

"Lo siento . . ." he began, Falk paying attention to the interpreter, who repeated the general's remarks in the typically stilted language of simultaneous translation.

"I am sorry for these circumstances that bring us together, Captain Lewis. In a moment we will transfer to your custody the remains of your soldier. But I must comment first that this troubles me."

"I'm troubled, too," Lewis answered. When Cabral heard the translation he shook his head.

"No, no. My troubles are of a different nature. You have a casualty, and for that you have my sympathy. But for me the problem is much larger. What am I to tell my commanders when they ask how it was possible for an American soldier—even a dead one—to come ashore and not be discovered for hours?"

Lewis opened his mouth, but Cabral raised a hand and continued, using the cigar like a prompter to punctuate each point.

"How are we to know for sure he was dead when he first reached our waters? Why, if he was only swimming, was he in uniform? Would that not suggest to you or to me, being military men, that he was either coming from a boat or was on some sort of mission?"

Good questions. All of them. Falk noticed the Cuban civilian taking notes.

"I can assure you, speaking for all parties on our side," Captain Lewis began, "that Sergeant Ludwig was not on any mission, official or otherwise. As for what he was doing out there in the ocean at all, much less on your side, it is as much a puzzle to us as it is to you. But I can say with complete confidence that he was acting as an individual, and not as a soldier of the United States. In fact, he was expressly acting against his orders as a United States soldier. As I told you by e-mail earlier today, his unit had already reported him missing, and some of his belongings had been found on one of our beaches, two miles from the fenceline."

Falk was mildly surprised by the detail of the captain's candor, but he supposed that it was warranted.

"It is reassuring to know of the 'missing man' report," Cabral replied through the interpreter, "although perhaps that, too, is a convenient circumstance for your side. But I will take it into advisement with my commanders. We have launched our own investigation into this matter, of course."

"And we as well. Meaning that any information you can offer as to the time and place he came ashore, his initial condition, and so on, will only help us both find the answers to your questions as quickly as possible."

"All in good time. We must first satisfy ourselves as to the nature of the sergeant's business."

Meaning that the wounds from this weren't likely to heal quickly. As if to confirm this, Cabral stood, signaling abruptly that the meeting was over. Lewis still held the rolled-up magazine in his right hand. Cabral nodded to a soldier by the door, who disappeared outside.

"They will bring the body from the truck. Your Marines will take it from here."

They'd zipped Sergeant Ludwig into a Soviet-issue body bag and placed him on a stretcher. The men in the room watched through a side window as the awkward transfer took place. Everyone stood in rigid silence, as if not daring to exit before the formalities of the transfer were completed. Lewis moved toward the door without a further word. No one shook hands or said good-bye.

"That was pleasant," the captain muttered as they walked toward the American side, trailing the meager cortege of two Marines and the laden stretcher. Falk said nothing in reply. Glancing skyward, he saw that the vultures had drifted south, toward the better pickings of the base landfill.

Back inside the observation post, General Trabert took Lewis aside for a few moments of grim-faced conversation that Falk couldn't hear. Lewis then made his exit as Trabert crossed the room.

"Sounds like they're taking it badly," the general said. "I suppose you'll need to tie up some loose ends as well."

"To put it mildly. We'll need an autopsy, for starters."

"Obviously. Although I gather the Cubans have concluded it's a drowning, or they'd have said otherwise."

"In the meantime I'll need his records, access to his colleagues, both here and in the States, and also to his family. Any recent letters from home, all that kind of thing. Plus all the rota listings from his unit, to show when he was last on duty, and who he was with. We'll need a full accounting of his movements for his last twenty-four hours."

Trabert seemed taken aback.

"Is all that really necessary? Unless you know something that I don't."

Was this the same man who, less than twelve hours ago, had been talking about the need for outside help?

"Well, even if he drowned, the Cubans are right about one thing. It's damned strange where he wound up."

"I'm not so sure of that. Captain Lewis says those offshore currents are trickier than you think. He figures Ludwig hit a funny tide or something."

So would this be the party line? A freak current? Maybe that was the real job of this incoming "special team." A PR chore of glossing things over. Either way, Falk would be checking the Navy's charts, and that's what he told Trabert.

The general gave him a long look.

"Fine. The Navy's port control office will have those. But you look like something else is bugging you. Speak your mind, Falk."

Speak your mind. Always a dubious proposition when it came from a man with two stars on his sleeve. He decided to be frank anyway.

"I guess I'm a little puzzled, sir. You're the one who called in this delegation from Washington, and as far as I can tell you'd arranged it before I even got to the beach."

At first the general looked stern, stroking his chin. Then he lowered his head and broke into a sheepish grin.

"My apologies, Falk." He lowered his voice. "Between you and me, I was using you."

"Sir?"

"This delegation has been in the works for weeks. I did happen to pass along word of the sergeant's disappearance as I heard about it, of course—it's that kind of crowd, one that wouldn't want any surprises. But any involvement in this affair would be secondary to their real work."

"Which is?"

"Classified. There's bound to be talk once they're here. The usual gossip. And if people want to believe that their main order of business is the sergeant's disappearance, fine by me. And fine by them."

"So will they have any interest at all in this case?"

"Only to the extent that it affects their work. Five minutes ago I would have told you that was a zero possibility. But with all that you're asking for, it may raise their eyebrows."

"It's really the minimum, sir."

"Fine. Just don't complain to me when they come crawling up your backside. Yours and everybody else's."

"Just what *are* they coming for, sir? Between you and me."

Trabert gave him a long look.

"Security matters. Some of it won't be pleasant." So maybe the rumors were true, after all, just as Tyndall had said. "But I'll tell you what, Falk. I'll keep them off your back as long as you do me a favor."

"What's that, sir?"

"Keep me posted. When they move, I want to know it. You be my eyes and ears on these people."

"I'm not sure how much good I can do you. I'm likely to be a little, well, preoccupied."

"You may change your mind once you've met them. There's a friend of yours on board. Or so he claims. Ted Bokamper."

For all the shock of hearing the general speak Ted Bokamper's name, Falk supposed he shouldn't be surprised, knowing what he did about the man. But it certainly made the nature of the team's work seem even more intriguing.

"Yes, sir. I know him, all right. I'll do what I can."

"Good. Then you'll join me in the welcoming party. Touchdown at Leeward Point at eighteen hundred hours. Be at the ferry dock at seventeen thirty."

"Wouldn't miss it for the world, sir."

For a change, he really meant it.

CHAPTER SIX

Miami Beach

WHENEVER Gonzalo Rubiero was homesick for Cuba—an almost everyday occurrence lately—he made his way by bus or bicycle to a small park at Collins and Twenty-first. It had clipped grass, stately palms, and a lush grove of sea grapes, but the real attraction was the view. It was one of the few places on South Beach where the ocean wasn't walled off by new high-rises or Art Deco revivals.

Gonzalo preferred mornings, seating himself on a shaded boardwalk bench that stank of cat urine and gazing out at the sea. Container ships lined up offshore like targets in a shooting arcade, red-and-white cutouts inching south on the blue horizon. If he stared long enough he could place himself on board—hands gripping the wet rail, sea breeze billowing his guayabera while dolphins leaped in the swells, guiding him homeward.

Suitably pacified, he then walked down the beach, taking an hour to reach the fishing pier and stone jetty at the lower end. The sight of fishermen produced further nostalgia—memories of his father in a wide-brim straw hat, knee-deep in the shallows, flinging a net at schools of minnows. When his aim was true, the clear water fizzed like seltzer.

Spies weren't supposed to get all mopey like this, especially old hands on hostile ground. But these were unsettling times, and the beachfront pilgrimage had become a means of collecting his thoughts amid growing disorder. That seemed especially important just now, at the close of a week that had brought two challenging new assignments in rapid succession.

The first began as a mere janitorial chore. There had been a lot of those lately—cleanup jobs and damage assessments after networks had been rolled up by raids and arrests. Cuban agents had been deported and carted off by the dozens during the past few years, and Gonzalo had always been left behind to suffer the consequences—radios gone silent, mailboxes looted, diskettes plundered. He moved stealthily in the wake of each disaster like an insurance adjuster in the wake of a hurricane, plotting reconstruction even as he scanned for leaking rooftops and cracked foundations. Too often he found both.

His employer's current problems dated back to a shake-up in 1989, but the worst of the recent miseries had begun two years ago, when an operative who had infiltrated the highest corridors of the Defense Intelligence Agency had been identified, arrested, then sent to jail. The latest fallout from that disaster had come only two months ago, when fourteen agents working under diplomatic cover in New York and Washington had been expelled. The casualties included Gonzalo's ostensible handler, a fluttery man in Manhattan who had played the stock market as impulsively as he had played the spy game, vainly trying to keep his four daughters in the right schools and the best prom gowns while still paying his rent on the Upper West Side. It was always nice irony when material attachments did in the enemies of capitalism.

Fortunately the man had never known Gonzalo's real name or address, and there was no shortage of operatives still in place. Gonzalo's boss, a wheezing old fixture of the Dirección de Inteligencia—the Intelligence Directorate, or DI—liked to joke that the South Florida payroll exceeded that of the home office.

But from Union City, New Jersey, down to Little Havana it was a good time for lying low. Which was fine with Gonzalo, seeing as how lying low had always been part of his duties. It had been his lot in life to spy on his own people almost as much as he spied on the Americans, watching carefully for weak links, chiselers, blabbermouths, and potential defectors.

Such a role, as might be expected, kept him isolated. In the upper floors of DI headquarters his existence was known to only a select few, who thought of him as one of a handful of Las Ranas del Árbol, the Tree Frogs, so named for a Cuban species that had invaded Florida's ecosystem eighty years earlier, establishing itself as a dominant but well-camouflaged predator in the state's dampest and darkest corners.

That is why even his handler, Fernandez—the stock player formerly of the Upper West Side—had known only Gonzalo's operational name of Paco. Fernandez was a mere conduit, ensuring that Gonzalo's occasional needs were attended to. His only attempt at independent supervision came just before his expulsion, when he rashly ordered Gonzalo to empty the mail drops of blown agents in Hialeah, Coral Gables, and Kendall.

Knowing it to be a fool's errand, Gonzalo ignored the edict, although out of curiosity he reconnoitered all three locations, discovering, as expected, that each had been staked out by special agents of the FBI. Two of them he recognized from a gallery of snapshots that he'd wrapped in plastic and taped to a cabinet door beneath his kitchen sink. The first of them had been seated by a window in a diner across the street. The second was dressed in painter's clothes at the next location, scraping woodwork at an abandoned storefront. Gonzalo recognized no one at the third drop, but eventually deduced that his rival was the fellow who kept coming and going from a Verizon van. He snapped the man's photo for his gallery, then celebrated the acquisition with a midday feast of roast pork and a papaya milk shake at the Versailles, a Little Havana eatery garishly decked out in wall-to-wall mirrors, the sort of excessive bad taste that always made Gonzalo smile at his fellow expats—in affection, not ridicule. Such misguided striving amid the whining babble of their enraged politics. They never stopped voicing their zeal for deposing El Comandante, yet if they ever succeeded he doubted even one in ten would actually return to Cuba for more than a visit—unless someone was stupid enough to put them in charge, a possibility he attributed only to ideologues at the U.S. Department of State.

Gonzalo was generous with the fruits of his triumphs. By late afternoon that day he had e-mailed a JPEG of the agent's photo to a secure intermediary in Union City, who erased Gonzalo's cyber-fingerprints before forwarding the image to Havana from an Internet café in Passaic. By week's end every field operative in the United States had a copy—except those among the recently disgraced, such as the luckless Fernandez, who was already packing his bags and breaking the news to his tearful daughters.

Word of Gonzalo's newest assignments had come via regular channels. Messages from the home office arrived as needed during an 8 a.m. broadcast by high-frequency shortwave radio. Setting up the radio and tape recorder for the daily transmission was a part of his morning ritual, like making coffee. If he happened to be out, or had company, there was always a repeat performance in the evening.

The signal never lasted more than a few seconds. It produced a series of numbers that Gonzalo taped while a television played loudly in the next room, in case the neighbors were listening.

He then typed in the numbers on a Toshiba laptop, erased the tape, and retrieved a decryption diskette from its hiding place behind the bathroom mirror. A professional search would have discovered it in minutes, but Gonzalo was more worried about the hazards of random chance—a burglar, an overly curious friend, or anyone else who might accidentally discover the diskette and wonder, "What have we here?"

With a few keystrokes, Gonzalo activated the program. Seven years ago it had been state of the art, and so had the Toshiba. Now both were dinosaurs. Any Dade County teenager willing to put aside his Game Boy for a few hours could probably pick apart the encryption. But budgets were in the toilet—had been for years—and shipments of the new equipment kept going to people who were getting caught.

The message produced a sigh of resignation.

K out. Janitor requested.

Another one bites the dust, he thought. A safe house in Kendall was about to be compromised, probably because of an arrest that had yet to hit the papers. It was Gonzalo's job to launder the premises, a chore about as touchy as a domestic call for a beat cop. It was a nuisance that could turn dangerous at any second. The sooner he got it out of the way, the better.

He wore painter's clothes for these occasions, and had after-hours access to a contractor's panel truck parked in Coral Gables. The house in question was in one of those bland condo subdivisions that looked pretty much like a hundred others in the flat, broiling suburbs off Dixie Highway.

Gonzalo arrived just after dark to find the place a mess—ashtrays full, unwashed pots in the sink, coffee rings on countertops. Dust covered every surface, and the digital displays flashed on the microwave and VCR, meaning they probably hadn't been reset since the last power outage. You could never teach spies to be good housekeepers, but this level of neglect was especially egregious.

The dirt and dishes, however, weren't his concern. His mission was a glorified scavenger hunt, to round up any and all traces of intelligence activity. The only mail to collect was a pile of ad flyers and pizza coupons that had been pushed through the front slot and now lay on the carpet, just inside the door. Judging by the postmarks, no one had been here for at least four days.

Next he checked for stray videotapes, finding the VCR empty. Then he methodically collected four tiny concealed microphones from their customary locations—one behind the bathroom mirror, one beneath the corner of a coffee table in the living room, and one behind the headboard in each of the upstairs bedrooms.

He dropped these treasures into a cloth sack as he moved from room to room, the Cuban Grinch here to steal the FBI's Christmas. In an upstairs hall closet he checked the recording equipment. Ideally the tape should be clear. Yet after rewinding it for a few seconds he heard muffled conversation on playback. He sighed but somehow wasn't surprised. He ejected it with a click and dropped another prize into the sack. The recorder went next, an angular bulge making the sack heavy enough that he had to shift the weight across his right shoulder. Now he really did look like Santa.

In the second bedroom he discovered the biggest security breach yet, after flipping back the dust ruffle on a queen-sized bed to spot a cardboard box hiding on the floor beneath the bed. He slid it across the carpet into the open, and saw to his dismay that it was half filled with papers—cables and faxes, e-mail printouts, just the sort of baubles that might bring down an entire network. Stupidity writ large. No wonder someone associated with this location had been caught. Another ex-military man, if Gonzalo had to guess, one of the hires during the big purge of '89 when Raúl Castro—El Comandante's brother, and the head of the military—had reached across the upper levels of Havana bureaucracy to install one of his generals atop the Interior Ministry, which ran the Directorate. The general, in turn, had recalled some of the Directorate's best and brightest, replacing them with loyal but untrained military hacks. Field men like Gonzalo had been paying for the mistake ever since. In recent years the Directorate had begun hiring back some of the older and steadier hands who'd been purged, but the damage was done.

Gonzalo hefted the box carefully, as if its contents were radioactive. If there had been a fireplace handy—about as likely in Miami as a jalousie window in Alaska—he would have burned the contents on the spot. He briefly considered dispatching the load to the oven, or checking outside for a grill. But the former would take too long, and he was too uncertain about the neighbors for the latter.

So he dumped the papers into the sack, and as he did so one of the sheets toward the bottom of the pile slipped free, oscillating like a parachutist to the floor. He was about to stuff it into the bag when the subject line caught his eye.

From: MX
Re: Desert Rose, via Guadalupe.

Well, now.

MX was the Directorate's top man, and the subject in question had been the source of abundant speculation and internal rumor during the past few months. He knew that if he held this document in his hands any longer that he would read it, and he didn't want that kind of knowledge. Too burdensome—the sort of information that might get wrapped around your ankles and drag you to the bottom of Biscayne Bay. He dropped the paper daintily into the sack, then bunched the top and slung it across his back, heading for the steps. Why would someone have kept a memo like that? And it was a photostat no less, suggesting that some local imbecile had actually run off a few copies for wider circulation.

Gonzalo was sweating by the time he was downstairs, partly from exertion but also from an onset of nerves. The sound of a slamming door stopped him halfway across the living room. Tensed and silent, he heard voices—the light chatter in English of two women, followed by laughter. They were outside, probably having just left the condo next door. Paper-thin walls and shabby construction were an unavoidable hazard of South Florida safe houses. During Hurricane Andrew they'd lost the roof off one near Homestead Air Force Base. The place stood open to the elements for a full week before anyone did a thing. Fortunately, the neighbors and insurance adjusters were slower to move than their operative, and the waterlogged equipment had been carted off as if it were just another ruined stereo system. If a hurricane had hit this place it might have sent those papers fluttering for miles.

Gonzalo peeped through the front blinds. The two women were getting into a Mazda parked at the curb, apparently harmless, but a reminder that he might soon have company. To be on the safe side, he dropped the sack by the door and quickly retraced his steps through the house, checking one last time for anything he might have missed. Almost as an afterthought he picked up the phone receiver and pressed the Speed Dial button and the number one. It beeped into action, dialing to God knows where. He immediately hung up, and then flew into a rage.

"Stupid, careless, lazy bastards! Fucking idiots!" After twenty-two years in Florida, Gonzalo now cursed mostly in English.

He wasn't quite sure how to deprogram the phone, so after fumbling with the buttons for a few seconds he simply unplugged it and tossed it into the sack. Then he retrieved the upstairs extension and opened the door to leave, checking his flanks from the small porch. The street was clear. The worst of the day's heat was melting into the streets and sidewalks, conserving its energy for morning. Gonzalo decided not to lock the door behind him. If thieves came along and ransacked the rest, all the better. Who knew what sort of mail might arrive in the days ahead, judging from the monumental foolishness already in evidence? Nothing he could do about that, however.

He tried not to drive too carefully on the way back, although he compulsively checked his mirrors for anyone following. The only thing more likely to attract the attention of a cop than drag racing up Dixie Highway would be scrupulously observing the speed limit. Blending in required tailgating, excessive acceleration after stoplights, and generally making an ass of yourself with frequent lane changes. If no one honked at you at least once every five miles, then you probably weren't meeting the standard.

He switched back to his own car, a nine-year-old Corolla, in the parking lot. He felt like a thief loading his sack into the car, and as he headed home he eyed it on the seat beside him. Somewhere inside it, perhaps growing like a tumor, was the memo from MX. It wouldn't have surprised him if it suddenly burst into flame, spontaneously revealing its presence to other drivers. There was a charcoal grill out back at his apartment building, and his neighbors were accustomed to his using it. He would light the papers beneath a pile of briquettes and destroy them. It would take only a few minutes, and the ashes would drift in the nightly breeze that would carry them out over the ocean. A burial at sea, all those forbidden secrets safe at last. Then he would grill some sausages, open a beer, and relax. He could deal with the phones and electronic gear later.

But by the time he was upstairs and safely indoors his curiosity had gotten the best of him. If MX was sending urgent memos and, worse, if station chiefs were daring to make copies for careless field men, then why shouldn't he at least know the latest, if only for self-protection? While his relative autonomy as a "Tree Frog" generally worked to his advantage, it also made him an easy dupe for supervisors eager to employ his services to undermine their rivals. What his taskmasters failed to realize in making such assignments was that in the process Gonzalo often learned as much about their weaknesses as about those of their targets. By imparting such knowledge they were violating the single most important rule of their trade: No one should ever be told more than he explicitly needed to know. Of course, Gonzalo would be making the same mistake by peeking at the forbidden memo.

He knew enough from previous findings that any directive from MX involving source Guadalupe and operative Desert Rose was a likely precursor to renewed upheaval. But as he stared at the sack on his kitchen table, he supposed that for a change it might be better to know more than he was supposed to.

He easily found the document, since it had been the last one into the bag. It was a little crumpled from its voyage across town, so Gonzalo smoothed it on his kitchen table.

First he checked the date. Nine days ago. New enough to be fresh, old enough to have been overtaken by events. He wondered if the imminent exposure of the local field man was somehow related.

The circulation list was intriguing. Besides Miami the memo had gone to station chiefs in Madrid, Khartoum, and Damascus. Madrid was the hub for Europe, Khartoum was at the heart of the current troubles in Sudan, and Damascus was a frequent clearinghouse for operations in the Middle East, although that theater had long been dormant, ever since the days of the Directorate's close relations with various Palestinian factions, some of which had long ago sent fighters to Cuba for training in arms and explosives.

The message was brief:

> Guadalupe reports abort incomplete. Desert Rose,
> José 1, and three others incommunicado. Request

> immediate assistance all locations. Utmost
> urgency.

Guadalupe, he knew, was a sort of glorified freelance, with duties similar to Gonzalo's but on a wider field of play. Desert Rose was a name he hadn't come across in years, dating back to the busiest days of cooperation with the Palestinians. José 1 didn't ring a bell, but seemed to have thrown in his lot with Desert Rose and the "three others." The Directorate was apparently trying to stop this quintet from whatever it had gotten up to, but so far had failed. If all five were now considered off the leash, then they must have crossed the bounds of Directorate orthodoxy.

Figuring there had to be more information on a subject of such importance, Gonzalo plowed through the rest of the pile, but it was all junk, as worthless as the pizza coupons shoved through the mail slot. Expense vouchers and office logistics. A few mild reprimands for overspending countered by a few plaintive requests for more money. The usual give-and-take between headquarters and any regional office, whether the product is shoes or secrets.

The memo was the only important item in the whole stack, so he reread it, in case he might have missed some implication the first time. The circulation list continued to intrigue him. He shook his head, figuring that he had better light the fire. Whatever was going on here, it seemed like a good time to keep his head down.

But he couldn't, thanks to the message that arrived the very next morning on the shortwave. Two in two days, like the bouncing needle of a seismograph. And the second, in its way, was every bit as disturbing:

> Peregrine in nest. Arrange meeting. Highest
> urgency. Further details Puma.

Gonzalo usually erased his messages as soon as he'd read them. This one he left on his screen for several minutes while he paced the kitchen and turned on the coffeepot. He lit a cigarette and returned for a second look. He pressed the Delete key, but only once, then retrieved the message a final time, if only to convince himself that it wasn't a mirage, a malfunction.

Peregrine was a name representing one of his most intriguing triumphs and dismal failures, although his superiors still held a generally rosy view of the operation. He had long hoped for an opportunity to salvage something from the wreckage, so in that sense he was gratified. But how strange that Peregrine had somehow returned to his original roost, or, as the message described it, "the nest." Perhaps the further details, soon to arrive at mailbox Puma, would clarify the circumstances of this mysterious development.

At any rate, he sensed that because of the names involved he would soon have to take risks. And in calculating the risks he realized something alarming: He was comfortable here. Settled. Happy, even. That, he now realized, was at the root of his recent bouts of homesickness. They were separation pains, an acknowledgment that he was breaking away. For all its faults, enemy territory had become home, a dangerous development in his profession.

He was also troubled by the timing of this message. Its arrival only ten days after the date of the MX memo led him to believe they must be connected in some way, even if Havana would never have wanted him to know about the former. Whatever storm was brewing, he had just been swept into it.

Gonzalo deleted the message for good, taking a few extra steps that the techies had assured him would wipe it from his hard drive. He hoped they were right. In the wrong hands, those few words would be as damning as a bag of cocaine or a bar of yellowcake uranium.

Then he got down to business, heading out of the parking lot in his Corolla, crossing MacArthur Causeway to Biscayne Boulevard, where he turned north and began scouting for a phone booth. None of the ones he had used before would do. But they were increasingly hard to find, especially ones that took coins. Some agents, he knew, had begun using generic phone cards. Sloppy. He finally spotted a phone in the parking lot of a Denny's. He decided to make the call, then enjoy an American breakfast, the greasy hash browns he'd developed a taste for. At $3.99, how could he resist?

After scanning the parking lot for anyone within earshot, he plugged in a few quarters, then punched in the number for a beeper in Long Island. All the Manhattan lines had been deemed too hot to handle. At the sound of a recorded prompt he punched in a sequence of numbers, a code of acknowledgment that would tell Havana, "Message received, urgency acknowledged, awaiting instructions." He figured that the postman for the Puma mail drop might not arrive until noon, so he decided not to risk a premature visit.

Now all he could do was wait. So he ate breakfast while reading both the English and the Spanish editions of the *Miami Herald*, amusing himself as always by the rightward drift of the politics in the Latin version—niche pandering at its worst. He then decided that a long walk on the beach was in order for sorting things out. Besides, he was due to meet Lucinda at noon, down by the jetty. Thinking of her, he smiled for the first time all morning. Then he frowned. Yet another reason to fear this assignment. Lose this time and he lost everything.

Gonzalo had found much to sneer at when he had first arrived in America. He had come ashore with the Mariel Boatlift, blending easily with the ten thousand refugees who had come north in the giant flotilla. It was now well known that Castro had released a few thousand prison inmates into the mix, helping set off a South Florida crime wave of epic proportions. Less well known was the dictator's insertion of a few dozen select operatives such as Gonzalo.

Miami offered plenty of easy targets for someone eager to find fault. So much wealth alongside so much misery. Gated communities of feudal poshness. He watched causeway drawbridges open for huge yachts while thousands waited in sweltering cars. Public officials squandered millions on sports arenas for rich athletes and their top-dollar fans while, blocks away, entire communities rotted. On a visit to Fort Lauderdale he watched a ragged Haitian fisherman trying to net dinner on a tidal canal from the edge of a parking lot where a sign said, "Valet only. No bills larger than $20." It was easy to see this place as Rome in decline, Babylon on the Bay. Gonzalo could be as smug as he liked.

The people in the middle ranks were the ones he couldn't comprehend, so in the evenings he often drove through their trim warrens of one-story homes in the suburbs, as if seeking entry through a last unlocked door. If only he might penetrate their stucco walls, join them on their couches before the flickering TV screens, or at their smoldering grills, or on their rumbling mowers.

No such luck. It was as if they existed in a different dimension, and he always arrived home thwarted and resentful, or cursing the traffic. So he gave it up, kept his head down, tended to his duties, relaxed, and slowly blended into the scenery. And look at where he had wound up—a man with a girlfriend, a steady income, and an apartment he liked on Washington Avenue, only four blocks from the beach at $550 a month. So what if his parking space was next to the Dumpster out back, and there were security bars across his windows, and his car insurance cost him an arm and a leg even for a nine-year-old Corolla. He had everything he needed over there on the beach, and all of it was within range of his bicycle, locked to a rack downstairs.

In thinking back, he supposed he had gotten the first inkling of his current predicament a few weeks ago, during one of his first trips to the park bench at Collins and Twenty-first. A snatch of graffiti scrawled on an emergency phone box had caught his eye: "Castro Fall—You Go Home"—a typical semaphore of rage from some Anglo fed up with Miami's bilingual bazaar. But to Gonzalo the message offered an unsettling truth. El Comandante wouldn't live forever, and when he went, so might Gonzalo's job, income, and passport. You go home? Yes, he just might have to.

All this was on his mind as he plodded down the beach after receiving his new assignment, sidestepping the seaweed and dead jellyfish. He wondered if the Directorate had already contacted others among Peregrine's old network. Perhaps wheels were already in motion. He would find out for sure once he retrieved the message from mailbox Puma.

On his beach walks, Gonzalo preferred to stay close to the surf, away from where the bulldozers groomed the sand for the hotel guests, with their loungers and cabanas. That was another reason he liked his little outpost down by the jetty. The bulldozers never journeyed that far, nor did most tourists. Instead there was a small corps of regulars who had gravitated to the spot just like him, seeking their own corner of paradise.

A Haitian family, the Lespinasses, came twice a week by bus from Allapattah—every Tuesday and Thursday, the father's days off. They always brought their three children, a big blanket, and a battered cooler filled with fresh fruit and Caribbean soft drinks.

There were also Karl and Brigitte Stolz, a retired couple from Germany who had decided to give Miami a try a year earlier, and still seemed stunned by its hyperkinetic brashness.

Then there was Ed Harbin—fiftyish, crew-cut, ex-Army, with a tan so deeply bronzed it seemed to have been applied in layers, each one thinner and harder than the last. Every day Ed swam out to the buoys that marked the exclusion zone for the fishing boats and Jet Skis that ripped up and down the shoreline, and the end of Gonzalo's walks often coincided with some part of Harbin's swim. Gonzalo would sit down to watch from the stones of the jetty while Harbin steadily came and went, never seeming to vary his pace or his stroke through rain or shine, hot or cold. Harbin was wiry, muscles stripped to their essentials except for a small potbelly. When he emerged from the water, two sets of dog tags jangled and glittered against the dripping silver hair on his chest.

Gonzalo had often wondered about those tags. Presumably one pair belonged to Harbin, but whose was the second? A son's? A pal's? Dead or alive? Gonzalo never had the guts to ask. Not much of a spy on matters like those, he supposed.

Harbin never failed to ask about the health and whereabouts of Lucinda, whom he had met a few times, and Gonzalo was always pleased and even proud to keep him informed. He liked to believe that after swimming Harbin indulged in a huge lunch somewhere up the beach, at Jerry's Famous Deli, perhaps, manhandling something sloppy like a cheeseburger with a thick shake. In truth, he had no idea where Harbin went. The shared world of these beachfront regulars was confined to their doings on their little stretch of sand, where they abided by an unspoken agreement that no one would ever pry further without an invitation.

Today Harbin was on his last fifty yards as Gonzalo arrived at the jetty. He watched the man step from the water and reach for a towel, brown eyes glowing in the sunlight of late morning.

"You did well today," Gonzalo said in greeting. "Almost to Bermuda."

Harbin smiled, toweling off as the tags clinked.

"One of these days maybe I'll head south, stop off in Cuba." He grinned, an opening for Gonzalo to offer more. But Gonzalo wasn't in the mood today, so he just smiled and said, "Make sure and say hello to my father then."

Harbin wouldn't have dared ask whether Gonzalo's father was still actually alive, just as Gonzalo wouldn't have dared ask whose name was on the extra set of tags. Maybe the man was childless and gay. It certainly would have been an easy fit with the culture of South Beach.

"Have you seen the Lespinasses?" Harbin asked.

"Charles said last week they might not make it today. A family birthday to celebrate. Some aunt of theirs in Overtown."

"Ah. Thursday won't be the same without them. Sort of like a Friday without the Stolzes. They're moving back to Germany, you know."

"No. I hadn't heard." Another little tremor in his safe world.

Harbin nodded.

"Saw them over the weekend at the Publix." Odd to think of ever bumping into each other anywhere but here. Gonzalo wasn't sure he would even know how to act.

"Brigitte's homesick, I think. Misses her sons."

"Who I gather have stopped visiting, now that they have children."

"Yes. Just when you want to see them more." The tags clinked again as Harbin fell silent. So perhaps they had belonged to a son.

"Well," Harbin said, neatly rolling up the towel as he always did, forming a bundle as tight as a sausage. "See you tomorrow."

"Until then."

No sense mentioning that he wouldn't be there, perhaps not for days. It was going to be hard enough telling Lucinda. Speaking of whom, there she was now. Gonzalo's heart lifted at the sight of her as she stepped from the park sidewalk onto the sand. She was waving now, golden eyes flickering like candlelight, her emotions playing in them like a flame.

"You're a lucky man, Gonzalo," Harbin said.

"As usual, you are right again, GI Joe."

Harbin laughed as he left the beach. Gonzalo watched him pause to speak with Lucinda. For the briefest moment he wondered what they were saying, and the slightest pang of mistrust registered in some quadrant of his mind that had been trained to be suspicious. He could never quite shut it down, especially after a message like this morning's. He would be edgy all day. Lucinda would notice and ask why—she always noticed, and he always made up something about the boss at his regular job. He was a security deskman at the South Bay Club, a condo high-rise overlooking the bay, which Lucinda liked because it gave them pool privileges. They had enjoyed many nice evenings grilling steaks out by the water, on a patio redolent with chlorine and sun lotion, a salt breeze stroking the palms. Perhaps that would be their destination tonight.

Harbin continued on his way, and Lucinda smiled toward Gonzalo with a generosity that melted every doubt and made him ashamed.

Her full name was Lucinda Bustillo. She was Venezuelan, having moved here as a teen when her father bought an apartment block on Key Biscayne. She had a slow smile and thick wavy hair that was a deep bronze, the sort of color you might come across in an old box of heirloom jewelry, although she never seemed happy with it—streaking it one week and frizzing it the next, a master of disguise without even trying.

"No bicycle," she said, looking around. "You took the bus today."

She liked it better when he brought his bike, even though it meant he had to push it alongside them as they walked to lunch. She thought the extra exertion was good for him, helping melt the little roll of fat around his belly, which she often pinched in bed. But that was a quibble. The only time she truly got irritated with Gonzalo was when he did volunteer work for the Cuban American organizations that he liked to keep tabs on.

"Right-wing crazies," she called them, hating them far more than Gonzalo did, not that he could ever confess his loathing. As a Venezuelan she found the politics of the expat Cubans ridiculous. During the Elián González fiasco she hadn't spoken to him for a week after hearing that one of the groups he worked for was at the forefront of the daily rallies and protests.

He had suggested that they stop discussing these matters altogether, in the interests of peace. So far she had been happy to oblige him, although lately she had begun to talk of a different solution. Why didn't they move, she suggested. Get away from South Florida and all of the whining.

She first brought it up when they were out walking on Calle Ocho, during one of their rare excursions as a couple into the heart of Little Havana. When they passed Domino Park she of course reminded him of the way the local merchants had tried to drive out all the old men and their game boards, by complaining that too many bums and drug dealers were hanging around. When they strolled across the "Walk of Fame," a latinized version of Hollywood's Walk of Fame, she couldn't resist joking about the way its sponsors had been accused of kickback schemes and of trying to arrange a hit on a city commissioner.

"And these are the geniuses who think they should be running Cuba instead of Fidel?" she said, her laughter filling the street.

"Nothing was ever proven," Gonzalo said testily, feeling as if he had to stand up for all Cubans, even the moronic ones. "No one was ever charged."

"No," she said. "No one is ever charged. But they keep on making the same stupid mistakes. And if we didn't live here anymore, we'd never have to argue about them again."

Moving was out of the question for Gonzalo, of course, but he couldn't tell her why. So instead he hemmed and hawed about wanting to stay close to his roots, and to the way he grew up. Rather than argue the point she had shaken her head.

"Someday," she said slowly and in a tone of deep sadness. "Someday you will tell me the real reason you continue with this fiction."

At that moment he realized she knew him better than anyone. Personally he was enchanted. Professionally he was alarmed.

Lucinda was predictably displeased when he told her that he would be busy for a while because he had just taken on a new assignment for the crazies in Little Havana.

"So you won't be staying over tonight?"

"There's too much to do. At least for a few days."

"Fanatics and fools. Always calling for change when they haven't been to Cuba in years. What do they know about what it's really like anymore?"

True about him as well, Gonzalo supposed. With regard to his homeland he felt like a pen pal who hadn't written in ages. The Havana of his boyhood—his father flinging the net, his mother working as a hotel maid for pennies an hour—now seemed closer to him than the Havana that had existed just before he left for America, when he had been a young man brimming with the passion of the cause.

"So you'll be doing some job for them," she said with a sniff.

"Please. No politics. We agreed."

"Just don't expect me to be so understanding. Not when they're taking so much of your time. Will you be finished by Sunday?"

"I wish I could say."

"This won't be dangerous, will it?"

She had never asked that before, but Gonzalo had already pondered the same possibility. He had also been wondering if he might need help this time, not from the Directorate's regular stable of operatives but from his own personnel, which he had personally recruited. They were illegal immigrants from other Latin American countries who didn't know his real name, much less his real employer. They knew only that he was the fellow who had provided them with fresh identities stolen from tombstones in Texas and California, from dead persons who shared their same years of birth. It made your employees more loyal that way, especially if you called on them for only one chore and then set them loose, which was Gonzalo's practice.

So, yes, maybe this job would be dangerous, and Lucinda had

apparently picked up on his anxiety. The way she could read him was almost unnerving, even though it was part of her appeal. He would have to lie to her all the same.

"Oh, no," he answered. "Nothing dangerous. Just busy. And I'm not the boss."

"Please. I don't want to know any more."

"That's the last you'll hear. Let's at least enjoy the afternoon."

Which they did, followed by an evening at poolside with a big porterhouse on the grill. Then he drove her back to her place off Alton Road, a quiet building in the shade of ceiba trees, perfumed by orange blossoms.

She opened her front door just enough to let him smell the essence of the place—the bouquet of her cleaning, her cooking, her soaps and scents, a combination that only made him want to step inside.

"Are you coming in?" she asked, her eyes offering a night of sweetness and languor. Behind her he saw the amber light of the lamp next to her couch, the same color as her hair. It was safe and comfortable here, and for a few seconds he wavered in a way that he never had before when duty called. How easy it would be to say yes, and to let the message from Havana rot in its mail drop while he slept, resting against her back while the noise of the traffic came in through the jalousies and the ceiling fan thrummed. A Cuban lullaby right here on Alton Road.

But his conscientious nature prevailed. And, truth be told, he was curious. Something important was waiting just around the corner, and he had to find out what.

"I'd better go," he said, braving her eyes a final time. "There's a lot to do, even tonight."

She scowled, not knowing it was for all the wrong reasons.

"Those crazy Cubans," she said, as if Gonzalo was from a different country altogether. "Always stirring things up."

Once again, her intuition was right on the mark.

CHAPTER SEVEN

The sleek little Gulfstream approached Guantánamo from the south like a mosquito, needling through the rosy dusk on the narrow flight path that pilots loved to hate. It was a toss-up as to what was the greater hazard—violating Cuban airspace or plunging into the Caribbean. Yet everyone always seemed to arrive in one piece.

The jet taxied to the yawning mouth of the airstrip's cavernous pink hangar, where Falk waited with General Trabert alongside the group commanders for detention and intelligence. Joining them were a few mechanics and an active cloud of midges. It was their feeding time, and Falk slapped one on his neck. They were tiny, yet drew blood and left a welt the size of a nickel—the perfect welcoming delegation for a team from Washington, as far as he was concerned.

The three visitors stepped to the tarmac, their hair blowing in the ocean breeze. Two wore suits, as if they'd been lifted right off K Street. The third wore a dark green Army dress uniform with enough campaign ribbons to cover a dashboard.

Bokamper, one of the suits, was the last one off. He spotted Falk immediately, signaling recognition with a familiar glint in his eye, the barely contained glee of a frat boy who has just short-sheeted every bed in the house. But, as always, he maintained an air of command—the upright carriage, the stride that was almost a swagger, an ease of movement radiating calmness and control.

Their friendship dated to the unlikeliest of beginnings. During basic training Bokamper had been the bright young officer to Falk's rebellious recruit. Without the guidance of the former, the latter might well have washed out. Without the prodding curiosity of the latter, the former might have settled into a military career path. Or so Bokamper later claimed.

They developed enough mutual respect that three years later Bo was the first person Falk turned to for fellowship and counsel when he left the Marines to enroll at American University in Washington. When Falk had shown an aptitude for foreign languages, it was Bo who steered him toward Arabic—"the real up-and-comer, just watch." And by then he was in position to know, as a new Foreign Service officer working just around the corner at the State Department.

From there, both men hit the road, Bokamper to a succession of embassies in Jordan, Managua, and Bahrain while Falk spent two years at American's campus in Beirut, for further studies in Arabic and Middle Eastern cultures.

A high priest of Foggy Bottom pegged Bokamper as a rising star and brought him home for grooming as an acolyte of the inner circle, that ring of professionals which forever steers diplomacy no matter who is installed at the helm. Falk spent a few more years abroad working as a corporate security consultant, and then signed on with the Bureau, which was desperate for his language skills. He arrived back in Washington within a year of Bokamper's return, which proved to be fortuitous timing. Without Bo's influence, Falk might have found his new masters a bit too gray and rigid, even though his polished Arabic virtually guaranteed a fast track. Falk's shared insights on the Arab world, meanwhile, helped Bo widen his audience of patrons among State's burgeoning influx of neoconservatives, even though Bo believed that that fashion, like many before it, would soon come and go.

Since then, their paths had occasionally crossed elsewhere—in Yemen during the *Cole* investigation, for example. Busy schedules permitting, they still got together in Washington every month or so.

Falk was nonetheless a little disconcerted that the fates were bringing them together at Guantánamo. They had a common link to this place, one with its own odd and unsettling history, which Falk would rather have left undisturbed. He would also be playing the unaccustomed role of host and mentor, after years of letting Bo set the tone.

"Let's make 'em feel at home," Trabert said as the three members of the delegation strolled forward. "You're to give them everything they ask for. You in particular, Falk."

"Yes, sir," he answered, a shade too quickly.

The general returned the salute of the Army officer, then announced, "Gentlemen, welcome to Guantánamo, the Pearl of the Antilles."

Bokamper was the only one to chuckle, which drew an irritated glance from the other suit, who Falk learned during introductions was the team leader, Ward Fowler, from the Department of Homeland Security. The uniform belonged to Colonel Neil Cartwright, from the office of the secretary of defense. Bokamper was presented as the new liaison to Task Force Guantánamo from the secretary of state, meaning he must still be moving up in the world.

Trabert introduced Falk not as an interrogator but as "the special agent investigating the Ludwig affair," which drew a smile but fortunately not another laugh from Bo. By the time the grip and grin was over, the atmosphere was already stiff and formal, and the general didn't exactly lighten the mood with his next remarks.

"The MPs will be using a canine to check your luggage for explosive materials. Then we'll take the ferry to the windward side, where you'll be shown to your quarters. For those of you who wish to socialize this evening, MPs are available to escort you wherever you like. But I'd offer a caution. Throughout your stay, bear in mind that there are operational matters we don't dialogue about in the open. We give no aid and comfort to the enemy. Questions?"

There were no takers, lest anyone accidentally offer aid and comfort.

"Then I'll be seeing you at my office tomorrow, per your schedule, at oh eight hundred hours."

He turned smartly on his heel to lead the way, everyone silently falling into formation.

FALK LEANED ON THE PORT RAIL as the chunky gray ferry plowed through the luminous chop on its twenty-minute crossing. Sternward, the last of the sunlight bled into the hills, and to the north the distant lights of a Cuban village twinkled on the horizon. Only eight passengers were aboard, which left plenty of room to spread out on the steel deck. Bokamper sidled up on Falk's left.

"Congratulations on the promotion," Falk said.

"Not sure I'd call it that."

"Sounded like one when I heard about it from the general."

"Do I detect an edge?"

"I'm not that hard to get in touch with."

"Maybe I wanted it to be a surprise. What with this being your old stomping grounds and all that."

"Yeah. All that."

Only they would have understood the freight carried by those words, but Falk glanced around anyway to make sure no one else was within earshot. It was the perfect opening for mentioning the letter from Elena that had arrived that morning, but he decided to wait for more privacy.

"The general's got quite a bedside manner," Bo said. "Really knows how to put the troops at ease."

"Figured you guys would hit it off. So what's with your bunch? Who are these guys, anyway?"

"Where do you want me to start?"

"How 'bout the top. The guy from Homeland Security."

"Fowler? If I had to pick his three biggest heroes I'd say George Patton, John Madden, and Dale Carnegie. Hit 'em hard, play to win, and always keep the customer satisfied. Bit of a prude, but a true believer."

"In what?"

"The Mission."

"Which is?"

"Whatever his boss tells him but doesn't tell me."

"But you're part of the team."

"Yes and no. Beyond that, I shouldn't say too much. They're already worried I'll spoil the party."

"Trabert said there would be surprises."

Bokamper nodded, gazing at the foaming wake. There was no sound but the rumble of the engines, which sent shuddering vibrations up through the deck. Bo tipped his head to the north.

"Those lights. Cuban?"

"Yeah. Caimanera, I think. Maybe some other village. You'll get used to it. What about the uniform, Neil Cartwright?"

"Fowler's errand boy. And considering that he's got the full power of the secretary of defense behind him, he should be a pretty handy errand boy."

"What's he like?"

"The quiet type."

"Meaning dangerous?"

"Or stupid. I don't know. Could be a cipher, could be the next deputy secretary. Seems like a good enough guy. About as warm as an undertaker, but that comes with the territory. He's been designated the chief springer of surprises. The one who'll light the candles on the cake."

"When's the party?"

"Soon. Maybe tomorrow."

"Am I invited?"

"You better hope not. But I haven't seen the full guest list."

It was a little too indefinite for comfort, or maybe Bokamper was just teasing, as someone who knew Falk's weaknesses all too well.

"What else?"

"That's the extent of my knowledge. I've known Fowler for a while, but Cartwright I hadn't even heard of until yesterday. Met him on the plane."

Falk raised his eyebrows.

"Like I told you, I'm not an original member of the Brady Bunch here. Last-minute adoption. The boss wanted me to get my feet wet, and this seemed like a good opportunity."

"Speaking of the Bradys, how are Karen and the kids?"

"Growing up too fast. Karen's great, volunteering for everything in sight. Turning into a Democrat, but I guess that's a hazard of living in Bethesda."

Bokamper had four children and counting, with each seemingly more contentious and rambunctious than the last, just like dear old dad. He was building a big, noisy brood along the lines of the one he'd grown up in. A visit to their home a year ago had been one of the few times when Falk had been tempted by the idea of being married and having children, of settling in one place long enough to watch your seeds grow and flourish while you pruned and weeded and prayed for the grace of the elements.

In visits to the homes of other friends he often glimpsed quarrels and attitude, the dammed-up pressures of overscheduling, or the bitterness of a wife whose career had been trampled in the stampede of child-rearing. He usually departed with relief, taking deep breaths all the way home. After leaving Bo's he felt only envy, having witnessed that fierceness of love that develops when every turn of fortune is embraced at full energy, both spouses working at close quarters, too busy protecting each other's flanks to notice any threats to their own.

It was the children's bedtime ritual that moved him most. Tiny heads poking from pajama tops as they dressed for sleep. A look of complete trust and comfort on their faces as Bo tucked them in. Falk supposed he could have all that, too, if he worked on it, tried harder. But some people weren't cut out for that life, even if they wanted it.

They talked a while longer about Bo's kids, until the ferry bumped the pilings at Fisherman Point, engines churning in reverse. Schools of striped fish hovered in the current below, illuminated by the dock lights.

In the neighboring slip, four members of a Coast Guard crew were putting covers on the deck guns of their Boston Whaler, a tidy patrol boat that Falk coveted whenever he saw it zipping nimbly around the bay. With a boat like that you could make a living out here. A woman, tall and blond, toweled sea spray off the biggest gun, a .50-caliber cannon mounted at the bow.

"Got many of those here?" Bokamper asked.

Falk knew he wasn't referring to the boat or the gun. The family man had never lost his roving eye.

"Not nearly. But if you want to see the entire field, I know the place. You guys had dinner?"

"They catered one for the flight. Not half bad."

"Meaning not half good."

"You know me. Palate of a stevedore."

"When you're finished unpacking, come down to the Tiki Bar. The place to be and be seen on the Rock."

"What's with the transportation? Do we get cars, or is the general going to have us driven everywhere?"

"I'd guess the official line will be that everything's rented out, which is true. But also convenient."

"You think he wants to keep tabs on us?"

"Wouldn't you?"

"If I was a nosy, insecure little hard-ass paratrooper like him, yeah, I guess so."

The boarding ramp thudded onto the shore. The voice of General Trabert piped up as the new arrivals reached for their bags.

"Gentlemen, I've got work to complete, so I'll be taking my leave." He gestured toward his office at Task Force Guantánamo headquarters—the so-called Pink Palace—which was just above them atop the facing coral bluff. "Your billets are a few miles from here. That's your bus waiting with the headlights on."

"First class all the way," Bokamper muttered.

"Get used to it, soldier," Falk said.

CHAPTER EIGHT

The Tiki Bar offered the military's idea of tropical island ambience—a little palm thatch, a few paper umbrellas for the fancier drinks, and enough cases of beer to sink an outrigger canoe. It wasn't much to look at—white plastic tables on a plain of concrete—but the drinks were cold, there was a pleasant view of the bay, and prices were at subsidy levels. Better still, its location just a few blocks off the main drag of Sherman Avenue offered an escape from the swarms of the MP underclass, who now had their own open-air bar, Club Survivor, down on the sands of Camp America.

So the Tiki Bar had become the locus of evening social life for Gitmo's chattering class—its interrogators, linguists, and analysts—although there were few more disorienting experiences than spending six hours in a bare room pumping a stubborn old Saudi about life among the sand fleas, then kicking back with a Corona beneath a palm frond while your buddies rehashed an old episode of *Seinfeld.*

Even at the Tiki Bar the crowd tended to subdivide by team, rank, or organization. Most cross-pollination involved females and featured all manner of awkward mating dances. Every knot of males gathered near the bar usually had a woman at the center—"the prize in the box of Cracker Jacks," as Falk's roomie, Whitaker, had once described it.

Falk made a quick reconnaissance to see if Pam had arrived, but instead spotted Whitaker, who had grabbed an early seat in hopes of glimpsing the visitors from Washington. He had already predicted they'd be the source of much entertainment in the days ahead, and he didn't want to miss the opening act.

Bokamper and the others arrived a few minutes later, all three stepping off a yellow school bus. Everyone but Fowler had changed into his own idea of sportswear, which in Cartwright's case meant cargo shorts and a T-shirt. The midges would eat him alive. Fowler had at least left behind his jacket and tie, and made it a point to buy the first round.

Falk handled introductions, and for a while everyone made small talk about the trip down, the weather back in Washington, and the baseball season in Baltimore. Finally Whitaker could no longer contain his curiosity.

"So what can you guys say about what you're up to?" he asked with a smile.

Bokamper smiled back, but said nothing. Cartwright dutifully looked to Fowler, who seized the initiative.

"Not much, I'm afraid. We'll be talking to a lot of you in the next few days. You'll just have to trust me when I say that we intend to be as unobtrusive as possible. Believe me, we know the importance of the work you're doing."

Whitaker seemed unimpressed.

"I was kind of hoping for a little disruption. Give us something better to do for a while. Or more interesting, anyway."

Everyone laughed, if a bit politely.

"Be that as it may," Fowler said, holding his smile, "I'm not sure you fellows realize just how lucky you are to be here. You have no idea how many people in my shop would love to get a crack at this action. They'd give anything to be in your shoes."

"Anything? A sleeve of new Titleists would do it for me, if they're that hot on the idea. Especially if I could use 'em someplace where you don't have to hit off a toupee."

That brought more uneasy chuckles, except from Fowler.

"It's okay to joke about it, but you know what I mean. Or ought to. Other than Iraq, Gitmo's the single most important front right now in the GWOT."

"Gwot?" Cartwright asked, as he swatted at a midge on his thigh.

Falk supplied the answer.

"Global War on Terrorism. Gitmo acronym 12-b. You'll know 'em all within forty-eight hours. I'd urge you to start using the word 'robust' within the next twenty-four."

Fowler eyed him coolly, which pissed Falk off enough that he stared back, the beer hitting home a little too quickly after his marathon day. He hadn't eaten since breakfast. He decided it was probably best to make peace before things turned further in the wrong direction. Even the ardor of zealots tended to cool after some quality time on the Rock. In a week or so Fowler might actually be bearable, so Falk pointed to the man's bottle while raising his own, which was empty.

"Let me buy you another. You're half empty."

"C'mon, Falk," Whitaker said. "Fowler's a half-full kind of guy."

"Maybe you *should* pack it on home, with that kind of attitude," Fowler said.

"Easy, fellas." It was Bokamper, playing peacemaker, a role he tended to fill only after amply enjoying the sparring. "It's been a long day, but last time I checked we were still on the same side."

Whitaker said something under his breath and picked at the label of his Bud. Fowler made a show of checking his watch, then stood.

"Thanks, but I'll have to pass." His tone and smile were so curtly formal that Falk wouldn't have been shocked if he'd bowed, or told Whitaker to meet him at dawn with pistols and seconds. "I've got some work to catch up on before bed."

Cartwright also rose in a show of solidarity with the boss, but when Fowler seemed to dismiss him with a flick of the hand he sank obediently back into his chair. A real sacrifice given the fits he was having with the bugs. Whitaker by now was flushed with embarrassment, or maybe he was just drunk. Falk wondered how long he'd been at it. It was becoming a habit with his roommate. But as Fowler boarded the bus, Whitaker snarled back to life.

"Off to pray for our souls, I guess."

Bokamper grinned, taking a neat swig. "That *was* quite the sermonette."

"Ward's always been pretty gung ho," Cartwright said.

"But an intriguing piece of work," Bokamper said. "Give him time, Whit. He'll grow on you."

Whitaker normally hated being called Whit, but didn't seem to mind it this time.

"You know him pretty well?"

Bokamper shrugged.

"In the Washington sort of way. He used to work down the hall from me at State before making the jump to Homeland Security. One of the new breed, out to save the world one conquest at a time. I was out to his house once. Dinner party, probably his wife's idea. Nonstop shop talk. The world's most well-read man, judging from all the books. Practically had them classified by the Dewey Decimal System."

"Maybe he had 'em shipped in by a consultant. One of those clubs with leather bindings and blank pages. The Palace of Unread Books."

Bo grinned, shaking his head.

"Not his style. More likely he had them all memorized, cover to cover. The last thing you should do is underestimate him. Besides, it's easy enough to see why he's pumped. I mean, look at this place. It *is* amazing. Jihadists on the inside, Fidel on the perimeter. Half the corn-fed youth of the Midwest down by the sea in their barracks, chowing down in their cammies and saying 'Honor bound' every time they salute. At least that's what I read in the *Washington Post.* For anybody with an ounce of red, white, and blue it's a paranoid's paradise. Not that everyone isn't really out to get us."

Only Bokamper could blend reverence and subversion so artfully, then punctuate it with a verbal slap on the back. Cartwright seemed to decide it had been suitably laudatory, so he joined in the chuckling. The only one not laughing was Whitaker, still smarting from Fowler's brush-off.

"I understand General Trabert's made quite a difference," Cartwright said, in a tone that seemed eager for affirmation. "Intelligence volume is way up, in any event. I hear they're doing more than a hundred interrogations a week now. Pretty impressive."

"It's all about pushing the envelope," Whitaker said. "Buzzword of the month. But I'm a Bureau guy. What do I know?"

"Not everybody sees eye to eye on technique," Falk explained. "Especially those of us who've been trained to be a little more subtle. And I don't mean Miranda rights. I'm talking about excesses that in the States would get your confession kicked out of court."

Cartwright flicked yet another midge off his knee.

"Well, it's not like there isn't some pretty noble precedent for bending the rules. Lincoln suspended habeas corpus, shut down the secessionist newspapers, and arrested the mayor and police chief of Baltimore to restore order. Even jailed Francis Scott Key's grandson at Fort McHenry. But everything seemed to work out okay. There's a war on, even if a lot of people still don't want to believe it. And I guess we've got even more grounds for paranoia now that the Cubans are stealing our soldiers. Or so I heard on the way down."

"Yeah, what's up with that, Falk?" Whitaker asked. "Everybody says the tides should've pushed him our way."

Falk frowned.

"Depends on where he really went in. Or maybe everybody's looking at the wrong charts. Hell, I don't know. Maybe a dolphin took him for a ride. Ask General Trabert. He seems to be ahead of me on this one." He turned to Cartwright. "Not counting you guys, of course. I hear you may have some news for us in the morning."

"Oh, I'm pretty much where everyone else is, still trying to make the pieces fit." He slapped another midge, then stared at his knobby knees. You could tell he wasn't accustomed to lying. "We'll carry out our little assignments, then get out of everyone's way. Which reminds me, I've also got some work to do before I turn in. Better get moving if I'm going to be worth a damn in the morning."

So he, too, took his leave. The morose Whitaker retreated to the bar, where he lingered near a knot of revelers that actually included two females for a change, even though neither was the one Falk was looking for. Bokamper watched the departures in apparent amusement.

"Nice job, Falk. You and your roomie cleared the table. But now that I've got a private audience, what the hell *is* going on with this Ludwig case?"

"You mean with me trying to solve a drowning, or the shit storm it's stirring up?"

"You know me. The latter."

"The Cubans aren't happy, that's for sure. Both sides have ramped up patrols along the fenceline. I'd imagine they'll lodge some sort of formal protest. On what grounds I have no idea. An invasion by a dead man doesn't strike me as a major threat to sovereignty. Otherwise, I'm too near the bottom of the Gitmo food chain to know anything more. I thought maybe you'd have some answers, coming from Washington."

"Same boat as you're in. In this delegation anyway."

"Then what's your real role in the Brady Bunch? Or are you just here as a chaperone, keeping an eye on Greg and Marsha?"

"If only we had a Marsha. Let's just say that an interested party wanted to have a counterweight in place."

"A counterweight to what? Or who?"

"You'll see. If you pay attention."

"Who's the interested party?"

"Not open to discussion."

"C'mon, Bo. You're too old to start being a toady."

Then a pause, a few beats longer than necessary. From their long years of acquaintance, Falk knew that something significant was likely to follow.

"Sorry, but I can't say more. Doctor's orders."

It was all Falk needed. Bokamper's longtime benefactor at the State Department was Saul Endler, an aging sachem of high policy who had accumulated so many PhDs that Bo simply referred to him as the Doc. One part Kissinger and two parts alchemist, Endler seemed to get involved only when political conjuring was required and stakes were at their highest. Even then you hardly ever saw his name in the press, except in those obscure journals that published inside accounts months after the fact, in lengthy footnotes that no one but the experts read.

"Got it," Falk said.

"Thought you would."

"So you're not really here for the secretary."

"Oh, I'm doing his bidding, all right. Officially, anyhow."

"But it's also some kind of cover?"

"Officially? Not at all."

"Then why tell me?"

"Unofficially? Because I need your help." He leaned closer, lowering his voice. "With any number of things. Maybe even the Ludwig matter, depending on where it leads. As for the rest, we'll both have a better idea by the close of business tomorrow."

"Arrests? That's the rumor."

"Just keep your eye on Cartwright."

"And what will you be doing? Keeping an eye on Fowler?"

Bokamper shook his head, not in denial but in apparent refusal to offer anything more.

"Think OPSEC, Falk."

"Very good. You learn fast."

But Bokamper's attention had abruptly moved elsewhere. A look of appreciation creased his brow, an expression Falk had seen often enough to know that a woman must be approaching. Falk was on the verge of turning to make his own appraisal when a hand brushed his shoulder, followed by a familiar voice.

"Knew I'd find you here. Looks like your new friends have all gone to bed."

"All but one," Bo said, rising to his feet.

"This is Pam Cobb," Falk said. "Captain Cobb to you. And this is Ted Bokamper, who's also here for the sleepover. So watch what you say. He's very official."

"Just as well there are only two of you," she said. "It gets old being the only woman at a table for six."

"From what I've seen that's pretty much the norm."

"You told him how the Gitmo rating system works?" she asked Falk.

"It's the old ten-point scale," Falk explained. "Except the moment you step off the plane the rating for every male drops by three, and every female goes up by three."

"Which makes you what?" Bokamper said to Pam. "About a twelve?"

"See, you're already warped by the inflation. I'm a stateside six and a Gitmo nine, yet I still ended up with this guy," she said with a smile. Fortunately she no longer seemed peeved by this morning's news of the perfumed letter. Falk was about to offer to buy her a drink, but saw that she already had her usual, bourbon on the rocks. No umbrella.

"So what do you do here, besides keeping him in line?" Bo asked.

"Interrogator. Saudis, mostly."

"She's regular Army. Fluent in Arabic, so they sent her to the Intelligence School at Fort Huachuca."

"Ah," Bokamper said, "a ninety-day wonder. I hear it's been a struggle for some of you."

Falk winced, but Pam seemed to take it in stride.

"There's always a learning curve. But you could say that for the pros, too. I'd bet no more than five or six of them had ever dealt directly with Arabic speakers, much less Pashto or Dari, which is most of the Afghans. You could do a whole joke book on some of the cultural blunders."

"Except in the case of our friend here, Mr. Arabist," Bo said. She smiled for the first time since introductions. Falk wanted to seize the common ground and hold it, but Bo was already bolting for the next hill.

"I wasn't referring to cultural blunders as much as some of the other horror stories," Bo said. "Rookies losing control of the interview. Facing their interpreters instead of their subjects. Even being intimidated. I hear some of the hard cases were practically laughing in your faces."

"That must have been before I got here."

"Maybe so. But what's up with the sex stuff?"

"You mean the taunts? The 'Hey, big boy, how 'bout a good time' stuff some of the women were told to try out?"

"I heard it was a little worse. Rubbing their boobs against them. Painting the poor little pious fellows with nail polish and saying it was menstrual blood. Really freaking 'em out."

Pam's cheeks colored. Exactly what Bo intended, if Falk had to guess. It made him a little ashamed of all the times he'd tried for the same effect.

"That was never my department," she said tersely. "There was some of that, but it's been phased out. It was a disaster, which I could have told them after spending ten minutes with these guys."

"Oh, c'mon. Don't tell me you haven't batted your eyes now and then. Or wouldn't if they gave you the right signals. A come-on is a come-on. And if it makes 'em talk, why not?"

"You're not shooting for a come-on when you're trying to become their mom. Or their sister. Even if I did, I'm not into offering blow jobs for a few names in the network."

"Easy, sister. Or should I say mom? No need to bring blow jobs into it. I'm just pulling your chain."

"And where'd you learn all about interrogation?"

"Talking to people like this guy. Reading stuff."

"A ninety-page wonder. Pretty ballsy coming in here talking like a pro, don't you think?"

"'Ballsy'?" He smiled with apparent relish. Falk cringed in anticipation. "I know you're military, but you'd be doing yourself a real favor by toning down the tough-gal act just a notch."

Falk could tell from Pam's eyes that the remark stung and that she was itching to strike back with a quick "Fuck off." But she must have realized that would be playing right into Bo's hands. So instead she took a deep breath, turned to Falk, and said with forced calm, "Is your friend always such good company?"

Bo answered first.

"Falk's too polite to ever say this in front of me, but you've got to take everything I say with a grain of salt. Maybe even a whole box."

She didn't reply, but her nostrils were flared, and a glint in her eye warned that she was still seeking an opening for a counterattack. Awkward as it was to watch his two friends spar, there was another emotion behind Falk's uneasiness. He'd seen Bokamper get into these sorts of immediate confrontations with other women, and they always led to either lasting enmity or passionate affairs. Neither prospect would promote much happiness in Gitmo's close quarters. Blessedly, Bo seemed to back off a bit, lowering his shoulders and easing down in his chair. Then, as if reading Falk's thoughts, he turned to him and said in a stage whisper, "Don't worry, man, I *am* married. Besides, I don't poach."

"Did he really just say 'poach'?" Pam asked. "Unbelievable. So you've got an ego to match your big mouth."

"Easy," Bo said, chuckling now. "Don't take it personally. It's the way I was trained."

"Another Marine?"

"That, too," Falk said, "but he's referring to his family. If you'd met them you'd know. Six brothers and sisters and an argument every minute, with their dad egging 'em on like a pit bull trainer."

"Constructive engagement," Bokamper said. "That's what Pops called it. He was an old infantry sergeant, and it was his version of the Socratic method. Throw out a topic at dinner and let the offspring rip each other's lungs out. If you weren't the biggest mouth you got knocked off the podium. Sort of a verbal king of the hill."

"So did you ever tell your sisters to cut it with the tough-guy act?"

"Oh, far worse than that."

She smiled in spite of herself, then quickly shook her head, as if trying to take it back.

"So what have you come here to do?"

"I'm the new liaison to the task force from the secretary of state."

"I didn't ask your title. I asked what you're doing."

"See, you're getting the hang of it. But mum's the word. I've already told Falk more than I should have, so maybe you should ask him later."

Falk was relieved Bo hadn't used the words "pillow talk," and felt that the worst was over. A few moments of relative calm seemed to restore the table's equilibrium, and Falk seized the opportunity to fetch another round from the bar. If he wasn't around to provide an audience, Bo would probably play nicer, and he was eager for this cease-fire to hold.

"So how'd you guys meet?" Pam asked Bokamper, once Falk was out of earshot.

"I was just going to ask you the same thing."

"But I was first."

"I'll bet you always are."

"Do I get an answer?"

"I was his drill sergeant's CO. Parris Island."

"Not exactly the way most friendships get started."

"You got that right. But I was pretty new to the job, and he was fighting us. He needed some help getting over the hump."

"A father figure?"

"No, but that's what my sergeant kept telling me, only because everybody kept misreading the poor bastard. Falk was such a stubborn cuss they were sure he was never going to make it. Any kind of father act only got his back up. What he needed was a big brother, somebody to teach him how to deal with authority by example, not by layering on more."

"Sounds like somebody who'd had enough of his parents."

"He ever talk about them?"

"A couple of drunks, from what I gather. Died when he was in his teens. Pretty bad when your father names you out of spite."

"What's that?"

"He never told you how he got his name?" Pam's face flushed with the joy of a minor victory.

"Sure. He was named for Paul Revere. His dad was a big Red Sox fan pushing for any Boston connection, and his mom had already nixed 'Yaz.'"

"That's part of it. But it also had to do with some Maine connection. It seems that during the Revolution Paul Revere led this disastrous naval expedition up the Penobscot. Lost a bunch of ships and fled through the woods like a coward. So that's how he was known around Deer Isle, at least among the old-timers. Nice little joke to play on your son, huh? Of course, Falk got that from his mother, so who knows."

"Interesting. He told you all that?"

She nodded.

"Then I guess he also told you about his engagement?" Her jaw dropped. "Didn't think so. Don't worry, it was ages ago. He was barely out of college. Would have been a huge mistake, which I guess finally occurred to him. Ever since then he only seems to get really close to women when he knows he won't be around for that long. Like during his posting to Yemen during the *Cole* investigation. Or to Sudan after the embassy bombings."

"Or to Gitmo. Not that you were going to say that. How nice of you to warn me."

"Not saying it'll happen to you, of course. But you do know the three most important factors in relationships? Location, location, location. Just like real estate."

"So now I'm a piece of waterfront property?" She offered a smile carved in ice. "A perk of the current posting?"

"Weren't you the one just telling me about Gitmo's point system? Another variation on the theme, that's all. I'm just saying you should keep your options open, because he always has."

"Some friend. I thought it was all Semper Fi with you Marines."

"Oh, it is. I'd do anything for Falk. Even if he was over there robbing the bartender right now, if I saw an MP raise a gun to shoot him, I'd drop the guy. No hesitation."

"That loyal, huh?"

"Forever and a day."

"Maybe that's because you've never been on opposite sides when something really mattered."

Before Bo could answer, Falk returned to the table, followed closely by Whitaker, who seemed to have rallied.

"Was just telling Falk that I'm headed back to the ranch soon, if anyone needs a lift," Whitaker said.

"You've got a car?" Bokamper asked.

"Falk and I both. Tell Fowler if he's a good boy I might let him take her out for a spin."

"If you think of it," Falk said, "turn on my window fan when you get back."

"With any luck I won't need to. Repairman was out this afternoon, two days ahead of schedule. He remembered you from your Marine posting. Said to say hello."

Falk's stomach took a tumble. "You catch his name?"

"Harry. Which is funny, 'cause I'd have sworn he was Cuban, one of the old commuters. Anyhow, he said to come see him sometime."

Falk would be doing just that, he supposed. It now seemed clear that Elena's message was more urgent than he had thought. But with one soldier dead, arrests in the offing, and a team of Washington snoops on the loose, the timing couldn't have been worse. Gitmo was still shrinking by the minute.

The last thing Falk wanted to do after that exchange was to look Bo in the eye, so he turned to Pam, only to detect a smoldering anger. He wondered what Bo had said in his absence.

"I think I'll leave you boys to talk about guy stuff," she said, forcing a smile. "Nice meeting you, Bo." Her tone was perfunctory, but Bo smiled back.

Whitaker, oblivious to everything, started in on the subject of Fowler and Cartwright as soon as Pam left. But a few minutes later he, too, called it quits. Falk was inclined to do the same.

"Need a lift?" he asked Bo.

"Better not. Looks like the bus is still waiting. That's probably how Fowler wants to see me arrive home."

"Since when did you worry about appearances? This mission must really be serious."

"Now if I only knew what the mission was." He leaned across the table and said in a lowered voice, "We need to talk again. Soon. Someplace with privacy. Voice and otherwise."

"Well, now. How 'bout tomorrow after breakfast, a little walk on the beach?"

"Perfect."

"I'll show you where Ludwig went in."

"Even better."

"This really *is* serious, isn't it?"

"Tomorrow, Falk. Tomorrow after breakfast."

CHAPTER NINE

ADNAN AL-HAMDI had learned to think of himself as a mouse in a burrow, surviving in a desert filled with hawks and snakes. It was a scorched landscape where the white sun never set.

The hawks were a constant presence, their shadows flitting across his face at perfectly timed intervals, as if they circled to the beat of a drum. The drumbeat was their footsteps, the boot tread of guards relentlessly approaching, then fading in the corridors of Camp 3. Once per minute. Twice per minute. Every hour of every day.

Sometimes he watched them from his bunk, the mouse buried beneath the sheets with his nose to the air, twitching just enough to take a reading as they passed—talon, beak, and feather cloaked in military camouflage, gun at the ready—a menacing sight, yet harmless as long as he didn't cry out or stir, the way he often had at first. Careful observation had disclosed a weakness in their bearing. In the place on their uniforms where their names were supposed to appear, there were instead strips of tape. Apparently they, too, feared this place.

Adnan wasn't exactly sure how long he had been here, mostly because those first weeks—months perhaps? years even?—were now a blur, only some of which he could remember.

He had been captured on the battlefield after only a few months in Afghanistan, having departed his homeland with a sense of zeal and a spirit of adventure. Off to join the jihad. God's work was calling from across the seas and deserts. He landed in Pakistan, where holy men from the mountains drove him north from Karachi, and then west, across the barren passes. There were not enough guns to go around, and the snow on the ground at higher elevations had shocked him, numbed him. For weeks they did little but wait or march, and then the bombers came. Half of the men were dead within a week. Huge explosions all around, and then a chaotic journey south. A band of Tadjiks picked them up, packed them on a colorful truck, and then shoved them all into a stinking dungeon in the middle of an orange grove, stuck there for weeks until he was hauled out into the sunlight before two men in pressed pants and sunglasses. They spoke on two-way radios and drank water from clear plastic bottles. One spoke some Arabic, but not very well.

"You are a leader," the men told him.

"I am a soldier," Adnan replied. "A zealot, yes, praise be to God the most holy, but still just a soldier."

"No," they said. "The men who brought you here say you're a leader, an organizer."

Further questions followed. Where did you train? Who paid you? How did you recruit them? They mistook his ignorance for stubbornness, then drove him north, half a day up a valley, another two days in a hot metal crate at the edge of an airstrip, surrounded by mines. They dressed him in an orange jumpsuit, and then blindfolded him and bagged his head like a chicken for beheading, the sack coming down across his face while someone else shackled his wrists and his ankles. He was duckwalked onto an airplane, its engines already roaring, the floor vibrating beneath his feet. Then more shackles as he sat, binding him to the floor. A door slamming, then only darkness and the lift of take-off before a journey of what seemed like days. Swamped in his own vomit and shit and piss as the plane swayed in the cold skies, ever in the roaring darkness. He shivered, crying, but heard only the shrieks of his neighbors inside the hollow metal tube that carried them onward. At one point someone put an apple in his hands, and he was able to strain into position long enough to take a few bites, the flavor and juices overwhelming. But it was too hard to keep eating, bound as he was, and when the plane bounced through some turbulence the apple jostled loose. He felt it roll between his ankles across the floor.

Then, finally, after hours more, the plane thudded hard against the ground and came to a throbbing stop. Light poured in through the blindfold and sack as he heard the rear hatch wrenching open. There was shouting, some in a foreign tongue and some in a rudimentary Arabic, telling him to stand while someone unlocked him from the frame of the plane. His knees buckled as he tried to rise. Then a stick knocked against his calves, and someone shouted into his ear, incomprehensible, before hands grabbed him roughly beneath the armpits and hauled him forward, his legs full of pins and needles. He smelled sea air, and felt a windy blast of dust and grit rake across his hands. The air was a humid blanket that he would wear from that day forward.

When they finally took off the blindfold and hood he was in a chilly white room seated in a metal chair with his legs shackled to the floor. For hours on end they asked him the same questions that the two men in Afghanistan had asked. Where did you train? Who paid you? How did you recruit them? When he replied again and again that he didn't know, they shut him away in his burrow. Not the one where he lived now, but a sort of glorified cage among other cages. He had come to his present home later, while still clouded by fears and strangeness.

Weeks ago this new world had finally begun to come into focus for him. It happened after he realized that the only way to reclaim equilibrium was by imposing his own natural order. He would name and classify the things around him, sort and list them in his own fashion. And he had settled on the idea of hawks and snakes as the first zoological labels, a taxonomy that he hoped to expand through further careful observation.

Some aspects of this universe resisted easy categorization. Day and night, for instance. The fluorescent panels of Camp 3—he had overheard a hawk speaking the number of this place—cast a harsh permaglow. It was a chill limbo between sun and moon, which left Adnan's compass spinning without anchor until he rediscovered the lodestone possibilities of prayer. Now he oriented each day by the five calls that came regularly over the prison loudspeakers, falling to the narrow floor in famished zeal. He aligned himself toward Mecca by a small black arrow marked on the floor at the foot of his bed, then knelt on a thin foam mat.

There was little space for much else. The room was six feet by eight feet, eight inches, with the bed taking up about a third. It was his home for almost every hour of every day, except for those times when he was forced back into the white room, the clean but cold den of the snakes. Otherwise, there was only a once-weekly trip to the showers, when he was escorted at gunpoint to bathe beneath coils of razor wire, plus a half hour each day of "exercise," a bit of idling on a small cement corner while he stared across the grounds toward the burrows of other mice who spoke in other tongues.

He had few belongings, only what they had given him in a small bag on the very first day, replenishing his supply as each item ran out: his orange jumpsuit, flip-flops for the shower, a white cloth prayer cap, a foam sleeping mat plus a sheet and two blankets for his bed, a washcloth, two small towels, a stubby toothbrush that fit onto a fingertip, soap, shampoo, the prayer mat, and a copy of the Quran that came in a plastic bag.

The toilet in his room was a hole in the floor in one corner. In another corner was the sink, where the water emerged in a pale yellow stream that was as warm and stale as the air. He had to stoop to wash his hands, and he had to stoop lower to get a drink, gulping straight from the faucet. The hawks wouldn't give him a cup. A security risk, they said. You might use it to throw your own shit and piss at us, the way you did earlier—he didn't remember any of that now, but had no reason to believe it wasn't true. Or you might make something out of it, a weapon even. They told him the sink was built low to make it easier for him to wash his feet for prayers.

But Adnan no longer bothered with ablutions, because piety no longer motivated his prayers. He had been religious back in Yemen, and even more so in Afghanistan, when his hopes for adventure had turned bleak and hopeless in the face of gunfire and deprivation. Whenever death came near, God had seemed to lurk right over his shoulder, a fine warm breath upon his neck. But in this place he sensed God only as an absence, a void. God, in his infinite wisdom, had escaped and taken no one with him, vanishing without a word into the vapors of the heat. So prayer became merely a wheel in Adnan's timepiece and, when meshed with the clockwork of mealtime, told him the approximate hour of the day. In a world without horizons beneath a sky with no stars, calibration was its own salvation.

The wheel of his day turned like this: dawn prayer, breakfast, shower time (but only once per week), sick call, noon prayer, lunch, a half hour in the exercise yard, mail call, sunset prayer, dinner, evening prayer.

The only events that always came upon him without warning were the summonings to the dens of the snakes. In the beginning—or what he could remember of it—he had been taken to them daily, locked into chains and shackles by the hawks, then delivered to the dens. The hawks hobbled him onto a cart that glided across gravel paths. The vipers' chambers were divided into eight rooms all in a row, like a giant egg case, a place where perhaps they gestated, reproduced. Or, no, he decided, amending his version of the natural order, perhaps these rooms were instead aligned like the stomachs of a camel, each with its own digestive function. But he was always taken to the same one. Always the third door and, behind it, the same two men working in tandem. And sometimes a third behind a mirror, where he could detect just enough movement when the light changed to know that the mirror was really a window. Eventually he discarded this image of the camel stomachs and began thinking of the rooms instead as holes in the ground, deep places where the snakes lay in wait behind their mirrors and beneath their tables.

In the earliest days the snakes splayed him, stripped him, and held him wide open to their hissing. They circled and swayed in the manner of cobras, broadening to show their hoods, while the rollers of their chairs emitted mouse squeaks to echo his own as they circled toward him to strike. Prim men who spoke Arabic sat to one side—jackals, he later named them—translating snake words into Arabic. Sometimes the questioners rose up from their seats to tower above him, then pierced him with fang and venom. Other times they tried swallowing him whole, their bones crushing his own until every juice was ingested into their systems.

His vague recollection was that in self-defense he began to babble, to talk nonsense, but they only squeezed harder, until he was no longer sure of what he was saying. Or maybe he was saying nothing at all, the poison rigid in his jawbone, locking it shut. That must have been the case, because finally the day came when they left him alone, casting him back into his burrow for a few weeks of rest beneath the shadows of the circling hawks, who no longer came for him in the floodlit night.

It was during that interval that he began to recover his sense of order, the clockwork of his days, then began to name and classify. And it was around that time that the newest of the creatures arrived. He, too, demanded Adnan's presence in the lair of the snakes, but he was different. Quieter. Slower. He circled at a distance, and he didn't hiss in the tongue of the others, or depend on a jackal to interpret his words. His use of Arabic was at first alarming, as if he must have crept into the family home in Sana, stolen the words of Adnan's parents and sisters, and then twisted them almost beyond recognition with his serpent's accent. Even as his mouth shaped Yemeni vowels and offered the buzzwords of the bazaar, his accent betrayed him as an interloper. But at least he never bared his fangs. Sometimes he even chose to circle with the hawks, especially at night, in the quiet hours when the permalight was at its harshest, or in the bleakness before first prayers, when Adnan's sense of time was at its weakest.

Like every other beast inhabiting the world outside Adnan's burrow, this one offered no name. So Adnan came up with one of his own, settling on the Lizard. Still a reptile, but without the snake's bite. More like the big green creatures that he had seen beyond the fences, which were probably just other interlopers in disguise, waiting to shed their skins to take the form of humans.

Adnan decided that by keeping the Lizard happy he might gradually improve his life, and thus began their dialogue, cautious and wary at first, but harmless enough that Adnan began to almost welcome their sessions, now finding it a relief to leave the burrow. The Lizard never said much about himself, but he didn't have to. You could learn a lot about a creature like him just by paying attention. He had been a soldier once, that much Adnan was sure of. And he had lived in this place before, at a much earlier time. His lack of uniform meant he now must be working for one of the security services that practically everyone in the world had heard of, even in Sana—the CIA or the FBI. All of this had piqued Adnan's curiosity for reasons he wasn't yet ready to reveal. When Adnan returned to the burrow from one of their meetings he did something he had never yet tried—so far as he could remember—and shouted to the other mice in the cells all around him.

"I told them nothing!" he yelled, having heard others shout the same thing.

There was applause, a few words of encouragement in Arabic.

"Allahu Akbar!" someone offered, missing the point entirely. It was not about God anymore. It was about spreading the word, filling in the blanks, passing along the news of this new world that he was finally beginning to comprehend.

Up to now, he supposed, he had been a broken link in the chain of communication that often spread news among the cells of Camp 3. Newer arrivals had passed word to them that they were in Cuba. Others had told them that the whole world knew of their existence. Every bit of information added dimension to his new sense of things.

Word went around that a few dozen men had actually gone home, back across the water on the same plane that had brought them here. Adnan, who had always stayed out of these cell-to-cell conversations, mended his ways and joined in, telling the others even more than he had told the Lizard. Because he had secrets. And he now knew intuitively that if the snakes and the Lizard wanted those secrets, then perhaps they could also be of value to the other mice.

Last night the Lizard had surprised him, even scared him a little, by coming for him at the worst of hours. It had thrown him off balance and made him want to hasten their conversation along. Perhaps that was what had jarred loose one of his deeper memories from his days in Yemen, an item that until then had been irretrievably buried. It was the name of Hussay, the man who had paid Adnan's way across the seas. Both travel agent and sponsor, Hussay had been yet another foreigner with a bad accent.

But Adnan's revelation seemed to have no effect. The Lizard seemed to think Hussay was just another Yemeni, and he infuriated Adnan by insisting on asking for a family name, as if people such as Hussay ever gave them. To make matters worse, one of the snakes of old then burst through the door. Adnan immediately recognized the reptile grin, the gray coat that had always been shed like an old skin whenever the squeezing began, peeled off against the chairback to stay in place as the snake rose from his seat, preparing to strike.

So Adnan refused to say anything more, even when it seemed that the Lizard was as angry at the snake as he was, an oddity that he wasted no time in reporting to his neighbors once he had returned to the burrow.

Adnan was still contemplating the implications of the matter as he rose from his bed at the hour—by his reckoning—of about 10 p.m. It was time for a journey, a walk through his hometown of Sana. These walks were another recent addition to his schedule. By pacing back and forth in his cell, he dreamed his way back home, step by step. If he shortened his stride just a little, he could squeeze in four steps for each trip across the floor, then make four more crossing back. It generally took about ten minutes before he left this place behind and found himself upon the streets and alleys of home, where the odd and timeless architecture made every building look like an iced layer cake of pale stones and white paint, with adornments on every door and window. Where to go today, then, on this late afternoon with the sunlight creeping low across the mountains, a cooling butterscotch that softened every corner and roofline. He crossed cobbles, and then pathways of packed mud, working his way east through the alley of the qaat parlors, where everyone chewed the intoxicating leaves and spit gobbets of brown juice onto the floor. Men crouched on their haunches upon wooden platforms raised before every storefront along the way. Onward he walked, climbing now, first up a hill and then up some stairs, to a third-story roof and its view across the city, Sana spread below him with its marketplace sounds clanking up to him across the rooftops. The smells came, too, of cardamom and of clean mountain air. His bare feet were cool upon the plaster. Then down to the bazaar he went, passing Ahmed's butcher shop, where the severed heads of five goats dripped blood into a plastic tub by the door. Ahmed sang as he skinned and trimmed the carcasses, shooing flies with each whisk of a long, glinting knife. Then came a voice calling out from far away. Adnan stopped in his tracks and saw himself facing the wall of his cell.

"Adnan!" It was one of the hawks. The door of his burrow unlatched, and a flurry of words came at him, all of them incomprehensible except the last, which had become a countersign that meant it was time to see the Lizard.

"Get moving, Adnan. They want you in interrogation."

His first stop was at another burrow, a bare one where he always waited for the cart that took him to the lairs. But this time the routine was different. They bundled him onto a truck, a big green one like the ones that armies used on the march, with canvas flaps across the back. They bolted him down, then drove on. And, wonder of wonders, they drove through one gate, and then through another. He could see their progress through a space between the flaps.

Was it really possible? Was he leaving this place? Was he going home, back to the airplane that would fly him away to freedom, and to his mother and his sisters?

The ride proceeded into blackness, his first experience of true nightfall in ages. This natural darkness was like a balm, not frightening at all, and it was cooler out here as well, the air smelling like plants, like dirt, a world where your feet would feel the ground instead of concrete. In his growing excitement he allowed himself a sigh of relief. The bus climbed a hillside, and when the driver paused to shift gears, Adnan thought he heard the chorusing bugs of the night desert, which stirred him even more deeply.

His hopes sank, however, when the bus stopped at yet another gate, where hawks in smaller numbers circled with flashlights and shouted to one another, ushering the truck inside. He knew this place, he realized. It lived in his vaguest, most muddled memories from his arrival. It was where he had stayed for months before winding up in his current burrow. This was the place where the cages had been stacked from end to end. But now, even in the darkness, he could see they were empty and overgrown with vines that had spread across them from the adjacent hillside, this hated old home given over to the jungle.

They took him off the bus, his steps shortened by the irons around his ankles, and they shoved him toward a trailer like the one that contained the lairs. A door opened onto a lit room with a table, two chairs, and a mirror on the wall. But this time the Lizard was nowhere to be found.

Then the snakes arrived. There were two, both unfamiliar to him. One wore the mottled green plumage of the hawks. The other was in more typical snake's clothing, although not in the gray skin that some of them liked to shed. It was frigid in here. It felt about forty degrees after the heat outside, and the box in the wall blowing the cold air seemed to be turned as high as possible, wheezing loudly.

A hawk shackled his leg irons to the ring in the floor. Then the snake in mottled green muttered an order, and the hawk pulled Adnan's shirt up over his head. He knew better than to struggle, but it was freezing without his shirt. There seemed to be some confusion about what to do next, until finally the hawk unlocked his leg irons just long enough to strip off his pants, then his shorts, before hastily locking him back into place. When Adnan made a move to climb into the chair, the gray snake shoved him in the back until he fell to the floor. The hawk then handcuffed him and produced a chain, which he looped through the leg irons, pulling it tighter until the second snake barked a command. Adnan was hunched and chilly, a tickle rising in his throat and his sinuses clogging. A hood went over his head, and now he began to resist, but it was too late. Some sort of rope was pulled around his neck, just tight enough to keep the hood from slipping free. Then he heard furniture moving and chairs scraping the floor. A few moments later music began to play, like the screech of something electronic and rasping, a throbbing sound like a heartbeat, and all of it blended in a way that hurt his ears. Then it was louder still. He could barely hear the voice of the snakes over it all.

This went on for what seemed like hours until finally the music abated. His ears rang, aching from the noise and the cold. Then he felt one of the snakes leaning closer, the breath upon his ear, almost welcome if only for its warmth.

The snake spoke in its own tongue, then one of the jackals offered the words in distorted Arabic: "Tell me about Hussay, Adnan. Tell me about him and everyone else he worked with. Where was Hussay from, Adnan? You know, don't you? Where did he come from? Where was his home?"

Adnan didn't even bother to shake his head. The snake waited a while and then asked the same questions a second time. Then a third. Then a fourth. And when Adnan still did nothing he sensed the snake easing away from him. Then the music resumed, louder than ever. And someone took the chain bolted to the floor and wrenched it tighter. The aching in Adnan's bent joints and arched back made it feel like someone was wringing him like a wet rag, and the coldness made his bones throb.

What was it that he had called this bit of information about Hussay, this memory that he had offered up to the Lizard only yesterday? His great gift. Yes, a gift that he now wished he had never offered. One of the snakes, it seemed, must have figured out exactly how great, even if the Lizard hadn't. If that were true, there was probably no way they would be stopping this treatment anytime soon. Not until they had the rest of his secrets.

But he made up his mind that they would never have it. Not now. None of them, neither the snakes nor the Lizard. Even if they killed him. He was no longer the mouse. He was the mole, blind to their lights and to this world aboveground.

And with every passing minute he dug deeper.

CHAPTER TEN

> Our adversaries attempt to elicit information from us every day using all types of means. At times, they may even directly question you after you've spoken. . . . If someone other than another service member approaches you and questions you about our mission, units, or anything regarding our overall operation, you have an obligation to report it immediately. In the meantime remember that your conversations are never confidential in public or on the phones, especially in our environment. So do your part to eliminate our adversaries' ability to elicit information. "Think OPSEC."
>
> —From "OPSEC Corner," a regular feature of JTF-GTMO's weekly newspaper, *The Wire*

THE FIRST ARREST came before breakfast, when a grumbling convoy of Humvees arrived on the doorstep of an apartment at Villa Mar. The target was a translator, Lawrence Boustani, an Arabic linguist employed by one of the two big contractors, United Security. They handcuffed him in his pajamas while his housemates watched from the kitchen, blinking sleepily.

Boustani worked regularly with Pam's tiger team, so she immediately drew a crowd that morning at the mess hall. Everyone wanted details, but no one seemed to have them.

"His father's Lebanese, maybe that's the link," she said. The breakfast regulars, Falk among them, leaned closer to catch every word. Heads were hunched at every table across the room, and conversation was muffled. Everyone seemed convinced this was only the first of several such actions.

"Isn't he a Navy guy?" Whitaker asked. "Retired or something?"

"Army," Pam corrected. "Eighty-second Airborne. Bragg and a few overseas postings. Got out in '99. He's a good guy."

"Plenty of good guys have done us in before," said Phil LaFarge, a member of Falk's tiger team, an analyst from Army Intelligence.

"So we're assuming guilt now?" Whitaker said. "Remember, this is a Pentagon operation."

"Well, I know Tyndall never trusted him."

"Tyndall didn't *like* him. Never heard him say anything about trust."

"Maybe 'cause he doesn't trust *you*, being from the Bureau."

"Then I guess I'll be next."

Nervous laughter. Gallows humor. You could easily predict how the day would unfold. By lunch there would be newly minted jokes and a fresh set of suppositions. By dinner some of the jokes would have already been e-mailed to colleagues in Washington and at various military bases in the States. In some quarters Boustani would be deemed the greatest threat to national security since Osama bin Laden. In others he would be a scapegoat, the new Dreyfus.

"Guess this knocks you off the front page," Whitaker said to Falk, referring to the previous day's sensation over Ludwig.

"As if any of this stuff would ever make it into *The Wire*."

"Think OPSEC, fellas," Whitaker chirped. "Hey, speak of the devil."

There they were, the three members of the team, striding into the mess hall, fresh from the kill. Bland as ever, they certainly didn't look like spy hunters. Cartwright's uniform seemed to have gotten an overnight starch-and-press job. Fowler wore a gold polo and khaki slacks, looking like a real estate salesman. Bokamper lagged a few steps behind—intentionally, Falk presumed. He was sockless, wearing loafers, and he nodded across the room to Falk as they headed for a table in a far corner. Business breakfast.

"Plotting their next move," LaFarge said. "Whitaker, if you're lucky you can catch the ten-ten to Jacksonville."

"I'll hire some ambulance chaser and plead the Fifth."

Falk caught Pam's eye. She wore an expression like the others, one part worry and two parts excitement. It was like upheaval in any office or big organization. Even when the news was bad, it produced a shot of adrenaline, a burst of energy that spent itself on gossip, hand-wringing, and manic fascination. Productivity would be down the toilet for the rest of the week, which was probably exactly what Trabert feared most about this task force. Falk wondered if the prisoners would notice the difference, the subtle change in air pressure. The thought reminded him of Adnan. Somehow he had to find time for a follow-up session, even if other items were higher on his crowded agenda. He was already backlogged on the Ludwig case. Then there was the nagging matter of "Harry," who would have to be visited.

He looked up to see Pam still watching him. After leaving the Tiki Bar last night he had stopped by her place to pick her up, and they'd made a late night of it. They drove to his house, opening the front door to hear Whitaker's snores competing with the drone of the repaired air conditioner, which made the place as chilly as a hospital. They had another drink on the couch, then spent a pleasurable hour in bed. Falk found that he missed the heat, the usual slickness of their bodies, although fooling around in the cold reminded him of parking on a fall night in Maine—owls hooting in the trees while you kept an eye out for Deer Isle's one overnight cop.

Afterward he took her home. It was part of the charade here. Everyone back in his own bunk by dawn. They drove the narrow, twisting lanes past cactus plants beneath a deep, starry sky, headlights offering glimpses of a transplanted American suburbia.

When they pulled up outside her apartment at Windward Loop—no lights on, roommates presumably asleep—she leaned against the car door and stretched like a cat. She still smelled like the bed, and he knew that when he got back to his room the whole place would be heady with her perfume. The night air breezed through the car's open windows, a dry grassy scent baking off the land.

"So is it true what they say?" Pam asked with a mischievous grin. "That you love 'em and leave 'em? A girl in every deployment?"

Falk had a pretty good idea where that had come from, but given his track record he supposed the question was fair enough.

"It's been true at times. A few weeks ago I might have said it was going to be true here. But lately it doesn't feel that way. I find it hard to believe we'll just say good-bye once our posting's up."

"Me, too. That would be too painful. The kind of pain I like to avoid, if at all possible."

He supposed that was his cue to bow out gracefully if he was at all weak-kneed about a possible future together. He smiled, but at first said nothing.

"Are you uncomfortable talking about this?" she asked. "We can always do it later."

"No. Just out of practice. It's been years."

"It's okay to be out of practice. I was more worried you've had too much practice, that this was just another part of the routine."

Falk shook his head.

"It is funny, though, when you think about it, us having this conversation. Considering what we're doing down here. Asking questions for a living. Prying out information. I mean, it's not like we don't have the skills to get to the heart of it. But we're just sitting here, waiting for each other to make the first move."

"Maybe I'm just watching your nonverbal clues."

He smiled wryly. He supposed both of them were wondering how much scrutiny they could stand at this stage of the game. Whenever an interrogation reached a delicate point, the paramount rule was trust. Falk wondered if they were yet willing to test that trust by revealing all their feelings, and he flashed on the old advice from Quantico, the bit about "overcoming resistance through compassion." But would either of them admit to offering resistance just now?

"Well, seeing as how we're a couple of professionals," Pam said, "am I allowed one more prying question?"

Falk nodded.

"Is there anybody else I should know about? Either back in Washington or, well, any other place?"

Her way of asking about the perfumed letter, he supposed. Maybe that's what had triggered the conversation.

"No one who matters," he said, holding her gaze. "How 'bout you?"

"The same."

"So what else did Bo say about me while I was getting drinks?"

"That you were engaged once."

He blushed, thankful for the darkness.

"A mistake of my youth."

"Never to be repeated?"

"It can't be repeated. I'm no longer a youth. Any future mistake will be the fully informed error of an old pro."

"I can live with that."

"Of course, you do realize that now I'll have to ask Bo for a full scouting report on your end of the conversation."

"Feel free."

"Good. 'Cause I'm seeing him first thing in the morning."

Pam frowned.

"Be careful with him."

"Bo? Hell, I've known him for years. He's like a . . ."

"Big brother?"

"Yeah."

"He told me that, too."

"Well, there you go." Although now he felt a little trumped by his friend, which Pam seemed to notice.

"Don't feel bad. He was probably just trying to get in my pants."

"Gimme a break."

"Why, 'cause he's married?"

"For starters."

"Means nothing to guys like him. Neither does 'poaching.' Believe me."

"He's just a big flirt. Always has been."

"And has always followed it up, I'll bet. Not that he'd want his little brother to know. So don't be naive. Especially not until we know what those creeps are really up to. Remember, he's one of them."

"Bo says he's out of the loop."

She rolled her eyes, flashes of white in the starlight.

"Another likely story," she said, but with less of an edge. She reached over to caress his cheek, luring him across the vinyl seat, springs creaking. They were high schoolers again, locked in a prolonged smooch by the curb. Falk half expected an angry dad to shout from the porch.

"So is this just another part of my 'tough-gal' act?" she whispered, coming up for air.

"That really got under your skin, didn't it?"

"You're the only one who does that." Another nuzzle, a whiff of sweat and jasmine, so Falk let it rest. But he still wondered, because he'd seen this reaction before with Bo—the initial anger, the women claiming to loathe the man. Then they did a 180 and fell for him, crossing the line between anger and passion in a single nimble step.

A few hours later, when Falk was sleeping soundly, the phone rang. Whitaker knocked at the bedroom door to say that the call was for him. It was 6 a.m. He'd been dreaming of old Havana, he realized,

Elena's perfume mingled with Pam's. A hotel room with a ceiling fan, the sound of congas drifting in from the streets. All of that played in his mind as he stumbled to his feet. Muddled, he plodded down the hall, reproaching himself for not yet having seen Adnan. Too preoccupied with women and friends. The kitchen was freezing, the linoleum floor icy against his bare feet. Bokamper's voice fairly shouted over the line.

"Gotta cancel our beach trip, buddy. Urgent war party to attend."

Falk came instantly awake.

"So it's starting. Got a name?"

"Like I said, I'm just here to observe."

Now, as Falk sat at the breakfast table in the mess hall, he wondered if Bo had been leveling with him. Pam certainly wouldn't believe it, but Pam didn't know the man, nor did she know their history, the storms they'd weathered, the trust they'd built. Whatever the case, Fowler must have decided overnight to take immediate action, or else Bo wouldn't have set up their beach appointment to begin with. Maybe all the irreverent chatter at the Tiki Bar had convinced Fowler that he had to act right away.

"Well, would you look at that," LaFarge suddenly marveled.

Three new arrivals to the mess hall were striding toward the team. Fowler handled introductions while Cartwright pulled up chairs for everybody. By all appearances they were invited guests.

"What do you think?" Whitaker asked. "Victims or collaborators?"

"Captain Rieger's no surprise," LaFarge said. "Walt's the head of Army counterintelligence for the JTF, so they'd have to include him. Protocol."

"But Van Meter and Lawson?" Falk asked. He was referring to Captain Carl Van Meter and Allen Lawson. The former was in uniform. The latter wasn't.

"Lawson's corporate. Global Networks."

"Nothing puzzling about that," Whitaker said. "Lawson is Boustani's competition. Probably gets a bonus for helping send him up the river."

"Or maybe he's just doing the right thing," piped up Stu Sharp, an Air Force investigator. "Van Meter's the one I can't figure. What's his official title?"

"Intelligence officer for the security force," Whitaker said. "J-DOG's House Snitch."

"Only when it comes to House Arabs," Sharp said. "He gets pissed when he sees any of the Arabic linguists praying. Must think they're reciting the Pledge of Jihad or something."

"I have to admit, it gives me the heebie-jeebies, too," LaFarge said. "I know it shouldn't, but when you see the detainees doing it all day, then one of your interpreters starts in . . ." He shook his head.

"Van Meter told me once that he believes we're in a war for the survival of our culture," Whitaker said with amusement.

"He's right," LaFarge said.

"But with Boustani? *He's* the enemy? Hell, Boustani grew up in Brooklyn."

"Means nothing once you get religion. But I'll give you one thing. Van Meter does have it in for Boustani. Thinks he's too nice to the Saudis. Must've filed a dozen complaints about it to Rieger."

"Looks like it paid off."

"C'mon guys, none of us know what else they have. Or what they found at Boustani's house."

"Spoken like a true prosecutor," Falk said. "You sure you're not a DA, LaFarge?"

"Well, I'll guarantee one thing," Whitaker said. "This arrest will be a big hit with the rank and file. You should've seen the looks the MPs gave Boustani whenever he started in about the peace and beauty of Islam."

Falk thought back to his own days as a young jarhead. He, too, would have been put off by the prayers and the lectures. If his career had gone in another direction, or toward another language, he might still feel that way. And he knew from his experience in the military that a lot of the soldiers in the security force would never move beyond that point of view, whether out of intellectual laziness or blind loyalty to their own way of life. It was a view easily reinforced when the other side starting flying planes into buildings.

"Didn't Boustani get one of the MPs in trouble?" Sharp asked.

"Yeah," Whitaker said. "For tossing a detainee's Quran on the floor. Chewed him out in front of the detainee, no less. Lot of guys saw it, and it didn't sit well."

"Smart. Tactful, too."

"So were the MPs. The minute Boustani left, a bunch of them called him a 'sand nigger.'"

"Nice," LaFarge said. "But it doesn't mean he's not guilty as sin."

"What happened to innocent until proven guilty?"

"Fine. Long as you use the same standard for Van Meter. Who, by the way, isn't charged with anything."

"Except being a prick."

More nervous chuckles, everyone beginning to sense the way the aftershocks might rumble through this place for weeks, creating new stresses and fissures, especially if there were more arrests.

"This'll do wonders for teamwork," Sharp said with a weary sigh.

"Get used to it," Whitaker said. "With those six on the loose it's bound to get worse."

Interesting, Falk thought, the way some of them had already decided that all six people at the other table were part and parcel of the same "team." Another form of guilt by association.

"Well, don't include me among the naysayers," LaFarge finally said. "For all we know, those guys are doing us a huge favor. Don't forget what we're here for."

True as well, and Falk nodded along with the others. The prospect of real spies in their midst was perhaps the most sobering possibility of all. Maybe that's why some of them were so eager to laugh it off or to suspect an overzealous investigation. The consequences of a genuine security breakdown could be horrendous. For a few minutes the only sounds were the clank and scrape of forks against plates. Then Mitch Tyndall approached from the chow line with a steaming plate of eggs.

"Who died?" he said, chuckling. "If it's Boustani you're mourning, save it. You should be grateful."

"Don't try to reason with 'em," said LaFarge, relieved to have an ally. "It's like talking to the Camp Delta ACLU."

"Sounds like you know something," Falk said. "Were you out there, Mitch?"

Tyndall shook his head.

"Heard a little, though. He had some strange tapes on him. Audio, not video. Plus some questionable diskettes. And he had a list of detainee names on his laptop."

Whitaker snorted.

"Then I better erase mine. Hell, Mitch, probably everybody at this table has got something at their place or on their laptop that they technically shouldn't have. It's not like you can just drive out of here with a briefcase full of documents."

"He also had a stack of letters at home. From detainees. You got any of those?"

Whitaker shook his head, seemingly chastened.

"Apparently he'd packed them in his bags for the mainland and was going to mail them," Tyndall continued.

Falk thought of the letter in his possession. Not from a detainee, and it was written in English, not Arabic or Pashto. But the contents would still raise plenty of eyebrows in this climate, especially if anyone knew the reason behind it.

The table again went silent. There would be some late drinking tonight at the Tiki Bar. Loose lips to sink plenty of ships. Just not his, he hoped. Or Pam's. In some people's minds, any speaker of Arabic was probably now under suspicion. Things could get ugly in a hurry if this team wasn't careful.

Falk thought again of Harry, who would be waiting, impatient. Well, let him. There were other people to see first. He rose with his tray.

"Where you headed?" Whitaker asked. "Off to report our conversation to your buddy, Mr. Bokamper?"

"Relax, Whit. The guy I'm going to see knows how to keep his mouth shut."

"Must be Adnan, then." That finally drew some laughter.

"This fellow makes Adnan look like a chatterbox. His name's Ludwig."

"Oh. The dead guy."

"Waiting on the slab. Finish your bacon before it's cold, Whit. Until we meet again, gentlemen. And lady." A parting glance at Pam. At least everything in that department seemed okay.

"Give him our best," Whitaker said. He had covered his bacon with a napkin.

CHAPTER ELEVEN

As it turned out, Ludwig's body was no longer on the slab. It had already been boxed for shipment in a military-issue coffin, then draped with a flag. By the time Falk reached the hospital it was sitting on the loading dock, awaiting delivery to Leeward Point for the next flight out. An orderly took him down for a look, but there was little to see apart from the Stars and Stripes. Camp Delta's one and only casualty—unless you counted the suicidal detainee still vegetating in a coma—was ready to go home.

Falk was mildly perturbed. In the States he'd have chewed out the doctor for moving ahead without telling him. Here that would only make trouble, generating a retaliatory chain of paperwork. At least there was an autopsy report to read.

The doctor was a Captain Ebert, who seemed agreeable enough. He probably wasn't accustomed to dealing with law enforcement people, and was apparently oblivious to his faux pas.

"The toxicology tests are still pending," Ebert said, reading over Falk's shoulder. "But there was no alcohol in his blood. It was pretty much what you'd expect."

"Water in the lungs?"

"Chock-full. Although that would have been the case even if he hadn't drowned, after all that time in the ocean."

"How many hours, do you think?"

"Seven or eight. Maybe more. Being on the beach a while muddies it. What time did the Cubans find him? The paperwork was a little vague."

"Seven, seven thirty. They weren't exactly gushing with information, under the circumstances."

"In any case, it was a drowning. Nobody shot him, stabbed him, or strangled him."

"Or knocked him on the head?"

"That, too."

"Could somebody have held him under water?"

"Sure. No marks to indicate it, but that doesn't mean it didn't happen. The fish got to him after a while, so I'm not sure any marks would be all that clear."

"Find anything to explain why he might have gone swimming with his uniform and boots on?"

Ebert shook his head.

"Like I said, he wasn't drunk. Could have reached into the water for something, I guess. Gone wading and slipped, fallen down. Then the waves took over. It happens."

"But you said there was no blow to the head. So it's not likely any fall would have knocked him unconscious."

"True enough."

"And I guess he still could have been on some kind of drugs."

"From where? For all the stories I hear of the goings-on down in Camp America, that's one that has yet to come up. Drinking? Sure. The way of the soldier. Drugs? Not unless he was on some prescription medication. But I'll give you a shout when those tests come back."

"Which should be when?"

"A few days yet. Sorry. The samples go to the States. It's why I was in such a rush to get him out of here. They're shipping his body on the ten-ten to JAX."

"Here's my number."

"You'll be the first to know. You and General Trabert."

"Somehow I thought you'd say that. Has he been 'making inquiries,' as they say?"

Ebert smiled but said nothing, the good soldier honoring the chain of command.

Falk had yet to come up with a scenario other than suicide that would explain why Ludwig had removed his wallet but not his boots or uniform. As an accident, the death still made little sense.

His next stop was the port control office, where the comings and goings of every ship were monitored by radar and radio. It wasn't a busy place. Gitmo seldom got seagoing visitors apart from the Coast Guard and the supply barge from Jacksonville.

An Ensign Osgood was manning the post alone, and seemed eager for company. He obliged Falk by unrolling a huge white chart awash in gray, white, and pale blue, and covered with contour lines and depth readings. It was titled "Guantánamo Bay, From Entrance to Caimanera." Osgood began explaining what all the markings meant.

"Don't worry," Falk said. "I can read 'em."

"Ex-Navy?"

"Marines. But I grew up on the water."

"Whereabouts?"

"Up North." Keep it vague enough and they tended to drop the line of questioning. "So, tell me, Osgood. If somebody goes in here"—he pointed to a spot just off Windmill Beach—"then swims out maybe a hundred yards, max, and then turns parallel to the shoreline and swims, let's say, another hundred yards east . . ." In his uniform and boots, no less. Falk still couldn't get that out of his head. "And then let's say he drowns. Where do you think he comes ashore?"

"A hundred yards out?" Osgood mulled it over a moment, then slid his finger a few inches west, a half mile farther from Cuban territory, and pointed to a location marked as Blind Beach.

"This would be my guess. The chart says 'Blind Beach,' because you can't see it from the water, but everybody here calls it Hidden Beach. Of course, there's a chance you would drift even farther." Osgood moved his finger another few inches west. "Maybe all the way down to Blue Beach. The trade winds run pretty steady out of the east down this coast. The currents, too. Ships running against it say it usually takes a pretty good push to get around the horn."

"Did anything happen the night before last that might have changed the equation? A weather front? A big ship in the neighborhood, maybe? A freak wind shift? Hell, anything."

"I've been wondering the same thing, sir. I'm assuming you're asking about Sergeant Ludwig. After I heard where they found him I checked the wind readouts, the shipping schedules, the works. I also wondered about an offshore storm, something that might have caused a riptide, pulled him out to sea. But . . ." He shrugged.

"Nothing?"

"Sorry. The only thing I can't account for is the Cuban patrol boats. One could've crossed into our sector by mistake, I guess. Hit him or something. They've fucked up before, but it's been years. And they've never come this far. Not to Windmill Beach."

"As far as we know."

"Yes, sir."

"Wouldn't they have showed up on your radar equipment?"

"Not the smaller ones. But the seaward surveillance people would have spotted 'em. Or heard 'em."

"Seaward surveillance?"

"The 204th Mobile Inshore Undersea Warfare Unit, if you want the whole mouthful. A Naval Reserve unit. They've set up a couple observation posts in the hills since Camp Delta opened. If a Cuban patrol had come across that night, or any night, I think everybody and his brother would have heard about it by now."

"Good point, ensign."

Even in the unlikely event that the Cubans had blundered across the line undetected, long enough to either pick Ludwig up or accidentally kill him, in that case they never would have reported finding the body. They would have been eager to hush it up. By now he would have been buried on their side in an unmarked grave, or tossed back into the current to make his inevitable way west.

"Then let's try this," Falk said. "General Trabert seems to think—or maybe somebody told him—that the currents can be kind of tricky out there, right off Windmill. Undertows or whatever. He believes it's not that unusual that Ludwig washed up where he did."

Osgood practically stood at attention at the mention of the general's name. His face reddened as he began to speak.

"I can't presume to speak for an Army general, sir."

"Not asking you to."

Osgood blew air out of puffed cheeks.

"Well, you can see the contour lines and the depth markings as well as I can, sir. It's pretty straightforward. And I'll show you the wind readings from that night if you want."

"For the record, that would be great. But no need right now. There is one thing you can show me, though. Point out where you think he would have had to have gone down to end up where he did, which was approximately . . . well, hell, it's not even on this chart."

"I've got another one, sir. Covers more area."

Osgood retrieved a chart of slightly larger scale, labeled "Approaches to Guantánamo Bay." The eastern edge extended several miles past the Cuban fenceline, just past the entrance to a small inlet at Punta Barlovento.

"He made landfall right about here," Falk said, tapping the Cuban shoreline. "About a half mile past the fence. Your opinion only, of course."

Osgood hesitated.

"Could any report you make just state that it's actually *your* opinion? Based on available nautical and meteorological data from this office, of course."

"My pleasure, ensign."

He nodded, and the color returned to his face.

"Any way you slice it, he went down in Cuban waters, sir. By a good bit. And if he had gone much past here"—Osgood tapped a spot just offshore from where Ludwig beached—"then he probably would have been carried up into this little bay of theirs, at Punta Barlovento. I know they had a patrol boat hit a shoal out there once. Her engine died, and she washed right up the inlet. Broad daylight, too."

Osgood obviously didn't have a high opinion of Cuban seamanship.

"Meaning what, that he must have drowned fairly close to shore?"

"Yes, sir. I'd say within a hundred yards."

"But over on their side. At least a half a mile over."

Osgood nodded. Falk folded his arms, more stumped than ever.

"Doesn't make sense."

"No, sir."

"You think I could get one of these?" Falk said, pointing to the chart.

"Sure. C'mon back to the chart room."

Falk could have spent hours in there, unrolling them all to unlock their secrets. Nautical charts were tailor-made for daydreams. You stumbled upon markings for old mines and shipwrecks. When he studied depth readings for shoals and sandbars he almost felt the shudder of a hull scraping bottom. When reading the bigger numbers he imagined the inky depths of the troughs. All of that lore hidden beneath the waves—a silent world inhabited by fish, long-forgotten ships, and the drifting corpses of everyone who had ever been lost at sea and never recovered. Ludwig could easily have wound up like that. Two of Falk's childhood friends were still down there, lost in summer storms off Stonington, sons of lobstermen, just like he was. Sometimes when studying the contours he felt like a cop scanning a map of a city's darkest and most dangerous alleys. Other times it was like viewing one big escape plan, a variety of portals that led to any place of your choosing. Because once you were out on the water you could end up almost anywhere, as long as you knew what you were doing.

"We've got a whole set of these, you know," Osgood said. "Three charts of the area, if you're interested."

"Sure," Falk said. "Maybe I'll put one up in our kitchen. Spruce the place up. Might as well have something to look at besides the grease stains."

"Here." The ensign rolled them up into a cardboard tube. "We've got plenty, and we're due to get more. The Navy's always remapping the shipping lanes down this way for us and the Coast Guard."

"For chasing drug runners?"

"And refugees."

"Forgot about them."

"Busy place out there sometimes. Just not in our neck of the woods."

FALK MADE IT TO LUDWIG'S BARRACKS about a half hour before lunchtime. The unit's CO, a Reserve colonel, had warily set up the appointment.

Ludwig had bunked in a panel barracks, the latest style of housing at Camp America in an evolution that had earlier included tents and flimsy sea huts. The panel units had twelve beds arranged in two rows, with no windows but plenty of air-conditioning. Ludwig's building was the second one down in a row of five in one of the newer parts of the camp. A new outdoor basketball court was nearby, already doing a brisk business despite the midday swelter. The grounds around the barracks were gravel, not grass, which only added to the heat. Stand out here long enough and you'd start to hallucinate, Falk thought.

A Weber grill and a couple of bicycles were parked outside. By the door was a bulletin board where somebody had posted a flyer offering a fishing rod with a full tackle box for thirty dollars. Probably a soldier who was headed home.

Falk entered without knocking, and the first thing he saw was a full-color poster of the World Trade Center towers in flames, above the typically awkward wording of an Army propaganda poster: "Are you in a New York state of mind? Don't leak information our enemies can use to kill U.S. troops, or more innocent people."

"You must be special agent Falk."

"And you must be Colonel Davis."

"Correct."

A few other soldiers were also present, and the atmosphere was one of quiet hostility. Besides the usual tension common to any unit that had just lost a soldier, there was an element of the civilian-military mistrust that one often found elsewhere at Gitmo. This mistrust went double if they knew you spoke Arabic. These fellows tended to hear from their officers 24/7 that each and every one of the detainees was a hardened killer and an experienced terrorist, who in at least some way shared responsibility for 9/11. It was part of the effort to keep them motivated and boost their morale. Falk didn't find it at all surprising that given that sort of indoctrination, they were skeptical of anyone who believed otherwise. To them, Falk was among the accommodators and deal makers, a guy who not only spoke the language of the enemy but had also complained about some of the rougher treatment during interrogation. And now he had come here to ask them questions, not seeming to care whether or not he pissed them off.

"We've tried to keep anyone from touching his stuff," Davis said. "Not that anybody would want to. It's been kind of hard for them, having this empty bunk."

"I can understand that. I was a Marine once myself. Got a key for his footlocker?"

"Been saving it for you. Soon as you give the go-ahead we'll send his things home."

"This afternoon's fine with me for anything I don't decide to keep. His hometown's Buxton, Michigan?"

"Yeah. About a hundred miles from Lansing."

"Most of the people in your unit from that area?"

"For the most part."

Posted above the bed were the photographs he'd expected to find. A pretty wife, a healthy-looking daughter who was maybe four or five, and a baby not more than a few months old. Ludwig himself was in one shot, and Falk was momentarily taken aback. He recognized the face from some of his nocturnal rounds in Camp 3, Adnan's area. He supposed that made perfect sense, seeing as how Ludwig had been on the 8 p.m.-to-4 a.m. shift. And none of the JIG people like himself were supposed to know the guards by name, or vice versa, lest anyone mistakenly utter a name within earshot of a detainee. That was why the guards used fake nicknames, often Arab ones, just for kicks.

The footlocker was about half full. On top was a battered Tom Clancy paperback, but that was the only book. If you didn't read much here, then you didn't read much anywhere. There were some civilian clothes, another uniform, some shaving items, a few music CDs and a portable player with headphones. Celine Dion and Garth Brooks. Banker music for the new millennium. Some blank stationery for letters home and a couple of pens. A towel, a softball mitt, a pair of running shoes. But there were no swimming trunks, nor was there anything resembling a diary or a notebook. He dug to the bottom, expecting to unearth a cache of letters from his wife. But there was no evidence of that, either. Maybe Ludwig communicated only by phone and e-mail. Plenty of others did. He'd have to ask to see those records as well, although that would mean more hoops to jump through.

"What were his regular duties?"

"The NCOIC for his shift in Camp Three." Meaning noncommissioned officer in charge. Falk would need to see the duty roster, check with other soldiers on his shift.

"Has anyone said anything about his state of mind? Was he upset? Depressed?"

"Ludwig kept a lot to himself. But I've asked, and everybody says there was no sign of anything out of the ordinary. Private Calhoun here was probably his best friend."

Falk turned to see a moon-faced private seated three bunks down, cap in hand, as expectant as a job applicant.

"Corporal Belkin told me about you the other night on the beach," Falk said.

"Told me about you, too," Calhoun responded, in a tone suggesting he hadn't liked what he heard. Jesus, but these guys were touchy.

"These questions have to be asked, private, even if some of them are unpleasant. I'm told you were the last to see him. Is that still the case, as far as you know?"

"Yes, sir."

"And where might that have been?"

"Dinner. Seaside galley."

"Remember what you talked about?"

Calhoun shrugged, looking off toward the corner. Either he was hiding something or he didn't give a damn what Falk thought.

"Well? Football? Women?"

"Yeah. Something like that. Small talk."

"What time you finish up?"

"Around six thirty."

"And afterward?"

"A couple of us went to watch TV. He said he was going for a walk. He did that sometimes after dinner."

The banker taking his postprandial constitutional, just like on Main Street. Only this one never returned. There would have been a few hours of daylight left. Maybe he spent them on the beach, watching the sunset while he sank into a wallow of depression.

"And no one saw him after that?"

Calhoun shook his head, now looking at his feet.

"Were you guys friends from Buxton?"

"Yes, sir. Used to hunt together. Double-dated before we were married."

"How was his marriage?"

"Happy." Now he was looking up, an expression of defiance.

"What did he like to do down here in his spare time?"

"Same as the rest of us. Movies. Go online." Yep, an e-mailer for sure.

"He do any boating?"

"None of us did. Not much water around Buxton. This place is kind of wasted on us."

"Did he swim?"

"He'd go in the ocean." A tad defensive, it seemed to Falk.

"Just wondering, because it doesn't look like he had any trunks."

Calhoun shrugged. Not his problem.

"Sorry to be indelicate, private, but did he have anything going down here? A woman on the side, maybe?"

Parker reddened—in anger, not embarrassment.

"No, sir. He was straight as an arrow. A banker." As if that clinched the deal.

"What was the name of his bank?" Falk should give them a call.

"Farmers Federal. He'd been promoted to branch manager a month before our deployment. You don't get promoted at a place like that when things are funny, or you're having some kind of personal problems."

"Understood, soldier. Tell me one last thing. Even before those last few days, did he ever seem at all depressed? Uneasy?"

"Look around you, sir." Calhoun gestured to include the other three soldiers. "Do any of us look thrilled? We've been here ten months, with two to go. Anybody who doesn't get a little depressed about that is the guy who needs his head examined. But none of us thinks about killing ourselves. This is the last place we'd want to end our lives."

"I get the message, private." Falk shut his notebook, then the footlocker. "Send this home whenever you like, colonel. But I'd like a copy of his personnel records."

"Some of that I'll have to get faxed from unit headquarters, back in Michigan."

"Good enough. I'll just have a last look around, then."

The colonel nodded and left. Two of the other soldiers followed, but Calhoun stayed, as if keeping a vigil over his buddy's possessions. Falk glanced at the photos again. Posted next to them was a faded Christmas card. He checked under the bed, but there was nothing on the floor or beneath the mattress. He was still bothered by the absence of letters. There should be *something* besides e-mail, especially for a guy who had hung on to a Christmas card for more than seven months.

"You guys get much mail from home?" he asked Calhoun.

"They already came for his letters."

Falk looked up.

"Who did?"

"The security people. They said it was authorized."

"Was your CO with them?"

"No. But they had the key to the footlocker, so we figured it was cleared."

The key? Or some kind of universal key? Footlockers like this one were a piece of cake to open if you knew what you were doing.

"What do you mean, security people?"

"The security task force for J-DOG."

Van Meter's people. Falk should have been told.

"You catch any of their names?"

Calhoun shook his head.

"One was a captain, though. Saw his stripes."

Maybe it was Van Meter himself.

"Tell you what, Calhoun. Next time you see him around town, how 'bout you look for his name and jot it down. Then call me." He scribbled down his number.

This, at least, seemed to get Calhoun interested, perhaps by making him feel like a part of the process. Maybe that's why he offered his next bit of information.

"You might check the P.O. All they took was his old mail."

"You guys don't get delivery at the barracks?"

"No, sir. We have to pick it up. Earl checked every day. A lot of us do. If the line's long enough it kills a whole half hour sometimes."

Two days of mail had arrived since Ludwig's disappearance, so it was worth a try. Maybe a captain like Van Meter, accustomed to delivery straight to his office, wouldn't have thought to check.

"Thanks, private."

Calhoun nodded, sullen again. He stayed on the bunk while Falk exited.

CAMP AMERICA'S "POST OFFICE" was a converted panel barracks, and there was indeed a long line. Falk ducked past it to the counter.

"You looking for something?" a sergeant demanded.

He flashed his Bureau ID.

"I'm here on the Ludwig case. I need any of his uncollected mail."

"You'll have to do better than that if you want to see it, much less take custody."

"Would General Trabert's word be good enough?"

That at least tempered the sergeant's attitude.

"You got a written order?"

"No. You got a phone?"

"Not for unauthorized personnel."

Falk checked the name on the uniform. Keaton.

"All right, have it your way. I'll just drive over to the Pink Palace and tell the general that some goddamn Sergeant Keaton made me come over and interrupt whatever he was doing just to get a letter of authorization. Works for me."

"Phone's at the desk," Keaton said.

Not only was the general in, he'd been trying to reach Falk for more than an hour.

"Good morning, sir."

"Damned near good afternoon, but I'm satisfied to hear you're walking the beat. The quicker you conclude this, the better, given the day's earlier events. Guess you heard."

"Yes, sir."

"Which brings me to the point of this call." As if the general had phoned him. "One of the team members has been trying to reach you. They need an audience with you, and seemed to think I'd know how to get in touch."

Falk glanced toward the officious Sergeant Keaton, who had picked up a clipboard and was trying to act as if he weren't eavesdropping.

"Any particular reason?"

"He didn't say. It was your buddy, Ted Bokamper."

Falk relaxed. Just like Bo to try and reach him through the general. Managing to stir up both of them while getting what he needed.

"You're to meet him at thirteen hundred hours, at the marina."

He checked his watch. Just enough time to stop by the house for a quick bite and a change of clothes for sailing. Bo and he would have their private chat, after all, and he couldn't imagine a better place for it than the deck of a sailboat, out on Guantánamo Bay. It was a good thing the general couldn't see his smile.

"Yes, sir. I'll be there."

"Now. You must have called for a reason."

"Ludwig's mail. I'm at the Camp America P.O. and need authorization to pick it up. There's a cooperative sergeant here who says that a verbal is all he needs."

"Put him on."

Falk handed over the phone and watched as Keaton nodded rigidly, saying, "Yes, sir," three times in succession. After the third one he handed the receiver back.

"He wants you again. I'll get the mail."

Falk took the phone while Keaton disappeared.

"Sir?"

"One more thing, Falk. As you make your rounds, keep my wishes in mind. Whatever you're hearing, I want to know it. Before they do. In fact . . ."

You could hear papers being shuffled, a hand covering the mouthpiece while Trabert consulted with someone else. "Why don't you stop by my office this evening? Let's say eighteen hundred hours, for dinner and a debriefing. Just you and me. Better that way."

"It'll be my pleasure, sir."

That was one lie. Falk wondered how many more he'd have to tell before the day was out.

CHAPTER TWELVE

THE MARINA, NOT the Tiki Bar, was Falk's preferred means of escape at Gitmo. He tried to find time to go sailing once a week, having settled on a twenty-seven-foot Hunter as his favorite therapy. It was a little banged up, but the rental was cheap. And there was nothing further removed from the confinement of the interrogation booth than cruising the open water of the bay—salt spray in your face and sun at your back, perhaps with a manatee as an escort, a brown bulge beneath the waves. After the iron chill of Maine's rocky shoals that Falk had grown up navigating, Guantánamo Bay seemed like a big swimming pool, bathtub-warm and punch-bowl green. With a few beers aboard he could spend hours tacking and running, hauling the sheets until the sails were set to the edge of the wind.

It was where he took Pam for their first real date, impressing her with his easy seamanship. On a later weekend they piled camping equipment onto a skiff and motored out to Hospital Cay, a slender spit of land where they stayed overnight. It was the only time during the posting when Falk had felt like he was somewhere else.

Recently the authorities had eased up on the rules by letting boaters exit the bay, a concession mostly to fishermen eager to troll the ocean. Even then, you were pretty much restricted to an eleven-square-nautical-mile area known as the Tackle Box, to keep you from straying into Cuban waters. Up to now Falk had stuck to the bay, but today he had other ideas. This would be a working cruise.

As Falk prepared for sailing, he glanced again at the haul of Ludwig's mail from the post office. It was disappointing—one stamped letter with a handwritten return address in Buxton, Michigan, and a metered mailing from Ludwig's bank, Farmers Federal, also postmarked in Buxton.

Pushed for time, he tossed them on his bed and changed quickly into shorts and a T-shirt, grabbing a cap, a rain jacket, and a handheld GPS on his way out the door. The chances of foul weather were virtually zero, but Falk never underestimated the sea.

Bokamper was waiting at the marina snack bar, reading a week-old newspaper at a picnic table while a radio played the sort of public service announcement typical to Armed Forces broadcasting: "Your fingernails, use them in good health!"

"How'd you manage to shake the rest of the team?" Falk asked.

"The better question would be how I managed to hang around as long as I did. Fowler and Cartwright asked me to take a hike for a while."

"Off planning their next move?"

"With their new friends."

"Van Meter and company."

"Guess you saw the conclave at breakfast."

"Who could miss it? Was that intentional?"

Bo nodded. "Fowler wanted to show a united front with the locals, and they were his choice. Didn't put the troops at ease, huh?"

"Oh, the troops probably loved it. It's the Joint Intelligence Group that's spooked. Especially considering Fowler's taste in friends. Not Rieger, the other two."

"Van Meter and Lawson. Exactly who I wanted to talk about."

"On the water," Falk answered, nodding toward Skip, the marina manager, who was also reading a paper but was close enough to hear every word.

"Think OPSEC," Bo said in a stage whisper.

"Fast learner, but still a smart-ass."

On the counter, Falk unrolled one of the charts he'd picked up from Ensign Osgood and laid out his proposed float plan for Skip, a big fellow in his forties who wore cargo shorts and a Hawaiian shirt. He smelled like motor oil and suntan lotion.

"I'll be pushing the envelope a little," Falk said, amusing himself by borrowing the general's favorite term, "but I won't get anybody in trouble."

Skip frowned, then nodded slowly.

"You ought to take one of those Sea Chasers. You can get five-foot waves out there in a heartbeat."

The Sea Chaser was a motorboat. No deal.

"The Hunter will handle it fine," Falk said. "C'mon, Skip. You know I'm good for it."

"Fair enough. But I'll have to phone you in to the observation outpost. They're not used to seeing sails out there."

"We're leaving the bay?" Bokamper said as they walked to the dock.

"Figured I could look at where Ludwig went in from the ocean side."

"Any particular reason?"

"I'll know it if I see it. Fresh perspective, I guess. The ocean killed him, might as well get the ocean's point of view."

"Criminal profiling for a force of nature. That the kind of mystic bullshit the Bureau's teaching these days?"

"Easy. I'm captain, you're crew. Any further mutinous talk and I'm cutting your beer rations."

"Aye, aye, sir."

"How 'bout helping with these sail covers?"

A few minutes later they were under way, small waves slapping the hull as Falk steered up into the wind. It was sunny and hot again—another black flag day—but the breeze from the water offered relief, and in only a few minutes he began to relax. He braced against the heeling of the deck, hands on the vibrating wheel as a gust popped the big jib.

"Moves nicely," Bo said.

"Your tax dollars at work. She's very forgiving. Maybe even enough for you take the helm."

"No, thanks. Just let me know which ropes to pull."

"Sheets. Not ropes."

"Then how 'bout if we put three of them to the wind? Toss me a beer."

"The cooler's below, swabbie. Watch your head."

Few ex-Marines were as seemingly proud of their nautical ignorance as Bokamper. Falk had long suspected it was Bo's way of emphasizing that he wasn't one of those Naval Academy snobs. He had instead gone to Officer Candidate School after graduating from the academically rigorous but socially freewheeling University of Virginia.

Bo handed him a beer. It tasted better out here. Maybe it was the salt in the breeze, just like the flavor around the rim of a margarita glass. Too bad they had to talk shop.

"Tell me about Allen Lawson," Bo said. "The corporate guy. Hell, he's not even ex-military, is he? Not that there's anything wrong with that."

"He's the type who would have told you if he'd served. Been here six months. Mostly as an interpreter, but also does some interrogating. Point man for Global Networks, meaning he's Boustani's main competitor. Thank God I speak the language, or I'd have ended up in the middle of one of their catfights. Everybody else has. Nobody was surprised to see Lawson getting chummy with the guys who nailed Boustani."

"So you think they've cooked the books against Boustani?"

"You tell me."

"A lot of the evidence sounds like chickenshit. But they won't let me close enough to see it firsthand. Complications involving corporate privacy concerns, according to Fowler."

"That's bullshit. Just an excuse to shut you out."

"Probably. But do me a favor. I'd love to get a look at the interrogation schedules for the past few weeks. See who Lawson and Boustani have been dealing with. Van Meter, too. How does that work, anyway? You sign up on some kind of dance card?"

"Normally you hand in a list of your targets the day before, which goes up through the intel chain of command for approval. Perfunctory, unless everybody's asking for the same guy. A copy goes to the MP support unit, then when you arrive at the gates you log your ID number and pick up your man at the holding cage, or just go wait in the booth."

"And all those sign-up sheets will still be around?"

"Sure. But you don't need me to get them. Just check with the MP station."

Bokamper shook his head.

"Don't want to attract unwanted attention."

"What is it you're looking for?"

"Yemenis. Or any interrogators showing an undue interest in Yemenis lately."

"That would be me, everyone else on my tiger team, and about half the members of the Gulf group."

"Not from your team. Outsiders. People who otherwise would have no business talking to Yemenis."

"Interesting. Any particular reason?"

"None I can share."

"Then you can check it yourself."

"C'mon, Falk. Just take a look next time you're inside. Or do it as part of the Ludwig investigation."

"I do need to look up Ludwig's duty logs. Not that they'll have anything to do with what you're looking for."

"You might be surprised."

"What is it you're not telling me, Bo?"

Bo grinned. It was just like him to tease this way, to lead you to the threshold of a revelation then steer you in another direction.

"One thing I *can* tell you," Bo said. "Fowler was a very busy man last night."

"Setting up the arrest?"

"Among other things. Like stopping by Van Meter's place."

"Another busy man. He collected Ludwig's mail."

"Van Meter strikes me as a guy with his fingers in a lot of pies. Between you and me, he's the one who got the ball rolling on this arrest. His reports to Washington were setting off alarm bells all the way to the White House."

Falk couldn't help but recall Whitaker's description of Van Meter's grudge against Boustani. In Gitmo's command structure, Van Meter's close working relationship with Lawson made perfect sense, but their cooperation in this crackdown was unsettling.

"So when was Fowler at Van Meter's?"

"Late. Well after midnight."

"Sounds like you were a busy man, too."

"Not half as busy as you, I bet." Bo grinned rakishly. "She's a nice one."

He had wondered when the subject of Pam would come up.

"Wish I could say she felt the same way about you."

Bokamper laughed, almost a bark.

"She'll come around. Soon as she decides I'm not trying to lay her."

"You guys seem to have figured each other out pretty quickly."

"I'll take that as a compliment." Then his eyes got big. He looked sharply toward the bow. "Was that a manatee?"

Falk had seen the movement, too. "Port side?"

"If that still means left."

"Dolphin. They're all over the place. Rays, too, up in the shallows. Keep watching. He'll resurface."

A few seconds passed in silence while they squinted at the glare on the water. Then the gray body glimmered and broke the surface, moving at the same speed as the boat. It leaped gracefully through the air before again disappearing with hardly a splash.

"Beautiful," Bo said. "You ever miss it?"

"What?"

"Living on the water. Didn't you practically grow up in a boat? Before your parents died, I mean."

Even Bo, who knew more than most, wasn't privy to the secrets of Falk's supposed life as an orphan.

"Sometimes."

"Then it must be nice being down here."

"It's hard to think of this as 'being on the water,' in a way. Too warm, like somebody's fish tank. I keep thinking one day I'll look down and see one of those divers with bubbles coming out of his helmet, standing next to a fake castle. Real water is cold. It's where work gets done. This stuff is leisure, nonthreatening, like somebody pumped it in from Disney World."

"I dunno. It was pretty threatening for Sergeant Ludwig."

"Maybe he wanted to die. What bugs me is how he ended up floating east."

"Good question. Got any answers?"

Falk shook his head.

"But it's time for you to get to work. Uncleat that sheet and prepare to come about."

"Translation?"

"Pop the rope free, then move to the other side and crank in the opposite one. Another tack should get us out of the bay."

As they were leaving the bay, Falk pulled the GPS from his pocket. He wanted to plot some waypoints to check later on the chart.

"What's the gizmo?"

"A GPS. I'm checking our position."

"Afraid we'll get lost?"

"For fun. It was a gift."

"From her?"

Falk nodded.

"Nice gift. Not exactly the classic lover's present, but nice."

Falk smiled. Those were almost the same words he had used to Pam, which had made her blush, especially the word "lover." He had liked her answer even better.

"Well, I figured you're a sailor, and not the yacht club kind," she had said. "Besides, you seem like a guy who always wants to know exactly where he is."

She was right. He was ever conscious of getting his bearings, of knowing the set of his sails, particularly if there was a shoal ahead, whether in the form of troublesome authority or a woman hoping for more than he could deliver. Not that he had explained that part to Pam.

The jib luffed briefly as Falk drifted too close into the wind.

"Hey, lover boy," Bo shouted, "keep your mind on your sailing. One drowning in a week is enough."

ENSIGN OSGOOD HAD BEEN RIGHT. It was tough going heading east, once they cleared Windward Point. The trade winds were steady, and the current moved in concert. They tacked their way up the coast, hitting each swell in a burst of spray across the windward side of the hull. Bo looked a little green at first but persevered, and he soon got the hang of scrambling from one side to the other beneath the swinging boom, cranking in the jib sheet as Falk reset their course.

The coral bluffs of Windward Point glared at them from the left, giving way to the tiny crescent of Cable Beach. The shoreline looked more rugged than Falk had expected—rocky outcrops and reefs, with breaking waves revealing other shallow points along the way. A half mile later they passed another opening in the crags, at Cuzco Beach, where scuba divers liked to explore the reef. Falk spotted a few marker buoys on the surface, indicating the presence of divers below.

Hidden Beach, true to its name, was barely visible from the water. But Windmill Beach was impossible to miss. The wide crescent of sand smiled out at them after they'd been heading east for nearly an hour.

"What's the little house on the bluff, just past it?" Bo asked.

"Used to be an officer's place, long time ago. Now it's Camp Iguana, which is why there's a fence."

"Where they keep the kid prisoners?"

"Three of them. Ages twelve to fourteen when they got here. But that was a year ago."

They, too, had come from the battlefield of Afghanistan, and their continuing presence had created an international stir. The authorities kept saying they'd be sent home soon, but for now they remained. Falk had heard that for entertainment they sometimes coaxed iguanas through the fence, onto the small lawn where they tossed around an American football and stared at the sea.

"Maybe they saw something," Bokamper said. "The night Ludwig went out."

Falk shook his head. "Doubtful. They keep 'em indoors after hours. Besides, you'd probably have to move heaven and earth to see 'em." All the same, it was worth checking.

He scanned the beach. A few towels were spread on the sand. A striped umbrella sprouted like a blossom. Only one swimmer was out, head bobbing in the gentle waves. He wasn't sure what he'd expected to see from this vantage point, but it wasn't this tameness. The wind the other night had been stronger, but nothing out of the ordinary.

They continued past the big bluff beneath Camp Iguana until the sprawl of Camp America came into view. Beyond it sprouted the plywood guard towers of Camp Delta and the long cellblock rooftops, gleaming in the sunlight.

Falk tacked toward open water until they were far enough at sea to spot the opening to the little bay at Punta Barlovento on the Cuban side.

"Where's the fenceline?" Bo asked. "Oh, wait. I see it. And a watchtower." The tower was about a half mile beyond the line, and closer to the shore than Falk would have guessed.

"One of their morning foot patrols found the body," Falk said. "That must have been a shock."

"No wonder they're so pissed. A whole division of Marines probably could have come ashore."

There was little purpose in going farther. They were probably approaching acceptable limits as it was, so Falk turned the wheel through the wind and headed for home, sails flapping as they came about. Once they were running with the wind and the current it was as if someone had shut off a noise machine. The boat moved with ease, traveling faster down the coast but with none of the buffeting.

"So what did all this tell you?" Bokamper asked, no longer having to shout.

"That I'm hungry."

"Nothing else?"

Falk shook his head. "Bad idea, I guess. But a nice day for a sail."

"Anything that gets you off the Rock for a while can't be all bad."

They reached the mouth of the bay in practically no time, and not long after that they were within sight of the marina. It had been nearly four hours since they departed, and the sun was drifting lower.

"Will we make it to dinner?" Bo asked.

"You will. I've got a date with the general."

"You're moving up in the world."

"He wants to know what you guys are up to. What should I tell him?"

"Hell, he probably knows more than I do. But at least you'll get decent chow."

"You should eat at the Jerk House instead."

"Sounds like another name for the officers club."

"You're not the first to make that observation. It's a Jamaican barbecue joint, near the Tiki Bar."

"Sounds perfect. But one last question before we dock back in OPSEC Land."

"Go ahead."

"Now don't get offended, but I've been meaning to ask since I got here, and this might be my last chance for a while." He paused, as if to soften the blow. "You haven't heard from the Cubans lately, have you?"

Well, now. Talk about unexpected.

A fresh gust out of the east fluttered the edge of the jib, and the wheel hummed in Falk's hands. He found himself relieved, in a way. It was good to get the issue out in the open, although he wondered uneasily whether Bo's question had been a lucky guess or informed supposition.

"Funny you should ask," he said, his mouth going dry.

He didn't want to be sailing anymore. He would rather be off the water, with a beverage stronger than beer at hand, plus another few hours to kill. This was the stuff of barroom confessionals, of quiet nights when you put everything on the table and hoped for the best. A sunny day on the water wasn't engineered for such a weighty topic. The subject of Cuba loomed so large in their past that it might capsize the entire day.

Then again, maybe they really had come to the right place, because he needed only to glance toward the green hills beyond the marina to see where it had all begun.

"You better tell me all about it," Bo said. "And we better both hope Fowler and Cartwright haven't already heard it from someone else."

"Let's come about, then. We're closing on the dock, and you know how sound travels over water."

"Think OPSEC," Bo muttered again. Only this time he meant it.

CHAPTER THIRTEEN

It began during Falk's Marine days, when he was sent on the Gitmo equivalent of a snipe hunt.

He had been on base for all of three weeks when he made the mistake of asking his barracks sergeant how one might apply for permission to visit Havana—the real Cuba, as he thought of it, the one with mambo orchestras and women who danced with fruit on their heads. His sergeant, having encountered this callow brand of nonsense before, knew exactly what to do.

"Oh, it's easy," he said. "Tell you what, Private Falk. I'll even let you out of this morning's three-miler if you want to get the ball rolling now. How 'bout it?"

Falk nodded, hardly believing his luck. Hook, line, and sinker.

The sergeant turned, scribbled something at his desk, then sealed it in an envelope.

"Take this note out to MOP 31 at the North East Gate. Jenkins will drive you. That's where they arrange it. Who knows, maybe you'll be spending the weekend in Havana."

On the ride to the observation post even the usual clouds of vultures had looked like harbingers of good news, and the sentries at the North East Gate seemed eager to help, smiling as they tore open the note. Then they loaded a rucksack with fifty pounds of stones and showed him the message:

"Here's another one who thinks he can visit Fidel. Award the customary door prize and return him by the usual means."

"Can't go there, son," a sympathetic Georgian drawled as he

heaved the pack onto Falk's shoulders. "Not 'til Castro's dead, anyway. Try Little Havana in Miami next time you're in the States. It's the next best thing, and you'll be bored in an hour. Which leaves plenty of time for the beach and the women. Have a nice hike."

Falk slogged the five miles back to the barracks in the heat of the day, suffering more from the simmer of embarrassment than the sunlight. It took him another week to work up the nerve to ask if there really was a Little Havana. With no family to visit he decided to follow the Georgian's advice.

He got his chance a year later, by hopping a Navy flight to Jacksonville and catching a Greyhound to Miami. He found a cheap motel near downtown, just south of the Miami River. Then he set off on foot, passing beneath the long shadows of the trestled I-95 before reaching the main drag of Eighth Street, or Calle Ocho, which took him into the heart of Little Havana.

At first he was wholly unimpressed. There was heavy traffic and lots of sprawl—low-slung homes, cluttered stores, and signs in Spanish—pretty much like the rest of Miami he'd seen to that point. But he had come this far, so he kept walking, and in an hour or so he began to warm to the small touches that set it apart—tiny cafés with service windows open to the sidewalk, offering thimblefuls of *café cubano* or fried *croquetas* displayed in glass cases; the bodegas and *joyerías*, and the storefront cigar factories that smelled of cured tobacco; produce vendors with yucca, mango, and plantain.

The heartbeat of this commerce was salsa, blaring from what seemed like half the doorways. As he walked west, one song seamlessly gave way to the next, as if bands were marching past him in the street.

But the hypnotic background noise that drew him deeper was the sound of Spanish. Only by mastering it would he ever feel at home here, and suddenly that seemed like a smart thing to do. He still dated his passion for foreign languages to that moment, when he realized that such skills were even more important than passports or plane tickets.

He lingered a while at Máximo Gómez Park, where the click and clatter of dominoes punctuated the conversations of elderly men hunched over the tables as they plucked tiles from small wooden racks. No one seemed to mind the Marine with the buzz cut gaping over their shoulders. He might as well have been invisible. The language barrier again. Or maybe they were just accustomed to any Anglo viewing them as curiosities.

Falk was puzzled by the shaded boulevard of stone memorials on Thirteenth Avenue. The first and tallest was a marble column dedicated to "Los Mártires de la Brigada de Asalto" from April 1961. The Bay of Pigs? Had to be. It was topped by a forlorn "eternal flame," barely noticed by the kids roaring past on bicycles. Far more impressive than any man-made object was a huge spreading ceiba tree with shoulder-high roots.

He also wasn't sure what to make of the Paseo de las Estrellas, a puny, latinized version of the Hollywood Walk of Fame. Was Celia Cruz Cuban? He didn't think so. And he was downright jarred by the sudden presence of a McDonald's in a big parking lot with a life-size statue of Ronald McDonald. Or did one call him "Ronaldo" here?

Falk wandered the aisles of a supermarket called the President, shopped aimlessly for music, then ate a Cuban sandwich just to see what it was made of. After a bus ride to the beach and an afternoon swim, he returned that night to try out a dance club he had spotted. That was when the place won him over.

He couldn't salsa, of course, any more than he could understand a word of what anyone said. But a few beers and an excess of earnestness boosted him across both humps, and before long he felt he had arrived on some far frontier.

Later he would try to determine what must have made him such an easy target that night. Perhaps it was his military haircut. Maybe it was something he said. Whatever the case, after the first hour a friendly fellow sauntered over with a beautiful woman on his arm and addressed Falk in perfect English. Hungry for conversation, Falk opened up in a hurry, and he found the man to be immediately likable.

His name was Paco, a jovial sort with a little potbelly and a pack of Kents poking from the pocket of his guayabera. He had come to Miami in '81, he said with a groan. *Mariel, what a mess.* That bastard Fidel emptying the jails, which made it hard on everyone, all of them tarred by the same brush until things finally got sorted out. Now he had it made, of course. He loved America, even if he still got homesick sometimes.

"You think you've got it bad," Falk said. "I *live* down there but can't even see the place. I'm stationed at Gitmo." Then the rest of his tale spilled out—the Marine who could only peek through a chain-link fence, denied the passage that might satisfy his curiosity. Oh, well. Maybe someday.

"Oh, no," Paco said, eyes alight. "You are one of the lucky ones. If I ever tried to visit, they would keep me. Fidel would throw me in jail! But you? You can actually *go*!"

"No, I can't. I checked, believe me."

"Oh, not as a soldier, of course. But as a tourist! It can be done very easily."

"Legally?"

Paco held out a hand, waving it back and forth.

"Más o menos." More or less. "Some friends of mine run a travel agency. They arrange it all the time. Lots of Americans do it. They don't even stamp your passport."

Thanks, but no thanks, Falk said. It sounded like a quick way to land in the brig, and Paco had the good sense not to insist. But the next day on the beach Falk began to reconsider. When you're eighteen, "more or less" sounds like pretty good odds. So he returned that night to the same club, and there was jolly old Paco, only this time with a different woman.

"Sí," he said. "I will be happy to help you. Let me call my friends and arrange it, because their English isn't so good."

They set up the trip for December, two months down the road. Falk worried a little about the expense, but Paco took care of that as well, securing cut rates for the flight and the hotel, bargain prices that Falk hardly believed were possible.

"It's because they want dollars," Paco explained. "Fidel, he is so hungry for them, especially now that the Russians are leaving."

In his first few days back at Gitmo, Falk considered backing out. But the more he thought about it, the more the idea appealed to him. There was nothing like the hint of the forbidden to turn a mere vacation into an adventure. It would be his own way of settling the score with his smug sergeant. Besides, he had already put down two hundred bucks in cash, and he couldn't afford to go anywhere else.

His misgivings returned not long after his flight from Miami touched down in Mexico City. As promised, someone from the travel agency met him at the terminal, although the man seemed to be in a great hurry.

"Your passport, please."

Falk handed it over. The fellow took it, then handed him an envelope. Inside was his ticket to Havana along with another passport—British, not American, yet with Falk's picture. Now where had they gotten that? Then he remembered Paco's request for photos, which he had said were for vaccination records.

"What's this?" he asked in bewilderment. The name on both the passport and the air ticket was Ned Morris, with an address in Manchester. "I thought they didn't stamp 'em, so just give me mine back."

"Later. When you return," the emissary said, melting into the crowd before Falk could protest further. Falk realized he didn't even know the man's name. But just as he was about to panic, a second man arrived at his shoulder and, placing a reassuring hand at his back, said, "This way. You must hurry. Your flight, it is soon leaving. Your passport will be returned on the way home. It works this way for everyone. Your bag, please."

Falk didn't want to hand it over, but by now they were at the security gate at the mouth of the concourse, and the man was gesturing for him to place it onto the conveyor belt.

Almost before he knew it, the plane was taking off. Falk scanned the ticket again and saw that the price was about three times what he'd actually paid. A special deal, Paco had said. En route he began expecting the worst. He was certain there would be a welcoming party from the Cuban Army—Falk led away in handcuffs while the flashbulbs popped for the Commie newspapers. Castro's prize Marine, bagged like a chump.

But there was nothing of the sort, and by the time the taxi reached the hotel he had begun to relax. Sure, it was a shady arrangement, doubtless involving kickbacks and bribes. There would probably be extra charges from the hotel now that they had a captive audience. So what? He had already seen other Americans here, along with about half of Europe. None of them were talking about Castro, and none seemed the least bit troubled.

As he strolled around town he occasionally got a creepy feeling that someone was following, but otherwise he had a fine time despite the terrible food, which reminded him of Marine chow. Instead of local fare, all the hotels and restaurants offered a bland version of Anglo cuisine.

He quickly got used to being called Mr. Morris. It seemed to fit with the methods he had used for shedding his family. Just put a few words on an official document and they magically came true. What better way to hide yourself? He decided he could be quite comfortable being Ned Morris for a while.

Then he met Elena. He smiled at her at breakfast from a few tables away, and that seemed to be the end of it, because the next time he looked up she was gone. He was disappointed at first, thinking he had been onto something. But that night at the Amigo Club he saw her walk by while he was speaking pidgin French to a reasonably attractive woman who had been speaking pidgin English. There was that smile again as she headed for the bar. A few moments later she passed in the other direction.

"'Scusé moi," he offered clumsily to the Frenchwoman, then muttered something about "visiting the loo," figuring that from time to time he ought to sound British.

He found her at a corner table with two friends. No dates in sight. Her English was basic, but seemed to get better the more she practiced. He bought her a drink. They danced. Her face tilted toward his, full of promise, her perfume like something that a blossom offered to the night air after a full day in sunshine. She moved against him on the dance floor, a perfect fit. When they returned to the table her friends were gone.

Later, in his room, the possibility that a camera might be behind the mirror never occurred to Falk, nor did it for any of the next five nights, all of which they spent together. He would not learn of that little trick until the photos arrived a month later, by which time she had already convinced him of her sincerity with letters sent via relatives in Puerto Rico. She said that she worried that anything mailed directly from Cuba might get him into trouble.

She did not write to Ned Morris, of course. Because by the third night Falk had been smitten enough to confess all and to tell her his real name.

Elena, too, eventually confessed her duplicity, although not until months later, in a letter stained with her tears. So she said. But by that time the damage was done. The photos had arrived, wrapped inside a typewritten letter posted from New Jersey—sent by pals of Paco's, Falk presumed. It included blunt instructions that Falk should visit Gitmo's machine shop next time he was in the neighborhood—after destroying this letter, of course. Failure to comply would result in copies of the photos being sent to Falk's commanding officer, along with a photostat of Ned Morris's passport.

That was when he met "Harry," the commuting handyman extraordinaire, a Cuban who came to work each day from his home in

Guantánamo City. Harry set up a schedule for once-a-month verbal reports. The Cubans never asked Falk for much, and he often wondered why they bothered. Everything he told them they doubtless already knew. Perhaps someone in Havana simply liked being able to say he had an insider at Gitmo. He forwarded small items about ship arrivals, base scuttlebutt about transfers and troop strength, all of which they could see for themselves from their watchtowers. Just as well. This way he needn't feel guilty. Well, not too much. At least not for a while. Because by the third month his conscience got the better of him, and he decided to come clean.

The last person he would have told was his sergeant. No sense in rewarding the very man whose practical joke had helped push Falk over the line. Instead he shelled out for a long-distance call to Ted Bokamper, who by then was an up-and-coming young star at the Department of State, already working for one of the better-connected undersecretaries.

"We have to meet next time I'm stateside," Falk said. "I have some information that might help you, depending on what your boss thinks of it."

He didn't say more because even then OPSEC was a concern, although it went by a different name. A month later they met at Bo's house in Alexandria, his first kids already crawling on the wall-to-wall carpet. Bo took the news calmly enough, and they agreed to discuss it with his chief, Saul Endler, who Bo said had long-standing connections to the intelligence community.

They spoke briefly at the office, Endler maintaining a poker face and offering little comment. Then they reconvened the next night at Endler's town house in Georgetown, discussing their next move between wall-to-wall bookshelves while Stravinsky played at a discreet volume on very pricey speakers and Mrs. Endler served them iced tumblers of bourbon.

"Latin America and the Caribbean are a special part of my bailiwick," Endler explained, "and Cuba is my particular passion, so I can certainly understand how it so quickly became yours."

He relayed all this in the calm, superior manner of a professor who has agreed to extend office hours, just this once, for a wayward scholar. The words "betrayal," "treason," and "espionage" never came up. Between those tactful omissions and the bottomless supply of food and drink, Falk was soon hanging on the man's every word. In for a penny, in for a pound, as Ned Morris might have said.

"Let's play them a bit longer, and you can start reporting directly to me," Endler proposed, pleasantly making it sound as if the whole arrangement with the Cubans had been Falk's idea. Then he poured a final round of bourbon, one for the road. Falk sensed the guilt lifting from his shoulders along with his sobriety. Out of the corner of his eye he saw that a flushed Bo was beaming. Perhaps the intimacy of the occasion signaled some sort of ascension for him, up another rung on the Foreign Service ladder.

Well, if so, what were friends for?

"Will you tell anyone else?" Falk asked. It was the last worrisome question on the checklist of his conscience.

"Based on what I've heard, there's really no need. The information you provide will help inform my own judgment on certain matters. As long as Havana doesn't escalate its requests, there's certainly no need for anyone else to know."

"Not even the Agency?" Bo asked. It was his one faux pas of the evening. Endler scowled.

"The Agency," Endler said, assuming a lecturing tone, "would only screw it up for all concerned. Our friend here might even face charges."

"But what if, like you said, they escalate their requests?" Falk asked.

"A reasonable question." Endler nodded, again the old mentor. "Should that ever occur, we'll deal with it accordingly. Even then I wouldn't foresee an immediate need to reveal your name. The Agency expects us to have some of our own sources. You might have to carry out a few extra favors, of course. But nothing more. Don't worry, it's not likely to become an issue."

Bless me, Father, Falk felt like saying. It must be the way devout Catholics felt upon receiving absolution, and for the rest of the evening he levitated in a tipsy state of grace.

Soon afterward they said good-bye. Bo stayed behind for further consultation, while Falk offered a soulful handshake and wobbled down the brick walkway to a waiting taxi. As the cab pulled away he turned in his seat for a parting wave, but the door and the curtains were already shut tight.

The meetings with Harry continued a while longer, each request as mundane as the last. But after Elena's tearful apology arrived three months later, the requests stopped. Had they figured out he had told someone? All Falk knew for sure was that his next visit to Harry produced little more than a shake of the head.

"Our business is finished, señor," Harry said curtly, looking up from a workbench where he was filing down a hunk of metal in a vice.

Endler sent word to try one more time, but Harry wouldn't even let him in the door. During his next leave to the States, Falk returned to Little Havana on the State Department's tab and visited the dance bar for three nights running. But there was no sign of Paco.

There was no more Endler either, in Falk's world, and Bo never mentioned the man's name when the two of them met, usually either at a D.C. sports bar or at Bo's house, where conversation was inevitably swamped by the noise of the children.

The topic came up directly only one more time, when Falk was undergoing the FBI's background security clearance. Bo was one of his references, and when the Bureau called Bo for an interview he, in turn, telephoned Falk to suggest a meeting at a swank restaurant on K Street.

The surroundings made Falk uncomfortable from the start. It was more of a lobbyist haunt than the raffish sort of joint where they usually met, and Bo only added to his unease by getting straight to the point while they were slurping down a dozen raw oysters.

"You sure about this gig? I mean, the Bureau. Are you really the type?"

"Hell, no. I'm not the type at all. But the work sounds interesting, and with my Arabic skills I'm actually a hot commodity."

"Still."

"Still what?"

"Do I really have to spell it out for you?"

"Havana, you mean."

"Obviously."

"That's been over for years."

"That kind of thing is never 'over,' not when you're taking this kind of job."

"So you're going to tell them?"

"Of course not."

"Is Endler the one with the problem?"

"No. We're both uneasy. It's just awkward, that's all."

"As long as the two of you keep your mouths shut, like you promised, why should it be a problem? But just say the word, and I'll withdraw my application."

Falk's stomach sank as he said it, but he knew the offer was necessary.

"You'd really do that?" Bo said, and for a moment Falk was sure his friend was going to leap at the chance.

"Yeah." He sighed. "I suppose I would. You guys bailed me out, so it's the least I could do."

"Forget it. I'd never ask you to do that."

"Endler would."

"But he's not here, is he? Look, I guess I just wanted to remind you that by giving you a clean bill of health I'm putting my ass on the line every bit as much as yours."

"Understood."

It would later occur to him that Bo's choice of restaurant, with its hushed tones and starched tablecloths, had been his way of tipping Falk to the seriousness of what lay ahead, a signal to let him know that, if Havana ever got back in touch, they might not be the only three players in on the secret. His new job was raising the stakes, by pushing him—and any future entanglement involving the Cubans—into the thick of the Washington power establishment.

It was a sobering thought, but until yesterday morning when Elena's letter had arrived, it had never seemed like one he would have to take seriously. Now, out here on the turquoise waters of Guantánamo Bay, the matter was an angry cloud on the horizon.

Falk told Bo about Elena's most recent letter, then about Harry's secondhand request for a meeting.

"Harry's still the postman?"

"Yes. Unbelievably. I've always wondered how he kept his job."

"Endler thought about getting him fired. But it would have tipped them that you were blown. As far as the Doc knows, you were his only client. Besides, Harry is searched every day, coming and going. It's not like he can leave with the crown jewels. And it's not like he's in position to see or hear anything they wouldn't already know."

"And it's not like I ever gave them much. I always wondered why they bothered."

"I guess we're about to find out. Maybe they think of you as some kind of sleeper agent. Well placed and moving nicely up the food chain."

"Great."

Bo chuckled.

"Why do you think I had the heebie-jeebies right before you joined the Bureau?"

"I saw him one day, you know. Harry. My first week back here."

"Where?"

"McDonald's."

"I thought he hated McDonald's. Didn't you take him once?"

He had, as a gesture of normalcy, a halfhearted attempt by the naive Marine to justify his friendship with the little handyman, in case anyone ever asked about his regular visits to the machine shop. Harry had eaten only a few bites of his burger before rewrapping the rest and tossing it in the trash.

"Cuban food is better," he had said, sitting in silence through the rest of the meal while Falk's embarrassment grew.

"Yeah, he hated it all right," Falk said. "Which is why I figured the only reason he was there was to get a glimpse of me. Or to let me get a glimpse of him. Show his face so I'd know he was still around."

"How'd he know you were coming?"

"Good question."

"You've had no other contacts? From anybody on their side?"

"C'mon, Bo."

"A simple 'no' will do."

"No."

"Sorry. It's the business we're in. If this got out, all hell would break loose."

"You're telling me. So how did you know I'd heard from them?"

"I didn't. It was Endler's hunch."

"Based on what?"

"You'll have to ask Endler. But it's one of the reasons he sent me."

"What difference would it make? Unless Fowler's work has some tie-in to Cuba."

"Well, he's Homeland Security, and Cartwright is Pentagon. Not to mention that those two travel in administration circles that are sticking their noses into everything else these days, so why not Cuba?"

"You'd think they'd be a little preoccupied with Iraq right now."

"Mission accomplished, as far as they're concerned. They got their war. Maybe now they're looking for the next target. Fowler's one of the new breed, part of the bunch that think they can make up reality as they go. Their work is easier to understand if you think of them as mergers-and-acquisitions specialists. Only it's countries, not companies. The minute the ink's dry on the next set of papers they're looking for something new. They don't concern themselves with aftermath. They just want to be the first to broker the next deal."

"But with Cuba?"

"Or Iran, Syria, North Korea. Wherever opportunity knocks first."

"So this whole security investigation is a front?"

"Not at all. They definitely think of themselves as being here to break up a spy ring, make a few friends at Gitmo, score some points in Washington. I'm just saying maybe there's also more to it. Some tie-ins we don't know about yet."

"But would like to."

"With your help, of course. It's one reason I want to see those interrogation schedules. And it's why I want you to meet Harry. Find out what he wants. Who knows, maybe the other side has heard something, too."

"I'd planned on visiting him tomorrow morning."

"Perfect. Just keep in mind that this isn't the old days. Don't count on it being quite as easy."

"That's occurred to me. Van Meter's little witch hunt would have a lot of fun with a guy like me. Unless Endler intervened on my behalf, of course."

"It would be a possibility."

"But not much of one, I guess you're saying. Meaning I'm on my own."

"No. You've still got me. You might say we're literally in the same boat."

They chuckled, Falk somewhat uncomfortably.

"So what else does Endler think? About Harry and me, I mean."

"You really want to know?"

Falk nodded.

"He thinks Harry's going to suggest a little reunion in Miami."

"With Paco?"

"Yeah. And Paco is someone who Endler would very much like to get a look at."

"And how am I supposed to find time for this little reunion?"

"Things have a way of working out." Bokamper nodded toward the bow. "Isn't it time we came about?"

They were well up the bay, heading toward Hospital Cay.

"Better get back to the dock if I'm going to make my date with the general."

"I'll get the jib sheet."

"The old Bo would've called it a rope."

"Easy, Falk. We're still friends."

He sure hoped so.

CHAPTER FOURTEEN

THE SPREAD FOR DINNER at General Trabert's office was nothing special—beef stew, rice, salad, and a square of yellow sheet cake, all of it straight from the mess hall. Some generals were like that, sharing meals with visitors only when it was the common fare of the enlisted man, as if they ate that way all the time.

"They're doing a better job down at the seaside galley every day, don't you think?" Trabert said.

"The food? It's not bad."

"When I first got here the men were barely past MREs. Nothing hot unless you heated it yourself. Now they serve three squares a day to more than two thousand soldiers, with no single menu repeating for a three-week period."

"Maybe they need one of those scoreboards like McDonald's. 'Millions served.'"

Civilian humor. Not to the general's liking. Falk supposed that raves in the world of the brass about the new soft-serve machine earned as many brownie points as the week's best gleanings from interrogation.

"So tell me what you know," the general said, wiping his chin with a napkin. "What's the current situation?"

"On Ludwig?"

"We'll get to that. You just spent a few hours with Mr. Bokamper. What's his read on where this team is headed?"

"In terms of arrests?" He wished Trabert would get straight to the point.

"In terms of scope. How deep it's going to go."

All the way to Havana, he could have said, but he doubted the general would understand.

"Bo's a friend, but he doesn't tell me everything. I get the impression that in some ways he's as much in the dark as the rest of us."

It was a bureaucrat's response, but it seemed to reassure Trabert. Maybe that was what the general had wanted to hear—that Bo and he were still on the outside. It was impossible to say whose side Trabert was on, or what his agenda was.

"Well, they'll be wrapping up their business inside a week, I hope. We need to clean our stables and move on. I was damned pissed off about Boustani, I can tell you that. That man had our trust, and look what he did with it."

"Do they really have much on him?"

"He's got some friends back in the States you probably wouldn't be comfortable with. There and elsewhere. That's all I can say right now. How are people reacting?"

The general was a fast eater. He had already moved on to the sheet cake.

"About how you'd expect. A lot of gossip. Some think it's a witch hunt, some that it's the worst thing since Aldrich Ames."

The general nodded.

"Not good, either way. And your work? It's progressing?"

"I could use a little help. The J-DOG intelligence people took Ludwig's mail before I could get a look at it."

"My mistake," Trabert said. "I take full responsibility for that."

"So you'll speak to them?"

"They wanted me to speak to you, actually. Part of the reason for this dinner. Seems I've gotten some noses bent out of shape. I've decided it would be best for all concerned if you turned over your findings to J-DOG. That way you can be released back to your interrogation duties."

"Is this a suggestion?"

"An order. Effective immediately. In compensation for the time you've put in on this matter, I'm granting you a three-day leave to the mainland, with my compliments."

"Is that an order, too?"

"Are you turning down a leave?"

"I was thinking the Bureau might have something to say about it."

"What you do with your time away from here is up to them. Your time at JTF-Gitmo is my concern. When you return from R and R you'll start with a fresh slate."

"Who'd I piss off?"

"Like I said, my screwup. We should have handled Ludwig in-house from the get-go. There's a seat for you on tomorrow morning's flight to JAX."

"Will my furniture be in the street when I get back to Iguana Court?"

"You'll be more welcome than ever around here once the smoke clears. I'd imagine even your friend Bokamper would agree."

"Did he know about this?"

"This was my decision, Falk. Mine alone. You're to hand over your notes and any other findings on Ludwig to Captain Van Meter by twenty-one hundred."

Van Meter again. Another finger in another pie. Falk still had plenty of questions, but it was clear the general wasn't in the mood, and there was no food left on his plate. Maybe Trabert had worked out some kind of a deal. Consolidate all the dirty laundry into one tidy sack—the security investigation, Ludwig, the works—as long as everything was cleaned up fast. That way he won, they won, and everybody's new buddy Van Meter kept building his little empire.

Or had Falk's quick trip out of town been engineered by Endler, perhaps, as a backdoor way of making Falk available to meet Paco?

Trabert stood, signaling an end to the evening. Falk's plate was still half full.

"See you on Monday, then, when you can hit the ground at top speed."

"I'm certainly leaving at top speed."

The general stood ramrod straight, unsmiling. Falk had to restrain himself from saluting.

He phoned Bo as soon as he reached the house. He suddenly had a lot to do and little time for doing it, but the only thing he needed more than time was answers. The most onerous chore was his planned visit with Harry. He would have gotten it over with tonight if possible, but by now Harry was at home in Guantánamo City, twenty miles beyond the fenceline. The Cuban commuters arrived in the early morning, so that would be Falk's best opportunity.

He wondered what he would do on this forced leave, especially if there was no rendezvous with Paco. Maybe he would just hang around Jacksonville. Drive to a nearby beach and veg out. He thought fleetingly of catching a flight to Maine. The possibility of a long walk in the woods, alone and out of touch, sounded pretty good right now. It was strange how much he was thinking about home lately. Coming back to Gitmo had been like revisiting a room from his past. This was the first place he had come after leaving Maine and basic training. In a sense he had returned to the threshold of his boyhood, his point of departure, so why not use it as the portal for his return? He wondered if his father was even alive. Surely someone would know where to find him.

But first things first. Bo, fortunately, was easy to reach.

"It seems I've been voted off the island," Falk said. "General Trabert has magnanimously granted me weekend leave. Not that I had any choice. I'm on the morning flight to JAX. Any idea what he doesn't want me around for?"

"None."

"Positive?"

"How the hell would I know?"

"Just thought you might have had something to do with it. You or your boss man. Especially if he thinks my old pal wants a face-to-face." He didn't dare say the names "Harry" or "Paco" on this line, and hoped Bokamper was wise enough to take the same precaution.

"Easy, Falk. I wouldn't set you up like that."

"Your boss would."

"Not without telling me. Fowler's a likelier suspect."

"Why?"

"I guess we'll find out while you're gone. Which reminds me, do you plan on seeing your old friend before you go?"

"Tomorrow before breakfast."

"Good plan. So what happens with Ludwig while you're away?"

"Case dismissed. I'm to turn over all notes to Van Meter."

"Mr. Versatility. When do you get back?"

"Monday. Assuming Trabert doesn't have them bump me off the return flight."

"I wouldn't think the Bureau would like that."

"They don't like Trabert, either. So it would hardly matter."

"Well, I would promise to keep you posted by e-mail on anything you're missing, but from down here . . ."

"Don't even think about it."

"Speaking of which."

"I know. We've said enough already."

"Give me a shout in the morning. After your, uh, 'breakfast.'"

"Will do."

His next call was to Pam, who answered on the first ring, as if she'd been waiting. His news got a poor reception.

"So you're throwing me to the wolves? You know, my rating goes up another three points while you're gone." Falk couldn't help wondering what would happen if she and Bo came face-to-face. As if to allay such worries, she added, "I guess I could use some early nights. Today's been a drain, with all the uproar over Boustani. Everybody else seems to think it's great entertainment, but our team's a man down. They won't even let us have his notebooks. I had to interpret for two other people in addition to my own interrogations. What I'd really like to do tonight is get hammered, but what I need is a good night's sleep."

Her reference to work shook loose a thought.

"Adnan," Falk said.

"What?"

"Sorry. You reminded me. I should check in with Adnan before I clear out. Bad enough I haven't touched base since the other night. If I let three more days slip by who knows what he'll think. He's probably already feeling used and abandoned."

"Join the club. At least he gets a farewell visit."

"Hey, this isn't my call. Trabert practically ordered me off the base."

"Remind me not to be sitting with you next time the general walks into the mess hall."

"What's that supposed to mean?"

"It's a joke. Although I do think you've forgotten the way things work in the military. I have to be more careful about making an impression than you do, that's all. But you're right about Adnan. You need some face time, even if only on the dawn patrol."

"It'll take more than that. We need a sit-down. As if I didn't have enough to do. Long night ahead."

"Guess I won't see you 'til breakfast."

"Not then, either. Got an errand to run."

"For Trabert?"

"For Bo. Can't go into details."

She pouted after that, and the conversation didn't end the way he would have liked, only in a lukewarm good-bye that bothered him. He also wondered about her crack about being seen with him by the general. Maybe it was just a joke, but he could only imagine how she would react if she found out he was damaged goods.

He threw his suitcase on the bed, then noticed Ludwig's letters, still lying on the pillow. He was about to tear one open when something told him to slow down, use caution. Maybe it would be better to let Van Meter think he hadn't read them. Whitaker was still at work, so Falk took both letters to the kitchen, filled a teakettle at the sink and turned on the stove. When it began to steam, he held the letters in the jet, working the flaps free without tearing the paper.

It was a familiar routine, not from his days as a special agent—the Bureau had far more sophisticated methods for this kind of chore—but from his childhood. He had become a snoop in his own house, searching for hidden answers when things began to fall apart. As his mother disappeared and his father drifted into uselessness, Falk had watched the notices from the tax men and the bill collectors pile up on the couch, neglected and unopened. So he had steamed them open in an empty house and delved inside, secretly reading the signposts on his family's road to ruin. He had known before anyone else of the coming foreclosure and the tax auction, and also of the letter postmarked in Boston from a defiant wife on the run, vowing never to return. This, by comparison, was nothing. Just another sleuth's trick taken from the playbook of Frank and Joe Hardy at the Deer Isle public library.

He read the personal letter first, jotting down the name of Ludwig's wife, Doris, along with their address in Buxton, then the name of a brother-in-law, Bob, mentioned on the first page. Bob was eager to go fishing next time Ludwig was home, and wanted to know what was biting in the Caribbean. It sounded like Ludwig was at least somewhat comfortable on the water.

Most of the letter was small talk: The tomato plants had blossomed, but the fruit was small and the leaves were curling; the baby's ear infection was better; their daughter, Misty, still missed her daddy; Ed from the bank had called and said he would be in touch; that nice widower Mr. Williams from down the street had died and left everything to his next-door neighbor, Mrs. Packard, who for the moment was still married; a new Sam's Club was opening on the bypass, thank goodness, twenty miles closer than the one in Revell. Four pages later Falk slipped the pages back into the envelope, then smoothed down the flap. It opened back up, of course, and he had nothing with which to reseal it. So much for old tricks.

He considered leaving the letter from the bank untouched. But something about the first letter's reference to "Ed from the bank" nagged at him. He pulled it back out.

"Ed from the bank called to get in touch, so I gave him your address and he'll be writing. It's about business."

Wouldn't the bank have had his address already? This sounded more like a veiled warning than news, so he pulled the letter from the second envelope.

It looked official enough, typed and single-spaced, with the "Farmers Federal" letterhead across the top. The writer was branch vice president Ed Sample, a lordly title for a fellow who probably outranked only a handful of tellers and loan officers. The first part was boilerplate. Hope you are well, business has been steady, blah-blah. The rest was odd, to say the least.

"I am still wondering exactly what to do about the wire transfers you authorized last week involving the banks in Peru and the Caymans. I have placed a ten-day hold on the transactions pending your further instructions. Please advise."

Then, back to the boilerplate, as if the query about the transfers had been the sort of thing that any banker in rural Michigan might ask about. Mentioning "Peru," "Caymans," and "wire transfer" in the same breath was like waving a red flag to banking regulators and the Drug Enforcement Administration. In a game of word association the answer would be "cocaine money." It would take balls to authorize something like that from anywhere, but to do it from Gitmo seemed foolhardy in the extreme.

Falk jotted down Ed Sample's phone number from the letterhead. Then he tucked the letters beneath the pages of his legal pad. Van Meter could have the rest of his notes, but this might be something the Bureau would want to look into. Or that's what he would say if Van Meter ever asked why he had held on to these items.

He left the house for Camp Delta. The prison had four main sections, and Adnan was in the highest-security wing, known as Camp 3. Camps 2 and 1 had progressively more lenient rules, although Camp 4, counterintuitively, offered the easiest conditions of all, with communal cellblocks, white jumpsuits, bigger meals, and more time for exercise and showers. The guards called it "the Haj," after the pilgrimage Muslims make to Mecca.

By the time Falk made it past all four gates into Camp 3 the sky was darkening. It was the time of day when the place began to calm down. You could still smell the detainees' dinner on a cloud of their collective farts and exhalations, hundreds of them in their tiny cells, preparing for the night.

Falk hadn't had time the day before to sign up for a session with Adnan, so he went straight to the young man's cell, expecting to find him in the usual position—hiding beneath the sheets, in spite of the heat. Instead the cell was empty. Falk's reaction was immediate and visceral. Someone must be poaching. Someone was in for a world of trouble.

"Guard! MP!"

A private came running from around the corner, face reddening. He must have thought Falk was in some sort of trouble.

"Where's this prisoner, soldier?"

"He's signed out, sir."

"To who?"

"Don't know. I'll check."

"You do that. Fast."

Falk waited by the door as if Adnan might return any minute. Instead the private returned, walking briskly. He flinched as a detainee shouted something in a language Falk didn't understand.

"Well?"

The private leaned low, Falk not understanding why until it occurred to him that the guard was trying to keep the prisoners from overhearing.

"It was an OGA, sir," the guard whispered. The local acronym for the CIA. "Here's his ID number."

Falk wrote it down, but he already recognized the number because it had the prefix of his own tiger team.

"Goddamn it," he muttered. "And thank you, private."

A few minutes later he was strolling toward the interrogation trailer in a fury, flashing his ID at another MP before flinging back the door. Maybe this was why they were sending him away for the weekend. Lots of tidying up to do in his absence. He threw open the door to the first booth. Empty. Then the second. Empty. He got the same result at three and four, like a bad sitcom, the jealous husband checking closets for his wife's lover. Slam. Nothing. Slam. Nothing. All the way down the line until he reached the seventh booth, where an Army sergeant he recognized as one of Pam's classmates from Fort Huachuca looked up in irritation. Seated at the table in a relaxed pose was a prisoner in white, meaning he was from medium security.

"Sorry," Falk blurted. He then couldn't help but add, "You seen Tyndall?"

No answer. Just an enraged shake of the head.

Chastened, Falk gently shut the door before checking the last booth, again finding nothing at this slow time of day. He supposed Tyndall could have taken Adnan to the CIA's booths in another trailer, but generally that wasn't the man's style. Falk's anger was turning to panic, and he practically ran back to the cellblock, tracking down the MP as sweat rolled down his back.

"Private, what was the sign-out time on that detainee?"

"I was going to tell you, sir, but you were in too much of a goddamn hurry. It was last night. Or this morning if you want to get technical. Three a.m."

"Then where the hell's the prisoner?"

The private shrugged.

Falk went to Adnan's cell for another look, as if he might have somehow materialized in the interim. This time he also noticed that there was no toothbrush, no soap, no towel, and no prayer mat or Quran. The place had been cleared out. Even trips to the infirmary didn't warrant this kind of handling.

"There been any medical incidents today?" he asked the private, who was nearly out of breath, having followed him at a trot.

"No, sir."

"How 'bout transfers to Camp Four?" Meaning medium security. Perhaps Adnan had finally caught a break.

"No, sir. None of those, either."

For the intents and purposes of Camp Delta, then, Adnan al-Hamdi no longer existed. But Mitch Tyndall did, and Falk had a pretty good idea of where to find him.

Tyndall was indeed at his usual evening perch, holding court near the bartender with another Agency geek and a raptly attentive female officer from a unit of Kentucky Reservists. Falk didn't waste time with preliminaries. He planted a hand on Tyndall's right shoulder, exerting a little extra force.

"Hey, what's with the Vulcan nerve grab?" Seeing Falk, Tyndall colored immediately.

"A word, if I might. In private."

"I was going to tell you, but the orders were expedited and I couldn't find you."

"Likely story. C'mon."

The Kentucky MP's mouth was agape, but Falk ignored her. When the Agency colleague made a move to intervene, Tyndall waved him off.

"Save it, Don. It's personal. Keep my beer warm, will ya?"

Falk steered Tyndall to the periphery of the tables. It wasn't yet late enough for much of a crowd.

"Okay. What the fuck have you done with him?"

"Easy. I was going to tell you everything, but I couldn't get you at home last night, and this afternoon you were out on a boat or something."

"Convenient. So you were going to wait 'til I came back, I guess."

"Came back from where?" He frowned. If it was an act, it was a good one.

"Long story, but I'm out of here for the weekend. So where's Adnan?"

Tyndall looked around. Don was still watching from the bar. The pretty MP looked like she might not get over this for weeks.

"C'mon. Let's go down by the water."

"This place will do. Just whisper in my ear, like we're inside the wire."

Tyndall frowned again but complied, keeping his voice low enough that Falk had to bend closer.

"They've moved him to Camp Echo."

Camp Echo was off-limits to Falk. It was the CIA's prison within a prison, Gitmo's house of ghosts, where, officially speaking, no one had a name or a future. For a moment, he was too thunderstruck to reply. Then he boiled over.

"Jesus, Mitch. They've made him a ghost? Why?"

Tyndall shook his head.

"Keep it down. Please. He's no ghost. It's too late for that. The Red Cross already has his name. He'll be accounted for, one way or another."

"Then you're playing with fire."

"Tell me about it."

"So why do it?"

"Orders from upstairs."

"Trabert?"

He shook his head.

"My shop. Special request from the clientele, apparently."

"Which customer?"

Tyndall looked around again. Falk had never seen him so antsy. Tyndall waited while a couple of drinkers strolled past to another table, then spoke again, in a voice so low Falk could barely hear him.

"This can't go beyond you. And definitely not to Whitaker or anyone else at the Bureau."

"Go ahead."

"It was Fowler. Him and his lapdog Cartwright. They've been busy little beavers. Adnan's not their only acquisition."

"How many others?"

"Two that I know of."

"Names?"

"Adnan's the only one I know. Somebody else signed for the other two. It might have been Don. But they're all Yemenis, like Adnan. Maybe it's got something to do with Boustani."

"Boustani never handled Yemenis. He did Lebanese, a few Syrians."

"The detainee letters, though, the ones he was going to mail. They might have been from anybody."

"Maybe."

"Either way, this didn't come from me. But I figured I owed you from the other night."

"The way I see it, now you owe me another one."

"Whatever. As long as this stays between us. The last thing I need is to piss off those two."

Pretty impressive when you could scare a CIA man, but Falk could hardly blame him. He, too, was feeling the heat. He knew that the odds of Boustani's collecting letters from the Yemenis were slim and none. Only a handful of interrogators and analysts at Gitmo regularly had access to those detainees, and Falk was one of them. If Fowler and Cartwright were zeroing in on Yemenis, then he was almost certainly on their radar.

Getting out of town was starting to sound like a pretty good idea.

CHAPTER FIFTEEN

THE SUN WAS BARELY UP, but Pam Cobb was already dressed in her morning uniform—Army shorts, fatigue T-shirt, and a pair of running shoes that had carried her across miles of dusty, hardened trails. She sat on her rump to stretch, long legs splayed across the linoleum of the kitchen floor. It was the corner of the house farthest from the bedrooms, and she always stretched there to keep from waking her roommates.

Pam yawned, then bent forward at the waist and arched her neck, reaching slowly for her ankles as her calves tightened. She could have used some extra sleep, but there was strength to be found in this daily routine, a reassuring rhythm that kept her moving in the right direction even when everything else was veering off course.

The strategy had served her well on several occasions at Gitmo. She recalled the morning after she first heard about General Trabert's plan to sexually taunt some of the detainees. Pam spent all evening worrying about the possibility she would be roped into the effort, and managed only a few hours of troubled sleep. The next morning she ran six miles through the creeping heat of dawn and emerged with enough focus and determination to finagle a meeting with the general. She spent nearly an hour arguing against the plan's insanity, although she never dared use a word as impolitic as "insanity."

She instead took the subordinate officer's customary approach, deeming the plan a potentially fine idea that deserved a fair shot—just not the sort of shot that required her participation. Not right for her playbook, she told the general. Disruptive to her game plan. She had learned that in conversations with military superiors, especially males, it always helped to use football metaphors, just as it always helped in football conversations to use military metaphors.

Trabert let her off the hook, but made it clear that the dispensation was conditional. If the strategy worked for others, then she, too, would have to add it to her playbook. Yes, he said "playbook."

This morning, conditions at Gitmo again called for some grounding as she set her course for the day ahead. Boustani's arrest had shaken her. Either the investigators had screwed up or Boustani had hoodwinked her completely along with the rest of her tiger team. To top it off, Revere Falk, the only other dependable aspect of her life here, was about to depart for the weekend for God knows what reasons, and she wouldn't even see him at breakfast.

She bent forward again, fingers reaching the soles of her shoes and feeling a pebble caught in the tread. Above her, the sink dripped, a loud plop into an oily pool of dishwater. Did sinks in these billets ever do anything but drip? There was something inherently depressing about military-issue kitchens. She'd known several from officers' housing at earlier postings. Always the same outdated box of linoleum and Formica, as if stamped out at a munitions factory in the seventies. Avocado refrigerators and countertops. None of the appliances ever quite up to par. Stovetop rings that glowed brightly in some places and dimly in others, like dying stars. Not at all like the big farm kitchen in the house where she grew up, with its ceramic sink and propane burners, a stout wooden counter piled in a clatter of cast-iron skillets and stockpots, plus an oven large enough to roast whatever beast her father and brothers dragged in from the hunt. She thought of them on a fall morning, faces dewy and flushed, everyone smelling of damp leaves and warm blood.

What would they think if they could see her here, talking tough to generals and speaking earnestly to surly young Arabs, then dating an FBI man by night, fooling around in his car like a date at the town drive-in? She wondered what Falk was up to this morning. He had mentioned a vague errand that would keep him away from the mess hall. Doing it for his buddy, Ted Bokamper. What an asshole. Supposedly another suit from Washington, but more like half the officers she dealt with daily. From the way they sometimes treated her you'd never guess she was their equal or better in rank—their free and easy innuendos, the offhand sexual humor, always trying to get a rise out of her. She knew better than to take the bait. Well, most of the time.

But Bokamper wasn't in her chain of command, so she had cut loose for a while last night. Her reaction obviously made Falk uncomfortable, and for a moment she regretted her sharp words. Then she remembered Bo saying, "I don't poach," just loud enough for her to hear, and she swore under her breath. Her hands gripped hard against the soles of her feet, calf muscles stretched to the limit.

She let go, then stood up and leaned against the countertop, legs straightened behind her at a slant, feet flattened to the floor. Almost ready to roll. Well, with any luck, Bokamper and the other new arrivals would be gone soon enough. A few more arrests to further muddy the waters and generally make everyone's lives miserable, then they'd grow tired of the heat and the midges and fly away.

Falk offered a more complex set of worries. She recalled something the general had said a week ago at a beach bonfire after he'd spotted Falk and her strolling hand in hand. Her first instinct had been to pull away, like she'd been caught smoking in the girls' room. She recalled with embarrassment her flush of anger when Falk refused to let go—the dangerous boy determined to show defiance. Trabert had made a joke about "fraternization," then laughed. But she had seen his jaw tense, as if it pained him to make light of it. He then turned on his heel in the hard sand like a squad leader on a parade ground. Had that been a caution, a warning not to let things get out of hand? She knew the Bureau and the brass were at war over tactics. In Trabert's mind she was sleeping with the enemy, and Falk wasn't exactly the company man most people expected when they thought of special agents. That was part of his appeal, she supposed. That, and the way he saw through the shell she had built for professional survival. Most guys never got past that, or tried to taunt their way around it, like Bokamper. Falk had recognized it right away as a bluff, maybe because he had his own facades. She wondered again about the tale she'd heard in interrogation, the odd story of the Marine with the Cuban connection, the Marine who had become a fed.

"He talks with the Cubans, sells them secrets," Niswar had insisted. "He is one of your people, and he talks to the Cubans."

It would have been more disturbing if it weren't so ludicrous on the face of it. How the hell would a bunch of jihadists who had spent their entire lives in Arabian deserts and Afghan mountains know anything about Cubans, much less an American who talked with them? She well knew how easily rumor and fantasy took flight among the fevered imaginations inside the wire. Only three days ago yet another prisoner had told her about the cabal of Jews that was secretly advising the Saudi royal family.

All the same, maybe it would be safer to put it on paper somewhere official, strictly as a matter of housekeeping. But she would wait until Monday, after Falk returned. She had promised him that much. By then Niswar would probably have changed his story anyway.

Her stretching was done, and she looked out the window. It was already a half hour later than she usually set out, and here that could make a world of difference. She'd need a sweatband for her forehead now, so she padded down the hall to her room, passing a roommate who was stumbling bleary-eyed toward the kitchen.

"Made any coffee?"

"Sorry, Patty. Just heading out for a run."

Patty grunted in reply. She always needed a few cups to reach full consciousness.

Pam pulled open a drawer and rummaged through her socks for the sweatband. As she pulled it on she thought she heard a door shutting. Probably a kitchen cabinet, Patty on the prowl. Then Patty appeared at the bedroom doorway, her eyes as wide as if she'd already downed a full pot.

"What is it?"

"You've got company." Her voice was high. A visit from Falk would never have prompted this reaction. Was it Bokamper, then, already sniffing around before his "little brother" even left town?

"Who is it?"

"Three of them. A couple of MPs, plus one of the new guys from Washington. Fowler, I think he said."

Disdain gave way to alarm. Then she steadied. Boustani. They must be making the rounds with everyone on his team. Pretty strange time of day for a house call, though. And so much for setting herself back on course with a nice long run. At this rate, she might not get out of the house for hours.

CHAPTER SIXTEEN

THE CUBAN HANDYMAN known around Gitmo as Harry was sixty-seven, and he had been working on the base since he was nineteen. His real name was Javier Pérez. A few decades ago an overly familiar ensign had begun calling him Harry instead of Javy, and the label stuck. Not that it bothered him. He was trained to be accommodating, having been hired by the Directorate of Intelligence only a few months before he acquired the nickname. A man earning two salaries for one job learns to be flexible.

Despite what Doc Endler smugly believed, Harry had worked with other Americans besides Falk—a naval officer during the eighties, and another Marine not long after Falk departed. Both had been lured to Havana in a manner similar to Falk's. Three customers in two decades wasn't exactly brisk business, but Harry's clientele nonetheless became the object of a small shrine in the Havana cubicle of his handler, who posted compromising photos of the three soldiers in a place of honor above his door.

For all that, Harry's value had always been largely symbolic. His bosses at the Directorate liked the idea of placing someone in the middle of a U.S. military base, even though it was a base where they could already see and hear most of what was going on. And even though Harry never yielded much in the way of useful intelligence, they figured his presence would eventually end in one of two ways: he would produce an unexpected dividend through sheer luck—by having a former client return to the base as an FBI agent, for example—or he would be unmasked by military authorities. Either would be a coup, the former for obvious reasons, the latter by throwing the base into a tizzy of entertaining embarrassment. His bosses worried little about the possibility of betrayal, since Harry's only contact with the Directorate was through the man who had recruited him. There were no other operatives whom he could identify, with the possible exception of his neighborhood pharmacist, who Harry had always suspected was an informant for the Interior Ministry.

Harry put in long hours for his two salaries, and he began the morning of his rendezvous with Falk like every other workday. He rose at four at his small home in Guantánamo City and dressed while his wife brewed coffee and buttered a slab of bread for the skillet. She went back to bed while Harry tore off pieces of the crusty tostada to dunk in his mug of *café con leche.* He left the house just as the roosters were crowing, walking six blocks to the bus stop on a route that took him past the homes of six of his children and a dozen of his grandchildren. Two other sons lived in Union City, New Jersey, and a daughter was in Miami Lakes. They mailed letters to him through the base, letters that he knew better than to bring home—one of the few secrets he had never shared with the Directorate. Having learned to memorize information from his operatives for reports back to his handler, he had no trouble reciting the letters to his wife.

The bus picked up nine commuters. Four would be retiring by year's end, but not Harry. It then headed southeast from town on a twenty-mile journey, skirting the north end of the bay and bypassing the village of Boquerón before arriving at its final stop nearly a mile short of the North East Gate. By then it was around five thirty, and the summer sun had crawled above the cactus hills. They walked the last mile on a dusty, hilly path bordered by land mines, a passage known as "the cattle chute."

In the distant past, especially in the 1960s during the first years after the Revolution, the guards of the Frontier Brigade had made life miserable for the commuters as they approached the North East Gate. They jostled and jeered and searched everyone head to toe. Some of them used to spit, or take a swing, give a shove in the back. The dollar salary made up for it, barely, but as the years passed and the number of commuters dwindled, so did the abuse. Now the daily walk and frisking passed in tranquil silence. When Harry and the other eight cashed their U.S. Navy checks at Gitmo's bank every two weeks, they did so knowing that Cuba wouldn't be charging any taxes. They were perhaps the world's only employees simultaneously benefiting from the economic theories of Adam Smith and Karl Marx.

Once they reached the American side of the gate there was another security check, and by the time Harry cleared that—around 6 a.m.—a Marine was waiting to hand him the keys to a white Dodge van. Two other commuters climbed aboard with him. He dropped them off at the Naval Hospital before continuing to his final destination at a maintenance shed of corrugated metal. Years ago Harry had sprayed "Abato Fidel"—Demolish Fidel!—on the side of the shed in white paint. A fine bit of cover, Falk had always thought, even if Harry did it guilelessly. At the time he had been upset about food and pharmaceutical shortages in Guantánamo City. Another little quirk for the secret annals of Gitmo.

His job was as an all-purpose repairman, sometimes for household appliances, at other times for the cars, trucks, and buses operating on the base. Being a Cuban, he knew all about keeping old things running despite minimal access to replacement parts. He had kept his own 1959 Chevy running for more than four decades—how hard could it be to keep a seven-year-old Chrysler in mint condition?

About the time Harry reached the North East Gate that morning, Falk was awakening from a troubled night's sleep. He thought first of Adnan, now residing among the ghosts, shut away at Camp Echo beyond Falk's reach. He wondered what Adnan had said or done to merit such treatment. Or was it merely his status as one of Falk's subjects that put him in jeopardy? He had scarcely had time to think about Harry. If it hadn't been for Bo he might have left the matter until after the weekend.

Needing a pretext for his visit, Falk scanned the kitchen by the morning light and settled on the blender. To make it convincing, he tossed in a banana, a cylinder of frozen OJ and half a tray of ice, then pressed the Puree button. He would at least get a breakfast smoothie out of the deal. The ice cubes leaped and jolted as the little motor whined. Eventually the slush ground to a halt in mid-twirl. Falk watched the digital time display on the microwave change to 6:04 while he waited for the blender's motor to burn out. He didn't hit the Off button until smoke began seeping from the vents in the back.

After a quick drink and a rinse of the plastic container, he carried the blender to the Chrysler and set out across the base. He felt a little foolish about the ruse. As a Marine he had never taken such measures.

But that was before 9/11, Camp Delta, "Think OPSEC," and his weekend banishment by a two-star general.

No one was on Sherman Avenue. The ball fields and parking lots of the schools and stores were empty. The base always looked odd at this time of day, when hardly anyone was out and about. The residential architecture and layout, straight out of *Leave It to Beaver*, seemed out of place on this parched and exhausted landscape, like a skin graft that hadn't taken.

Harry's shed was atop a small rise. Falk turned up a long driveway of crushed coral as a big land crab skittered out of sight, red claws waving defiantly. Harry's face poked out the door before Falk had even switched off the engine.

"Buenos días, señor!" He was beaming. You'd have thought they were old friends. "So many years, Señor Falk. And you are so important now, yet I still think of you as a soldier."

"Yeah, well." Falk climbed from the Chrysler. "Old habits die hard, Harry. How's your family?" The conversation felt more bizarre by the second. Falk had never asked after Harry's family before, but Harry answered without missing a beat.

"They are well. They are well, señor. Please tell me what it is you need repaired. Ah, I see. The blender, no? Adelante. Come in, come in."

Inside it was already ninety degrees. The place smelled like machine oil. Harry's battered steel desk was covered by tools, spare parts, and repair invoices. He shoved the mess aside and set the blender in the clearing.

"Perfect, señor. So tell me, what is the news for you?"

"More of the same, I guess." Falk looked around warily. They seemed to be the only ones here. Harry's coworkers, a Filipino and a Puerto Rican, lived on base with a few hundred other contract workers in a dilapidated high-rise called Gold Hill Towers. They weren't due here for at least another hour.

"Actually, Harry, I was more interested in any news you might have for me."

Let's get this over with, he thought.

Harry nodded jauntily as he fingered the buttons on the blender, making tiny clicks as he progressed up the scale from Grate to Puree.

"These are all false, you know. So many names for these settings, but they all do the same thing. I suppose it is to make you feel like you are getting more for your money. It is very clever, yes?"

Falk nodded.

"I think I can fix it okay. But I may need a part from the yard. If you will follow me."

Harry nodded toward the rear door, which led to the scrap yard. Then he smiled and raised both arms, gesturing toward the walls and ceiling as if to say, "You never know who might be listening, eh?" He had never taken such precautions before. Perhaps he, too, was spooked by the new climate. Or maybe this time the stakes were higher. He picked up the blender and they headed for the door.

Being back outside was a relief, although the sun already glared harshly off cracked windshields and battered sheets of metal.

"Over here, I think," Harry said, glancing over his shoulder back at the shed.

"Yes," Falk answered, finding that the tension was contagious. He had known all along that this meeting could mean trouble. It was why he had put it off. But only now had he considered the real implications: Whatever Harry said next could change his life, and probably not for the better.

"Do you remember your friend Paco, in Miami?" Harry's smile had lost its wattage.

"I remember him well. You're also a friend of his?"

"Of course." Another glance toward the shed. Harry probably wouldn't know Paco from the minister of the interior. "He wishes to see you again. Soon. He says to me, and these are his exact words, 'Tell Mr. Falk to drop whatever he is doing and visit me in Miami.' Same accommodation as before, he said."

Presumably meaning the same ratty hotel near Little Havana. Damned if Endler hadn't been right, which made Falk wonder again about the origins of his weekend leave. It made him wonder about a lot of things.

"Did he say anything else?"

"No." Beaming again. Relieved, perhaps, that he'd remembered all his lines and that the performance was almost over. "But he insisted you come. And if you don't . . ."

"Yes?"

Harry assumed a grave and careful manner, fondling the blender pensively.

"Then he says he will tell all of your cousins and uncles that you have been an unfaithful friend."

"Well then, I'd better go see him, hadn't I? Tell him I'll be in Miami tomorrow. Maybe even tonight."

If Harry was surprised, he didn't show it.

"I will tell him," he said. "And your blender. When you return, it will be fixed."

"Very good."

Falk turned to go, taking the path around the shed.

"Perhaps I will even add another setting or two," Harry shouted from behind. "Make it even more clever than before."

"Yes," Falk said, not bothering to turn. "You do that."

EVEN WITH A GUARANTEED SEAT, Falk needed to arrive at the Leeward Point terminal an hour before take-off to deal with the security rigmarole. If his flight was like most planes out of here, it would be packed with noisy Navy families of sniffling children and screaming infants, the overhead bins bulging with strollers and portacribs.

He had just enough time to swing by Bo's on the way to the ferry to pass along the latest development with Harry. Endler, doubtless, would be pleased to have his hunch confirmed. Cartwright answered the door in his pajamas, coffee mug in hand. He seemed surprised by the visit, even wary. When Falk asked for Bo, he shook his head.

"He took off pretty early this morning. Got a phone call around five."

Endler, perhaps?

"Tell him I stopped by, and that I'll see him Monday."

"Will do."

He barely made the ferry. Dolphins were already leaping in the bay, flashing into the sunlight while Falk stood at the sternward rail, watching the base recede in their wake. He wished he'd had time to see Pam. It would have been even nicer having her next to him at the rail, headed to the States with him.

The waiting room at the hangar was a zoo, and Falk stood outdoors with the smokers as long as possible, which left him last in the boarding line. A soldier thoroughly checked his bags and his briefcase, but didn't show the slightest interest in the letters for Ludwig or any of his papers. He had made a copy of all his notes before dropping off the originals the night before at J-DOG headquarters, in a big envelope for Van Meter.

The tarmac was already soft from the heat, and the runway was rank with jet fuel. The idling engines were loud enough that he could barely hear when an MP next to the stairway said something as he was about to climb aboard.

"What?" he shouted over the noise.

Instead of yelling again, the MP pointed toward the hangar, and Falk turned to see Bo sprinting toward them, with another MP in angry pursuit.

They both reached Falk at about the same time, although the running MP got in the first word.

"Sir, you're unauthorized!"

"I told you, goddamn it, I've been cleared." Bo flashed a piece of paper that Falk glimpsed just enough to see General Trabert's letterhead. It seemed to do the trick. The pursuing MP even saluted, then retreated to a safe distance while Bo leaned closer to shout in Falk's ear. The engine wash flapped their shirts like flags.

"Hell of a morning, huh? What happened with Harry?"

Falk cupped his hand at Bo's ear and shouted back.

"I tried to find you at your place. Endler was right. Paco wants a meet."

"In Miami?" Bo yelled.

Falk nodded.

"I'll be staying at the same fleabag as before."

Bo reached into his pocket and pulled a card from his wallet, nearly losing it in the wind.

"Call this man as soon as you're stateside." It was like having a conversation in a wind tunnel. "Use a pay phone."

The card had a State Department number and title, but Falk didn't recognize the name. His immediate reaction was outrage.

"I thought only you and Endler knew about this. How many people have you told?"

"He doesn't know the details. He just knows you're a player. I can't run this from here."

"And Endler can't bother to get his hands dirty?"

"It's not like that, believe me. Just call him. Keep it as vague as you like, but call him. I'd have thought you of all people would understand a little confusion after everything that's come down this morning."

Had there been another arrest?

"What the hell are you talking about?"

Bo gave him a hard stare, hair blowing wildly as the shrieking engines revved another notch. The nearest MP stepped forward, reaching to tap Bo's shoulder.

"Jesus, didn't you hear?"

"Hear what?"

"Pam. She was arrested."

The bottom dropped out of Falk's stomach. The noise and wind became a huge ringing in his ears. The MP tugged Bo by a sleeve, and then shouted toward Falk.

"Sir, you've got to board the plane. We have to pull away the steps. It's time for your friend to leave the runway."

Bo took a step back, but Falk held his ground, still too stunned to move. He felt like a bull in a ring that had just taken a sword between the shoulders. Faces stared down from the small windows of the jet, everyone watching him crumple, the engines roaring like a crowd calling for blood.

"For what?" he called out, but Bo either didn't hear or didn't know, and just shook his head.

"On the plane, sir. Now!"

Falk turned dumbly, and as the MP nudged him in the small of the back he wasn't sure whether to feel enraged or betrayed, so he settled for both, and a knot of impotent anger exploded from the base of his throat.

"Enough, goddamn it! Take your fucking hands off!"

He plodded up the steps, the MP on his tail.

Falk turned at the top of the steps. "I'm going!"

The MP retreated at the sight of his face. A stewardess with a worried look stepped from the cockpit to take him gently by the elbow and steer him aboard, shutting the door behind him. That put a lid on the noise, and Falk found himself bewildered and staring at the head of the aisle, every face looking forward, soldiers and their families wondering what the hell all that had been about.

They were rolling almost the instant he buckled his seat belt. Then another thought brought a fresh burst of rage. No wonder Trabert wanted him gone. So they could arrest his girlfriend without protest, question her all weekend without fear of interference. Within the past twenty-four hours, two of the three people he was closest to at

Gitmo—it was odd admitting to himself that one of them was a detainee—had been moved beyond his reach, one of them dispatched to Agency oblivion, the other to points unknown.

Then there was Bo, who may or may not have been lying about having kept Falk's involvement with the Cubans a closely held secret all these years. He looked at the business card again, and read the benign-sounding title. "Special assistant to the undersecretary." Him and how many others? How many files out there now had Falk's name in them, and how widely did they circulate?

The plane accelerated, then tilted upward as it left the ground. Two rows back a baby began to wail. You and me both, kid. He glanced out the window for a last look at Gitmo as the jet banked over the glittering sea, and he wondered if he would see this place again. If he'd been faced with that prospect a few days ago, he might have said good riddance and opened a cold beer. Now it seemed like the most important thing in the world that he somehow make it back, welcome or not.

CHAPTER SEVENTEEN

FALK FELT WATCHED and harried from the moment he landed. He checked his flanks as he waded through the crowd of relatives waiting outside the Navy terminal. Then he caught a base shuttle bus to the Yorktown Gate on Route 17, where he had arranged for a rental car to be waiting.

Barely pausing, he headed straight for southbound I-95. But once he hit the open road he realized how shaken he was and pulled off at the first exit, then sat for fifteen minutes in the parking lot of a convenience store, sipping overbaked coffee and chewing a stale doughnut.

Between the shock of Pam's arrest and his nervousness over what lay ahead, he felt like a man on the run who had lost a step, a magician without his props. All through his life he had kept a place of refuge within easy reach, whether it was the clapboard library in Deer Isle, some mossy nook in the woods, or, in Washington, a quiet bar just off the Metro's Red Line, a dim and musty place in Northeast with no Bureau people, no lobbyists, and no staffers from the Hill. At Gitmo there was the relative freedom of the bay. Here, not even the miles of flat, open countryside and the thousands of passing cars could convince him that he had blended into the scenery. He felt exposed at every turn.

As for Pam, where the hell must they have put her? A cell at Gitmo? Or might she already be en route via charter to a Navy brig in Norfolk, or South Carolina? Perhaps they had only confined her to quarters. Bo had said "arrested," but he hadn't said "charged." It was a distinction to cling to, the only item of hope still afloat in the wreckage.

Falk found himself wondering how he would approach her as an interrogator, knowing what he did of her wants and weaknesses. She had grown up on a farm, self-appointed peacekeeper between a strict father and a weary mom. The constant between then and now was the call of duty or, from Falk's point of view, the rituals of obedience. The military's itinerant lifestyle demanded plenty, but in return you were freed from making many of life's toughest decisions. If they needed something from her it would be pretty easy to get it simply by threatening her way of life. Just tell her that they were going to pull the plug on her career, withdraw support of the one institution she relied on. Then show her how its needs were the same as hers, and appeal to her loyalty, her deep need to make things right.

Those same factors made it unlikely she would have done anything to jeopardize all that. Had she unwittingly colluded with a detainee? Even that seemed out of the question. If true, then she had fooled everyone—but hadn't Falk already done that for years? Maybe they were well matched in ways he hadn't fathomed.

He thought back to their recent conversation at breakfast, when she had warned him about a tale making the rounds inside the wire. Falk had been so preoccupied with other matters that he'd barely given it a second thought—something about a Syrian babbling about an ex-soldier and Cubans. Impossible, yet there it was—a thread of truth somehow plucked from his own life by a jailed Arab.

So maybe all they wanted from her was information, secrets she would otherwise be reluctant to give up. Involving him? Boustani? Her notes?

Falk turned the key in the ignition, then sat a moment longer. He fished out his wallet and retrieved the business card Bo had given him on the tarmac. Chris Morrow. An unknown. This had always been his worst nightmare about the setup with Endler and Bo—that they would widen the loop. Or maybe Bo had told the truth, and this fellow Morrow didn't know any details. The only way to find out was by calling, as Bo had instructed, so he shut off the engine and walked to the pay phone at the corner of the parking lot.

He called collect, and Morrow picked up on the first ring. It was a young voice, mid-twenties at the most, Falk guessed, feeling insulted. Morrow's damn-glad-to-meet-you enthusiasm made him sound like just the sort of fellow who would be talking about this over lunch.

"I was expecting you," he said. "Bo said you'd call."

Bo. Like they'd been friends for ages.

"You spoke with him?"

"Got an e-mail. All I know is that you're to be looked after once you reach Miami. The boss is making the rest of the arrangements."

"Endler?"

"Affirmative."

"Did Bo say anything about Pam?"

"Pam? Was he supposed to?"

"Guess not. Next time you hear from him, tell him I asked."

"P-A-M? Like the cooking spray?"

Jesus. "Yes."

"Will do. And he, uh, he said I should ask you for the latest. See if you had set up the meet. Get your whereabouts."

"The meet with who?"

"He didn't say."

"Good. My whereabouts are Florida. I expect to be in Miami in six or seven hours. I doubt I'll know more 'til then."

"He mentioned some fleabag motel where you're supposed to be staying?"

"That's right."

"Got a name?"

"I'll get back to you."

"A forwarding number?"

"Like I said, I'll call later. And, Morrow?"

"Yes?"

"Next time I want to speak with Endler. Him or nobody."

"I'll pass it along."

Before Falk even shifted into reverse, he began to worry about the rental car. He had phoned in the reservation yesterday, which left plenty of time for someone to have arranged for a bug, or a homing beacon. An outlandish idea, perhaps, but the conversation with Morrow bothered him enough that he checked the map for the nearest Hertz office. When he saw it was only ten miles away, he turned the car north. He would backtrack a little, demand a new car, and then watch the attendant to make sure there was no funny business.

The move cost him forty minutes, and the counter clerk eyed him like he was crazy. But by the time he was again headed south for Miami he had regained at least a semblance of peace of mind. Maybe all he had needed was to begin taking action, no matter how minor. Gitmo had a way of smothering such impulses, but here on the mainland he needed to think differently.

DESPITE ITS NAME, the Mar Azul Motor Court was nowhere near the ocean. It hadn't changed a bit, except that rooms now cost thirty dollars more per night. Otherwise there were the same watermarked walls, the same stale smell of cigarette smoke, and the same rubbery shower curtains. There were even the same palmetto bugs—Florida's chamber-of-commerce name for cockroaches—running for cover when he switched on the bathroom light.

Falk hadn't even unzipped his bag when the phone rang. If it was Morrow or Endler he was going to go ballistic. Instead it was a husky voice with a Cuban accent—nothing unusual here—but it definitely wasn't Paco. Even after all this time, he'd have known.

"Mr. Falk?"

"Speaking."

"Tomorrow. Twelve thirty, for lunch. You have a pencil?"

"And a notebook."

"Café Casa Luna, 100 block of Northeast First Street. It's downtown. Sit at a table out front. Carry a Walgreens bag with a bottle of water. If there are others in your party, even those who might not be with you at the table, place the bag beneath the table. If you are unaccompanied, put the bottle on top. Here is what you will wear. Blue jeans, a white oxford shirt with sleeves rolled to the elbow, sunglasses, and a blue Miami Dolphins cap. It won't be hard to find one."

Nor would the rest of the wardrobe. Except for the cap, it was exactly what he was wearing now. He leaned toward the window from the bed and flipped back a curtain to scan the parking lot. Nobody in sight with a cell phone, and no one in the phone booth. His car was still the only one parked.

"Anything else?" he asked.

"Come alone, or put the bag beneath the table. Otherwise the meeting is off."

After hanging up, Falk found the location on his city map, then went for a stroll, taking his briefcase as a precaution. Before he knew it he was back on the route into Little Havana, just like old times. He stopped at the next pay phone and punched in Morrow's number.

Endler answered.

"What happened to the errand boy?"

"Easy, Falk. He's not in the know. Just a facilitator."

"Anyone who knows my name is in the know as far as I'm concerned. I'm on for twelve thirty tomorrow, by the way. Lunch date."

"Paco?"

"That's what Harry said. Someone else just phoned to set it up."

"Got a location?"

"A café downtown, Casa Luna on Northeast First. A block north of Flagler."

"Got it."

"I won't wear a wire."

"We're not asking you to. It's the first thing he'd check for."

"They said no babysitters."

"Of course they did. What's the all clear?"

"Water bottle in a Walgreens bag on top of the table. Goes underneath if I've got company. Said they'll take a pass if they spot any lookouts."

"Which is why we're going to be extra careful. You won't even know we're there. Anything else?"

"There's a dress code. Jeans and a white oxford, sleeves rolled, plus a Dolphins cap."

"They told you what to wear?" Endler chuckled, the reserved patrician laugh of a cocktail guest. "If I didn't know better I'd say that he's forgotten what you look like. Maybe he's not as good as I thought."

"You sound like you know all about him."

"We've heard plenty over the years, but no one has ever gotten his name, address, or photo. Every time we stake out a mailbox he leaves it alone. He's careful, he's good, and he's pretty much a lone wolf. This is our one chance to blow his cover."

"Or blow mine."

"Which is why I'm torn. I'd very much like to gig this frog—that's what they call them, you know, these autonomous operatives like Paco. Las Ranas del Árbol, the Tree Frogs. But I also want to protect you, and I'd certainly like to know what he has in mind for you. One last thing. We have a parcel for you. A cell phone, which would do you some good anyway. Save you a few quarters."

"I'll stick with pay phones."

"You don't have to use it, or even turn it on. Just carry it."

"A locator beacon?"

"In case he's cleverer than we think. Where do we make delivery? The No-Tell Motel, is it?"

Falk hesitated, but figured they'd be on his trail tomorrow in any event. And if they got what they needed, maybe this would end the affair, a welcome conclusion.

"The Mar Azul Motor Court."

"You travel in style. Room number?"

"Twelve."

"It will arrive in a pizza box. Hope you like pepperoni."

"It better not be Bureau people making delivery, or doing the babysitting tomorrow. I know about half the Miami field office."

"We have our own resources."

"Yours or the Agency's?"

"I'll sweat the details, Falk. You just show up. And bring the phone. If this works out, it's your curtain call. I'd expect you'd like that."

"Understatement of the year."

Falk returned to his room, and the pizza arrived cold twenty minutes later with a knock at the door. The delivery man was mid-twenties, blue and red Domino's uniform and a face that Falk didn't recognize, thank goodness. The phone was taped inside in a Ziploc bag. He was hungry enough to eat a few slices right away, and then he went shopping for the hat, which indeed was easy to find. Afterward he drove up Calle Ocho and stopped off for dessert at the Versailles. Its mirrored walls were just as garish as he remembered. The babble of Spanish was all around him, and he scanned the room as he dipped into his flan, half expecting to spot Paco lurking in a corner. In his current mood Falk wouldn't have been all that surprised to see the shaved head and sunburned face of his younger self seated at another table—the eager explorer with a thousand questions but, when push came to shove, none of the right ones. And now Paco was about to reel him in a second time. Maybe this time he would pull the fisherman out into the deep with him.

He returned to the motel at dusk, needing a drink. He tore the paper cap off a motel glass, then filled a plastic bucket with ice from a humming machine down the breezeway. The minibar was chock-full, and he began working his way through the selections, starting with a gin and tonic. Except for the occasional beer, Falk generally avoided drinking alone. He had witnessed far too much of that earlier in life. But as he drained the gin, and then a bourbon, and then the first half of a Scotch, he began to get an inkling of just what had driven all those blurry sessions by the woodstove for his dad. At some point, he thought, propped against a pillow, the only place left to hide was within. So you worked your way deeper inside, a swallow at a time.

He reached for the remote, which was bolted to a swivel on the bedside table, in the manner of all cheap hotels. After flipping through a few channels—no news of more arrests at Gitmo, thank goodness, either in the headlines or on the crawler—he turned off the TV. Then he took the remains of his fourth drink to the bathroom sink and poured it down the drain with a clatter of ice cubes. There was no refuge, after all. Nothing but confusion and worry. It was time to get some sleep, uneasy or not. See you in my dreams, Paco.

But his last waking thoughts were of Pam. Chin up, he told her. And sleep well, wherever you are. He hoped it was someplace where they actually turned out the lights.

CHAPTER EIGHTEEN

HE AWAKENED AT SEVEN, still on Gitmo time, even if his stale breath and throbbing head reminded him immediately of his poor OPSEC of the night before. He dragged himself to the shower, where a huge brown bug skittered down the drain when he threw back the curtain.

During the night someone had shoved an advertising flyer for another pizza joint beneath the door. Falk was about to throw it away when he saw handwriting at the bottom: "Ditch the phone. Too risky."

Just as well. Now he wondered if it had been a ruse just to get his location. They'd probably been watching him 'round the clock since. He pulled the curtains tight.

Before breakfast he checked the papers for news of Pam, but there was nothing. He supposed that was a good sign. On the cable news channels they were again buzzing about Boustani. Fox was already referring to him as "the traitor translator." He wondered what they'd say about an FBI man with long-standing ties to Cuban intelligence.

Badly needing coffee, he walked into Little Havana for a sugary double shot of *café cubano* and a greasy tostada. The place was just waking up, traffic building and the heat still at bay. The music vendors were silent. Without the pulse of salsa, an air of suspended animation prevailed.

He debated the idea of another circuit through the neighborhood, but any nostalgia had dissipated the night before, so he returned to his room. Checkout time was in two hours, and the meeting was another ninety minutes after that. The day seemed destined to move at an agonizingly slow pace, so he might as well do some work.

Opening his briefcase he came across the letters to Ludwig. From here—better still, from a pay phone—he could call the banker and Ludwig's wife. Unless one of them blabbed, no one at Gitmo would be the wiser. If Van Meter and company were going to lock up his friends, then what was the harm in a little retaliatory poaching, especially if it killed time? He walked back to the pay phone up the street.

There was no point in calling Farmers Federal on Saturday, so he got Ed Sample's home number from directory assistance. His wife answered. Falk identified himself as a special agent for the FBI, and she warily told him to call back at eleven.

Doris Ludwig answered on the third ring, and sounded angry from the get-go, although she calmed a little when he told her he was still looking into the matter.

"Well, it's about damn time, but I'm glad they reconsidered."

"Reconsidered?"

"They told me the case was closed. 'Drowning by misadventure,' or some crap like that. As if he'd really go for a swim at night."

"Somebody must have gotten their wires crossed. Who told you that?"

"What was your name again?" Now she, too, was wary.

"Revere Falk. Special agent. I've got about a dozen different numbers you can call, both in Washington and Guantánamo, if you need to verify my credentials." But please, please don't, he thought.

"Sounds like you fellows don't know what you're doing. One guy calls to say everything's taken care of. Swept under the rug, if you ask me. I guess I'm just glad somebody came to their senses."

"This earlier call. That was from . . . ?"

"Captain Van Meter. Officious and rude, under the circumstances. Two kids and a widow and all he wanted to talk about was protocol and due diligence. You name it, he had some official excuse for it."

"But he said the case was closed?"

"Don't you fellows talk to each other?"

"Not always, dumb as it sounds. He's Army, I'm Department of Justice. Sometimes we get our wires crossed." Or that's what he'd tell Van Meter if questions arose. He could always finesse the date and time of the call, at least for a while.

"Well, if you knew Earl, you'd know it's crazy for him to be swimming in the middle of the night."

"He didn't swim?"

"He swam. It wasn't like he was afraid of the water." A tad defensive now. "Hold on a minute." Falk heard a squalling child. The receiver drummed on a countertop. She was probably in the kitchen, a summer Saturday morning in the Midwest. She shouted a command to the daughter, the one who had been missing her dad at the time of the letter.

"Misty, put that down before you break it! Now!"

Given that tone of voice, Falk bet, Misty would shape up pronto. It occurred to him that maybe Ludwig hadn't minded his little Cuban vacation all that much. He would have been deployed just as the weather was getting cold, leaving behind a nine-to-five bank job, a new baby, and a wife who sounded like she knew how to keep people in line. Or maybe she was just having a bad day, one of many. There were probably a lot of those when you'd just heard your husband was dead, drowned while guarding locked-up kooks more than a thousand miles from home.

"Where were we?" she said.

"You said he wasn't afraid of the water."

"Right. He could swim. Usually in a pool. Sometimes in the town lake. It is true that the ocean gave him the creeps. Lake Michigan, too. Any place where he couldn't see the other side. It was the undertow he hated. That's why the idea of him going in at night is crazy."

Or suicidal. He thought again of the suspicious letter from the bank.

"Who else feels this way? Anybody who knows him pretty well who I should talk to?"

"There's my brother, Bob. Bob Torrance. They've been friends longer than we have. Says he can't believe the Army's not doing more. And I can't either."

He remembered Bob's name from her letter, the guy who'd asked about the fishing in the Caribbean.

"Got his number?"

She rattled it off, then asked a question.

"The funeral's in two days. Will you be coming?"

"I'm afraid not," he said, and heard a sigh of exasperation. "Who's the Army sending?"

"A color guard. A few guys to shoot off some rifles. His CO's flying in from Cuba, but everybody else has to stay at Gitmo. I hear they did a little memorial service for him, down on the beach."

That was the first Falk had heard about it, which made him feel pretty stupid.

"Stay on top of this, please," she said. "And let me know what you find out."

"Will do." Another stretch. "But, look, there's one last question I have to ask."

"Go ahead." Terse, as if she had already guessed it.

"Was there anything going on—at home, at the bank, at Gitmo, anywhere—that could have made him feel like he had to do this?"

"My God, you're just like the other one. You're all in this together, aren't you? The goddamn Army and everybody else. Point the finger at anybody but yourselves."

"No, ma'am. It's not like that at all. We just . . ."

Click.

He could hardly blame her. Yet another doubter suggesting her husband had wanted to escape this world—and, by implication, her and the children. So of course she'd be grasping at any straw that might suggest otherwise.

Falk got an answering machine at her brother's place. He still had time to kill before calling Ed Sample back, so he went up the street for a second jolt of coffee and then checked out of his room. He was already dressed in the day's mandatory uniform—jeans and white shirt—and had tossed the Dolphins cap on the front seat of the car. He left the cell phone behind.

He began making his way toward downtown, and soon spotted a Walgreens, so he pulled in to pick up the required bag and a bottle of water. Then he waited in the car until the dashboard clock rolled over to 11:00 before he called Ed Sample from a phone outside the store. This time Ed answered.

"Mr. Sample, I assume you've heard about Captain Ludwig's death down in Cuba."

"Yes, sir. We were all pretty shaken up. Our bank's kind of like family. Not at corporate level, of course, but around here. We were pretty much a mom-and-pop outfit until Farmers Federal bought us out."

"And when was that?"

"About a year and a half ago. Earl was one of the few local managers they kept and promoted, mostly because there would have been a depositors' revolt if they hadn't."

Just like the old Building and Loan in *It's a Wonderful Life*, Falk thought, although it was hard imagining George Bailey approving a wire transfer to the Caymans. He wondered if Sample would bring up the subject without prompting.

"Was he staying in pretty close touch with bank business while he was down there?"

"About as much as you'd expect. He always wanted to see the monthly totals, hear about any special problems."

"Anything else?"

"Oh, I don't know. This and that. I guess you'd have to know the business."

"Would 'this and that' include foreign banking transactions? Like wire transfers?"

There was a sigh at the other end.

"Look . . . What'd you say your name was again?" Falk heard him scribbling on a pad.

"Revere Falk. FBI." He repeated the song and dance he'd done for Doris Ludwig about numbers and verifications. Hardly anyone ever took him up on the offer, and Sample was no exception.

"I'll cut to the chase," Falk said. "I read your last piece of mail to him, and I'd wager you were as curious about those transactions as I am."

Sample paused, perhaps weighing the bank's reputation against his loyalty to his late boss.

"Is this part of some banking investigation?"

"Banking's not my area, Mr. Sample. That would be Treasury, or other people at the Bureau. If you hear from anyone on that matter—and I'm not saying you will—it would most likely be an assistant U.S. attorney. But I won't be in touch with them, if that's what you're wondering."

Sample exhaled, presumably in relief.

"It's the amount that surprised me most. I mean, two million? Around here that's more than we might turn over for months."

"Yeah, that's a lot, all right."

"Especially under those terms."

"Which were what?"

"I thought you knew all this?"

"Only what I saw in your letter. The one dated last Thursday."

"That was just my way of registering disapproval, in the mildest possible terms but without being too specific. He'd led me to believe that sometimes people read their mail."

"So you were covering your ass?"

"I guess that's one way to put it. This thing came out of the blue. No phone call, no letter. Just a transfer form on a fax, followed by a letter he'd signed on bank stationery, giving us the go-ahead."

"He had stationery with him?"

"Must have, 'cause he sent it. Then three days after the money was to come in he wanted to ship the whole amount back out, to First Bank of Georgetown, down in the Caymans. On his signed approval again."

Any banker knew that the Caymans were the funny money capital of the world.

"When was that supposed to take place?"

"Friday a week ago, the day after I sent that letter. So you can understand why I was a little upset. Hardly worth our trouble or risk for just three days of short-term interest."

"Unless he was planning on making this a specialty."

"Earl Ludwig? You must not have known him."

"Straight arrow?"

"The last thing you'd ever call Earl was a high roller. He'd lose sleep when our mortgage rates shifted by an eighth of a point. In *either* direction. Anything that looked the least bit risky and he was on the phone to corporate for a second opinion. It's one reason they liked him. Local goodwill was one thing, but they knew he wouldn't play fast and loose with their money, not even for somebody he might have known for years."

So, a little of the Mr. Potter along with the George Bailey.

"Had you ever done any business with this Peruvian bank? What was it again?"

"Conquistador Nacional. I'd never heard of it. Which is another reason I was kind of anxious for Earl to reply. But of course the next thing I heard he was dead."

"Any theories on what he was up to?"

"With anybody else I'd guess the usual. A woman. A secret drug habit. With Earl? No idea. And he's been in *Cuba* all this time. Practically the end of the earth, from the things he says—excuse me, *said*—about the place. It sounded like the last kind of place where you would get into this kind of trouble."

"Exactly what did he tell you about Gitmo?"

"Oh, you know. Hot. Strange. Big lizards. Everybody was lonely. Some of the guys in his unit were drinking too much. Patriotic work, and a lot of school spirit, but after a few weeks everybody thought it sucked. He said the Arabs threw stuff on 'em, but some of 'em weren't too bad. He said it was corporate, too. I think that part surprised him."

"What do you mean, 'corporate'?"

"Sort of like when Farmers Federal bought us out. Took a nice little operation and made it bureaucratic as all get-out. Everybody with his own rules and procedures, with five layers above your own breathing down your neck for results. I think the pressures of all that surprised him."

"Yeah, well, that's the Army. A big corporation, with everybody wanting to cover his ass."

"Like me, huh? Now I'm wondering if I should have tried to call him. Offered a sympathetic ear."

"I wouldn't blame myself. The best thing you can do for him now is to pass along anything that might occur to you later, or anything you hear." He gave the man his e-mail address. "And one other thing. We've had some of our own bureaucratic screwups on this, as you might expect. I need to know if anyone else from Gitmo called you about this."

"About the transaction, you mean?"

"That, or Sergeant Ludwig's death."

"No. You're the first. And frankly I figured if anybody called, it would be like you said, some prosecutor checking on the bank. Any advice if they do?"

"Can't help you on that one."

"Thought you'd say that."

Now Falk was more curious than ever, and there was still enough time for another call. Better from here than from Gitmo, where the general might be all over him, not to mention Van Meter. He glanced around the Walgreens parking lot to make sure nobody seemed too interested. Then he took another crack at Bob Torrance, the brother-in-law.

"Doris?"

"No. This is Revere Falk, FBI."

"Speak of the devil. She'd just called about you, but had to hang up. Something with one of her kids. You got her pretty upset."

"Sorry to hear that. I think she may have a few misconceptions about what I'm after."

"That's what I told her. Said you guys have to check every angle, even the ones we don't want to hear about." The guy had obviously been watching cop shows, which for once seemed to have done some good. "Truth is, suicide crossed my mind, too."

"How come?"

"Only 'cause nothing else fits. Earl's a guy who plays by the rules, even when it hurts." Tell it to the Treasury Department, Falk thought. "When he got an order, he did as he was told. I guess that's always made him a little tightly wound. Nice a guy as you'd want to meet, but maybe there was more going on than any of us realized. But, hell, just walking into the surf like that? Doris told you about him and the water, I guess."

"She said he wasn't too fond of waves. Or any big water."

"Even Town Lake, if you were going out very far. The smaller the boat, the worse it was. It was all I could do to get him to come out on my bass boat. Wore a life jacket the whole time. Wouldn't even take his wallet and keys on board."

"How's that again?"

"His wallet and keys. He left 'em ashore in case we capsized. I had to wait ten minutes while he walked 'em back to my car. At first I took it as an insult. Figured he didn't think I could handle a boat. But he was fine on my cruiser, even on Lake Michigan. So I think it was the size of the boat that freaked him out. A bass boat sits right on the surface."

"How big's your cruiser?"

"Twenty-seven-footer with a cabin. I guess that made a difference."

"Did he take his wallet and keys on board that one?"

"Oh, yeah. Like I said, no problem on the big one."

They chatted a while longer—mostly small talk about the town and the upcoming funeral—but Falk couldn't shake the image of Ludwig's wallet and keys in the neat little pile that night on Windmill Beach.

By the time he hung up it was a few minutes after noon. It was time to get to the rendezvous point. He slipped on the Dolphins cap and headed downtown.

CHAPTER NINETEEN

FALK WAS SURPRISED to discover that parts of downtown were as latinized as Little Havana. Café Casa Luna was wedged between a *joyería* and a bodega. He parked in a decked garage a few blocks away, then paced the area on foot, nervously biding his time until twelve thirty. At the appointed moment he seated himself at an empty table beneath a Cinzano umbrella, removed the water bottle from the Walgreens bag, and set it on the table.

He looked around for a possible shadow, but spotted no obvious suspects. There was no out-of-place Anglo—well, except for him—and no one in an ill-fitting suit. No sign of Paco, either.

A flower salesman approached in sunglasses and a straw hat to show off a bouquet of carnations. Falk was about to shoo him away, figuring the vendor had pegged him as a tourist, when the man said in a low voice, "There is a message for you in the men's room. Leave the water bottle on the table." Then, much louder: "Floras, señor? Por la mujer?"

Falk shook his head and rose from his chair as the vendor melted into the sidewalk crowd. The men's room was down a small corridor between the café and the *joyería.* Inside, the lights were off, and as Falk fumbled for the switch a hand covered his mouth from behind and a gun barrel poked his back. He knew some escape moves from Bureau training, but remained still.

"A moment, señor," said a voice in his ear. "You are quite safe."

The lock clicked on the doorknob, then the barrel moved away from his back. Falk relaxed, but when he tried to turn a hand stopped him.

"This will only take a second, but face in that direction. Empty your pockets."

It was still pitch-dark except for the crack of light beneath the door. The place smelled like one of those scent cakes they put in urinals. The only sound was the dripping of the faucet and the rustling of his clothes as he took out his keys, wallet, and passport. Next the man frisked him, cool hands without a hint of sweat as they patted his shirt, then checked his armpits. A quick check of the crotch and both legs, inside and out, with a slight tickling sensation at his ankles.

"Remove your shoes."

Falk nudged them off with his toes. He didn't recognize the voice, but it wasn't Paco. He heard the rustle of a plastic bag, which the man pushed into his hands. It felt like there were clothes inside.

"Go into the stall and change into these. Hand me your own clothes over the top."

Falk gave him the Dolphins hat first. By now his eyes had adjusted to the darkness, and there was just enough light to at least get a general orientation. He glanced through the stall opening toward the sink, hoping to catch a glimpse of his escort in the mirror, but someone had removed it. Inside the bag were a pair of shorts, a baggy guayabera shirt, and a pair of sandals. He heard the man also changing clothes, presumably dressing in Falk's. Then there was a beeping noise, probably a scanner checking his wallet, keys, and passport, which then came sliding across the floor into the stall.

"I am leaving now," the man said. "When you hear the door close you will count slowly to thirty before you go. Exit to the right, not the left. An escort will be waiting to make sure you find the way."

The light flashed on just as the door shut. Falk squinted in the sudden glare and came out of the stall while counting slowly to thirty. Then he turned the knob and stepped outside. He went right as directed, but needn't have worried about a wrong turn because the flower vendor swooped in from the left and took him by the arm, steering him across the corridor into a doorway that opened onto a kitchen.

A burly cook in a soaked white T-shirt looked up from a hooded stove and shouted angrily in Spanish.

"Sí, sí. Un momento," the flower vendor shouted back. They hurriedly crossed the wet kitchen floor to a rear exit into a narrow alley that led to Flagler Street. Emerging onto the block, Falk saw a high platform across the street overhead, with concrete trestles and an escalator to the top. It was the Downtown People Mover. The flower vendor handed him a pass and spoke into his ear as they rose.

"Southbound. The next train. One stop. You'll be met. If you don't board, or don't exit, no meeting."

Their trip up the escalator was timed perfectly. A southbound train slid into the station just as they cleared the turnstile. Falk didn't take a seat, but the vendor did. Through the windows he saw a woman running toward the train, red-faced, then cursing and skidding to a stop as the doors shut and the train pulled out of the station. She immediately pulled a cell phone from her purse. A thwarted babysitter, he guessed, while wondering how many pieces Endler still had on the table.

The train was agonizingly slow, but a glance at the street below explained the rationale behind this leg of the journey. They were moving against the grain of one-way traffic, and at every stoplight the lunch-hour crush was at a virtual standstill. All the usual chaos of Miami traffic was in its full glory: snowbird retirees inching along in Caddies with tags from Connecticut and Jersey, delivery trucks double-parked at every angle, vacationers ogling maps, impatient white-collar workers glued to cell phones, and fresh arrivals from who knew where—Haiti, Cuba, you name it—still getting their bearings.

So, slow or not, the train easily outpaced the mess below as it glided around a corner to the right, drifting down Biscayne Boulevard toward an unsightly brown skyscraper at the point where the Miami River flowed into the bay.

The car wasn't crowded, and only two others got off with him at the next stop. The flower vendor wasn't one of them. Falk's new escort was a man dressed like a stockbroker and carrying a folded copy of the *Wall Street Journal.* He stood up from a bench on the platform, then tucked in behind Falk on the escalator, speaking on a cell phone as brokers often do, even if his words were clearly intended for Falk:

"Your ride is a blue Datsun, waiting downstairs. You will board in the rear door."

It was indeed. The driver, also speaking on a cell phone, had just pulled to the curb as Falk stepped off the escalator. The back door opened, and the banker continued on his way. Once inside, the door locks went down and they pulled briskly away. On the opposite side of the backseat was a boy who looked about fifteen, although the tip of a gun barrel was just visible beneath his loose shirttail. Up front were mom and dad, or so anyone looking in on the scene would have surmised. Falk's new wardrobe was a perfect match with their attire, even if he was still very much the Anglo along for the ride.

The car headed north on Biscayne Boulevard, where the extra lanes made for less congestion. Already they were making far better time than any of the vehicles locked inside the grid around the Casa Luna. Falk couldn't help but admire the efficiency of the pickup. Nothing fancy, and from the look of things Paco had used a bare minimum of personnel. Three others plus this trio, which he was now convinced really *was* a family, even if the car, the tags, or both were almost certainly stolen. Perhaps one or two others had been posted as lookouts, to help synchronize his arrival at the train stop. A minimum of technology was involved, yet it had obviously been carefully planned and impeccably executed. Just the sort of work the Cubans used to be known for, but apparently hadn't pulled off in years. No wonder Endler wanted a name and a mug shot. Paco was very good.

The last of the touristy Bayside Marketplace development passed on their right. You could hear music playing over speakers and smell fried food on the bay breezes. They were moving smoothly now, squeezing past a weaving bus, which then ran interference for them by sluggishly crossing lanes to make a left turn. Falk gazed out the back window for possible pursuers, but they seemed to have left Endler's people in the dust.

"Face the front, please," the boy with the gun said.

A short while later they turned up a ramp onto the MacArthur Causeway, heading out across the bay. The *Miami Herald* building loomed to their left like a giant egg crate, a major story passing beneath its nose if the reporters had only known to look out the window.

While crossing the water, the woman up front rolled down her window to let in more air, a warm and briny smell. The bay was an unearthly cloudy green, glittering in the sun. Long white cruise ships were moored to their right like big wedding cakes. The ride was like a movie in need of a sound track, something with a plucked bass and electric drums. Perhaps the driver thought so, too, because he clicked on the radio as he glanced at Falk in the mirror, offering a smile that was almost a goad: Look as close as you like, but you will never see us again.

The boy in the back asked a question in Spanish that Falk couldn't decipher, but for a moment the three of them chattered with great animation. All that Falk was able to glean was the two-word phrase "*todo claro.*" All clear.

He had no doubt they were correct. Not bad for a lone wolf. Or what was the term Endler had used? The Tree Frog. Physically it was a nice fit, from what he remembered of Paco. A chubby face glistening with sweat, the slightly labored breathing of a smoker, a paunchy belly. He thought of a bullfrog with its loose skin and bulging air bladder. No, that was an exaggeration. Then just as suddenly he couldn't remember Paco's face at all. Too nervous.

They hit some congestion, slowing as they passed the Parrot Jungle on the left, then regained speed, flying past the gated causeway to Star Island with its huge homes tucked in the trees, a massive yacht bobbing at every dock. Finally they reached Miami Beach, heading south off the ramp. Toward Joe's Stone Crab, he remembered, wondering if the place was still in business. The waiters had all worn dinner jackets when he had visited before. No reservations, and Falk hadn't wanted to wait, so he had just had a drink at the bar. A splurge at those prices, especially for a young Marine. Funny what you thought about at times like this.

After a few blocks and a few turns they crossed the parking lot of a marina and stopped at the dock. The kid got out with him, not showing the gun this time. Falk looked over his shoulder for a tag number, but the car was parked sideways. The kid punched in a security code to open the gate of the dock and led him to the end, to the tie-up for visiting boats.

The only visitor at the moment was a modest cabin cruiser, easily the smallest, plainest craft among the marina's vanity fleet of overmuscled behemoths. Falk guessed that the boat was borrowed, not rented. A closer look revealed that the registration numbers on the hull had been carefully covered in white tape that blended with the paint job. Another set of numbers was pasted on top. Bogus, no doubt. No detail had been overlooked. Not yet, anyway.

A head of dark hair emerged from below.

"Come aboard," a voice said. It was Paco. Falk's heart was beating rapidly, yet he found himself oddly enjoying the moment. He stepped onto the deck while the kid unhitched the bow and stern lines from the dock. This would be Falk's second meeting on a boat in three days. Maybe it was the only remaining place where you could get away from the watchers, the minders, and the microphones. But he felt almost as if he were back on his home turf.

Paco turned to face him. He hadn't bothered with sunglasses, and seemed quite willing to show himself. He had changed. There was some gray at the temples now, a few more laugh lines. But he was in better shape, even if he still carried a pack of smokes in his T-shirt pocket. More tanned, not as flabby. The frog's skin had tightened. Maybe there was a woman in his life. Before, something about him had seemed unattached, overly restless and watchful—and not just in the manner of his profession. Or maybe Falk's hyper-attenuated mind was cooking up these conclusions out of nervousness.

"Vamos," Paco said, and the boy cast off the lines and turned without a word toward the waiting car. The boat's engine was already idling, so they were away from the dock in seconds, plowing toward open water. Paco seemed to be aiming for the gap between Lummus and Fisher islands, where a car ferry was crossing in the near distance. Paco eyed it warily but didn't seem overconcerned with being observed. And why should he be? They were alone now, no escorts or bodyguards.

Falk could detect no telltale bulges of weaponry in Paco's clothing. He supposed there must be a gun somewhere on board, but the man seemed too preoccupied with handling the boat to have made any sudden moves in self-defense if Falk had decided to rush him.

But why spoil the afternoon? He decided instead to relax and let events unfold at their own pace, so he took a seat toward the stern and stretched his arms along the gunwales of the starboard side, turning his face to the sun. He would let Paco break the ice.

Overhead, the grumble of a single-engine plane caught their attention. Surveillance? No, it was headed straight for the beach, towing one of those long advertising banners, red lettering aflutter: "Best party on the Beach. Sex@Crobar. Come and get it 2nite." Now what would a good communist make of that? Falk wondered, but Paco had already turned his eyes back to the water.

"You know," Paco said, "I've considered just spending the next hour cruising, without saying a word to you."

"Fine by me."

Paco actually smiled.

"I thought it would be. Unfortunately, I have my orders." Falk sat up a little straighter. "You see, I don't really believe in you. I'm not sure I ever have. And when you joined the FBI, that clinched it for me. You're damaged goods, that's what I think."

"Is that why I never heard from you again?"

Paco nodded.

"And it's why we put on the little show for you today. In case you had company."

"Did I?"

Paco shrugged, shaking his head.

"You would know better than me. But they weren't doing their best, that's for sure. In a way I was hoping they would try harder."

"You wanted to be caught? Not that anyone was necessarily following you."

"I wanted them to show they were more interested in me than in whatever it is I had to say."

Interesting. He'd read them perfectly.

"Then why am I here, if you think I'm worthless?"

"Because my superiors still think of you as a great catch. A well-placed asset. Or, at worst, a risk worth taking. I gather that opinion is divided."

"They sound desperate."

"I think your assessment is correct. Which is why I'm not sure I believe in them anymore, either. Or in their capabilities."

"Anything you *do* still believe in?"

"Oh, yes. I believe that long ago a young soldier did something very stupid. A mistake of youth. He betrayed his friends, his officers, his country. A small betrayal, really. Some weekend foolishness in Havana. But he knew that it was a crime that would only grow larger with time. So he told someone. Not his officers. They would have thrown him in the brig. We would have known. Not the CIA. They would have overreacted, run amok. Not the FBI, either, because he never could have gone to work for them later with that item on his résumé. So it had to have been someone outside the usual community. Someone closer to his circle of friends. How am I doing so far?"

He was batting a thousand, but of course Falk couldn't say so.

"Interesting story. But I think you're giving the stupid young soldier more credit than he deserves."

"Or maybe he's giving me less credit than I deserve."

Falk studied Paco's face while wondering how he had pieced it together. Not so hard, he supposed, if you had a dozen years to work on it.

"Please, have something to drink." Paco gestured toward a small cooler near the stern. Falk rooted through the ice and found two Cokes and two Piñas, a pineapple soda the Cubans liked.

"Get you one?"

"Coke," Paco said, so Falk went against type as well, taking a Piña.

"Nice day for it, huh?" Paco said, popping the top and taking a long swallow, looking for all the world like a fellow enjoying his day off.

"This your boat?"

"What, you think I'm crazy?"

"I did notice the fake numbers. A friend's, I guess. A rental would be too easy to track down." Paco didn't answer, just sipped the Coke. "So you were saying earlier that you have your orders."

"I am supposed to deliver a message."

"But don't want to."

"Correct."

"So don't."

"I have no choice. I am not like the foolish young Marine. When I am duty bound, I follow orders."

"Whenever you're ready, then."

Paco shook his head, scowling, and when he spoke the words came quickly, as if he wanted to get the chore out of the way as soon as possible.

"There is a prisoner at Guantánamo. Adnan al-Hamdi. You are to either silence him, by whatever means, or see that he is sent home. End of message."

Falk nearly choked on a swallow of Piña. He couldn't have been more floored if Paco had informed him that Pam and Bokamper were married and double agents. He thought right away of Adnan's "great gift," the name "Hussay." Could that be what the Cubans wanted, or were worried about?

Falk's bewilderment must have showed on his face, but for the first time Paco misread him, saying, "If you are not familiar with this prisoner, I am told he is a Yemeni."

"I know who he is," Falk said, realizing as he spoke that he probably should have remained silent. He was at a loss for what to do next, having reached the impasse that everyone trying to play the double game must eventually come upon, especially rank amateurs such as him. Should he try to lead them on—even if Paco wasn't buying it—by vowing to do his best? Or would it be better to play it sphinxlike, accepting the message with a mere nod? There was also a third option: Throw them for a loop by coming clean and admitting that, yes, you're right, I'm blown, and now your people are really up the creek. Endler had offered no instructions.

Paco maintained his silence, and Falk eventually decided to discard all three approaches. He would instead play the role of himself—the confused man in the middle, half in and half out, not trusted by either side as he groped his way through the dark, a man who, like Paco, was still looking for answers. He would give a little in hopes of getting a little.

"I'm afraid I can't help you," Falk said. "Adnan's been moved beyond my reach, and I can tell you for certain he won't be going home anytime soon. Believe me, I already tried to get them to do that." Foolishly so, it would seem now, if that was also what the Cubans wanted.

"I will pass that along," Paco said, turning the wheel as they skidded against the wake of the ferry. "Anything else?"

"Yeah. How'd they come up with that name? If it came from someone inside Camp Delta, then they shouldn't have needed my help."

"Even if I asked them these things, they wouldn't tell me. And if I knew, I wouldn't tell you."

"Did you ever consider the possibility, then, that I'm just as much out of the loop as you are? That I'm only following orders for whichever side, maybe both, but really have no idea what any of this is about?"

Paco looked at him long and hard as the engine droned, as if trying to figure out why Falk was suddenly so talkative.

"Our situation reminds me of an old joke in Cuba," Paco said. "A political joke. You'll like it. It's about two old friends who haven't seen each other since before the Revolution. Then one day in Havana they walk into the same bar. Neither of them wants to mention politics, of course. They're too scared they'll say the wrong thing. But they're both dying to know where the other one stands, so finally the first one gets up his nerve and says, 'Tell me, amigo, what do you think of our socialist regime?'

"The second guy is also cautious, so he answers, 'Why, the same as you, of course!' So the first guy frowns, and says, "Then I will have to arrest you for being a counterrevolutionary!'"

Falk smiled.

"Yeah, that sounds pretty much like us. So maybe we should level with each other."

"What, pool our secrets and sell them to the highest bidder? That would be a very American solution, letting the market decide."

"I'm just saying it might be in our own best interests to be better informed."

"In theory. The problem is that one of us has to go first."

"True."

"After you, then."

Falk laughed.

"I thought it was up to the host to break the ice."

"To quote that culturally sensitive expression of yours, 'No way, José.'"

Falk smiled again, figuring that was that. But Paco's words had snagged on a shard of memory. Not the words, he realized now, but the pronunciation.

"Say that again?"

"What? 'No way, José'?"

It was the "José." Anglos, himself included, always pronounced the "s" like a "z." Paco gave the "s" a quick hiss, winding up with a name that sounded more like Ho-SAY. And that's how you would hear it in Arabic as well.

"All right, Paco," Falk said slowly. "I'll go first, as long as I can start with a question. Have you got any field men out there—out toward Yemen, for example, say, two or three years ago—who go by the code name 'José'?"

Paco glanced over a little too quickly.

"Interesting question. What made you ask it?"

"No, no. Your turn."

"Like I said. Your plan works only in theory. So you are back where you started."

"Not really. You're forgetting what I've been doing for a living. Interrogations, day after day. Your reaction said plenty. Didn't have to say a word 'cause it was all over your face. We call 'em nonverbal clues."

"You mean the same way you gave away so much with your choice of questions?"

"True. That's always a risk for the interrogator. That he'll give up more than he gets. Either way, I think we both know more than when we started."

Paco smiled ever so slightly, as if in appreciation. Then he turned the wheel slightly, the boat banking to starboard. They were beyond

Lummus Island and curling toward the northwest. The Miami skyline loomed before them like a postcard, brilliant in the midday sun.

About then a helicopter buzzed overhead, circling a little lower as it passed. Paco looked up in irritation, probably thinking the same as Falk. He couldn't tell if it belonged to a local television station or was private.

"Friends of yours?" Paco asked.

"Who knows?"

Then it kept on going, speeding down the bay toward Coconut Grove, passing too quickly for anything beyond a cursory glance at this tub plying the waves. But the interruption was jarring enough to throw them back into silence. It seemed clear there would be no further revelations. Or maybe they had both said too much.

From the look of their course, Paco was headed toward Bayside Marketplace. You could already smell the grease and hear the canned music.

"I'm going to drop you at the Miamarina," Paco said. "From there you'll only have to walk a few blocks to your car."

"Very accommodating of you. Will I hear from you again?"

"That's not my decision."

"Well, if you change your mind, you know where to reach me."

When they arrived at the dock, Paco didn't even bother to tie up. He held on to a cleat as the boat rocked while Falk stepped onto the planks. Falk turned to say good-bye, feeling awkward once again, but Paco spoke first, and for the first time in their conversation he sounded uncertain, tentative.

"Maybe you are right. Maybe we should maintain, for lack of a better word, an open channel of communication. Unofficially, of course."

"I thought you considered this a case of good riddance."

Paco looked around quickly. The only person nearby was a hired hand swabbing the deck of a yacht four slips down, radio blaring. At this location, with the right equipment, almost anyone could have snapped their photo or recorded their words.

"Operationally, yes."

"But?"

"But I have a feeling we may yet need each other's help."

"You and me, or our employers?"

"The two of us. Because of the positions we are in, being outside the conventional community. In your case more than mine. Tell me, don't you have a sense that something is about to run off the rails?"

"Yeah. I suppose I do."

"Well, if that day comes, I'll want to be able to step out of the way of the oncoming train, and so will you. And it never hurts to have someone else to call on."

Was Paco suggesting a possible defection to the United States, or was he offering Falk safe passage elsewhere? It made him more curious than ever to learn what Paco must know.

"Fair enough. We'll always have Harry, I guess."

"Speaking of damaged goods. But sometimes you have no choice."

Paco looked around nervously, still holding on to the cleat as the boat bobbed.

"And now, my parting gift to you for the afternoon. My secret to match yours. You are right about the operative named José. Yemen? That I can't say for sure. But somewhere in the Middle East. Our people are looking for him. Or were, as of last week. Now it is your turn to say something."

"In theory, you're absolutely right. But I'll have to get back to you."

Falk left without another word, not daring to look over his shoulder. He hoped Paco was smiling.

CHAPTER TWENTY

FALK KNEW ENDLER'S PEOPLE would be trying to find him, so he threaded briskly through the weekend crowds of Bayside out to the street for a cab. He had more than a day to kill before his flight to Gitmo, and the last place he wanted to spend it was on the wrong side of an interrogation table, being debriefed by some assistant he neither knew nor trusted. He would save his secrets for Bokamper, who might even be able to make sense of some of Paco's revelations.

It was time to ditch the rental car. That was probably where they were waiting for him, sitting patiently in the shade of the parking deck with their two-ways and their sunglasses, watching tourists come and go. He would have to leave behind his clothes, shaving kit, and briefcase, but the rental company could forward them.

"Airport," he told the cabbie, who, as luck would have it, was an Arab, worry beads dangling from the rearview mirror. It reminded him first of Adnan and then of Pam. Their world, our world, Paco's world—all of it mixed up in his head, a jumble of jihadists and Cubans and misshapen secrets. The odd thing was that for the moment he felt as much kinship with Paco, a man whose real identity he didn't even know, as with anyone else. Paco was willing to give something to get something. Unlike Endler and his people, who only demanded. Paco was like him, groping his way forward without a map.

At least now he felt he had solved the puzzle of Adnan's "great gift." If Adnan's financial sponsor back in Yemen had indeed been a Cuban—and one who had now slipped the leash, no less—no wonder Adnan was such a hot property. The question was whether he had yet revealed the secret to Fowler and Company now that he had disappeared into Camp Echo. Falk felt sorry for the young man. God knows what sort of tactics he must have faced by now. "Robust action." That's how they would characterize it, the new euphemism for quick and dirty. He doubted it would do them any good with Adnan. The harder they pushed, the further he would retreat from sense and sanity, and this time he might never return.

Falk turned in his seat to scan the traffic. The Cubans knew the drop-off point at Miamarina and might still be on his tail. The windshields behind offered nothing but the glare of the afternoon sun, each vehicle seemingly as aggressively in pursuit as the next.

"I changed my mind," he told the driver. "Head south, toward Coral Gables. Use Dixie Highway." The cabbie nodded, turning the wheel without a word as the beads clicked and swayed. Minutes later they were whipping down Brickell Avenue, past brightly colored high-rises lined up like giant crayons along the bay. Falk was still pondering his next move as they eased onto Dixie Highway when he spotted the Metrorail tracks merging from the right, towering overhead on concrete trestles. A mile or so later a stop loomed up on the right.

"This is good. Pull over."

He flicked a twenty onto the front seat and bolted from the back, making it through the turnstiles just in time to catch a northbound train heading back toward downtown. Lucky timing, but he would take his breaks where he found them. He rode the train another twenty minutes, all the way through to Brownsville. By then hardly anyone was left on board, and his was the only white face to exit. He had to walk six blocks before he could find a taxi, then he rode to the airport, finally confident he was on his own even though he had gone about it sloppily, strictly on the fly.

Inside the terminal he checked the departures board and bought a United ticket on the next flight to Jacksonville, making it a round-trip to minimize attention. Then he handed over the car keys at the Hertz counter and told them where they could pick up the car.

"I was in a hurry to make a flight and had to leave behind a few things," he said to the puzzled clerk. "Could you forward my bag and briefcase to your office in Jacksonville? I'll pick them up early tomorrow. It'll need some gas, too."

The service charges would be horrendous, but he would let the Bureau's bean counters sort it out. No one would raise a red flag for at least a few weeks. Besides, after today he'd be paying his own tab as he moved around, and by cash. He withdrew three hundred dollars from an ATM and bought a change of clothes at an airport shop, keeping an eye out for a tail as he went. With two hours to spare he caught another taxi, this time to a nearby bank, where he withdrew an additional twelve hundred in cash advances off his personal plastic. Might as well get what he could now, he reasoned. If they bumped him off the Gitmo flight out of JAX he might have to lay low for days longer, and he wouldn't want them tracing his movements by a trail of credit transactions. He also had a gut feeling that it was time to prepare for the worst, like a sailor securing his supplies belowdecks before a storm. He sensed that he was being pushed toward the middle in a struggle between powerful but unseen adversaries, so why not start scouting for an emergency exit?

After landing in Jacksonville, he paid cash for a one-day car rental, then found a motor court off Highway 17, where he parked in the back and registered under a fake name. He quickly scanned the cable news, but there still wasn't a word about Pam, and he began to wonder if maybe Bo had been misinformed. It wouldn't be the first time a hot rumor had proven false at Gitmo.

A fast-food dinner of burritos and soda left him feeling bloated, so he slouched on the bed watching baseball until he fell asleep with the TV on, awakening with a start when a late-night show blared on at 1 a.m.

He slept in the next morning, relieved not to be facing any meetings or deadlines. Endler's people were probably frantic by now. Or had they expected this of him? A harmless disappearing act before he turned up back at Gitmo. The sensation of having slipped through the cracks was familiar, like comfortable old clothes, and throughout the day he found himself thinking of Maine, and of his father. Had he, too, had frantic moments of worry once Falk had disappeared? Only when he was sober enough. Maybe he had accepted his son's vanishing act as inevitable.

In late afternoon he placed a call on a pay phone to a buddy at the Bureau, Cal Perkins, an expert in money laundering. At the sound of the beep, he began his message, only to have Cal pick up.

"You're working on a Sunday?"

"Speak for yourself, Falk. This must be urgent."

"Not really. Just wanted to pick your brain on something. The names of a couple of banks. As long as you're not too busy."

"You know how Sundays are. The place is like a morgue. Just catching up on some paperwork. What are the names?"

"The first is Peruvian, Conquistador Nacional. The second—surprise, surprise—is in the Caymans, First Bank of Georgetown. Ring any bells?"

Cal chuckled.

"I'll say. Both of them were big DEA targets a while back. Conduits for the Peruvian cartels, and if I remember correctly they were able to place an undercover agent inside Conquistador. Accumulated enough dirt to convince the bank's board that they would be thrilled to cooperate."

"When was this?"

"Five, six years ago. I'd have to check. Why the interest? Their names come up in one of your interrogations?"

"Should they have?"

"Well, drug money wasn't their only sideline. They also handled accounts funneling U.S. donations to some of the less savory Middle Eastern charities. Conquistador had some of the first overseas assets frozen in the wake of 9/11, mostly because of what this insider had picked up."

"Did DEA share much of what they got?"

"So they told us. The Agency probably got more, but you know how that goes. In any event, we got enough to keep a couple grand juries busy. The one in Chicago's still at it, last I heard."

"Who was the insider?"

"Good question. A well-kept secret at the time, but the name is bound to be floating around by now. Want me to see what I can find out?"

"That would be great."

"Any particular reason?"

"Professional curiosity."

Perkins chuckled. Most people he knew at the Bureau were used to the way Falk liked to operate, even if some didn't care for his style. Perkins, fortunately, never minded as long as Falk was willing to return the favor.

"I'll get back to you. But it's kind of funny you should call. There's been some curiosity about you lately. You're not at Gitmo right now, are you?"

"No."

"Where, then?"

"Can't say."

"You don't have to. The number showing is from Florida. Jacksonville?"

"A pay phone by the highway."

"Ah. A man on the move."

"Weekend getaway. Believe me, you'd understand if you'd ever spent more than a couple of weeks at Gitmo."

"So I've heard from Whitaker. Says if he doesn't make it out of there in a month he'll be an alcoholic."

"Him and plenty of others. So what have you heard about me?"

"Oh, the usual. Doesn't play well with others. Not a team player."

"Seriously?"

"I wouldn't sweat it. It's coming from the outside, and around here that's a badge of honor, given the run-ins we've had down there."

"Yeah, well. If you hear anything more specific, do me a favor and shoot me an e-mail. And send me that insider's name if you get it. Careful, though. Our data lines are supposed to be secure, but you never know."

"Gotcha. Typical DOD."

Falk drove to the Hertz office early the next day to pick up his bag and briefcase. Then he went straight to the naval air station, even though the flight wasn't until midday, figuring he might as well get the check-in and security searches over with. Besides, if Endler's people were really still looking for him, they would have reestablished contact at the Hertz office, so there was no point to any further wandering. Even so, he saw no evidence of a tail.

The surprise came at the check-in counter, when he handed over his ticket and was told, "You're in luck. Some families canceled this morning, so you ought to make it on standby. Otherwise you'd have been waiting until at least Thursday."

"What do you mean? I was confirmed."

"Until you canceled. What happened, change your mind again?"

"Canceled when?"

The man tapped a few keys.

"Yesterday, according to what's on the screen."

Falk leaned across the counter, craning his neck while the guy swiveled the monitor so he could see.

"See, here's the cancellation code."

"But I never called in."

"Maybe it was your CO."

"I'm not military."

"Your boss, then. Could have been a computer glitch, for all I know. Wouldn't be the first time. Either way, you ought to make it now. We've had ten cancellations already and will probably get more after the latest weather report."

"What's the forecast?"

The clerk gave him a look as if to ask if he had been living in a cave. "Tropical Storm Clifford. Nothing major, but it's headed toward eastern Cuba. Landfall in a day or two."

"Great."

"That's what everybody's saying. Look on the bright side. It got you on board."

The flight indeed had plenty of empty seats, but you never would have known a storm was approaching from the weather at Gitmo when they landed. Same blue sky and crystalline green water, with every brown hill still crying out for rain. It was also dead calm, and Falk gasped for air as he descended the blazing metal steps to the tarmac.

Bo was waiting in the shadow of the hangar. Better than a troop of MPs, Falk supposed, but he had been hoping against hope to see Pam. Bo now had a tan, Falk noticed, and wore a flowered shirt that would have gone well with a piña colada.

"Well, if it isn't Tommy Bahama."

"Hey, you're the one who went MIA in South Florida. What were you doing all that time, beachcombing with Paco? I had to put up with whining all day yesterday from that kid Morrow. Said you left them in the dust. I think they finally got the message you didn't want to see them when the guy from Hertz showed up at the parking deck."

Falk chuckled, and so did Bo, who didn't seem to care any more for Morrow than Falk had.

They went around the corner to where the dogs had just finished sniffing the luggage. Falk, his heart climbing toward his throat, leaned toward Bo to whisper, "Anything new on Pam?"

Bo just shook his head, the smile gone, then glanced around.

"We can talk more about that later."

Everyone chattered about the approach of Clifford as they waited for the ferry. Falk noticed a new sign with the task force logo posted at the dock: "In Partnership for Excellence." Another morale booster from General Trabert.

It was noisy on board, even against the sound of the engines, with people crowding the rail and kids squealing in games of tag across the swaying deck. Everyone seemed almost giddy at the prospect of riding out a storm. The swells coming in from the sea were larger than usual.

"They don't expect it to reach hurricane status," Bo said, looking out at the water. "Top winds now are only fifty."

"You'd never say 'only fifty' if you'd ever been out in a gale. Rough stuff."

"Looks like you always made it back in one piece."

"Sheer luck. So where can we talk? Another sail?"

"Not enough time. I was thinking we'd drive to Windmill. Finally have that walk on the beach."

When the ferry reached Fisherman Point, Bo pulled out a set of keys for Falk's car.

"Commandeered your vehicle in your absence," he said with a grin. "Hope you don't mind."

"Long as I don't have to fight you for it now."

"Hey, what's yours is yours."

Presumably he'd gotten the extra set of keys from the rental office on the base. Only Bo could have talked his way into a deal like that. He had left the windows rolled up, and it was broiling inside. Falk thought he picked up a whiff of Pam's perfume, which produced a stab of nostalgia until he began wondering how fresh the sample might be. But this old car had been picking up smells for more than a decade. At times he still detected the greasy whiff of old French fries and spilled beer, so why not perfume from less than five days ago?

"Tell me about Pam," Falk asked as soon as they were under way. "What happened while I was gone?"

"She hasn't been charged. That's the good news. They questioned her for about a day and let her go. Then last night they put her back under house arrest."

"What the hell's that all about?"

"You, apparently. Whoever's behind this wants to keep the two of you from comparing notes. Either that or they're worried you'll be angry with her, so they're doing it for her protection."

"Angry with her?"

Bo shrugged his shoulders.

"Think about it. Maybe she's been saying things you wouldn't want her to. Telling tales. Anything she knows that you wouldn't want repeated?"

"Nothing that would be anybody's business here."

Then he remembered the rumor from breakfast, the one about the ex-Marine. Now that he knew a Cuban had once worked with Adnan, he could begin to fathom how the story might have spread. Office gossip from Havana making its way to a field man in Yemen. Pam had agreed to keep what she heard under wraps, but maybe it had come out under pressure.

"Looks like you thought of something."

"Nothing concrete. What are you hearing?"

"You'll have to ask Fowler. They don't tell me specifics."

"Is that who questioned her?"

"Him. A few others."

"And you've heard nothing about it?"

"No *specifics*. But the general implication is that you'd better watch your step. Hardly surprising, given what's been going on around here."

"More arrests?"

Falk was trying to keep his tone light, but his stomach felt like lead. Would Pam do that to him? Would he have done it to her, if the roles were reversed? Who knew what you might say when they had enough leverage, plus all the time in the world? And down here they would have both, the same way it worked with the detainees.

"Are you listening or what?" Bo must have been going on for a few seconds now.

"Sorry. What were you saying?"

"I said the word is that more arrests are coming by the end of the week. No names, but as many as a dozen people are under suspicion."

"A *dozen*? Where the hell is this coming from?"

"Where isn't it? It's all anybody's talking about. That and goddamned Clifford. Everybody has a favorite theory, and everybody's got a scapegoat. You should have stayed at JAX, buddy."

"Somebody wanted me to." He told Bo about the canceled reservation.

"Fowler or Trabert would be my guess. Guess they didn't want to be too obvious, or they'd have just nixed you altogether. Trabert can do that, you know."

"It crossed my mind. So am I one of the dozen?"

"Like I said, no names. But it's apparently not a good time to know Arabic."

Another strike against both him and Pam. There was an awkward pause, then Falk posed the question that had been prowling the back of his mind since they got in the car.

"So did you see her while she was out? Pam, I mean."

"Just once." Bo kept his eyes on the road.

"And?"

"And what? I got the impression she doesn't like me. So it's not like she told me a hell of a lot. Mostly we talked about you."

"Anything you can share?"

"Look, Falk." Bo slowed down, turning to speak. "I'll level with you. She's up against the wall. Whatever it is she knows about you, she's either already told them or will before it's over."

"And you know this how?"

He accelerated, turning his attention back to the road.

"Because that's the kind of person she is. A careerist."

"Like us, you mean. Or like you, anyway."

"No. Like every other woman in the military who wants to climb the chain of command. The only way they can make the grade is by showing they're even tougher and more willing to take one for the team than the boys are, even if it means burning their friends. Not fair, but that's the way it's set up, and she knows it."

"So you think she'd give me up for another stripe. Assuming there's anything to give up, which there isn't."

"Forget the stripe. She's just trying to survive. Get out of here in one piece before Fowler tears her career limb from limb. Between her closeness to Boustani and now to you she's practically radioactive by current standards. Don't ask me what it is about you that makes the needle jump—our little arrangement aside, of course—but you've apparently earned a prominent spot on Fowler's latest little flowchart of Gitmo conspiracies. And if Pam can sketch in a few more arrows for him, she'll do it. So don't mourn her loss, that's all I'm saying. You two would have been finished when this gig was over anyway."

Would they? Maybe Bo was just jealous. Either way, now Falk was pissed off.

"Hey, just because a woman doesn't fall for you doesn't mean she's bad news for every other male."

Bo grinned sardonically.

"I hope you're right. But keep it in mind. No need to go to the wall for her if she's the one who's placed you there. That's all I'm saying."

"In your opinion."

"Yes. In my humble opinion."

THEY WERE QUIET for the next quarter mile, then pulled up to the checkpoint leading to Camp Delta. The sentry leaned in the window to see their papers.

Having been away for a few days, Falk discovered that he again had a fresh eye for the sights here. It hadn't occurred to him until now how much a military operation—even one that only builds a prison—puts its mark on a landscape. He couldn't help but notice the sandbagged positions dug along the dune line near the beach. The ground had been slashed open for fencing and bunkers. On the camel hump of a mountain in the near distance to the east he saw a Cuban watchtower in plain view. Perhaps someone up there was following their progress at this very moment. Up to the right, on a rocky cactus hillside looming over the barracks of Camp America, military patrols had painted their unit numbers and other graffiti, their dubious reward for having completed a climb to the top, often out of boredom.

Finally they arrived at the beach and parked on the shoulder. No one was on the strand or in the picnic area, but Bo didn't get to the heart of the matter until they were down by the ocean, where every word would be swallowed up by the sound of the pounding surf.

"So I'm assuming you didn't spend the entire two days with Paco."

"We had about an hour together, tops."

"Where'd you finally meet up? Endler's people lost you at the People Mover."

"Thought so. They took me to Miami Beach. Some marina at the south end. He was waiting on a borrowed boat with a fake registration number."

"Sounds like he thought of everything."

"I was impressed. We took a little cruise across the bay. Dropped me about four blocks from the car."

"Which you then left behind, you sneak. So what did he want?"

"He gave me an assignment. One he didn't believe in, mostly because he was convinced I was blown. I didn't bother to tell him he was right. But he passed it along anyway. It's funny, I got the idea he *wanted* our side to know. Either way it was a damned weird request."

"Which was?"

"To take out Adnan al-Hamdi. *My* Adnan. The one who is now in Camp Echo. The Cubans want him either silenced or shipped home. Anything to keep more Americans from getting a crack at him."

Falk figured he should also tell Bo about Adnan's "great gift" of the name "Hussay," or, as he now understood it, José. But he bit his tongue without being certain of why. This was a dangerous place for loose information, even among friends, as Pam's arrest had already showed him. He would hold on to what he could until he learned more.

"That's pretty amazing," Bo said. "They sound desperate."

"That's what I said, and he agreed. And it gets better. He told me some off-the-books theory of his about a Cuban op in the Middle East who's gone AWOL."

Bo raised his eyebrows.

"He laid it out for you like that?"

"Yeah."

"You're right. They do want us to know, as long as it's the right people."

"And who would the 'right people' be?"

"Endler and me, of course." Bo grinned.

"How does any of this tie in with all the arrests?"

"I'm not convinced it does. Maybe they're just a smoke screen."

"Pretty damned destructive for a smoke screen."

"All the more reason I need you to go back inside the wire and get those interrogation schedules for me. When this team departs, I'll have to go with them, and I'm running out of time."

"And it's still the Yemenis you're interested in?"

"Them and whoever's been talking to them."

"Adnan's a Yemeni."

"I'm aware of that."

"Well, somebody certainly took an undue interest in him, if he's been moved to Echo."

"That's been established. So focus on the other ones now."

"Do you think they've got some sort of Cuban link?"

"It's one of the many things I'm trying to find out. With your help, of course. I need dates and times, anything that looks out of the ordinary. And I don't just want copies. I want the originals."

"Whoa, now." Falk stopped in his tracks, the waves coming within a few feet. "You're asking me to steal the pages?"

"It may be the only way to nail this down."

"Then I'll copy the info. Not in my notebook—on a machine. If there's anything incriminating you can get the originals later."

Bo shook his head, adamant.

"Once they hear you've been poking around in there—and believe me, they'll hear—the first thing they'll do is go back in to clear out anything that might hurt them. Hey, it's not like you can get into any more trouble than you're already in."

"Thanks for the vote of confidence."

"Yeah, well, joking aside, it's worth the risk."

"For you, maybe. Maybe I don't share your urgency."

This time it was Bo who stopped, digging in his heels as he pivoted quickly in the sand, face stern, the look of a man prepared to give anything to do his job. It was the loyal soldier in him that Falk sometimes forgot about when they were laughing or sharing a beer.

"Do you have any idea what some people could do with certain kinds of information from down here, even if it's only remotely close to being true?"

"What, some vague Cuban link to al-Qaeda, you mean? Embarrass Fidel, I guess. Make a stink at the UN for a few days."

"Make a war is more like it. If it fell into the wrong hands, with the right spin behind it. Cuba as an al-Qaeda sponsor would be diplomatic dynamite."

"Then why not just ask us to get it for them?" Especially considering that Falk had probably already gotten it.

"Because you guys will put it in its proper context, and that's how the clientele would receive it: a dumb cowboy in the field who overstepped his authority and mixed with the wrong crowd. Which would let Havana wriggle off the hook. Context is everything. And whoever gets the information first controls the context."

"Still." Falk shook his head, skeptical.

"How do you think Iraq got started? Four or five neocon theorists, totally committed to the cause, taking a few discredited reports from a handful of paid informants, completely unreliable, plus one forged memo on yellowcake uranium and a satellite photo of a mobile chemical lab that turned out to be making insecticide instead of anthrax. Pretty thin stuff, huh? But next thing you know, 135,000 troops are slogging through the desert toward Baghdad. Context is everything. And if you don't think this anti-Castro crowd could pull off the same trick, then think again. Besides, it's good politics. Which voting bloc do you think decided the last presidential election? Good old Little Havana. And you've got to keep the customers satisfied, at least until the next one. It's all about who gets the information first."

"Okay. You've made your point. Or Endler's point, anyway."

Falk gazed out to sea, wondering if he really believed it. It seemed unlikely. But a few years ago, the idea of a war with Iraq would have seemed just as outlandish, and now half the globe was seemingly on alert, waiting nervously to see where the American hammer would fall next.

As he watched the waves he thought again of Ludwig's body, tossing in the sea until it somehow wound up two miles to windward. Even now a rising breeze was pushing the surf west. He scanned the horizon as if it might hold a hint to the anomaly, but there was only the blue line of the sky. When he looked up he saw a bluff, and, at the top, a fence lined with green mesh. Behind it was Camp Iguana, the mini-prison holding three juvenile detainees—and the only place on the island with a commanding view of Windmill Beach.

"So you'll do it, then?" Bo asked, interrupting his thoughts. Still prodding, like a hungry dog demanding a treat.

"Do what?"

"Get those pages from the logbook."

"I'll try. Let me get back in touch with my tiger team first. Pick up a few fresh names for interrogation, to give me a pretext to get back inside."

He didn't need to explain to Bo why he felt the need for a pretext. The landscape had changed. His previous habit of strolling the cell-blocks after dark wouldn't cut it anymore, now that the place had gone into virtual lockdown, even for the jailers. He checked his watch.

"I better get moving. Our team's weekly debriefing is in half an hour."

"I'm sure they'll be thrilled to have you back."

"No doubt," Falk said. "Everyone loves a pariah."

CHAPTER TWENTY-ONE

THE MEETING WAS in session by the time Falk arrived. Most of the usual cast of characters had already assumed their customary Monday afternoon pose, slouched in chairs around a table that was covered with folders and legal pads, a few canned sodas. Two people had plugged in their laptops. The air conditioner was set high enough for fur storage.

The atmosphere was like that of a teachers' lounge or a captain's stateroom at sea—familiar but respectful, a tepid brew spiked with inside jokes and wry allusions to the high command. Oftentimes there were fresh tales from the front lines of interrogation: "You'll never believe what that wild ass Mahfouz is saying now about his network . . ." and so on.

What Falk wasn't accustomed to was the effect his arrival had upon the tableau.

Conversation halted. No one said hello. All four colleagues sat up a little straighter in their chairs, gave him a quick once-over, then looked down at their notes. All except for Phil LaFarge, the analyst from Army intelligence, who held his gaze with an expression of absolute disdain, like a party host who'd just spotted a drunk dipping into the silver.

"Was it something I said?" Falk asked.

"Well, no," answered Jerry Parsons from DIA, the polite one of the bunch. "It's just that we'd heard you might not be coming back. To the team, that is."

"Where else was I supposed to go?"

Parsons shrugged, looked around the table for help but received none. "They made it sound like you had other fish to fry, that's all."

"Or maybe that I was one of the fish?"

Parsons smiled, but his cheeks reddened.

"You know how rumors are."

"Yeah, well, I'm here. And needing some work to get back into the flow. Where's Mitch Tyndall, by the way?"

"You know how it goes with the Agency guys," LaFarge said. "Sometimes they're with us, sometimes they've got . . ."

"Other fish to fry?"

"Those weren't the words I was going to use."

"Never mind. I'll track him down. We're still on speaking terms last I checked."

Falk had nothing to contribute to the proceedings, having either been away or preoccupied with other duties since their last meeting. He sat back to listen to what the others had to say, but sensed that they were watching their words carefully.

Not that there was ever much of substance reported at these meetings. In the perfect world envisioned by Camp Delta's creators, Falk supposed, these weekly forums were to have become the intelligence equivalent of quilting bees—each person offering a patch of vital information to be fit into the grand design, while everyone looked for patterns, alignments, links.

It rarely happened. Mostly what people offered were threads, not patches, and even then it was often the same frayed material from one week to the next. Of all Gitmo's secrets, this may have been its deepest and darkest. The more the daily millstone of blab turned, the less it produced. The bulk of Camp Delta's population had been tapped out for months. Anyone of real value had either been sent elsewhere in the CIA's unseen archipelago or eased into Camp Echo. Yet this was the one conclusion never mentioned in the reports that reached the public.

It took some prodding, but Falk convinced the team to toss him the name of Khalid al-Mustafa, a young Saudi, for further interrogation. Even by Gitmo standards al-Mustafa was of low value. No one had spoken to him in weeks, and Falk knew him only in passing as a smart-ass who spoke decent English, a wealthy man in his early twenties, college educated, who, with a little more indoctrination and a few more years under fire, might have ended up like a junior bin Laden, having crossed into the realm of the fully committed with the family bankroll at his disposal.

Instead he had proven too soft and spoiled for what he'd gotten into, which was one reason he was captured. According to field reports he had been almost happy to be picked up, until he wound up with a one-way ticket to Gitmo.

Al-Mustafa was supposedly the source of a popular joke that had made the rounds when Falk first arrived: "How do you break up an al-Qaeda bingo game? By yelling 'B-52!'"

Several weeks ago he had moved to the Haj of Camp 4, with its white jumpsuits, bigger meals, extra exercise, and barracks-style cell-blocks.

Tyndall finally showed up toward the end of the meeting. He, at least, didn't seem at all surprised to see Falk, and he offered a nod and a smile, much as he always had. Afterward, Falk took him aside, which wasn't hard since everyone else exited as quickly as possible.

"I'm cashing in my chips on that favor," Falk said. "I need to get inside Camp Echo to see Adnan. The sooner the better."

Mitch blew air out his cheeks.

"Wow, you're asking a lot." He looked around to make sure the others were out the door. "It's not impossible, but I'm assuming there are certain parties you wouldn't want to know about it."

"You sound plugged in."

"Not as much as I'd like to be. Maybe you could tell me what's going on between Fowler and Bokamper."

"You'll have to get that from them."

"Fair enough. But I can't get you into Echo without Fowler's security team hearing about it. Maybe not right away, but soon enough. And believe me, you don't want to get dragged into what they're doing."

"People seem to think I already have been, so I'll take the chance. All I need is an hour."

"I can get you half."

"Better than nothing. When?"

"Let me check. The problem is that he may not be there much longer."

"Maybe I should just wait 'til he's back in Camp Three."

"No. They're talking about a rendition."

"To Yemen?"

"That's the word."

"From Fowler?"

"Sorry, Falk. I'm really not at liberty."

"I can read between the lines."

"I'm not sure you can. But I can't help you further. Half an hour, but keep it to yourself. And be ready to move at a moment's notice."

"You know where to find me."

"I did until this weekend. What was the vanishing act all about? And with Pam in the pokey, no less."

"If you really don't know the answer, this is worse than I thought."

Tyndall said nothing, just shook his head and went out the door.

FALK FINALLY GOT a chance to drop off his gear at the house. The air conditioner was still working, at least. Nice job, Harry. He checked for mail, but there was only a folded note from Whitaker:

"Finally got a leave from this wretched place. One week (hot damn!). Sorry about Pam, but I hear it's not so bad. I'm betting she'll be out by the time I'm back. Fingers crossed. Keep the beer cold. Whit."

So Whitaker had finally gotten his wish. Good for him. Or had he, too, seen the writing on the wall and decided he didn't want to be around when things went south for his roomie? Maybe someone else made the decision for him. They would certainly have more flexibility dealing with Falk now that Whit was out of the house.

Falk pulled back the shade in the living room, half expecting to see a parked Humvee and MPs heading up the walk. The sky caught his attention instead. A bank of clouds was creeping in from the southeast, the first trace of Clifford.

His stomach growled, reminding him it was dinnertime. The seaside galley didn't seem like an appetizing option just now. There would only be more stares and further questions. He scrounged up some limp lettuce and a slice of ham from a package three days past the sell date and slapped them between stale slices of wheat bread, then chewed the sandwich at the counter. Gloom settled over the house to the drumbeat of the dripping kitchen sink.

He rinsed the plate, then turned the valve extra hard but still couldn't stop the drip. Another job for Harry. Falk wondered what to do next. There was a night to kill, but he didn't feel like reading and there was no TV in the house. He decided to check his e-mail, logging on via the line the base had installed at the house. He wondered idly if Harry did that work, too, but figured it was probably handled by some private contractor. In a way, those employees were no more secure than Harry. Typical. You build the world's most secure prison, surround it with 2,400 soldiers, then let some private contractor bring in low-wage workers from all over the world to install your most vital lines of communication.

Falk logged on to find that Perkins, his pal at the FBI, had replied only an hour earlier.

"FYI: Insider's name was Lawson," the message said. "No longer with DEA. Cheers, Perkins."

Lawson. Almost certainly Allen Lawson, now of Global Networks, and Van Meter's ally on the security team, as well as the corporate rival to the disgraced Boustani. It seemed almost too good to be true, so Falk sent a reply asking for a first name or initial. If it was indeed the same guy, then Lawson would have been cozy enough with the Cayman and Peruvian banks to rig up some sort of quickie transfer through Ludwig's bank. But why, unless Lawson wanted some kind of leverage over Ludwig? His buddy Van Meter already outranked Ludwig. What more leverage could they have possibly needed?

The thought reminded him of Camp Iguana, and its prime vantage point. Even if they turned him away, a visit would sure beat hanging around an empty house.

It was time for a drive.

CHAPTER TWENTY-TWO

Camp Iguana was a source of embarrassment in a place that otherwise offered no apologies. It was a white bungalow on a small grassy lawn, perched atop a rocky bluff and surrounded by a single line of fencing. Unlike the barrier around Camp Delta, this one was a mere twelve feet high, with neither razor wire nor guard towers.

It was the prisoners themselves who were controversial—three Afghan boys, ages twelve through fourteen when they first arrived. Since then, each had spent a birthday in captivity.

General Trabert still referred to them publicly as "juvenile enemy combatants," but the MPs who attended to their daily needs simply called them "the boys," and they had become an international cause célèbre among Gitmo's critics.

As a result, Camp Iguana was now a regular stop on Gitmo media tours, so the authorities could show off the spotless, roomy, and air-conditioned quarters. The boys themselves were always hustled away to another room, kept silently out of sight while reporters inspected the bedrooms and the common area.

One of the mandatory parts of the tour was a twenty-foot-long viewing hole that the authorities had cut into the fenceline's green mesh. This gave the boys a gull's-eye view of the sea, and it was the possibilities of that view that intrigued Falk.

By showing up uninvited, he found it a little harder to get inside than the tour groups did. An MP retrieved a Staff Sergeant Wallace, who wasn't impressed by Falk's Bureau ID.

"The boys are doing a math lesson," he said. "We could set up a time for tomorrow."

"I'm in kind of a hurry."

"Maybe they are, too."

As if any prisoner at Gitmo were in a hurry. Falk raised his eyebrows, and Wallace seemed to realize the folly of his statement.

"Sorry, it's just that we get a lot of requests, and I'm kind of protective."

"Understood," Falk said. "This won't take long."

When Wallace wasn't doing Reserve duty, he was a teacher. In middle school, no less, and he had discovered that his wards here had many of the same quirks, anxieties, and ephemeral moods as his students back home, except theirs also came with the emotional freight of war and imprisonment.

"Let me get 'em squared away," Wallace said. "They should probably be in their rooms while we talk."

A minute or two later the MP ushered him inside. The door opened onto a small kitchen and a smaller TV room with a couch and coffee table.

"They got cable?"

Wallace smiled.

"I wish. Videos only."

There was a stack of VHS tapes on the TV table. *National Geographic* fare, mostly, plus a couple of movies—*Old Yeller* and *White Fang*. Nature stuff with leafy trees, the great outdoors, and very few people. A chessboard with a game in progress was open on the coffee table. Over in a corner was a boxed Parcheesi set, and stacked at the end of the couch were three notepads and math textbooks. The only other book in sight was a copy of *Curious George* in a language that looked like Pashto.

A short hallway led to their bedrooms and the bath. None of those rooms had doors, presumably to reduce the chances of suicide. Now that would be embarrassing.

A brown face poked out from one of the bedrooms, with large dark eyes and an inquisitive stare. The face quickly darted back inside when the boy saw Falk watching him. It was hard to imagine that face on anyone toting an AK-47 or scuttling for cover behind some dusty boulder in the Afghan hills, but he knew it happened often enough.

"What do you need?" Wallace asked. Before Falk could answer, a kid's voice piped up from down the hall.

"Meester Wallace, please?" Timid, a supplication more than a question.

"Hold on a sec," Wallace said to Falk. "I'll be right back."

Falk took the opportunity to snoop a little more. He stepped into the small kitchen, which was spotless except for the remains of the evening meal on four stacked trays in the sink. Wallace must have eaten with them. Falk opened the refrigerator and saw cartons of juice and milk, a chocolate bar, a few carrot sticks, and a packet of beef jerky.

"Hungry?" Wallace asked in an edgy voice. Falk hadn't heard him return.

"No. Just curious."

"Everyone is," he said, in a weary tone. "They're just kids, really. No matter what they might have been when they got here."

"I'm sure you're right. Everything okay back there?"

"Just a homework question."

Falk nodded toward the gleaming white stove.

"They cook their own meals?"

"It's not plugged in. Aesthetic purposes only." A line right out of the media tour, no doubt. But it was an odd touch, all the same. All that trouble to haul an oven here, just to give the place an extra measure of domesticity. Or maybe it had been here all along.

"So how 'bout you get to the point?" Wallace said.

"You heard about the soldier's disappearance, I guess. From down on Windmill Beach?"

"Christ, that again? Didn't the captain get enough?"

"The captain?"

"The security guy."

"Captain Van Meter?"

"That's him. Barged in like Sergeant Hulk. Scared the boys half to death. Sat on their beds and grilled 'em for half an hour. Of course, I lost it and got everybody even more upset. So forget it, no way we're covering that ground again."

"Sorry. I had no idea."

"Don't you guys talk to each other?"

"There's a question over jurisdiction. We're not exactly sharing notes."

Wallace shook his head.

"Just like every other goddamn thing down here. Not that I should be using that language in front of the boys. You should've seen the catfights over how much to pump 'em. How long to keep 'em. Have you ever tried requisitioning textbooks through the Pentagon? I finally just went and borrowed a couple from the school up on the base. Unbelievable. But you can get what you need from Captain Van Meter."

"It's not that easy, I'm afraid."

"It never is."

"Look. I don't even need to bother the boys. I'm just wondering if any of them saw anything that night."

"They're pretty much under lock and key after dark."

"Don't they have windows?"

He nodded.

"Can't see the beach from them, though. Not with all the screening on the fence. You only see the horizon, way out at sea. And at night, nothing."

"So all three would've been indoors?"

"That's what they told Captain What's-his-name, and that's what they'd tell you."

"Then I'll be on my way. Mind if I have a quick look outside first?"

"Whatever gets you out of our hair."

Wallace walked him to the door, and then turned. When he spoke next he had lowered his voice, as if he didn't want the boys to hear. "Didn't mean to bite your head off. It's just that one of the boys had bad dreams for two nights after that asshole came by, and I don't want an encore. Shakeel was the biggest head case to begin with, but with counseling he's made a lot of progress. Would hate to see it come to nothing."

"You should tell the general."

Wallace shook his head. Maybe he had already tried.

"C'mon, I'll show you the grounds of the estate."

The lawn out back was a patch of brown grass about fifteen by twenty-five feet, with a picnic table and a small soccer goal at one end. An American football lay on the ground.

"They ever use that?"

"They throw it around. They're pretty good. They'd rather play soccer, but the ball went over the fence a few days ago."

"Ah. More requisitioning."

"You got it."

As advertised, there was a long cutaway across the mesh. The view of the sea was spectacular.

"No wonder they like it out here."

"It's why they have all those nature videos. They can't learn enough about the ocean, fish, anything to do with the sea. They'd never even seen an ocean before they got here."

What a strange place for expanding your horizons. He supposed if they ever got home, the experience might actually do them some good. Falk strolled over for a closer look. Only by putting your face up to the fence could you see Windmill Beach. And after dark, like Wallace said, you probably saw nothing. They would have been in their rooms anyway. A waste of time for him to have come, in other words.

"Okay, that'll do it. Sorry to be a bother."

"No problem," Wallace said. They walked toward the exit.

"They going home anytime soon?"

"There's been talk. And lots of paperwork. But so far that's all it's been."

Falk drove back past Camp America and the prison, clearing the checkpoint, then heading for home. It was dusk, and a sense of desolation settled in as he navigated the curves. On impulse, he decided to swing by Pam's apartment on Windward Loop. At the very least he would find out what kind of attention they were paying her. With luck she would be looking out her window and see him. Yet another similarity to a high school romance, he supposed. The lovelorn boy cruising the street of his dreams.

The neighborhood was quiet, and Falk approached as slowly as possible, without attracting too much attention. A Humvee was parked out front, and there was a sentry by the door. Even though he knew she was under house arrest, the extra security dismayed him. She hadn't even been charged with a crime. Was all this just to keep him away? What if someone else visited? Van Meter could probably waltz right in. And what about Bo? What were the rules for him, and how had their one visit gone in his absence? He wondered how her roommates had reacted. Maybe they were still one big happy family, the usual sorority house atmosphere, except with an extra touch of sternness to ensure that their dates dropped them off on time. No more stolen kisses on the porch.

He resisted the urge to stop and drove on through to Sherman Avenue, turning left to loop back toward Iguana Terrace. In the mood he was in he might as well stop at the Tiki Bar, if only to seek out some company. With a few beers maybe he would sleep easier. If he was lucky the gossips wouldn't be out in force.

The bar was hopping. The arrests may have damaged morale, but they hadn't killed anyone's thirst. Falk decided to go with something stronger for a change and ordered a gin and tonic. It was well watered, so he soon returned for another, loitering at the bar while scanning the crowd for a familiar face.

Seeing none, he picked up a stray copy of *The Wire* from a barstool. The movie schedule was always worth checking, but otherwise the rag was worthless. He was mildly surprised to see a small story inside about the arrival of Fowler's team. The official line presented by the public affairs officer who had written the story was that the team was here "to evaluate the security and efficiency of current J-DOG and JIG operations." The story urged everyone "to offer all possible assistance as they fulfill their important duties." Blah blah blah. Next to it was their picture, all three of them squinting into the sun like golfers waiting for the last member of the foursome. Bo stood slightly apart from the others.

The only coverage of Sergeant Ludwig's disappearance was a brief story on the memorial service Falk had missed. It said Ludwig had drowned during a late-night swim from Windmill Beach.

He was rolling up the copy to take back to the house when he was distracted by some noisy new arrivals, led by a couple of MPs still in uniform. One gave him an odd look, nodding in recognition, and then whispered something to his buddies.

Great, Falk thought. Just what he hadn't wanted. Now the guy was walking toward him, beer in hand and nodding again.

"You were just over at Iguana, right? The FBI guy?"

"How'd you know?"

"I was in the back with the boys. Saw you out the window when you and Wallace went for a walk. I got off shift right after you left."

"Your sergeant's pretty protective."

"He's a good man. And they're good kids, really. Deserved better than being kidnapped by the Taliban and having an AK put in their hands. Hard to imagine, isn't it?"

"Yeah, well. That's war in their part of the world, I guess."

"Ain't it the truth."

Neither of them said a word for a while, and Falk figured the guy was about to head back to his friends. Instead he lingered awkwardly, looking down at his feet while peeling at the label on his beer.

"So Wallace said you weren't working with that other guy, Van Meter."

"That's right."

"Some kind of jurisdictional snafu?"

"Something like that." Falk shrugged, trying not to lie any more than he had to.

"Well, don't ever tell Wallace I said so, but it's probably my fault that asshole came around to begin with."

"How so?"

The MP looked around warily. Falk, paying closer attention now, saw that he looked to be about nineteen, only four years older than the oldest kid at Iguana. Children watching children, all of them far from home.

"Maybe we shouldn't talk about it here," the soldier said.

"C'mon." Falk shook the ice in his empty glass. "Let me freshen this, then we'll go for a walk."

The kid went to tell his friends while Falk ordered a third gin. Then the two of them strolled off past the tables toward the water, down a small slope to a narrow floating dock where pleasure boats sometimes pulled in. A runabout droned past offshore in the deepening darkness, headed for the marina with its green and red running lights on. The dock bobbed up and down on the waves of its wake, groaning against the pilings.

This was a convenient getaway for the bar crowd at times. For those who felt a sudden pang of homesickness between drinks, it was a refuge for collecting yourself before rejoining the gang. It also served as a testing ground for men and women contemplating pairing off for the evening, a place to see how things went with a little privacy. Pam and Falk had come here the night she first bought him a beer, a memory that put a small stab through his chest. He thought of her locked in her house, grounded without privileges, all because her bad boyfriend had somehow pissed off the teachers.

The only other people down here tonight were a guy and his date, smooching off to the side in the glare of a streetlight. Falk led the MP toward the opposite side, down by the water's edge.

"What's your name, soldier?"

The kid looked down and saw that his nameplate was still taped over. So much for trusting the kids completely, Falk supposed.

"Sorry," he said, tearing off the duct tape. "Specialist Hilger. Out of Kentucky."

"Tell me what happened."

"It was all 'cause of something I let slip. I told some of the guys at dinner one night about one of the kids, Shakeel. He's thirteen and he has these nightmares. Some weeks it's every night. Wakes up shouting, in a full sweat. We finally figured that the best way to calm him down was to take him outside. It's against regulations—they're not supposed to be out after dark. But, hell, it works, and it's better than having him wake up the others. He walks it off in the moonlight, out where he can hear the waves on the rocks. So, anyway, word got around the way it always does, and this Captain Van Meter must have heard."

"And figured he'd have a chat with Shakeel."

"Exactly."

"Might have been nice if Wallace had told me this."

"I guess he figured there was no point. Shakeel told Van Meter he hadn't even been out that night. So why put him through the wringer again for nothing."

"For that matter, why tell me now? I can't do a damn thing about Van Meter."

"Because Shakeel *was* outside that night. And so was I. It was my last week on overnight duty, and I was sitting at the picnic table, having a smoke while Shakeel walked it off. We were both too scared to tell that asshole Van Meter, so we ended up not telling Wallace, too. But I figured somebody ought to know. Just to set the record straight."

"Or to cover your ass."

Hilger shook his head vigorously.

"No. I'll be glad to take the heat for it. Hell, maybe they'll send me home. It's Shakeel I'm worried about. He's due to go home. All of them are, if the brass ever stops putting it off. But if Van Meter finds out Shakeel lied to him, well . . ." Hilger shrugged. "God knows what would happen. He could be stuck here 'til he's eighteen. Then they'd move him to Delta and nobody would give a fuck."

"Point taken. I'll keep it quiet."

"You still don't get it, do you? Shakeel wasn't just out there, he saw something. Out on the water. The same night that sergeant went missing."

Falk checked their flanks, stunned and suddenly worried. He would hardly have felt more vulnerable if someone had just rolled a live grenade beneath their feet. The smooching couple, still going at it some twenty feet away, was by all appearances completely preoccupied. But, hey, think OPSEC.

"Let's move onto the dock," Falk said, glancing around. "And I don't want a word of this going elsewhere. Understand?"

"Sure. That's the way I'd prefer it."

The planks creaked beneath their feet as they walked to the end, just beyond a circle of light thrown by a lamp on a piling. A fish flicked at the surface, then vanished.

"So what did he see?"

"A boat. Not a big one. One of those little rubber ones."

"An inflatable?"

"Yeah, like the commandos use."

"Did you see it?"

Hilger shook his head.

"I was zoned out, half asleep. He didn't tell me 'til the next night. I think it scared him, like he knew it was something he wasn't supposed to have seen."

"But you can't even see the beach from there."

"It wasn't on the beach. The boat was passing by, just beyond the breakers."

"In what direction?"

"East."

"Back toward Camp America? Toward the Cuban side?"

Hilger nodded. "All three of them."

"Three boats?"

"Three people. One boat. That's how many people Shakeel saw."

Falk considered this for a moment. Something didn't add up.

"There wasn't even a moon out that night. How could he have seen anything, much less made a head count?"

"By the lights from our place. They keep 'em on all night. It's not as bright as the ones at Delta, but still. He saw it, all right. He'd have no reason to make it up. And I know he never heard anything about that sergeant."

"And he was sure there were three of them?"

"Yeah."

"So why didn't you tell Van Meter?"

"Like I said. The kids. I wasn't there when Van Meter came by. I just heard about it later. I could never live with it if Shakeel got busted, held here for life."

"And you think that's what would happen?"

"Van Meter said as much, to all three of 'em. 'Lie to me and you're never getting out of here.'"

"Prince of a guy." Not to mention an idiot as an interrogator. Another dope who'd watched one too many cop shows where confrontational assholes got the goods.

"Besides, I figure if three guys are out horsing around in a raft, and one of 'em drowns, eventually one of the others is going to 'fess up, right? And if not . . ." He shrugged. "Then I guess they'll have to live with that."

"So that's what you think it was? Three guys joyriding after dark? Maybe taking a little cruise to the forbidden zone, just for kicks?"

"What else would it be?"

"I don't know."

But to Falk, any fellow who'd go to the trouble of first removing his wallet and keys didn't sound like the joyriding type. An inflatable was just the sort of craft Ludwig would have been least inclined to board.

"Well, don't worry, Hilger. You did the right thing in telling me."

"I hope so. I'll admit, I almost didn't because of, well, because of what people are saying."

"And what might that be?"

"Oh, you know. The usual stuff you hear about Arabic speakers. One of the guys in my group said he thought you were one of them."

"Well, you know how rumors are. Like I said, you did the right thing."

"Thanks, sir."

Hilger took his leave, trooping back up the hill to his buddies without another word as Falk watched from the swaying dock. The amorous couple had disappeared. Falk shook his head as he thought about all the tales that must be making the rounds. It made him wonder again what Pam must be saying. Maybe Bo was right, and she was telling all to save her own skin.

He brooded about it further as he walked to a lonely table at the periphery of the Tiki Bar, finishing the third gin, then starting on a fourth. By then he was just stewed enough to come up with a plan to find out more, and he knew of only one person who could help him carry it out.

He returned to his car, groping the key into the ignition before pausing to lean against the wheel as he marshaled the remnants of sobriety. The last thing he needed was to run the car into a ditch or a big cactus, or to get pulled over by a security patrol for drunk driving. He fired up the engine and set off into the night, checking the mirror at every curve to make sure no one was following.

The turnoff was hard to find in the dark. It was even tougher negotiating the coral lane with the headlights off. He rolled down the window as he came to a stop outside the corrugated shack, listening to the engine tick, a metronome for the ratcheting chorus of night bugs. Switching off the dome light before he unlatched the door, he turned in his seat to make sure no one had followed him in.

He pulled a notebook and pen from his briefcase, then sat for a few seconds as he considered what to say. If the wrong person saw this first, he wanted the instructions to be vague enough not to arouse suspicion.

"Need you to check the air conditioner on Iguana Terrace one more time," he scribbled in the dark, hoping it would be legible. "Something is rattling behind the vent screen. Thanks. Falk."

Reconsidering, he added a P.S.—"The sooner the better."

He folded the note twice, scribbled "For Harry" on the outside, and then walked to the padlocked metal door and wedged the note behind the hasp. He checked the sky. Still cloudy. With any luck the rain would hold off until morning.

By the time he reached the house he had decided what to say in the second note, and he wrote it down while he sat in the driveway. This time he folded the note even tighter before making his way behind the house in the dark. He pushed aside the low limbs of a rubber tree to reach the air-conditioning unit that protruded from the living room window. Then he squeezed the note up into a slot of the vent. The foliage would keep any neighbors from seeing either it or Harry. The question was whether Harry would have the balls to actually carry out Falk's request.

In the privacy of the house he popped three Advils to ward off the headache he almost always got from gin. Then, with a sense that he had done all he could for now, he stripped to his boxers and crawled between the chilly sheets.

No sooner had he laid his head on the pillow than he wondered if Perkins had yet replied from Washington. He fired up the laptop on the foot of the bed, the screen casting a vaporous glow as he pecked his way to the e-mail server. There was no further word. Strangely enough, the earlier message from Perkins seemed to be gone as well.

Had he accidentally deleted it? It wasn't in the Delete basket. With a lump of panic in his throat, he clicked into the Sent basket. His own message to Perkins had also vanished. Erased by either an intruder or an e-minion elsewhere on the base, locked in some windowless room where OPSEC never slept.

Falk wasn't sure whether to be outraged, frightened, or both, but he leaped from the bed in his bare feet. What he needed most was a beer and a stroll on the lawn to calm his nerves, but that didn't seem like the wisest move after four gins. Besides, he would feel vulnerable out there. An easy mark.

So he sat tight and considered his options. Just him and the four walls of the bedroom, far more confining than they usually seemed. Even on his worst days as a Marine, the Rock had never felt quite this small.

CHAPTER TWENTY-THREE

SEDATED BY THE GIN, Falk slept until nine thirty. Just as well, he supposed. If the day went as planned, he would need every spare ounce of energy.

Fortunately there was no trace of a hangover. In another stroke of luck, it hadn't rained. He checked the air conditioner to find that Harry had retrieved the note while he slept. So far, so good.

His first order of business was to check the interrogation sign-out sheets inside Camp Delta, so he made coffee while flipping through the file for the Saudi he was scheduled to interrogate, Khalid al-Mustafa. The information confirmed that Mustafa had been pretty well exhausted as a useful source. The observations of the Biscuit team were particularly revealing:

"Aristocratic background and university educated in London. Polished diction. Generally cooperative attitude toward questioning. Khalid al-Mustafa is a dilettante among the committed, a 'gentleman jihadist,' as one examiner observed. The idea of adventure abroad appealed to him more from a standpoint of personal conquest than of religious fervor. Often embellishes narrative accounts, a tendency springing from a desire to burnish his self-image as a man of action. Accounts of contemporaries make it apparent that during his eleven months in Afghanistan he accumulated little if any leadership responsibility. It is most likely that the casual tenor of his participation was tolerated due to the value of his family's financial portfolio in Jeddah. Appears eager to offer whatever information necessary to secure his release. Highly recommended that any actionable intelligence from this subject be double-referenced."

Great. He was about to waste an hour chatting with a glib fabulist, an al-Qaeda sugar daddy who liked being photographed with a scimitar but was handier with a checkbook. Small price to pay, he supposed, for getting his hands on the records.

Security had tightened in his absence. It took more than half an hour just to get through the gates. Procedures that normally lasted a few seconds stretched into minutes, as first one, then another sentry checked and double-checked IDs and authorizations. Hardly surprising. If a guard from Camp Iguana was hearing rumors about Arabic speakers, he could only imagine what the ones inside Delta were picking up.

A cooperative sergeant greeted him at MP headquarters. Falk logged Mustafa's name onto a clipboard along with a series of code numbers and letters. He wrote seven characters in all, with a hyphen after the first three, like a phone number. The prefix—a letter followed by two numbers—identified your group and tiger team. Falk's was S04, the number four team in the Saudi-Yemeni group. The last four numbers identified the individual.

Some interrogators had made a hobby of trying to spot and memorize the numbers of friends and colleagues, turning it into a parlor trick to amuse (or horrify) their drinking buddies. Falk had stumbled onto Tyndall's number after following him inside the wire one afternoon, committing it to memory if only because he felt that a Bureau man should keep tabs on the competition. One rumor had it that the CIA knew all the numbers anyway, with full access to the master list on file at the Pink Palace.

"Oh, you're here for Mustafa," the sergeant said. "He'll be thrilled. Hasn't had a customer in weeks. Ought to have all kinds of news for you."

"So he's still a talker?"

The sergeant smiled and made a yakking motion with his hand.

"When he's in the yard it's all the others can do to shut him up. And his English isn't bad either, so all the MPs get an earful."

It was a wonder none of the detainees had tried to do him harm. Blabbermouths were generally frowned upon by the Camp Delta population. Then again, anyone inclined to vengeance probably wouldn't have made it into the Haj of Camp 4.

"We'll bring him over to the booth," the sergeant said.

"Great. Oh, and if it's not too much trouble, I need to check some of the recent sign-out sheets. Refresh my memory on some ground I've been covering."

"You mean these?" He tapped the clipboard.

"That plus the last few weeks' worth. I need a look at the duty rosters for the MP shifts, too. You know the Bureau. Got to dot our 'i's and cross our 't's or they think we're spending all our time on the beach."

"No problem," the sergeant said, apparently not in the mood to make an issue of it. "I'll round it up while you're talking to Mustafa. You only want the MP records for Camp Four?"

"Three, actually. That's mostly where I've been working lately."

That seemed to slow the sergeant down. Camp 3's detainees were the hard cases. But eventually he nodded and said he would do what he could.

"Perfect. I'll make sure and report your willingness to go the extra mile, Sergeant . . ."

"Badusky," he said, flipping back the line of duct tape like a flasher opening his trench coat. "Sergeant Phil Badusky. From the 112th."

MUSTAFA SEEMED THRILLED to have gotten out of the yard. The idea of a little air-conditioning couldn't have been too disagreeable, either. The MP didn't bother to bolt his leg irons to the floor once they arrived, and Mustafa insisted on speaking English. His command of the language was better than Falk had remembered.

"I have been practicing," he said with a flourish. "When I went to school in London it was always good, but then I became rusty. So every day now I speak English. I teach it to others in my block. It will be good for business when I am home."

"Assuming you get there."

"It will happen. Someday we will all go home. Even Donald Rumsfeld does not want to feed us forever. That reminds me, you must please tell the cooker in the kitchen. Cooker? Is that correct?"

"Cook."

"Cook, then. Or chef. Yes, chef is better. If you can please tell the *chef* for me, no more boiled eggs at breakfast. They are green inside, and dry. Enough of boiled eggs."

"I'll put in a word."

Falk covered some old ground for the sake of protocol, and they spent a few minutes going over names from Mustafa's unit, reviewing their roles and their movements during his time in Afghanistan. Both of them soon grew bored, and Falk didn't resist when Mustafa simply wanted to chat. It was then that Mustafa caught him off guard.

"So tell me, which one among you is the Marine? Is it you, perhaps?"

"The Marine?"

"The one of whom they speak who knows the Cubans. Is it true, this story?"

Falk felt the heat in his cheeks. He knew that to a trained eye he must be lighting up like an alarm. Was this the same thread Pam had unraveled?

"Look, I really don't . . ."

"Surely you must have heard this, too?"

"Can't say that I have. Is this how you guys inside the wire kill time now, making up stuff about us?"

"Oh, no, this did not come from one of us. It was from one of *you*."

"From us?"

"From interrogation. From questions, not from answers. The new people asking questions, they have been saying this."

"Which new ones?"

"Two of them. With so many strange questions. You must have heard this yourself. You are playing games with me."

What could he say? Every possible response led somewhere dangerous. He was just glad he had recovered his composure before the glib Mustafa had noticed. A more attentive detainee—like Adnan, for instance—would have noticed right away. He considered asking more about the "new ones," but that would only have added fuel to the rumor mill. So he sat up straighter in his chair, tried to look as disinterested as possible, and steered Mustafa to another topic. Within a few minutes they were both bored again, the light gone out of Mustafa's eyes.

Later, back at the MP station, Falk was still mulling the implications of Mustafa's tale when Sergeant Badusky burst through the door holding a ledger and a green file folder.

"Here you go, sir. MP duty roster for Camp Three in the book, interrogation sign-outs in the folder. They go back about a month."

"Thanks. Shouldn't take long."

"Take your time. Business is slow. Has been all week."

Falk was looking for Yemenis, which wasn't hard because he knew all their names, even if at times a roster from any Islamic country seemed to include at least a dozen guys named Muhammad.

He started from four weeks back, and the first name he found was Adnan's, a 4 p.m. session twenty-four days ago in booth three. The team and interrogator ID numbers were his. Two more Yemenis were on the same page, both signed out to other members of his tiger team. In the following week he found more such notations, with some of the Yemeni subjects signed out to other teams that were also part of the Saudi-Yemeni group. He tried recalling some of the names and faces from those teams. They were reasonable people who would have been interviewing these subjects as a matter of course. Whenever Adnan's name turned up, his own number followed. He wouldn't have expected otherwise.

Nothing seemed out of the ordinary until a reference from two weeks ago, on a Tuesday at 8:20 p.m., when another Yemeni had been signed out for an interrogation. It was an awkward time of day for business, during the customary lull between the daylight hours and the spike of activity that usually commenced at 9 or 10 p.m. It was an hour when most analysts and interrogators were relaxing after dinner, either in their quarters or at the Tiki Bar.

Falk drew a finger across the page to the final column, but in the space where the number of the interrogator and his team should have appeared there were instead the initials "OGF-NCOIC," scribbled in a rigid hand.

"What the hell," he muttered.

"Problem?" Badusky said, looking up from his magazine.

"Yeah. Tell me what this means." He turned the page around while Badusky walked over for a look.

"Well, NCOIC is . . ."

"Noncommissioned officer in charge. That I'm familiar with, but what's it doing in place of the interrogator's ID?"

"Because the NCOIC was signing out the prisoner for an OGF, a session at an off-grounds facility. Camp X-Ray, usually. The abandoned camp with all the old cages. Some guys like to take the detainees there for the change of scenery. Truck them down to the jungle at night. Supposedly scares the shit out of them."

Falk had heard of the tactic, but didn't know anyone who had actually tried it. It sounded almost farcical, a touch of tropical Gothic. He supposed it might be pretty spooky being taken to the deserted Camp X-Ray, which was now nearly overgrown by vines.

"I guess that makes sense. But shouldn't there still be an ID number?"

"You'd have to ask the NCOIC from that shift. And that'll be in the ledger."

First, Falk scanned the rest of the sign-out sheets for more of the mysterious notations. There was one on each of the next five days. Each involved a Yemeni detainee, and each occurred between 8:10 and 8:45 p.m. That meant there were six in all, on successive days. Each involved a different Yemeni detainee, with the last one occurring on a Sunday, nine days ago. Why had they stopped? He knew of at least six other Yemenis they hadn't yet talked to, and one was Adnan.

He flipped open the MP duty ledger, spent a few seconds getting his bearings, then turned to the Tuesday of two weeks ago. He found the 8 p.m. to 2 a.m. shift for Camp 3 and recognized the rigid handwriting that he had seen on the sign-out sheet. It was the signature that threw him for a loop: "Sgt. Earl Ludwig, 112th MP Co."

Ludwig was the noncommissioned officer in charge at that hour for each of the next six days. He was also on duty the following Monday, when no one had been signed out to Camp X-Ray. On the next day, a Tuesday, Ludwig never showed up for work. It was the night he disappeared into the sea, on an inflatable bound for Cuban waters with two other men.

Falk went back to the sign-out pages and reviewed the last few weeks more closely. He returned to the page for last Wednesday—the day after Ludwig's disappearance and the day Falk had last spoken to Adnan—and checked for Yemenis. He quickly found his own sign-out of Adnan, high on the page at 2:30 a.m. Just as it should be. But at the bottom of the page he saw that Adnan had been signed out again, at 11:54 p.m. It was another OGF reference, meaning someone had taken him down to Camp X-Ray even before the transfer to Camp Echo. This time there was an interrogator's ID number, one that Falk didn't recognize. He knew only that it didn't come from one of the three teams that regularly dealt with Yemenis.

Falk thought back to that day, trying to remember what he had been doing at that hour. Mostly he remembered how tired he had been, from all the long hours of work following Ludwig's disappearance. He had been called to the North East Gate to retrieve Ludwig's body in the afternoon. Then they had welcomed Bo and the investigative team at Leeward Point around 7 p.m. before retiring to the Tiki Bar, followed by a late date with Pam. He must have dropped her off at about eleven. The sign-out had occurred during the following hour.

Falk couldn't imagine the tactic working, not with the way Adnan was wired. Maybe that was when they had decided to move him to Camp Echo. He jotted down the ID number, then flipped through the rest of the pages, but found nothing to further stir his curiosity.

It was then that he remembered Bo's request: Bring the pages, not just copies. It was a tall order with Badusky sitting a few feet away.

"These ID numbers for interrogators—do you guys keep a master list?"

Badusky shook his head, now eyeing Falk warily.

"That's all up at Command," he said. "Which reminds me, you never gave me your name. I mean, normally I'm not supposed to ask, and you mentioned something about being with the Bureau, which is fine. But I thought you were just backtracking your own schedule. If you're checking up on others, I'm gonna need some better ID. So if you don't mind . . ."

"Falk. Revere Falk, special agent with the FBI."

Badusky got him to spell it, and then wrote it down.

"What about these OGF exceptions in here? Shouldn't they have all included an ID number, instead of just the NCOIC?"

"Probably," Badusky said, beginning to sound like he wished he'd never gotten into this. "I did kind of wonder about that when you showed me."

"Are there any other records for those sessions?"

"Not that I know of."

"Could you check, just to make sure? Who's your CO?"

"I'll get him," Badusky said, tight as a drum.

As soon as he slammed the door behind him, Falk carefully tore out each of the pages with OGF references, plus the sheets for the corresponding days from the MP duty ledger. He folded them away in his briefcase, then put everything back in order before placing the ledger and sign-up folder back on the sergeant's desk.

A few minutes later, Badusky entered with a disgruntled-looking captain, who spoke up loudly before Falk could even introduce himself.

"Sorry, sir, but I'm going to have to ask you to leave the premises, effective immediately."

"No need to get upset, captain, I'm on my way. Just one last question about those special notations."

"The answer is no, we don't keep a separate log. If you want any particulars, you'll have to ask the NCOIC in question."

"That's going to be kind of hard," Falk said. "It was Sergeant Earl Ludwig."

Badusky and the captain exchanged surprised glances, suddenly at a loss for words.

He eased past them out the door.

OUTSIDE THE GATES, Falk eyed the sky. Clifford was beginning to make his presence felt. The wind had picked up, and ragged clouds were racing west. It felt like rain, but there still hadn't been a drop. It was too hot to just sit there in the car, so he started the engine to run the air conditioner while he checked his map of the base. The road he wanted was unpaved, and it wouldn't be easy to spot unless he knew exactly where to look. He drove back through the checkpoint, looping up and around Kittery Beach Road toward Bay Hill. Then he turned left up a winding paved road that led to the highest point on the base, John Paul Jones Hill.

Marines liked to run to the top of this hill on occasion, just to prove they could do it, setting their sights on the American flag that waved from the top. The hill was rich with Cold War relics: artillery emplacements that had long since been abandoned, a radar station, plus dugouts for riflemen, also vacant.

The latest Pentagon plans called for the construction of a row of big white windmills along the ridge, to help take up the slack for the base's diesel-burning power plant, which grew more expensive to operate every day, thanks to the same upheavals that had brought prisoners to Camp Delta.

Falk drove by the radar station, offering a halfhearted wave to the crew seated in a shaded tent. A little farther on he stopped when he thought he had found the turnoff, a track of hammered coral leading down the face of the ridge. He turned and inched onward, the Plymouth creaking on its aging springs and shocks.

After a quarter of a mile he reached his destination. It was another tented position dug into the hillside, inhabited at the moment by a few Navy Reservists from New Jersey, members of a Mobile Inshore Undersea Warfare Unit. They had mounted an oversized pair of binoculars to a swivel along the wall facing the sea. From up here nothing could move out on the ocean below without these guys seeing it, although Falk wondered how much was visible after dark, even with night-vision lenses.

The two men on duty got to their feet, stepping from the shade as Falk climbed from the Plymouth.

"Howdy, fellows."

"You lost or something?" No hint of sarcasm. They seemed genuinely puzzled to have a civilian visitor.

"You're the guys I wanted to see, believe it or not. Revere Falk, FBI."

The Bureau ID generally cut more ice with Reservists than it did with regular Army, especially once you were outside the wire. The two fellows seemed suitably impressed.

"Just double-checking some items from events last week, and you were on the checklist."

The vagueness didn't seem to bother them, and they both nodded.

"Is there ever much to watch out there? By way of boat traffic, I mean?"

They smiled and shook their heads.

"Sometimes you get small craft like fishing boats, or maybe a yacht on a Caribbean cruise, a mile or so offshore," one answered. "Anything closer and it's usually either the supply barge out of JAX or a patrol boat. Ours will come right down in front, and sometimes you see theirs over in that direction." He pointed east. "But you can bet that if it's out there, we'll spot it."

"Great. You keep a log of every sighting?"

"Sure," the second one piped up.

"You still have it from a week ago, say last Tuesday?"

"Probably." He turned back toward the tent to fetch it, still talking as he went. "What's your authorization on this?"

"General Trabert," Falk said without missing a beat. It was true enough, even if the general had later rescinded his authority.

"Good enough for me," the first one said.

"How you guys like it up here?"

"Better than being down there," the first one said. He nodded toward the distant rooftops of Camp Delta, which even from here looked like they were broiling in the haze. "Decent shade. Steady breeze. Maybe a little lonely."

"Here you go," the second guy said, approaching with a logbook encased in a metal box. "The page for last Tuesday looks pretty open."

Standard stuff. A mention of weather conditions and visibility, all clear and normal. No overnight storms or rain or notable wind shifts. Just like the guy at the port control office had said. The only mention of boats was a Cuban fishing vessel, far in the distance to the east, plus a Navy patrol boat sighted during daylight hours.

The rest of the page was blank, with no activity after dark. With so little to keep them busy, Falk wondered if they napped, or played cards. He sure would have as a Marine. And all the more reason they wouldn't have missed anything. They'd be downright eager for business.

"Thanks," he said, handing it back. "Must get pretty boring."

The first guy shrugged. "Some of the foot patrols stop by. They get kind of bored, too. Of course they think we've got it made. One of them calls this place the gazebo, like we've got our feet up all night, drinking beer. Same with the guys in the inflatables. They'll pay us a visit on their way to the put-in, and sometimes they'll make a crack too."

"Inflatables?" He tried not to sound too interested.

"Army counterintelligence runs 'em into the surf sometimes," he said. "They run sort of an informal coast patrol after dark. Not that anybody's supposed to know about it. Which is why we don't write it down."

"But Trabert okayed it," the second guy said.

"Yeah, it's kosher and all that."

"How often do they run it?"

They both shrugged.

"It's not like they post a schedule," the second one said.

"What's their put-in?"

"Blue Beach. They pass here to get to the access road."

It was a few miles west of where Ludwig went in.

"They come by here last Tuesday night?"

The two of them thought about it for a minute, and then shook their heads.

"They'd have stopped. They almost always do."

"*Almost* always?"

"Always."

"Same crew every time?"

"Don't know if I'd call it a crew. Two per boat. Different guys. I guess they've got a rotation."

"Who's their admiral, for lack of a better term?"

"Captain Van Meter. He always stops. He's a good guy."

"Yeah. I know him. Very hands-on."

"That's why his men like him. Never asks them to do anything he wouldn't."

Such as riding an inflatable through the surf at night. But not that night, apparently. Or not from here. In fact, if you were putting in for a quick trip down to Windmill Beach, Hidden Beach would have been a more convenient choice than Blue, especially if you didn't want to be spotted on the way to the put-in. Not only was the beach more secluded but Falk had just noticed on his map that it was officially off-limits, closed in order to protect the fragile ecosystem. One of those quirks you found from time to time on military installations, like an eagle sanctuary located next to an artillery range.

"The general give you any kind of orders you could show us?" the first one asked, perhaps beginning to have second thoughts. "Anything on paper?"

"Nope," Falk said, turning to go. "Just a verbal. You'll have to take it on trust."

"Trust?"

"Yep. And I thank you for it. One other quick question. When's the last time you had any rain up here?"

The second guy, still seemingly okay with everything, flipped back through the log, then whistled.

"Not a drop in twenty-two days."

Meaning well before Ludwig disappeared. Good.

"Thanks, fellows. Have a quiet night."

"We always do."

HE DROVE NEXT TOWARD the road that led down to Hidden Beach. It took a couple of false starts and wrong turns, but eventually Falk found a track used by the mechanized patrols that seemed headed in the right direction. Fortunately there was still plenty of light, even though the clouds were heavier than ever. Up here the wind was getting fierce, a good fifteen to twenty knots. The last he had heard, Clifford was in no danger of strengthening into a hurricane. The storm was supposedly weakening, but it was still brisk enough that the Coast Guard would probably soon call in its Boston Whalers from patrol. No sense risking a rescue of your own boats when no one else was out on the water. The air felt as if the heavens were about to open at any moment, and Falk knew he had to hurry.

He parked after following the track as close as he could get to the beach. Then he located a wide trail that led downhill, and he walked several hundred yards toward the beach. It was crushed coral, meaning it wouldn't easily show footprints.

The moment he set off down the hill he was startled by a sudden rustle in the brush to his left. He froze, tense, hands out in front like a wrestler's to fend off an attacker. It was like being back on duty along the fenceline, only now he was deep inside American territory. He listened a while longer, but there was no further sound or movement. Probably just an iguana, running for cover.

Falk hoped Hidden Beach had some sand. Some of the strands around here were all stone and pebble, the stuff that the British called "shingle." That wouldn't do him any good.

It turned out to be a mixed result. Most of the beach was shingle, but fortunately there was about a ten-foot-wide band of sand that stretched across it a few feet behind the beach, right where the trail came in, and that's where Falk found what he'd come looking for. With no rain in the past three weeks to wipe it away, and with enough protection from the sheltering rocks and underbrush to hold the wind at bay, the sand above the tide line offered a tabula rasa for anyone who would have crossed it during the past week or so. And there in the middle, on a direct line between the trail and the sea, was a faint but unmistakable track, a smooth imprint about five feet wide across the sand. It was a pattern that you'd make by pulling something heavy down the hill, like an inflatable with an outboard motor. He unfolded his map, which he'd brought from the car, and checked the distance against the scale, just to make sure he wasn't overestimating the convenience. Windmill Beach was a mere half mile away, just around the corner to his left as he faced the sea.

As he refolded the map, the first drops of rain began to fall. By the time he reached the car it was pouring, smearing the haze and dust from the windshield into a milky brown ooze. He looked up, face to the storm, refreshed by it in the way that only a mariner could be. By now the flattened little path to the beach would already be gone. The raindrops tasted salty, a gift from the Caribbean, blown here by forces from afar.

Bring them on, he thought. He was ready.

CHAPTER TWENTY-FOUR

FALK WAITED UNTIL dark to make his move. By then it was pouring, the rain sheeting at wild angles against the windshield as he prowled up Skyline Drive. He parked about a half mile from his destination, resigning himself to a good soak even though he had thrown on his rain slicker and a wide-brimmed hat he sometimes wore sailing. A flashlight was zipped into a side pocket.

He had never bothered to eat dinner, instead grabbing a prewrapped sandwich from the Naval Exchange after his visit to Hidden Beach. He was too nervous for anything more, and all he could think about was Harry, who by now would be warm and dry at his home in Guantánamo City, relaxing after another commute home through the North East Gate. Falk hoped the old man had managed to hold up his end of the deal.

He had to guess on where to cut between the apartment houses as he stalked across the darkened lawns of Windward Loop, heading for the backyard of his eventual target. He lucked out, missing by only one building. The rain, he supposed, was a blessing. It kept everyone indoors and provided a wet veil against prying eyes.

As he approached the back of the apartment he was all too conscious of leaving footprints, already imagining an evidence technician making molds. Reaching the wall, he felt his way along the rough bricks like a rock climber at the base of a cliff.

Her window was the third one down. This was the moment of truth. Rain sluiced off the hat brim as he searched for the all-clear sign. Without it he would turn back and head home, knowing that either

Harry had failed or Pam had forsaken him. After what Bo had told him he supposed he wouldn't be that surprised. He reached for the small flashlight, slippery in his wet hands, then flicked it on for barely a second, just long enough to see a small strip of silver duct tape stuck to the bottom right corner of the sash. His heart leaped at the sight, as welcome a sensation as hearing a bell buoy ring out in the fog.

Falk tapped lightly at the window, three times only, just as he had said in the note. The curtains flicked, and he saw a pair of hands working at the latch. The sash came free with a squeak and a slide.

"Quick," Pam whispered, barely audible above the downpour. "Climb in. I've put towels on the floor."

The threshold came up to about thigh level, and Falk struggled across the sill, dripping like an old dog and wishing he could shake like one, too. The room went silent as she shut the window against the pelting rain, and then he unzipped his jacket and shed it behind him onto the muddy towels. It was such a relief to see her, to know she'd been waiting. They exchanged an excited glance in the dark, her glimmering eyes looking keyed up, perhaps a bit worried. She was taking quite a risk. Was that really what he had wanted most? A proof of her loyalty? He was about to speak when she placed a finger to his lips and shook her head.

"Not yet," she mouthed, pointing next door. "Roommates."

Then, before he could make another move, she slid her arms around him, all warmth and comfort against the dampness of his shirt. He had been on edge for the better part of the afternoon, and it was almost a shock to his system. But in a moment his body relaxed as if he had slipped into a warm tub. Then came the excitement, the smell of her skin and hair, the feel of her hands on his back—all of it producing a surge of attraction that was never far beneath the surface when they were together.

When the first flush of the moment passed she backed away, turning her ear to the door and listening. She reached to a radio on the bureau and switched on a sudden blare of salsa beaming from across the fenceline, another reminder of just where they were.

Their next embrace lasted longer, with a deep, slow kiss tacked on. But neither of them was taking this risk for an amorous liaison, and as soon as they came up for air the many unanswered questions suddenly loomed between them like another threshold to be scaled. Falk sensed the awkwardness, and since he had called this meeting he felt obligated to speak first.

"Good to see you." He kept his voice to a whisper.

"I wasn't sure they'd let you back on the island."

"They probably wouldn't have if they hadn't been afraid to be too obvious. How are you holding up?"

She shook her head.

"Going stir crazy. Cabin fever, plus the worry. Sleeping a lot, if you really want to know, and always wondering if this is the end of my career. Every night it's a different dream, all of them bad."

Falk winced at the remark about her career. Exactly what Bo had alluded to.

"What about you?" she said. "What's going on out there? My roommates don't tell me a thing. I've become a leper. 'Oh, we'd better not,' and a lot of other OPSEC bullshit. Guess I've been blackballed from the sorority."

"Same here. My team would barely speak to me yesterday. And I guess that kind of made me wonder."

"Wonder what?"

"What you've been telling your interrogators." Her eyes darkened. "Let me rephrase that. I've been wondering what they've been asking you."

"So that's why you wanted a meeting? To find out if I've spilled your secrets? Maybe you're forgetting that I'm the one under house arrest. Did you ever think that maybe it's you who's the problem for me?"

"Sorry. It's just that Bo said—"

"Bo?" She frowned. "Who do you think these jerks are reporting to?"

"Fowler."

"He's not the only one. It's a lot more complicated."

"Who says?"

"No one. You can just tell from what they ask, the things they say. Something funny is going on at the Pink Palace, but I'm not sure even Trabert has a handle on it."

"What *are* they asking?"

"Who's been talking to the Yemenis? Who shapes the questions? How did your friend Falk end up as Adnan's sole interrogator? Whose idea was it? Who let him do it? Who sees our reports? And they wanted to know about the rumor, the one behind the wire."

"The one about the ex-Marine? I think I—"

Her eyes widened in alarm and she abruptly put a finger to his lips. She looked toward the door, where Falk heard footsteps passing down the hallway. They held their breath, and then Pam slowly exhaled and turned back toward him.

"Yes, that rumor. The one I mentioned at breakfast."

"But wouldn't tell me any more about."

"That was for your benefit. I was hoping that would be as far as it went."

Falk shook his head.

"It's making the rounds. Even I've heard it now from a Saudi."

"In a way I was hoping you *wouldn't* come back. Much better to be stuck in JAX than here, believe me."

"Then who would have looked after you?"

"What, by breaking into my room?" She smiled. "It's okay. I was all for it, if only to tell you to watch your step. And to trust no one."

"No one?"

"Except me, of course. And your deliveryman. What's he all about?"

"Harry? Long story."

"Another one going back to Marine days?"

"Later, when we've got more time."

"If we've ever got it. Oh, and he also brought this. Said it was for you. Compliments of someone named Paco."

It was a shock hearing Paco's name at this time and place. He hoped that the darkness hid his surprise. She handed him a brown envelope with a Department of the Navy letterhead. It was used, with an old postmark and a return address from some supply officer in Washington. It was grease-stained, obviously from the machine shop, and Harry had sealed it with electrical tape.

"So are you going to open it?" Playful, not challenging, but there was no way he was going to unseal it in front of Pam. If Harry had taken this kind of risk, it figured to be something urgent.

"I'm sure it's not important," he said. "Besides, there's a lot I need to ask you. Who does all the questioning, for starters?"

"Fowler mostly, and he's the most insistent. But sometimes it's Van Meter."

"They work together?"

"No. But they ask a lot of the same stuff. I'm beginning to see why it drives the detainees nuts. Same questions, over and over. You'd think they'd compare notes. The only time Fowler didn't come alone he brought Cartwright, the one in uniform. Just what I need, having a lieutenant colonel breathing down my neck."

"And Van Meter? Alone?"

"Except once."

"With Lawson or Rieger?"

"Neither. With Bokamper."

"Bo?"

She nodded, as if that closed her case. But Pam didn't know Bokamper the way Falk did. He had probably come along to keep tabs on Van Meter. Snooping on the snoop. Maybe he had also been keeping an eye on Pam, on Falk's behalf.

"Well, say as little as you can to Van Meter."

"Easy for you to say."

"I'm serious. He's mixed up in something that goes way beyond this mess. And if—"

She shushed him again, the footsteps returning, this time stopping just outside the door, followed by a muffled knock.

"Pam?" One of her roommates, sounding concerned.

"What is it?"

"You okay in there?"

"I'm fine."

"It's just that I thought I heard—"

"What?"

"Crying. I don't know. Sounded like a sob." Or a deep voice, perhaps?

"Really, I'm fine. Just talking to myself. Playing music and babbling away. That's what happens when people cut you off."

"It wasn't my choice, you know," she replied with the aggrieved tone always adopted by those who are only following orders. The footsteps retreated without a further word.

"You should go," she mouthed, barely whispering. "She'd report me if she knew. Seriously. Maybe she already is."

"The phone is still hooked up?"

"Only the one in her room. Which she keeps locked when she's not here."

"Lovely people."

"No worse than your friends, believe me."

"I'll keep that in mind."

It was apparent that the dislike between Pam and Bo was still mutual, and this was how it was playing out under pressure, with each pointing a finger at the other. Not particularly becoming of either. But where did that leave Falk?

They kissed again, lightly this time, the commuting husband on his way to catch the train. Then they flinched as she unlatched the window, the sash squeaking open onto the industrial clatter of the storm. He clambered across the sill and turned to say good-bye. When she whispered now it was all he could do to read her lips. "Leave that way," she mouthed, pointing in the opposite direction from the way he'd come. "So you won't have to pass her window."

"Thanks," he mouthed, water pouring off his hat. "I trust you."

Right now he figured that was the best he had to offer. But instead of nodding or mouthing anything back, she leaned across the sash, out into the rain, her face close to his, and he instinctively turned an ear for her parting message.

"When we're out, when this is over—if it ever is over—I want you to be there for me."

"I will," he said, knowing then that he meant it. So he said it again, if only to convince himself. "I will." Like a vow, an advance to higher ground that would have to be held at all costs.

She nodded, brushing his lips with hers, and drew back inside. Her hair dripped onto the floor as she slid the window shut, still gazing at him. Then she pulled the curtains back into place, the line of communication severed. Falk felt his stomach knot, and he took a step in the wrong direction before catching himself, a soldier who'd nearly tripped the mine.

Already he could think of a dozen questions he had meant to ask. But of all of them, the most crucial was this: When all of this was over, would she still be there for him? He knew what her answer would be now, but what about when she found out more about his own involvement, his own past missteps? His track record wasn't exactly the sort you could afford to be associated with when you were trying to climb the chain of command.

Watching warily for a burst of light, or the appearance of a sentry, he headed across the soggy lawn and between the buildings to the rear, back through the rainy night toward his car.

He was still soaked by the time he pulled into the driveway fifteen minutes later, and after switching off the engine he sat for a few seconds as rain hammered the roof. It was a relief that it had gone off without a hitch. Now he even felt comfortable enough to check on what Harry had delivered. Falk flipped on the dome light, then tore back the tape on the old envelope and reached inside, reminded of the days when he poked his hand into boxes of Cracker Jacks, groping for the prize at the bottom.

Inside was a British passport, belonging to Ned Morris of Manchester, with Falk's picture inside. It was an updated version of the one he had used on his trip to Havana. The photo was also new. Now when had they managed that? he wondered. Sometime in Miami, perhaps. There was no note inside.

His first impulse was to come up with the quickest possible way to destroy it. Were they trying to set him up? Then a sharp rap on the passenger window nearly made him jump out of his skin. A pale, dripping face peered through the glass. It was Tyndall.

"Let me in!" A muffled shout. "Open up!"

Falk shoved the passport and envelope into a jacket pocket, then unlatched the door. The noise of the downpour entered with the CIA man, who was almost as wet as Falk. A flash of lightning lit the sky, and you could see the rubber trees out front whipsawing in the wind.

"You scared me half to death," Falk said. "Where were you hiding?"

"Didn't you see my car parked out front? I kept waiting for you to get out so I could follow you inside. Then I finally gave up."

"Sorry," Falk said, pulse still on overdrive. "Didn't see it in this mess."

"I've been waiting half an hour. You've got your wish, but it has to be tonight, and you can't tell a soul."

"What are you talking about?"

"Adnan. Your half hour of glory inside Camp Echo. Now or never, take it or leave it."

"I'll take it."

"Then let's roll."

"My car?"

"Do you really want to get soaked again switching?"

"No."

"Besides, I'd prefer not to be seen leading this expedition. But hurry. We don't have much time."

Hurried or not, Falk had to go slow in the rain, the water running now in wavelets across the banked pavement of the curves. The landscape was drinking it in as fast as it could, as if aware it might have to live on this one big gulp for weeks to come, but the ground was already choking on the excess, and streams poured through the gaps between scrub and cactus.

As they swerved around the orange barriers up to the checkpoint, a pair of headlights bobbed up behind them, nearly blinding Falk in the glare of the rearview mirror.

"Who's the asshole?" Tyndall asked.

"Don't know."

"Anybody know you'd be coming here?"

"No."

"Maybe it's just a night owl, then. But in this shit?"

The checkpoint MP, draped in a drenched parka, glanced at their IDs and waved them through. The trailing driver must have had his pass ready, too, because he was soon right back on their tail.

"Go past the main entrance to Delta and take the next right."

He did, but the other car still followed.

"What the hell's he up to?" Tyndall said, turning in the seat. "Maybe we should turn around, get out of here."

"Too late," Falk said. They were pulling up to a gate, where another MP in a parka leaned toward the window.

"Park over there," the MP shouted, pointing to a small gravel lot to the side. "Then come inside the hut. They'll get you squared away."

They pulled to the side, and the second car sidled up beside them.

"Well, here goes nothing," Tyndall said, and they unlatched their doors to run for the cover of the MP hut. No sooner were they inside than Falk heard a familiar voice.

"Wait up, fellas!"

It was Bo, who was just coming through the door. Falk sighed with relief. Bo was still in his shirtsleeves, not even wearing a windbreaker.

"It's okay," Falk said to Tyndall.

Tyndall said nothing, but didn't look so sure, maintaining a grim expression as Bo stamped his feet, shedding water from his pants. An MP eyed them somewhat incredulously from the security desk.

"How'd you know where to find me?" Falk asked.

"Dumb luck. Was on my way to your house when I saw your car

turning off Iguana Terrace. Figured I'd catch up to you. Where are we, anyway?"

"You really don't know?" Tyndall said.

"Hey, I'm still the new guy. I was just following my pal here."

Falk tried to read his face for any hint of urgent news, but couldn't decipher it. Bo would be thrilled with the findings from the sign-out sheet and the MP duty roster. But that discussion would have to wait.

"This is Camp Echo," Tyndall said.

"Well, now."

"We get cleared here," he said, turning to Falk, his body language indicating an almost purposeful snub of Bokamper. "Then an escort will take us to a booth. I'll have to be present, too, I'm afraid. House rules, since it's technically our shop."

"I'm going in to speak to Adnan," Falk explained to Bo, which didn't seem to win him any points with Tyndall.

"Mind if I tag along?" Bo asked. "Watching from behind the glass, of course."

"Three's a crowd," Tyndall said.

"Not always." Bo slipped a folded sheet of paper beneath Tyndall's nose, so close Tyndall had to back away to read it. Then he snatched it back before Falk could get a look.

"Your friend's well connected," Tyndall said. "You mind if he's in there?"

Now Falk wasn't sure, but there was no time to debate it.

"Long as he stays behind the glass." He turned toward Bo. "What's on that letter? And who signed it for you? For that matter, where'd you get the car?"

"Technicalities, gentlemen, technicalities." Spoken with a Cheshire-cat grin. "Let's get going if we're going, Mr. Tyndall. I thought you said time was short."

He had, Falk thought, but not while you were present.

Tyndall opened the door, and the three of them ran back into the rain.

CHAPTER TWENTY-FIVE

THIS TIME, AT LEAST, they didn't wake him with loud music. Or with shouting, or water, or a prod to the chest, a slap on the face. Nor did they force him to his knees and bend him over, then leave him there for hours, until his joints locked and the blood stopped and his muscles cramped into hard balls of frozen rubber. No hoods, no strobe lights, no chains—well, no more than the usual ones—and for the time being, no snakes in gray suits, hissing into his throbbing ears.

In this new place where Adnan lived you could burrow as deeply as you wanted, but it was never deep enough, because the hawks and snakes simply climbed in with you. So he had retreated to the only remaining sanctuary—a silence within the remotest reaches of his mind, protected by a shield that became harder and thicker by the hour, almost organic in the way it grew.

They had brought him here nearly six days ago, on the morning after the midnight interrogation by the snakes at the place of the cages, with all the vines. It was a cell unto itself—one of a cluster of about a dozen, judging from what he had seen on his way in—a hut built of concrete blocks with no view of the outside. Inside was his room, even smaller than his earlier burrow. There was also a second room with a table and chairs, the place where they strapped him down and tried to talk to him, visiting several times a day.

For a while he had still tried to think of himself as a mouse who had become a mole, but when the extra burrowing proved ineffective he resorted to this other refuge. The taxonomy he had developed so carefully no longer worked in this new place. Everything here was too programmed and artificial to be populated by real creatures. And there were no more calls to prayer to set his inner watch by. Meals still arrived, but seemed to do so at irregular intervals, by whim. Nor was there any network of gossip and shouting. He sensed from the noises—or lack of them—that this was a smaller world. He wondered sometimes if that earlier place even existed anymore. It was as if the snakes and hawks had eaten their fill and denuded the plains of all prey, leaving behind this isolated wasteland. In that sense, he supposed, he was a survivor.

But in keeping with the man-made aspect of his new surroundings, he began to think of his existence as comparable to a single pixel on a TV screen that someone had just switched off, a glowing dot at the center of a blankness that would inevitably swallow him as he shrank and faded from view.

Yet for the moment he must still be visible, because they had found him again and were fetching him in a far more gentle way than was customary. An MP stood at the door, calling his name. Behind the MP was a second man, waiting silently. Then the second man called out, speaking Arabic in an accent he instantly recognized.

"Adnan? Are you okay? You don't look so good."

It was the Lizard, the patient one who lay still and brooded and watched him with what Adnan had thought was sympathy. Now he knew it for deceit, because no sooner had he given up his one big secret than the Lizard had betrayed him to the others, who had brought him here.

That first night had been almost like the plane trip again, with its vomiting and chill and shivering, teeth chattering so hard that it was like biting concrete, again and again.

Now he heard the Lizard speaking in English to the guard, who was shaking his head, speaking back. The guard pulled him over to a chair, saying something. Was he supposed to sit now, here at the table? The others never had let him sit. They stood him in a corner, or squatted him before a strobe light, or a speaker blaring music. Then they leaned low with their questions: "Tell us about Hussay. Just tell us about Hussay and you can go home."

The MP nudged him toward the chair, so Adnan sat, still eyeing the scene through the opaque layers he had built around himself. He tried brushing them away, but his hands wouldn't move, still locked behind his back. They must have done that before waking him. But he was determined to climb back to the surface, if only for a moment. The Lizard had to hear what had become of him. Had to know the price of betrayal. So he would emerge, if he could, just long enough to vent his anger. Then he would retreat. There would be plenty of time later to rebuild all the layers of his shell, to again become the pixel on the screen, the lone dot of light fading to darkness.

CHAPTER TWENTY-SIX

FALK HAD TO SPEND at least ten minutes of his precious half hour getting Adnan settled down, and it was easy to see why. The young man was bruised, pale and gaunt, looking as if he had lost fifteen pounds. He had been here only six days, but it might as well have been a lifetime.

The props of his destruction were plain to see. A pair of strobe lights sat on the floor in a corner, next to a tape deck and a hundred-watt speaker—only one, no need for stereophonic quality when volume was your only concern. There were no truncheons, prods, or extra shackles, but that kind of equipment was portable.

Under these circumstances, Falk didn't want anyone at the table but Adnan and him, but first he had to argue with the MP.

"I'm not supposed to leave, sir, and this one's been trouble. They said to never let him out of my sight."

Falk would have asked who "they" were, but knew he'd get nothing. He had noticed on the way in that no one filled out any forms or otherwise noted their presence for the record. Maybe that was because this visit was off the books. Or maybe every visit to Camp Echo was off the books. His bosses in Washington would have blanched to know he was here, and there was no way he would ever volunteer the information.

"Don't worry, soldier. I take full responsibility. Just lock him to the floor and wait outside. I'll call if I need you."

"Okay, but it's kind of hard to hear from out there."

No doubt, Falk thought, eyeing the walls and door. Whoever

had built Camp Echo had thought of everything, including sound insulation.

Tyndall and Bo were behind the mirror, waiting for the show to begin. It was cramped and stuffy back there, but so be it. With the time limit, they wouldn't suffer long, and judging from what Falk had to work with, the half hour wasn't likely to be productive.

Falk had insisted that neither of them show his face or speak up once the session began. As damaged as the young man was, the last thing Falk needed was another intrusion that might set him off, or push him deeper into whatever place he'd retreated to. Adnan might well remember Tyndall from last week. Even an unfamiliar mug like Bo's could upset the balance.

Adnan was breathing heavily from the moment he entered the room, and the hyperventilation scarcely improved when he recognized Falk. He said something, but it was unintelligible, coming out as a grunt, and even that took so much effort that it sprayed a white foam of spittle across his chin. His eyes were burning, with either rage or eagerness, maybe both. But it seemed clear that he had something to get off his chest.

"Easy, now. Easy, fellow." Good Lord, it was like talking to a child, a dog. It was all Falk could do not to reach across the table and stroke him on the head. "It's going to be okay now." But it wasn't, of course, not if Adnan was being handed over to Yemeni intelligence, whose tactics would only be worse.

"I don't know if they've told you, but they'll be sending you back to Yemen in a few days." He resisted the urge to say "home," because it wouldn't have been true. He was through lying to Adnan. Or so he vowed.

"I'm told that the move is going to happen for certain." But leaving it at that, of course, would have been a lie by omission, so Falk came clean. "You'll be released to the authorities, not to your family, although with any luck, maybe they'll let you go soon."

He thought he heard a cough from behind the mirror. Was Tyndall trying to tell him he was speaking out of school? Too late now.

"But before you go, Adnan, you have to tell me who has done this to you. You have to tell me who brought you here to this room, and who has been coming to see you."

"Betrayer!" Adnan finally spluttered, the word seeming to geyser from some deep recess where it had bubbled and stewed for ages. "You and the snakes. Betrayers!"

"The snakes?" It was the first time Falk had heard him use the word.

"All of you! All snakes."

The outburst released enough pressure to calm him, and as the eruption subsided Falk leaned forward ever so slightly, not close enough to be threatening, but enough that he could lower his voice and still be heard.

"Listen to me, Adnan. Look at me." A glance, almost holding it. Then Adnan looked off to the usual corner where his eyes went when he had nothing further to say. "You are right, Adnan. You are right about the snakes. They have betrayed you, but I want to punish them for it, and you can help me."

He waited, and Adnan's head swiveled slowly back, a pivot that stopped just short of face-to-face. But the eyes kept coming, halting briefly as they met Falk's, then wavering and flicking back toward the corner.

"You can help me," Falk said. "You can help us both."

Well, there it was—deceit creeping back into his approach in spite of his best intentions. But there was no taking back the words now, especially since they seemed to be showing results. Adnan's face had moved, and now his eyes were locked onto Falk's.

"Good," Falk crooned, master to dog. "Good. Now I am going to show you some pictures, Adnan. Some of the snakes. So don't be upset, because they're not here, and they're not waiting outside, and they're not going to hurt you again." Another promise he couldn't keep, and he knew he would keep offering them as long as they kept working.

Falk pulled from his briefcase the copy of *The Wire* with the article on the investigative team. He had folded back the photo so that only Fowler's face was showing. He slid it onto the table where Adnan could see it, doing it slowly, careful not to break the spell. Snakes, indeed. He felt like a cobra, trying to stare his victim into a trance.

"This one," he said, still holding eye contact even as he tapped the photo. "Do you recognize him? Look down at the picture, Adnan. The picture can't hurt you."

Adnan looked down, and for a fretful moment Falk thought he had lost him, such was the blankness of the young man's expression as he stared at the photo. It was as if he were peering deep into a well, the focus not quite right.

"You know him?" Falk asked. "Has he been here?"

Adnan slowly shook his head, expression neutral.

"No?"

"No," Adnan answered, mildly, as if he were declining an extra helping of dessert. "I do not know him. He is not among the snakes."

Falk got the same result with Cartwright's photo. Then he showed the picture of Fowler once more, just to make sure, and also as a sort of test. If Adnan reacted as if he were seeing it for the first time, then maybe his mind was blanking, repressing the memory of everyone who had done him harm.

But that's not what happened.

"You have asked me already about him!" Adnan said, voice rising. "He is not among the snakes!" He was back to the precipice. Falk withdrew the photo.

"Very good, then. Very well. It's all right. You won't see that picture again."

To Falk, this meant that maybe whoever had done the interrogations of the Yemenis at Camp X-Ray was the same person who was doing them here. If that was Van Meter, then he would have had an interpreter in tow, and Allen Lawson would have been the logical choice. Perhaps Fowler only watched from behind the mirror.

Unfortunately, he had no photos of Van Meter to show, and he doubted he could get one before either Adnan departed or General Trabert found out what Falk was up to and shut him down. Miracle enough, he supposed, that he had gotten in here at all.

"Okay, then," he said, changing tack. "Let's talk about these snakes."

Adnan shook his head.

"Don't you want them punished?"

Adnan looked down at his feet.

"Well, don't you?"

A slow nod.

"Then describe them to me. What they wore. What color their hair was, their eyes."

Adnan looked up at Falk as if he were a dolt. He seemed furious.

"They are snakes!" he shouted. "What else do you need to know? They look like snakes, they bite like snakes, they coil and strike like snakes. They are snakes!"

So this was where the damage showed itself, he supposed. Which might explain why none of the pictures registered. Show him a photo of a timber rattler and perhaps he would jump to his feet, pointing wildly in recognition. But Falk soldiered on, keeping his voice low and his posture neutral. He did not again lean forward and he did not stand. He folded his hands in front of him, on the table where Adnan could see them.

Adnan responded in kind, to a point. His demeanor calmed, and he did not again raise his voice. But no matter how many different ways Falk tried to elicit a description of his tormenters, or even a hint of one, Adnan always responded the same way.

"It is all I can say of them," he said wearily, in apparent exasperation. "They are snakes."

"Okay, then. Fine. But how many? How many snakes have come here?"

"Three," he said. Certain of it. "Three in this place."

"And in the other place? From before you were here?"

"Too many. Many more."

"But some here are the same as before? Or are all the ones here new ones?"

"Two are the same as before. One is new. Here and from the last time in the jungle."

"The jungle?"

"The place where the monkeys lived."

He must have meant Camp X-Ray. That last session before they brought him here. All other snakes must be those he had talked to before Falk had taken over his handling. Falk wondered what Bo and Tyndall were making of all this. Neither understood Arabic, so they would only have noticed the gestures, the changes in inflection and volume. They would have seen Falk hold out the newspaper, but wouldn't have known what it was or what he was asking. Just as well, especially in Tyndall's case. Or was the CIA man somehow taping this? Possible, he supposed, but it was too late to worry about it.

Checking his watch, he saw that only a few minutes remained. Tyndall had promised to cut him off promptly when the time expired. For all Falk knew, the rendition was scheduled for daybreak, although air traffic was likely to be grounded at least until Clifford passed through.

He made one last stab at getting a description of the newest snake, and when that failed he sighed, feeling there was nothing left to ask, if only because it seemed there was nothing left to retrieve. Adnan was calmer now, but accompanying the calmness was an expression of such vacant resignation that Falk was oddly devastated by the sight. All that was missing to complete the effect was a straitjacket, or the stitch scars of a lobotomy. Adnan was an empty vessel, thoroughly spent.

"Okay, Adnan," he said gently. "That's good. You did well today. This will help you."

Not even the lies seemed to matter anymore. Adnan's face remained as rigidly placid as a frozen pond. Falk got up and knocked lightly on the door. The MP was inside immediately, looking excited until he saw that everything was in order.

"All done," Falk said. "You can put him back."

The words in English brought a response from Tyndall, who cracked open the door of the observation room just enough to mutter, "You've still got three minutes, you know. If you want it."

"He's running on empty," Falk said. "Nothing left to get."

"Empty?" Bo snorted, not bothering to whisper. "I don't speak Arabic but, hell, you hardly tried. You looked more like his therapist than his interrogator. That what they teach you at Quantico?"

There was a sudden commotion behind him, then an agonized groan from Adnan.

"Snake!" he said in Arabic. "It hisses! I hear it!" Falk turned to see Adnan's eyes glowing in fear.

"What the hell's he saying now?" Bo said.

"Snake!" Adnan struggled with the MP, who was pulling a truncheon from his belt.

"Shut up!" Falk muttered to Bo over his shoulder. "And shut the door. I want those three minutes. MP! Hold him, but don't dare hit him. Keep him there by the door, just one second more!"

Falk's stomach turned as he pulled the newspaper back out of his bag, but he mustered enough composure to catch Adnan's eye, beseeching the young man to calm down enough for one last question.

"Is this the snake?" he asked, keeping his voice low and even. He folded back the picture to the one face he hadn't showed, that of Ted Bokamper, hovering to the right of the frame.

"Yes!" Adnan said, nodding quickly, then looking wildly toward the mirror on the opposite wall. "He hisses, and he is there. He lives *there*!"

"Easy, Adnan."

But Adnan would no longer be calmed, and even in his leg irons and handcuffs he was a handful for the young MP, who ended up simply shoving Adnan onto his bed, still locked at his wrists and ankles, then slammed home the cell door.

"Man's out of control," the soldier said scornfully. "No wonder he's in this place."

"Yeah," Falk said. "No wonder."

By the time the three of them had run back through the rain to the entry station, Falk had regained his composure.

"Bo, why don't you follow us back to my place. You and I need to talk."

"My sentiments exactly." Falk shot him a questioning glance, but got only the usual wiseass grin in return. "But unfortunately I can't do it right now. Previous obligation."

"At eleven o'clock at night?"

"Hey, you know me."

"Thought I did, anyway."

But Bo was already out the door, sprinting for his car through the downpour. Tyndall and he followed suit, and after slamming the door of the Plymouth, Falk sat for a moment with his hands on the wheel as he sorted out the implications.

"I'm getting some weird vibes from all this," Tyndall said.

"You should be."

"What just happened back there?"

"I'm not sure. But thanks for getting me in."

"Sure. I think."

He was about to turn the key when he suddenly thought of something.

"Shit!" he said, feeling like an idiot.

"What? What is it?"

He pulled out his flashlight and bent as low as he could in the seat, peering beneath the wheel.

"Feel under the dash on your side," he told Tyndall.

Tyndall tapped feebly beneath the glove compartment.

"What am I looking for?"

"Anything that shouldn't be there."

"You mean like this?"

There was a sharp clicking sound on Tyndall's side, and when Falk turned the beam Tyndall was holding a small metal disk.

"It was hooked to a wire," Tyndall said. "Probably goes straight to your radio. That way it broadcasts off your antenna."

"Meaning they can hear me, what, a mile away?"

"I'm no expert, but probably something like that. Maybe more." Tyndall was a smart fellow, so he added up the rest of the evidence pretty quickly. "I guess this explains how we ended up with an escort."

"Yeah. My old pal."

"Hardly a surprise."

"What do you mean?"

"Him. And his employers. Part of our special clientele for product from down here. You didn't hear that from me, of course."

"Special clientele? Since when?"

"Since forever. Or the last change of administrations, anyway. You're his friend. I'd always assumed you two were working together."

"What, for the Bureau?"

"Not really for the Bureau. Just as part of their, well, whatever they call themselves."

"And what might that be?"

"Nobody's ever told me. All I know is that certain people in my shop have asked me to cooperate whenever they ask. But I am surprised you didn't know. The way you guys pal around and everything."

Maybe he and Bo *had* been working together, Falk supposed. Just not in the way he'd imagined.

"As long as everybody else knows so much, tell me this. Those three guys on the team—Bo, Fowler, Cartwright—were they assigned security numbers for signing out detainees inside Delta?"

"That would be a safe assumption."

"I don't want an assumption. I want an answer."

"The answer is yes. But I'm not telling you their numbers."

"Fair enough. All I need is a yes-no on one."

"You're asking too much."

"C'mon, Mitch. It's one fucking number. I name it and you tell me if it's Bo's."

"And you think my memory's that good?"

"For those three? Damn right I do."

"Okay. For those three, maybe. But it's not like I've got the whole of Camp Delta memorized. To hear some of you guys talk, it's like we're snooping on everybody. Fowler makes an arrest and we get blamed."

"I'm not here to blame, I just need information."

"You and the whole fucking world. What's the number?"

Falk dug out his notes by flashlight, and then read aloud the digits that had been logged in for Adnan's interrogation last Wednesday at Camp X-Ray.

"Bo's, right?"

Tyndall shook his head and gave him a funny look, seeming more embarrassed than puzzled.

"Van Meter's, then. Has to be."

"What is this, twenty questions? Goddamn it, Falk, enough. But of all the numbers, I would have thought that would be one you'd know."

"Well, it's no one from my team."

"Of course not. It's from hers."

"Hers?" A pause while everything clicked. *"Pam's?"*

"Satisfied now? No more questions, okay? I think we've both had enough."

"Okay," Falk said weakly.

And for the second time in ten minutes, his world turned upside down.

CHAPTER TWENTY-SEVEN

AFTER TYNDALL SPRINTED to his car, Falk sat for a few minutes in the driveway with the engine running. His first impulse was to head back to Pam's—bang on her window until he awakened the entire household, roommates and all, then demand an explanation as he stood dripping on their floor. He would throw himself on the mercy of the MPs.

Maybe it would get him kicked off the base. They would put him on a flight, banish him from all this misery. He would take the evidence with him and embarrass them all. Leak it to the press, burn every bridge. Why not, since half his bridges were already ablaze.

But on whose behalf, or for what cause, were his friends betraying him? As far as he could tell, both Pam and Bo had interrogated Adnan. Yet, unless their antipathy for one another was an act—a prospect raising possibilities Falk didn't care to consider just now—then they had been coming at Adnan from opposite agendas. Was Pam working for Fowler, meaning her arrest was some kind of cover? None of it made sense, and all of it made him feel used. They must have been laughing to themselves as he scurried between them, so eager to please and keep the peace.

He turned off the ignition and unlatched the door. The noise of the storm swallowed him in a sheet of rain that slanted right onto the seat. Let it. So what if he was soaked. There were four beers in the refrigerator, and there was a bottle of gin in the cabinet. The idea of a temporary oblivion had its charms just now, so he wasn't bothered in the least as raindrops hammered him all the way up the sidewalk.

Slamming the front door behind him, he was quickly chilled to the bone by the air-conditioning, and he paused to behold the calming groan and hum of the window unit while his eyes adjusted to the darkness. The only light came from a kitchen window to the right, where the orange glow of a streetlamp wavered, filtered by the sheeting rain. A palm frond brushed like fingernails against a screen. It was a nasty one, this storm, perhaps not quite a gale but still a corker for anyone unfortunate enough to be out on the sea. For the slightest moment his heart went out to them, wherever they were, tossed and alone and just trying to stay afloat.

As he stepped toward the refrigerator he was startled by the chirp of a cigarette lighter and the sudden glow of a small flame from the living room. Someone was sitting on the couch.

"Who's there?"

No answer.

"Bo?"

"Instructive response." Falk didn't recognize the voice.

Then the lights came on, blinding him momentarily.

"Care to explain why you expected Ted Bokamper to be waiting for you at this hour of the day?"

It was Fowler, and he wasn't alone. An MP stood in a far corner, gun holstered and hands behind his back.

"What's this all about?"

"I've got a few questions. Have a seat."

"How 'bout getting the hell out of here. I'm tired and need a drink, and I'm definitely not in the mood for a chat."

"Go ahead with the drink. But I'm not leaving until we've talked."

"You here to arrest me?"

"Should I be?"

Falk shook his head and turned down the hall, away from the kitchen. "I'm going to bed. Turn out the lights on your way out."

But there was a second MP blocking the entrance to his room, and when Falk stopped to ponder his next move a hand slapped against the wall from behind. Fowler's. He had moved from the couch with the rapid stealth of a commando and was close enough for Falk to smell the toothpaste on his breath.

"All right." Fowler was all business now. "Enough playing around. You can make this as hard as you want. But don't give me any guff about warrants, or your rights as a civilian, because you know exactly where we are and what that means as far as anyone's rights are concerned.

The Constitution? Never heard of it. We're in the zone of exclusion, and I've been authorized by the highest authority possible, so pay attention. Now how 'bout if we both have a seat?"

Falk returned to the living room while wondering what Fowler meant by "highest authority possible." On the base? In the task force? Or back in the States? Which would be a different matter altogether. Maybe Fowler was bluffing. But he was right about one thing. No one would be reading Falk his Miranda rights anytime soon.

"Maybe you should take that wet jacket off," Fowler said, settling back onto the couch. "This could take a while."

As Falk unzipped the jacket he felt the rigid wafer of the fake passport in his right pocket, and it was all he could do not to flinch. One quick patdown by the MP and he'd have been a goner. He gingerly placed the dripping jacket on a coat hook by the door, as if it had been wired to explode. Then he sat down in a chair opposite Fowler.

"Frankly I'm surprised you came back from Jacksonville," Fowler began. "When I heard you'd skipped town I figured you'd hang out there until everything blew over, then come creeping back like nothing had ever happened."

"You've obviously never spent much time in Jacksonville."

"You haven't either, from what I've heard. Took off due south and weren't seen again until the day of the flight. Care to tell me where you went?"

"I've got to account for my leave time now? Hell, I'm not even military. I'm civilian. I don't have to tell you anything."

"Look, I know you may think of me as an overly patriotic blowhard. Plenty of others around here do. It's like some sort of Gitmo combat fatigue. Two months of mission and everyone's a cynic. So go ahead, but be forewarned. Right now your loyalty is in question."

"Loyalty to what?"

"This task force, and everything it stands for. Your country, your employer."

"Care to explain what makes you think that?"

"Do you really want the list?"

"Yes. Because frankly I'm not sure who's working for what anymore, or why. And that includes my closest friends and colleagues, and it certainly includes you."

"Since you brought it up, let's discuss your friends. Ted Bokamper, for one."

"What about him?"

"What's he up to? And what's your role in it?"

"Look, I'm not sure what delusions you're operating under. But I'm not involved in *anything.* Whatever my friend Ted Bokamper does is his business. If I've done a few favors for him along the way, then that's all they've been, favors for a friend, and maybe I'd like to know what the hell they were for, too, now that they're attracting so much unwanted attention."

Besides, he just bugged my goddamn car! Falk wanted to say, but he restrained himself.

"So you *have* been helping him."

"I've passed along the usual rumors. Offered him my opinion on the lay of the land. It's no secret that your little team hasn't exactly been the happiest development in the history of Camp Delta. Some see it as a needed cleansing, some see it as a witch hunt. But everybody I've talked to seems to be as much in the dark as I am about what's really going on."

"I'm not here to talk about the arrests, or our little security investigation, and I think you know that. I'm talking about the extracurricular activities that your friend Mr. Bokamper and some of his local colleagues have been involved in. Van Meter. Lawson. And you. That's four pieces I know of, and we're looking for more, so how 'bout some straight answers."

Every time Falk thought he had something figured out, the tables turned again. He was more confused than ever.

"Then you'd better ask Bokamper. Because I'm not a part of it, and don't want to be."

"You really still think you're immune, don't you? Is it because you work for the Bureau? Or because of Bokamper's sponsors, and who they represent? I'm here to tell you that you're not protected by either. In fact, you've got a couple of major weaknesses that none of them have."

So here was where Fowler began talking about Cuba, Harry, and Paco, he supposed. Here was when they decided to search the house, and turn the place upside down.

"All right. Tell me about my weaknesses."

"One is that you're here, and already in our custody. With no lawyers and no phones. Yours has been disconnected, by the way. The bigger one is this: There's no one back in the States who'll miss you. I've checked. No wife and kids. No mom and dad. No bro and sis. No steady. No rich uncle or doting aunt. Hell, Falk, you're alone in the world except for your employer, and trust me, they'll agree to play along once they know the stakes. As for your girlfriend, she's under house arrest. And your best buddy, well, maybe we can't touch him yet, but if you think he'd lift a finger on your behalf then maybe you really *don't* know what he's up to. But I still think you're playing dumb, and I won't tolerate it."

Falk shook his head, saying nothing. Fowler continued.

"Okay, then. Let's talk about the Yemenis. Seven of them in all, I believe, all but one signed out by interrogators who withheld their ID numbers. Why'd you authorize that?"

So Fowler had also seen those records, which put his theft for Bo in an entirely new light.

"I never authorized anything, especially not that. I'd like to know who those people are, too."

"For a Bureau man you're not very good at lying, you know."

At that moment Falk could see himself as if in a mirror. Or, more apt, as if he were looking at himself through a two-way mirror, from the viewing room of an interrogation booth. He was there on the couch, still dripping wet, face startled, the light a little too bright in his eyes as his weariness began to show. He was hedging his answers and looking off into the corner. He was avoiding eye contact, professing ignorance even as he admitted knowledge.

Fowler was right. Falk was being sloppy and acting stupidly or, worse, acting like a liar. Well, he was done with that now. Time to tighten the ship. He turned and looked Fowler straight in the eye while keeping his hands in his lap. No gestures of evasion or futility. He struck the relaxed pose of a man with nothing to hide, but also nothing to offer—well, nothing except one small item to cover the misstep he'd just made by admitting to knowing about the interrogated Yemenis. From here on out he wouldn't leave a single track for Fowler to follow.

"Look, I checked those sign-in books, too. Just like you must have done. But I did it in the course of the Ludwig investigation. I was checking all the sign-outs done during his watch. A matter of routine. But none of those people were me, and none were authorized by me. I've spoken to probably three of those Yemenis in all, but primarily Adnan. And now he's been removed beyond my access."

"Ludwig? The soldier who went missing?"

"The soldier who drowned. Then washed up on the Cuban side.

You should look into it. Maybe you'd find the tracks of some of your buddies. Van Meter, for one, although you seem to be implying he's no longer on your side."

Falk knew he had gone too far with the remark, but it would keep Fowler busy for a while.

"Your story doesn't wash," Fowler said, but no longer with his previous conviction. "We know that you've been after *all* those Yemenis, and we know—repeat, *know*—that you're doing it in tandem with your friend Ted Bokamper."

"Sorry. You're just wrong." He held the gaze. Kept his hands folded.

"Then let's move back to more fertile ground. Bokamper. You still haven't filled in the blanks on him."

Falk was beginning to realize that Fowler wasn't very good at this, so he decided to say nothing more, not because he was protecting anyone—were any of his friends even worthy of protection now?—but because he had no idea which end was up. There was a new dynamic at work, one that he had never encountered before, a new code, a new language even. He spoke Arabic as well as any of the non-Muslims here, but in this strange realm dreamed up by Bo, Fowler, Van Meter, Tyndall, Paco, and yes, perhaps also Pam, what he needed most right now was an interpreter, someone to point out all the loaded words and to separate the treasonous from the loyal, the duplicitous from the straightforward, and, frankly, the murderous from the merely pragmatic.

Until he could speak that language, he was determined to keep his own counsel.

Fowler played one last card, but it was a pretty powerful one.

"I'm going to give you a proposition to consider overnight," he said. "How would you like to end up inside the wire? Someplace where you would be ours and ours alone? I could make it happen, you know. Put you on the wrong side of the table, and for good. You'd be one of the ghosts, with no sponsor, no advocate, and no one back home to ask whatever happened to old what's-his-name? So think about that tonight while you're trying to sleep. In the meantime, I'll post these MPs out front to keep you safe. Not that there's anywhere to go. In the morning, we'll talk again. And if you're still not in the mood, we can try a little of what General Trabert calls 'pushing the envelope.' Sleep well."

Fowler got up to leave, and the two sentries followed. Falk kept his seat on the couch.

Snakes, indeed.

CHAPTER TWENTY-EIGHT

FALK DID SLEEP WELL, at least for a while, thanks mostly to exhaustion, a couple of beers, and the hypnotic drumming of the rain.

Besides, what else could he do? After Fowler left he looked out the front window and saw a sentry on the porch and a Humvee at the curb. At the rate Fowler was going there would soon be a Humvee and a sentry on every block. Maybe the Pentagon would have to call up another Reserve unit, just to tend to all the misfits and security risks.

Falk awakened to a knocking and scratching sound, as if a giant rodent were trying to come through the wall. Sitting up in bed, he realized it was coming from the window. He thought first of Pam. A return visit? His second thought was to wonder if he would let her in. Instead it was Bo, soaked to the bone in a T-shirt and shorts as he forced back the screen. Falk unlocked the sash. This was becoming Gitmo's preferred method for social calls.

"Easy," Falk said groggily, raising the sash. "Don't tear it off. I'll pop it loose."

Once again, the security of Fowler's "house arrest" had proven quite porous. But, again, it wasn't as if there were anywhere they could go.

Falk fetched a towel from the bathroom, and by the time Bo was drying off he had remembered all the reasons not to offer a warm welcome.

"What's the occasion?" he asked. "You here to bug my bedroom, too? Or have you already taken care of that?"

Bo shook his head. "Did the living room instead."

"When, if I may ask?"

"While you were gone. After Whitaker left."

"So you must have heard Fowler's little visit?"

"Most of it. You did well. After kind of a rough start, anyway."

"Let's see what you say tomorrow, after he's stuck me in Camp X-Ray."

"Relax. He's bluffing."

"Easy for you to say. Why doesn't he just run you in?"

"Maybe he thinks you're calling the shots."

"Wonder who gave him that idea."

"Maybe he just knows I'm better protected."

"If it's true, why are you sneaking around at—what time is it?"

"Half past midnight."

"Jesus, Bo. Well, as long as you're up, how 'bout getting rid of the goddamn microphone? I don't want to waste the whole morning looking for it before the Inquisition arrives."

They padded down the silent hallway toward the living room.

"Just keep your voice down," Bo said in a stage whisper. "The sentry's on the porch, staying out of the rain. Don't turn on any lights."

Falk answered in a normal tone of voice.

"You think I'm actually worried about you getting caught?"

Bo reached under the dining room table and, with a small popping sound, tore loose a device much like the one that had been wired to Falk's car radio. Then he actually grinned, more impish than embarrassed.

"So I guess you're really pissed off, huh?" he said.

"Wouldn't you be?"

"Definitely. I plead guilty with an explanation."

"Let's hear it."

"First I need a beer."

Falk found himself oddly ambivalent as he stepped toward the fridge. Yes, he was angry. Bo's cavalier attitude was especially infuriating. But maybe their friendship still counted for something if Bo was here now. And if Bo had helped back him into a corner, at least Bo seemed to be in the same tight space.

He grabbed the beer, plus a glass of water for himself. Bo turned on a radio and jacked up the volume. More salsa from across the fenceline. Nonstop, like a heartbeat.

"You were sleeping pretty soundly for a condemned man."

"Is that what I am now?"

Bo shrugged, finally seeming a little unsure of himself. In a way, it was the most encouraging sign Falk had seen yet, so he pressed the advantage.

"You're not exactly flying with the angels on this Cuban mess, are you?"

"I'm flying with Endler, period. I work for people, not causes. I trust the Doc to get it right, and usually he does."

"Except this time he threw in his lot with the zealots. It makes me wonder why you didn't try recruiting me from the beginning. I certainly had all the right qualifications: Talks to Yemenis. Gets results. You could have lied to me just like you did anyway and gotten exactly what you wanted."

Never mind that Falk already had exactly what Bo and Endler wanted. But he would rather have shared Adnan's bombshell with Paco than with this bunch.

"Believe me, you would've been first on the list. But Endler came late to the game, and by then his sponsors were using Van Meter and Lawson. Those guys didn't think you were ready for prime time. They said you weren't their style."

"Best thing I've heard about myself all week."

"I agree. Dumb and Dumber, those two. Why do you think I wanted those sign-out sheets? I needed to see how much of a trail they'd left."

"The way I remember it is that you wanted me to steal them. To erase the trail altogether."

"Did you?"

Damned if he'd say so now.

"Couldn't. The MP was right there the whole time. But I saw their trail, all right. I guess you must already know they killed Ludwig."

"Suspected it, anyway. They'd said all along they had an insider, somebody to cover their tracks and keep their names out of the books. Then he got cold feet, so they were going to strong-arm him, put the fear of God in him."

"They did that, all right. Fucked around with his bank and then took him for a little boat ride."

"Is that what happened?"

"Met him on the beach. Then probably rode him toward the boundary just to shake him up. Only I guess they didn't know he tended to freak out in small boats, so they must have lost him overboard. Or maybe they pushed him. Either way, like you said, Dumb and Dumber. Is that why they sent you down once Endler signed on? To clean up the mess and keep Fowler's hands out of the pie?"

"Only because the Doc told his people he had an insider who could help."

"Meaning me. But they still didn't have the information they wanted. So you decided to get Pam involved."

"Pam?" Bo initially looked flabbergasted, then seemed on the verge of laughter. "For that last interrogation at X-Ray, you mean?"

"Yeah." Falk wasn't smiling.

"Sorry. My little prank."

"What do you mean?"

"That happened my first night here and—how can I put this nicely?—she hadn't exactly made a good impression. So when we needed a crash interrogation I just told Van Meter to use her number."

"Nice guy." Falk tried not to show his sense of relief. At least someone hadn't lied to him. "So how'd you get her number? Tyndall?"

"The Agency? They're out of the loop on this."

"The Pink Palace, then. I guess as chief of security Van Meter had the connections."

"Believe what you want. I've said enough already. I'm just sorry it came to this."

"Why? You're getting exactly what you want. You even got Adnan moved into Camp Delta."

"That was Fowler's move, to keep him away from us. They've been pumping the poor bastard to find out what we're after. Hasn't worked, of course."

"So you piggybacked on me to get inside Echo. And now, let me guess, Endler's the one who pulled a few strings to make Adnan a rendition. Let the Yemenis do the dirty work for you."

"Sorry, Falk. No more explaining."

"Until after you get your war. Or whatever it is everybody's hoping for. That'll be a huge public service."

"Getting rid of Castro? Damn right it will be. And if some Cuban operative strayed from the leash long enough to crawl into bed with an al-Qaeda recruiter, why not make the most of it? It's like I told you, it's not the information, it's who controls it. If we get it before Fowler, we own it."

"Castro will probably die soon anyway. I thought you worked for people, not causes."

"I am working for people. You included. You know what Endler wanted? He was getting worried about your reliability, so he wanted you arrested as soon as you were done with Paco in Miami. A trumped-up charge that would let him stick you out of sight until we finished our business. The only reason he didn't was because I talked him out of it."

"Out of loyalty, of course."

"Hell, yes, out of loyalty."

"But that's not how you sold it to Endler."

"Of course not. I told him I still needed you to get to the bottom of things on Van Meter."

"You sure that wasn't your real reason?"

"Believe what you want, but you're here and not in jail."

"Yeah, I'm much better off. Under house arrest, and about to be drawn and quartered."

"Endler will do what he can. Just don't expect it to happen right away."

"So as long as the Doc gets his war, I'm a free man. Otherwise, nice knowing you."

"You might have to stay under wraps for a while, that's all. It will all be explained to the Bureau."

"And Van Meter? He gets away with murder?"

"He'll be dealt with."

"I'll bet. What'll it be, another boating accident, or killed in action in Iraq?"

"Look, if you really need someone to blame, then blame the stupid young Marine who decided it would be just great to go down to Havana for the weekend. Everything goes back to that. But Endler won't write you off, because I won't let him. You know how it works in the Corps."

"Yeah, we never leave our dead behind. I guess that's me right now."

Bo shook his head, as angry as Falk had seen him since basic training.

He departed shortly afterward, leaving a disconsolate Falk on the couch to ponder his future. The choices seemed clear. Tell everything to Fowler and be swept up in the net by the other side, and possibly face espionage charges in the bargain. Or keep his mouth shut and hope that a splendid little war would come along to save his ass. Nothing like having that on your conscience, even if matters never came to it. The thing that rankled most was that Bo's last comment had been true: The only person he could really blame was himself. Falk had struck the bargain, and he was still making payments.

He got up, prowled the kitchen, opened then closed the refrigerator without making a selection. Now he really was sleepless. Pacing back to the living room, he gazed up at the nautical chart Ensign Osgood had given him. A thing of beauty, a blueprint for a lifetime on the water. Maybe he should have toughed it out and stayed in Maine all along. He might have ended up drunk or drowned, but it was a kind of life that came with a refreshing clarity. Success and failure were measured by the weight of your traps, and every day that you made it home safe was another small victory.

The palm frond scratched again at the window on a fresh blast of wind, and Falk was struck by an inspiration, an idea. It was downright foolhardy, yet it seized him like a powerful current, just the sort of idiotic plan that you would expect from the son of a drunken lobsterman after a few cups of courage, except that by now Falk was stone-cold sober.

Pulling the thumbtacks from the wall, he carefully took down the chart and placed it on the table. Then he slid the other two charts from the tube. It was just after 1 a.m.

He strolled down the hall to pack his gear.

CHAPTER TWENTY-NINE

It was sloppy going once Falk climbed into the storm. He had half a mile to cover through the brush, heading downhill toward Sherman Avenue. The route wasn't steep, but the wet ground seemed to move beneath his feet. Once he lost his balance and slid feetfirst into the base of a big cactus. As he lay in the muck the sound of pelting raindrops was deafening. Fortunately none of the needles pierced the soles of his shoes.

While scrambling to his feet he thought he heard someone approaching from behind, so he remained still a moment longer, on edge, the Marine back on patrol. He concluded it was the noise of the storm playing tricks on him, and he continued downhill as the water popped off his hat brim, the whole night wild with wind and rain.

The duffel bag slung across his shoulder didn't make the journey any easier. He had spent half an hour preparing, first by packing, then by charting a rough course at the kitchen table.

The heaviest part of the load was a pair of one-gallon milk jugs that he recovered from the recycling bin in the kitchen, then rinsed with hot steamy water before filling them from the tap. He also threw in a change of clothes, a second pair of shoes, and all his notes from the past week, along with the stolen sign-in sheets and the two letters to Ludwig. He wrapped everything in a plastic garbage bag, which he tied off before dropping it into a second bag for extra protection.

He put the British passport, his wallet, and the cash from Florida into double Ziploc bags, then made a couple of peanut butter sandwiches and grabbed two bananas from the kitchen counter.

Before wrapping the tube of nautical charts in plastic he spread one of them on the table and fired up the laptop. They had cut off his phone, but apparently forgot about his data line, another sign of their overconfidence that he had no way out.

He went to the Web site for the National Oceanic and Atmospheric Administration for the latest information on the storm. An update had just been posted. Clifford was weakening, thank goodness, still just barely a tropical storm, with its highest sustained winds at about thirty-five knots (or forty miles per hour) and falling. The radar image showed its cyclonic motion disintegrating as its whirling arms raked southeastern Cuba. As of 1:25 a.m. the center was at a latitude of 19.3° north and a longitude of 74.5° west, moving west-northwest at about twelve miles an hour.

Plotting the projected path of the storm, Falk figured that by the time he was under way it would be about thirty miles southeast of the mouth of Guantánamo Bay. For the first few hours he'd be braving the worst winds on the upper or right side of the storm's counterclockwise pinwheel. It wasn't what he would have preferred, especially in the type of boat he'd be using. The alternative was to wait another few hours, but that would cut deeply into his head start, and would offer calmer seas and skies to any pursuers. With luck—and he would need plenty—by leaving early he would have nearly reached his destination by the time anyone knew he was gone.

The last thing he did before clambering out the window was to write down some waypoints he hoped to hit. He put those into a smaller Ziploc and stuffed it into a jacket pocket next to the handheld GPS.

It took about ten minutes to reach Sherman Avenue, and from there he kept to the shoulder, ready to dash off into the brush or a drainage ditch if a security patrol came along. There wasn't much cover, but at this hour the roads were empty.

From the few fishing trips Falk had taken at Guantánamo, he was familiar with the selection of powerboats. The pickings were slim—a few Bayliners and Sea Chasers. The Bayliners were your typical pleasure craft with sleek lines and a small cutty cabin, built more for speed than for battering the waves. His preference was the twenty-four-foot Sea Chaser, with an open deck that drained quickly and a hull that rode better in rough weather, although he'd obviously never piloted it in seas like tonight's.

Falk heard the marina before he saw it, from the almost manic sound of the halyards pinging wildly against the masts of the sailboats, a noise that at any harbor was like the pealing of tiny warning bells, telling you to stay off the water. The rental office was dark and silent. He easily broke in by punching out a pane of glass on the front door. On the mainland the office undoubtedly would have been armed with a security system. Police would have arrived within seconds. Yet, for all of Gitmo's security on the perimeter and at Camp Delta, there was little concern over petty theft and burglary, especially on this side of the base. He had heard once that when Gitmo was measured against American towns of its size, the crime rate here was by far the lowest.

Falk groped through the darkness toward the back of the shop, where Skip, the marina manager, kept the keys for powerboats hanging from a board behind the counter. Falk found it on the floor, propped against the counter just beneath the cash register.

He would have to fill the fuel tanks on the way out, a tricky proposition with the way the waves were rocking the docks. The Sea Chaser's 140-gallon tank should give him more than enough to make his destination, even if its usual rate of 1.5 nautical miles to the gallon were reduced considerably by the pounding of the storm.

What else? He looked around in the gloom of the shop. A life jacket, of course—never the first thought of a lobsterman but a necessity for Falk. He took a coil of extra line so he could tie himself a lifeline. Then he grabbed another line and searched among cleaning supplies in a broom closet for a pail to use as a sea anchor.

But as he shut the closet door the lights flicked on, and Falk looked up in astonishment. There stood Van Meter at the front door with a gun leveled at him.

"Little rough for a boat ride, ain't it?"

"Where'd you come from?"

"Did a little check of your perimeter and saw that a back screen was off. From there it was easy. I've seen wounded deer leave less of a trail than you did."

"So where are the flashing lights and the siren? The big show for the boss?"

"That comes later. Those dumbshit MPs of Fowler's don't even know you're gone."

Falk didn't know whether to be pleased or alarmed by that bit of news, but it certainly fit Van Meter's style.

"Still the Lone Ranger, huh?"

"Fewer people to fuck it up."

"Is that what happened with Lawson along, out on the raft with Ludwig?"

Van Meter momentarily betrayed himself with a wide-eyed look of astonishment. Then he broke into a grin.

"All the more reason to take care of this on my own."

Falk checked his flanks for anything usable as a weapon. Van Meter's last remark made immediate action mandatory. Would he really be stupid enough to plug a special agent? Oh, yes. And Falk had already provided plenty of evidence to suggest a provocation: an escape from house arrest and a break-in at the marina, with the key to a boat in one pocket and a GPS in the other, plus all the supplies and a plotted course. It wouldn't be hard to convince the authorities Falk had made some sudden or threatening move.

But no move came to mind that seemed likely to succeed. Throwing the bucket wouldn't do much good. A few feet to the right was a spare anchor that might have come in handy in medieval combat, but it was no match for a semiautomatic 9 mm Beretta pistol, the standard sidearm of an MP.

Van Meter stepped toward him, never lowering the gun as he moved to within about six feet—just out of reach but well within the can't-miss range of the gun. Perfect technique, in other words. Van Meter may have been a dumb cowboy, but he followed his training.

Falk was about to sling the bucket when he saw movement at the doorway. His eyes must have betrayed it, because Van Meter flinched.

In walked Bokamper.

"Well, I'll be damned," Bo said, as relaxed and cocksure as ever. "The mystic mariner, heading back to his roots?"

Falk saw the disappointment in Van Meter's face. Obviously he'd hoped to finish the job before witnesses arrived.

"Should've called me on the radio, Carl. Lucky for you I must have been making the same rounds. And lucky for all of us the MPs are half asleep back there. Fowler's a trusting soul about some things, I'll give him that. You weren't just about to do something you'd regret later, were you, Carl?"

"Nothing I'd regret, I'll guarantee that."

"Thought you'd say that. How 'bout if we de-escalate a minute and figure out what to do next?"

"What's to figure?" But Van Meter lowered the gun, which finally allowed Falk to breathe. "Your friend here was about to blow town on a stolen boat, not to mention he seems to know everything we've been up to. If you want that kind of knowledge running free, that's your funeral."

"Yours, too," Bo said.

"In that case, I've still got a job to do."

He quickly raised the gun back to firing position, and Falk was about to dive for cover when Bokamper lunged at Van Meter from behind, striking the gun hand just enough to send the shot wide, an explosion of sound that shattered a plate-glass window overlooking the bay. Wind and rain tore through the opening in a rush of noise and water. In the ensuing scrum on the floor between Bo and Van Meter the pistol sprang loose, twirling free in a metallic clatter. Falk stepped forward and picked it up, as easily as he might have retrieved a dropped pencil.

"Break it up, guys," he shouted over the wind, while the two men awakened to the new reality. Windblown rain sprayed all three of them, and the noise of the storm was everywhere. To Falk, the clanging from the mast tops sounded like applause.

"On your feet, but slowly. C'mon."

"You can't stop both of us," Van Meter said, inching forward, still spoiling for a fight.

"Yeah, but he'll shoot you first," Bo said. "Guarantee it."

"Whose side you on, asshole? I had him dead to rights!"

"At this point it's not about sides. But you wouldn't understand."

Marines, he meant. Brotherhood of the Corps. Or maybe just of friends. But Falk, like Van Meter, had a job to do.

"Inside the closet, both of you."

Bo grinned and shook his head, as if he had been victimized by a particularly clever practical joke and had decided to be a sport about it. Van Meter was another matter.

"You're gonna have to shoot me first!"

"Then hold still, 'cause I'd be happy to. Or else get in the goddamn closet."

That drained some of the heat from his defiance, and the two men climbed in.

"Now, put your radios on the floor and slide 'em over."

Van Meter tossed his, clearly aiming for the gun but missing by several feet. It convinced Falk that he should shut and lock the closet right away. The door was industrial strength, and in all likelihood so was the lock. Sometimes government extravagance had its virtues. Falk shoved a rubber wedge from the washroom beneath the door for good measure. As cramped as they were in there they would have a tough time crouching low enough to push it free or, for that matter, applying enough leverage to shove hard enough to snap the lock. They would be out of commission until Skip opened for business at nine. And with this kind of weather, maybe Skip would sleep in.

Falk walked to the front door and flipped off the lights, plunging the room back into darkness, an act that immediately calmed his nerves. The only sounds now were of the storm, moaning eerily through the shattered window. Poor Skip. The whole place would be drenched.

"Bon voyage," came a muffled shout from Bo. The best Van Meter could offer was an anguished "Fuck!" which was more satisfying than Falk cared to admit. They'd have a fine time in there. He smiled for the first time in hours.

But this had been the easy part of the night. The sea was far more cunning than Van Meter, and it would come at him with everything it had. Evasive maneuvers—every seafaring trick he'd learned as a boy—were his only hope. Flinch once and he was dead.

TEN MINUTES LATER he had filled the gas tank and was crossing the foaming wildness of the bay, which was sheltered enough for him to hold a speed of nearly twenty knots as the hull banged and slopped against the waves. Channel markers bobbed crazily, red and green lights winking. He turned on the marine radio, and all was silent on the local channel. If his departure was showing up on anyone's radar—doubtful—or if his engine had been overheard by anyone ashore—even more doubtful in this maelstrom—then no one had yet thought to sound the alarm or to try hailing the madman at the helm.

Falk's general strategy was simple enough. The storm was centered just to the southeast, meaning the wind and waves would initially charge at him out of the east as he cut across the upper arc of the pinwheel. The prevailing current also moved in that direction, for a double dose of wave strength. Rather than slam against them and risk broaching—a helpless drift to broadside that would allow the next wave to flip him—he would at first head southwest, pushed onward at an angle by a following sea. Then, as the pinwheel tumbled through, Falk would gradually adjust his course southward to keep the shifting wind and waves coming at him from behind.

It was a harrowing tango, and the first few hours would be the most dangerous. No matter what NOAA said about Clifford's weakening, the storm's upper or right side still packed its sucker punch, with winds blowing in the same direction as the cyclone's progress.

By daybreak, if he was still afloat, Falk should be well into the bottom half of the pinwheel, where wind and wave would be moving in the opposite direction of the storm's progress, softening the blow. By then he planned to be on a southward course running at an angle against the sea. It would use more fuel and slow him down, but as he left the storm behind he could increase his pace accordingly.

He braced himself as the boat cleared Windward Point, and the sea did not disappoint him, slamming home with a high whistling sound as the waves built quickly from foothills to mountains. The next half mile would be the trickiest, until he reached deeper water.

Falk had navigated plenty of storms, even a few after dark, but the surprise of this one was its warmth, its tropical fug. Muscle memory told him that weathering a storm meant a numbed face and aching limbs, perhaps even a glaze of ice on the gunwales and the footing gone to hell. This, by comparison, was a smothering stewpot in heaving darkness. But as he clung to the wheel he soon grew accustomed to the idea that, yes, you could even drown in a sauna.

The little boat took her punishment surprisingly well, or at least more nimbly than any craft that his father's circle of lobstermen had ever put to sea in. The initial blast came at him from the east, and he steered to starboard, finding the optimum angle by feel since he couldn't really see the approaching waves until they were practically atop him. He could only sense their lurch and shove beneath his feet as the hull literally rose to the challenge.

There was little to see other than his running lights or, when he had the time and the wits to check, the small ghostly rectangle of the GPS display. The only other illumination came from blowing spindrift, shreds of cotton streaking past him in the driving rain. He sometimes looked over his left shoulder at a wave rearing up on his stern, and he would glimpse the white streaks of foam down its side, like a massive striped whale breaching, giving him the eye.

Yet at moments he almost felt like laughing. There was a deranged glee to it once he found his rhythm, as with the Nantucket sleigh ride of the New England whaler, dragged to glory or doom on the tethers of impaled harpoons. He remembered the old terror and thrill—one never came without the other—of beating homeward to Stonington before one particular squall. All their barrels had been filled to the brim with clicking, banded bugs hauled all day from the lobster pots. His hands had smelled of bait, with fish oil smeared across his face as he stood awestruck, watching the waves build walls around their retreat.

But this sense of rhythm could be dangerous, a sinister lullaby, because inevitably there were surprises to jar you awake.

One came upon him toward the end of the first hour, just as the storm seemed to be weakening. There was a flash of white over his shoulder. A bolt of spindrift raced past as if pursued by something terrible. Then his stomach dropped as the boat skidded down the side of a sudden trough, which told him that something huge was rearing up from behind. Falk turned his head to see the wave towering like a bluff, a thirty-footer that came upon him from a crazy angle so suddenly that he barely had time to turn the wheel, desperate to move the hull to forty-five degrees. The stern lifted with a sucking sensation, as if the wave's force had momentarily leached all rain and noise from the air. It was a wonder he wasn't already swamped, that the stern wasn't submerged, but that was only the first hurdle to be cleared. Half a second later the boat perched high on a precipice. It was the sensation of reaching the top of an incline on a roller coaster, that point where you stare into the nothingness below while the breath catches in your throat before the plunge. He heard the rushing of the sea, and then his stomach soared as the hull tore downward across the face of the wave, surfing now, far too fast, and the last thing he wanted to do. The slide seemed to last forever, the boat with a mind of its own in a dive toward the seabed. He watched the prow, certain that it would pierce the foaming blackness and dig in, pitch-poling the boat forward into a flip upside down. Then he would sink, the lifeline dragging him toward the bottom until he could free the knot.

But the wave overreached, water rushing across the transom from behind. That provided just enough counterweight to lift the bow ever so slightly, so that in the nick of time it planed rather than spiked. The backwash tore in across the deck and took Falk's feet from beneath him, one last bit of deadly mischief. He fell hard on his ass but managed to keep his left hand on the bottom of the wheel, or else he would have been washed to the limit of his tether in the swamping. But his frantic grip swerved the wheel, turning the boat violently to port, and when he stood and tried to correct course the engine whined in protest, the prop having momentarily risen above the waterline. The boat was like a climber who had lost his grip, and the next wave was approaching to topple him.

Then there was a coughing sound, a smoky gargle as the prop bit into the sea. The hull turned to starboard, finding the correct angle just as the next roller coursed beneath her. He held on, steadied himself, and thanked his luck.

There were two more rogue waves in those first hours, but none quite as menacing as the first, and by the time a faint peep of grayness began to show itself in the east, Falk felt as if the worst of the journey was behind him. He checked his position on the GPS and determined that he had crossed the midsection of the pinwheel. From here on out conditions would only improve. Maybe it was the added comfort of finally seeing light, but he would have also sworn that the waves were already abating. Just as forecast, Clifford was weakening with the dawn, and moving on, up the Cuban coastline.

When Falk checked the wind gauge a half hour later, the reading was eighteen knots, with gusts to thirty. Still quite a blow, but manageable. As the sky brightened, his certainty grew. He was going to make it.

The challenge then was maintaining his concentration against the onslaught of fatigue. Even the dim light of dawn made his eyes ache. Hours of blinking against salt spray had made the stinging almost unbearable. What he wanted more than anything was to curl up on the deck and sleep, while the warm film of water sloshed back and forth, rocking the boat like a cradle.

He wondered what was happening back at Gitmo, now some fifty miles in his wake as the gull flies, although his arcing course had crossed perhaps sixty-five miles of open water. Even if Fowler came calling for him at around eight—assuming that the MPs outside had never checked on him—he would probably be okay. And if Fowler waited until later, then his absence wouldn't be discovered until Skip arrived at the marina, around nine. He could only guess what kind of story Bo and Van Meter would concoct. Both, in their way, would put themselves in untenable positions by telling all. And neither was likely to agree with the other's preferred cover story.

In any event, by nine the worst of the storm would have moved well past Guantánamo. The air search team would rule the skies. Perhaps the helicopter crew would get lucky and spot him, although he doubted it. Looking for a single small boat was a difficult business. He'd seen searches of far smaller patches of ocean drag on for days.

More worrisome was that there were only a limited number of anchorages at his eventual destination. The Navy would alert port authorities and harbormasters in western Haiti and eastern Jamaica to be on the lookout for a stolen piece of U.S. military hardware, even if it was a pleasure craft. While Haiti might not offer the most efficient assistance, the authorities would be ill-equipped to restrain any direct U.S. search efforts.

Those circumstances had weighed heavily in Falk's choice of landfall. He had picked Navassa Island, an uninhabited two-square-mile lozenge with steep bluffs and hardscrabble soil, about a hundred miles due south of Guantánamo and roughly a third of the way between Haiti and Jamaica.

During his Marine days a Coast Guard ensign had told him about the island, because the Coast Guard had then maintained a lighthouse there. The place had a strange history. It was rich in guano—the bird shit that through centuries of accumulation formed much of the island's landmass. Guano was a prized fertilizer, so the United States had claimed the island just before the Civil War and turned over the mining to a U.S. phosphate company. Slavish working conditions led to a bloody revolt, but it was the declining market for guano that finally shut the place down at the turn of the century. Seven years ago the Coast Guard had also closed the lighthouse. Nowadays the only official American visitors were biological survey teams from the Department of the Interior. The island's more common visitors were Haitian fishermen, who often camped there overnight, especially when they needed to ride out an approaching storm such as Clifford. At least, that's what the Coast Guard ensign had told him long ago. He hoped it was still true.

Only the GPS made it possible to find his way. Otherwise, the island was so small that he almost certainly would have passed wide of the mark. But with the rain gone and his speed up to twenty knots on a choppy but navigable sea, he now saw Navassa Island dead ahead, an emerging forehead of gray bluffs sprouting a green hairline of scrub.

Anchorage was easier than he'd expected, via a scantily sheltered cove at Lulu Bay on the southwest side of the island. The better news was that a single battered fishing boat also lay at anchor. The engine looked suspect, and the red and white paint job had seen better days, but if she had survived last night he supposed she could last a few hours more.

Getting ashore was trickier. He had to swim for it, thrashing twenty yards across a sea that was still coursing with deep swells. He grabbed at an iron ladder suspended sixty feet down the side of the bluff, and was shocked at the weakness of his arms and legs as he clambered onto a slick lower rung. An incoming swell pressed his chest against the metal. He held on tightly as the wave receded, his soaked clothing pulling like an anchor. It was all he could do to keep from tumbling back into the emerald sea. Then he caught his breath long enough to begin the long, slow climb. Halfway up the sun broke through the fleeing clouds, warm against his back. Finally he reached the top and heaved himself onto a platform of rough concrete, exhausted. From there he could scale an old concrete stairway the rest of the way to the top of the bluff. But for the moment he was too tired, and he quickly fell sound asleep.

He awakened in what seemed like seconds, startled by a shadow across his face and the gritty scrape of sandals on concrete. It was an opportune moment, he supposed, because he had been dreaming of helicopters arriving in droves to drop ladders from the sky, each with a dangling Van Meter at the bottom. He opened his eyes onto the dark leathery face of a wiry man in tattered shorts. The man, shading his brow with a hand, stared intently.

Falk checked his watch. He had been asleep for only an hour. His thirst was overpowering, and a thick knot of bile in his stomach made him want to retch. But first things first.

"Speak English?" Falk offered.

The man shook his head and replied in a patois Falk couldn't understand. The language was probably Haitian Creole, but a little French might do the trick. He hoped so, because that was all he had.

It seemed to work, because within minutes they had arranged the necessary transaction. The old fisherman, whose name was Jean, was now the proud owner of a twenty-four-foot Sea Chaser, formerly belonging to the Morale, Welfare and Recreation division of the U.S. Navy. Falk was the new skipper of the battered white fishing boat.

For both men, it was the deal of a lifetime.

CHAPTER THIRTY

Miami Beach

GONZALO HAD BEEN WATCHING his back closely in the five days since his meeting with Falk. He wasn't sure what he dreaded more: federal agents arriving on his doorstep or henchmen dispatched by Havana.

Either visitation seemed possible following his indiscreet words on the boat. But after two decades of operating largely on his own, he had sensed the need for an ally as he and Falk bobbed in the waves of Biscayne Bay. Odder still, he had sensed the same need in Falk, an amateur on this field of play if there ever was one, yet a kindred spirit.

Or so Gonzalo hoped. How else to explain why he had taken the additional risk of asking their old middleman, Harry, to deliver an updated passport, if only because he believed that Falk, like him, might soon need more flexibility. It was the sort of hunch that either paid off handsomely or mired you deep in trouble, and he had been having second thoughts ever since. Maybe he had finally succumbed to the recklessness that afflicted the entire Directorate.

He was also anxious over the possibility of losing his posting. Lucinda had a lot to do with that. Being recalled now would be a personal disaster. He would be lost and lonely, rattling around Havana like an exile.

The good news was that so far there was no cause for alarm. There had been no unexpected visitors to the apartment, no unsolicited painting crews or telephone repairmen. His core of regulars on South Beach had remained steadfast and friendly, the same creatures of habit as always. If any of them had been approached by strangers asking about Gonzalo, they would have told him. Yes, even the old GI.

What troubled him most was the eerie radio silence from Havana. Not a single message had come across the shortwave since he had filed the report of his rendezvous with Falk.

"Message conveyed to Peregrine" was all he had said, and all they had wanted.

He had then disbanded his team of operatives, paying dollars for a job well done and telling them their services would never again be necessary. You used up a lot of personnel that way, but the reward was almost always an airtight job.

The performance of the Americans that afternoon hadn't impressed him—a skeleton crew, he concluded, and not very experienced. It was further confirmation that he was dealing with some unofficial structure, an off-the-books outfit without the polish or professionalism of his usual adversaries. Experience had taught him that in America a newcomer flying by the seat of his pants usually ended up either testifying to a congressional committee or sowing the seeds for spectacular mischief. The ones who didn't go to jail either ran for office or got a show on talk radio.

Whatever the case, Gonzalo was jumpy enough to have begun monitoring an emergency mailbox he had set up years ago, in case his boss ever needed to reach him without going through the usual channels at the Directorate. He had changed the location every six months, but up to now it had never been used. Even so, he checked it every morning, pedaling there on his bicycle before his first cup of coffee. On the way back he bought a bagel with cream cheese and a double espresso, then took his usual walk on the beach.

The mail drop's current location was behind a loosened brick along the back wall of a commercial parking lot bordering Flamingo Park, a shaded sanctuary of green with ball fields and tennis courts. Gonzalo had been dismayed to see a construction notice go up recently at the parking lot, signaling the imminent arrival of yet another condo complex. Soon he would have to scout out a new location.

Last night, at least, had offered a welcome respite from such worries. He met Lucinda for dinner at 10 p.m., the sort of late hour she preferred for its Continental feel, as if she were back in her hometown of Caracas, or abroad in Spain. The only blemish on an otherwise spotless evening was when she insisted on talking again about moving.

"Why not Arizona?" she said, having given up on Manhattan and L.A. "There are still plenty of people who speak Spanish, and it's nice and warm. Okay, it's in the desert, but I can handle the desert as long as you're standing next to the cactus."

Gonzalo, too restless to argue, only shrugged in response, which Lucinda misread as a sign of progress.

"Is it the money you're worried about?" she said, trying to coax him further. "Because you know that I'd be happy to—"

"Please, Lucinda. Do we have to go through all this again?"

He immediately regretted his abruptness, especially when she pushed aside her half-finished dessert and muttered, eyes downcast, "No, I don't suppose we do. Maybe I should never bring it up again."

The signal for a full mailbox was a red thumbtack poked into a palm tree along the sidewalk in the park, a block from the mailbox itself. For four straight mornings now Gonzalo had pedaled past the tree and, seeing nothing, continued on to the bagel shop.

This morning he saw with excitement that there seemed to be a red dot on the smooth gray bark, about six feet up. Drawing closer, he was certain. He dismounted long enough for a quick glance around before he stepped across the grass and pulled out the tack, then tossed it down a storm grate. He pedaled harder now, trying to keep a lid on his anxiety.

No attendant was yet on duty at the parking lot. It was one of those places where you took a ticket on the way in, then paid at a small booth at the gate. Gonzalo scooted to the back left corner, stepped across the low wall, and then found the brick by counting from the left and the bottom. He pried it free, and beneath it was a folded scrap of paper, which he stuffed in his pocket. He replaced the brick, glanced around once more, then pedaled away for his breakfast as beads of sweat trickled down his chest.

He didn't read the message until he had picked up his bagel and a copy of *Diario Las Américas*, and was seated at the usual park bench at Collins and Twenty-first. There he saw the graffiti once again—"Castro Fall—You Go Home"—like a taunt. Gonzalo looked furtively around and unfolded the paper.

Peregrine departs nest by sea. Destination unknown. Eagles in pursuit.

Was he reading this correctly? Falk had gone AWOL from Guantánamo? Gonzalo had never heard of such a thing. And on a boat, no less. He seemed to remember a mention of some tropical storm down there, and he flipped hastily to *Diario*'s weather page. The paper, exhibiting its usual homesick obsession with everything Cuban, had a story saying that Tropical Storm Clifford had fizzled out, dissipating wetly in the seas north of Jamaica as it crossed into southeastern Cuba.

Fleeing a naval base in that fashion was the sort of rash, bold stroke that only an amateur would attempt, presumably an amateur who had decided to break ranks with the professionals. The news seemed to confirm his instincts about the man. He wondered if Harry had yet delivered the British passport.

The very presence of this message was a sort of implicit warning, a signal that both his boss and he were temporarily operating in a danger zone, beyond the usual bounds of what the Directorate considered proper. Such behavior in Cuba earned neither a run for office nor a radio talk show. The prize was a firing squad.

Gonzalo tried to work out the timing. A message arriving overnight by this channel would be at least twelve hours old, meaning that Harry—the only plausible source of the tip—would have heard the news yesterday and then phoned it to Havana last night from home. That meant Falk must have taken off sometime between Tuesday evening and midday yesterday. If "the eagles," meaning the U.S. military, were truly in pursuit, then maybe he had already been caught. If not, he might be anywhere by now. As long as he hadn't drowned first.

Not just any FBI man could have piloted a boat through that kind of mess. But Gonzalo, with his usual thoroughness, had never relied on secondary sources when it came to selecting and running operatives. Long ago he had learned much more about Falk than the man had probably ever told his superiors at the Bureau. It was hard to say for sure what had made Gonzalo dig so deeply, but when you were in the business of manufacturing false identities, you became pretty good at spotting them, and something about Falk had set off his alarm. So he had researched the man's background much more doggedly than, say, a Marine Corps recruiter in Bangor ever would have. It was one reason Gonzalo had chosen a boat for their meeting, as if to convey the message "See, I know all about your secrets, and the places where you are comfortable."

In any event, the news meant Gonzalo didn't have time for his usual morning stroll. There was urgent business to attend to. He climbed back on his bicycle and pedaled through the park, crossing Collins to Washington Avenue and heading for home.

He approached his apartment as he always did when bicycling—not from the street out front but by looping around back and entering the parking lot from the rear, threading between a Dumpster and a large bush of sea grapes, where the bike rack was.

He locked the bike and headed for the stairwell. Through the breezeway he spotted an unfamiliar car at the curb out front, a black Lexus in a No Parking zone. No one except deliverymen ever dared to stay there more than a few minutes. His antennae twitched.

He crept slowly up the stairs in a half crouch. When he reached the second floor he poked his head just far enough around the corner to look at his doorway. All quiet, so he crept closer. The door was shut, the window blinds still drawn. If anyone was inside they'd be watching for his approach from the bedroom or living room, keeping an eye on the street and the small lawn in front of the building.

He placed an ear to the door. Nothing. His heart began to calm. The Lexus probably belonged to a visitor at some other apartment. He was overreacting. He was just about to reach for his keys when he heard a mutter—a few words only, unintelligible, and the sound of a shoe sliding on a gritty floor. His poor housekeeping suddenly seemed like a boon to his well-being. Then more words were spoken, a low conversation in Spanish, barely loud enough for him to pick up a few words. At least two men were in his apartment.

He backed away from the door and eased around the corner, then crept down the stairs as silently as possible. They should have spotted him coming, of course. Should have posted a lookout for the rear as well as the front. But they were sloppy, the way things had been going for years.

So he got back on his bike and, deciding that they probably still weren't looking in this direction, he pushed between the Dumpster and the sea grapes, making the big waxy leaves rattle like plastic. He headed for the alley that connected to a side street.

Where to now? Not Lucinda's. They might be there as well. He should warn her. It was almost time for her to leave for work. What he really needed was a safe house, but none was safe enough for these circumstances. Should he call on one of his recruits? Perhaps even they couldn't be trusted now.

Then he thought of his friends down on the beach, his loose corps of regulars. It was time to take that next step, to dig a bit deeper into their lives, or to let them a bit deeper into his. But which of them should he ask for help?

Not the GI, Ed Harbin. He would ask too many questions. The Germans, Karl and Brigitte, would be welcoming and want to do the right thing, but they would also want neatness, order, everything in its place, which would require explanations, a logic he couldn't offer.

The Lespinasses, on the other hand, were from Haiti. They, better than anyone, would understand the importance of not asking questions at the wrong time. And it was a Thursday, so they should be there. Gonzalo turned his bike south.

Everyone was on the beach, just as if they'd planned it in advance. A little send-off for a friend they didn't even know was leaving. Harbin was in the surf, stroking steadily for the buoy, his bronze back glistening in the sunlight, hard as a tortoiseshell. The Stolzes sat beneath their striped umbrella, sun hats flopping in the breeze around their pale Nordic skin. And there were the Lespinasses, seated by their cooler, the bounty of a tropical feast spread before them on a tattered white sheet.

Their four-year-old daughter, the youngest of their three children, got up and ran toward the turquoise surf.

"Hello, Gonzalo," Charles called brightly. Karl and Brigitte waved.

It was rude to rush things, but conditions were urgent.

"I need your help this morning," he said in a low voice, looking Charles in the eye. "A ride somewhere, as soon as possible. Two places, in fact, and one is in Fort Lauderdale. I can pay for the gasoline. Jeanette and the kids can stay here."

Charles didn't hesitate.

"We will all go," he said firmly, already gathering a pineapple and some oranges from the sheet. "Whatever you need. And you will pay no money. You are a friend."

And so the wall was breached, just that easily. The children protested a bit or they wouldn't have been children. Two hours of sitting on hot vinyl seats with the itch of sand and salt on your backside was asking a lot. They were sullen for most of the ride. But Jeanette and

Charles moved with a sense of mission, having come from a place where one never questioned the need for urgency once someone had whispered a cry for help.

The first stop was at a bank up in Aventura, a high-rent district where tellers and managers were accustomed to asking no questions, even if they weren't accustomed to having their customers pull into the parking lot in a rusting old Chevette with all its windows rolled down and three dark children crushed together with their mother on the backseat.

The transaction went smoothly. Gonzalo showed his ID, presented a small key that he always kept on his chain, and then was escorted into a paneled office, where an assistant manager brought him a safe-deposit box, then left him alone. Inside were a New York State driver's license with Gonzalo's photo and several charge cards. All carried a name that Gonzalo's employers, even his boss, had never heard of. There was also an envelope with ten thousand dollars in cash, his entire savings from years of work as a security guard and deskman. Wasn't this, after all, the American way? Building that nest egg for the future?

On his way out of the bank Gonzalo spotted a phone booth and decided to make a quick call. No telling when he might next see one that still took coins.

"Lucinda?"

"What a nice treat to have a midmorning call from my lover." Then, as if the urgency of his tone had just registered, "Is something wrong?"

"I have to go out of town for a few days. For work, of course."

"Oh." The enthusiasm gone. "Of course." Some remark about "the crazies" would doubtless follow unless he acted promptly.

"Lucinda, there may be some people who will be asking about me in the next day or two. They'll be looking for me, saying they're my friends. You're to tell them nothing, but don't act alarmed."

"Gonzalo, what is it? What's happened?"

"Please. Trust me. It will be over in a few days. Then we can talk again about some of your ideas about moving, okay? I've been giving them some serious thought."

"Yes?" He could tell she couldn't decide whether to be elated or alarmed.

"Yes. This Saturday maybe?"

"Of course. My apartment?"

"Well, it may be a little more complicated. You may need to pack a bag. But we'll discuss it later."

"Okay." Her tone went flat, dumbfounded. "Gonzalo? You're not really one of the crazies, are you." A statement more than a question.

"No."

"Maybe I always knew that."

"It's fine. Just keep it to yourself."

"I will. Be careful."

"Of course."

Traffic was heavy as always on I-95, but in another forty-five minutes they were pulling to the curb of the departures lane at Fort Lauderdale's international airport. Before hopping out of the Chevette, Gonzalo pressed five new twenties into Charles's hand, and then spoke over the man's protests.

"Please. It is only fair. For all I know, you've saved my life. And if anyone asks about me, say nothing. Even if it's Ed Harbin, or Karl and Brigitte."

Charles nodded, his face resolute. Jeanette did the same. Everyone said good-bye, but it was the parting words of Joseph, their eight-year-old, that snagged Gonzalo as he turned on the sidewalk to go.

"Will we see you again, Mr. Rubiero?" he piped sweetly, his little round face poking from the rear window.

"I don't know, Joseph. I really don't know."

Then he was off to tend to his business.

CHAPTER THIRTY-ONE

FALK SUPPOSED HE HAD known all along where his journey would end, no matter how roundabout the course. But it wasn't until he was on the phone that night with an airline reservation clerk that he acknowledged his choice by finally stating it aloud.

He called from a cheap hotel on the outskirts of Kingston, where he sat exhausted on the edge of a swayback mattress, clinging to consciousness after a hot scrub in a closet-sized shower. He had dined at a nearby bar on conch fritters and two bottles of Red Stripe.

The last leg across the water from Navassa Island covered eighty miles. He and the old fisherman had collected their gear from each other's new boats. Then Falk napped a few hours in the sun while the sea continued to calm. Around 1 p.m., having gulped down nearly a gallon of water and devoured both peanut butter sandwiches, he deemed himself fit for another long spell at the helm.

Despite a scouring by the tropical rain, the old boat stank of dead fish and machine oil, but it handled better than expected. The engine was another matter. His speed topped out at fifteen knots, meaning he didn't reach Jamaica's Port Antonio until six thirty that evening. He could have made it to Haiti in a third of the time, but entering the United States via a Haitian airport, especially under a British passport, would have been far trickier, not to mention the hazards of dealing with Haitian authorities.

Not once during the crossing did he hear a helicopter. The silence told him that they'd written him off for dead, were looking in all the wrong places, or had decided to hush things up. The rumors on the base would have been rampant, and mounting a noisy search-and-rescue operation would only have spread the word elsewhere more quickly. Better to keep it discreet. They must be counting on him to turn up at some border crossing under his own name. Or, who knew, maybe they thought he had sailed a little ways down the coast to give himself up to the Cubans—the wily old traitor finally showing his true colors. He supposed Fowler might believe that, once he heard the backstory. Bo would know better. Pam, too, he hoped.

Hardly anyone gave him a second look on the docks at Port Antonio—another encouraging sign—so he slung his duffel on his back and hailed a wheezing cab for the twisting, hour-long ride to Kingston, skirting the foot of the Blue Mountains.

And that was where he sat now, tethered to the phone in the stale-smelling room as the sunset bronzed the window. He reserved a seat on a 6:45 a.m. American Airlines flight to Boston, via Miami, in the name of Ned Morris of Manchester, U.K. He told the clerk he would pay at the counter in cash. On such short notice the costs were exorbitant. At this rate he would be out of money by Saturday.

He then called Hertz to reserve a car in Boston, only to hang up after the first ring when he remembered that Ned Morris didn't have a driver's license. Shit. He would either have to hop a smaller plane up to Bangor, then thumb the rest of the way—another few hundred dollars tossed into the wind—or take a bus from Boston, which sounded interminable, especially to someone whose eyelids were nearly drooping to the floor.

Tomorrow, he told himself, sinking back onto the bed with a creak of rusty springs. Tomorrow he would sort things out. Then he drifted into deep sleep, still feeling the motion of the waves in his weary muscles, as if bracing for a big roller to chase him down in the dark.

Next morning, bleary-eyed, and with barely enough time for a cup of coffee, he rushed to the airport to make his early flight. He didn't bother with a British accent—too tired—and he slept through the short layover in Miami. It didn't occur to him until the leg to Boston was under way that his face might now be getting some airtime, even though there had been nothing about Guantánamo on that morning's news broadcasts. So, he spent the rest of the flight huddled behind an in-flight magazine, lest anyone recognize him.

He was nervous in the passport line at Logan, but breezed through with hardly a pause. It was the Jamaicans who were getting all the grief, nodding repeatedly as they answered question after question. The customs agents smiled and nodded as Falk strolled past with a wave, trusty duffel stained with salt water. Thank goodness they weren't yet fingerprinting incoming Brits. Then he burst through the doors and past the babbling line of welcomers and limo drivers with their hand-lettered signs.

He'd made it. He was officially in the country. But there were still miles to go before he slept, and after buying a ticket on a 5:17 Delta flight to Bangor he rushed to a newsstand for copies of the *Globe*, the *New York Times*, and *USA Today*. A quick scan didn't turn up a single dispatch from Guantánamo. Not a word. The same was true of the news channels airing loudly in the concourse bar. Perhaps General Trabert was still coming up with a cover story. In Gitmo, it seemed, Washington had finally achieved its ideal in media management. No news was emerging without consent, or at least not without a delay of weeks, or even months. Falk was not naive enough to feel smug or secure about this, even if for the moment it was working to his advantage.

By the time the plane landed at Bangor, shortly after 6 p.m., he had napped and snacked enough to regain his energy, and he set out in excitement for the final sixty miles. It took only a few minutes to flag down the first ride, which carried him to a turnoff just past Bucksport. Waving good-bye as the car disappeared around a bend, Falk experienced a deep sense of comfort in the silence of the narrow roadway. The evening sky tinted the scene a glowing pink. Spruce and poplar leaned in from both shoulders of the road, and the rough pavement was buckled and bowed. The air smelled of resin, grass, sunshine, and the slightest hint of brine.

The second ride got him to South Penobscot. The driver of the third vehicle, a refrigerated truck that had just delivered a load of lobsters, said he was going all the way to Stonington. And just like that, before he had really had time to prepare, Falk was riding home, bouncing across the humpbacks of Highway 15 as they passed familiar inlets and the homes of long-ago friends

Just before passing the town of Deer Isle they drove by the house where he had spent his earliest years. The clapboard sides were spruced up, the whitewash replaced by robin's-egg blue. The roof was patched, the flower bed weeded. Across the road, the McCallum place had gone beyond gentrification and become an art gallery. But next door he saw Mr. Simmons—he must be in his eighties—out riding his mower just as he always had, bobbing along in an oily cloud of exhaust while he navigated between the same five birdbaths that had stood in his yard forever. In one of Falk's earliest memories he was setting paper ships afloat on their placid waters.

The sights multiplied, and the trickle of memory became a deluge. There was the field that led to the trailhead for Lily Pond, his old swimming hole. The town of Deer Isle flashed by, and he glimpsed the small library where he'd spent so many hours. It would be closed for the day by now, yet he could imagine peering in through a windowpane at its silent shelves, the oaken table, a ticking clock on the wall. He saw tourists strolling past antiques shops, but they might as well have been ghosts haunting this museum of his childhood. Yes, he would be able to hide here well enough, because there were a thousand nooks and crannies where he had already learned to do so.

When they reached Stonington, literally at the end of the highway, he found a room at a small B&B with a French name that was much fancier than the plain but immaculate decor. It was a gray clapboard house on a leafy rise overlooking Greenhead Cove, the small inlet where his dad and all their friends had moored their lobster boats during the season. The only room available was a single by the kitchen, no view, with a bath down the hall.

"Two-night minimum, breakfast at eight," said the innkeeper, who smiled but gave him the once-over. She wasn't familiar to him, or he to her, which was just as well. He was painfully aware of needing a shave and a shower, and his duffel suddenly seemed suspiciously insufficient for a tourist on the move.

"We don't take plastic," she added.

Fine with him.

As soon as he had paid up, he strolled outside to gaze upon the calm waters of the cove, gilded by the sunset. He searched in vain for the familiar white hull and its dark blue trim among the dozens of boats bobbing on an incoming wake. As a boy he had been able to swim in this chilliness at least two months out of every summer, as sleek as a young seal. After his first Marine year at Gitmo, Falk had visited the Massachusetts shore—as close to home as he had ever dared to venture until now. He had discovered then that he could no longer stand the icy temperatures of the North Atlantic for more than a few seconds. At the time he had decided it was a good thing, a sign that he was acclimating to other places. Now he wasn't so sure.

It was well past closing time at the docks of the Stonington Lobster Co-op, where some old-timer might know what had become of his father, so he instead walked over to the town's tiny main drag. A bike-rental kiosk was just about to close, so Falk signed one out for the next twenty-four hours under the name of Ned Morris. This way he could make his first stop, a few miles away on Airport Road.

He pedaled hard to get there while there was still enough light. The exercise felt good in his thighs and calves as he inhaled lungfuls of the clean and bracing air. But when he saw the trailer his spirits fell. It was empty and sagging, every window cracked or missing. The yard was overgrown with thistle and tall grass, and the old lobster boat was up on blocks. Weeds sprouted like a green geyser from the staved-in hull. Nothing was left of the paint job but a few peeling strips. The rest of the wood had bleached gray. It would have taken years of inattention to reach this state.

Only then did Falk admit to himself that he had been holding out hope of finding his father here. He had built a mental image of a quiet old man, demons tamed, who would be washing the dinner dishes while a Red Sox game played on a radio by an open window.

Falk could have forced open the trailer door easily enough, but the place was so obviously abandoned that he didn't care to move closer. He just stared from the pavement as the light faded, listening to the tree frogs tuning up for the night. Then he pedaled back to his B&B and strolled across town to a local restaurant, the Fisherman's Friend, where he decided to splurge on a lobster. He needed an extravagant taste of home to dispel the ghosts of the trailer, which seemed to have followed him back into town.

In a booth across the room he thought he recognized an old classmate, although she was about thirty pounds heavier and had three children, the youngest of whom kept running away from the table. She glanced once at Falk with a quizzical look, a hint of recognition, and he overcame his jitters long enough to nod and smile. But she was distracted by the boy, who was now behind the cash register, helping himself to a fistful of mints.

"Jeffrey! Get back over here. Now!" Jeffrey received a brisk pop across the seat of his pants. Then he shot back across the room toward the coatrack by the door.

After dinner Falk walked the town streets and passed a busy ice cream shop, but all the customers seemed to be from out of town.

Maybe he would feel more welcome here in the morning, when the community of fishermen and others who made their living from the sea were back on the job.

As his dinner settled, exhaustion crept in. In preparing for bed he threw open the window of his room to a briny chill that he had not felt on a summer night for what seemed like a lifetime. As he pulled up the sheets and listened to the night bugs and the lapping of the water, he was overcome by a strong sense of his father's presence, as if he could hear the man's breathing in the next room.

Next morning, after a huge breakfast and three cups of strong coffee, he set out for the docks of the co-op. A bell jangled as he opened the door to the office, and an older man looked up from the counter. It was Bob Holman, who recognized Falk right away.

"Revere? Revere Falk?"

"Howdy, Mr. Holman."

"Good Lord."

The old man stepped from behind the counter and gave Falk an awkward slap on the back. It felt good to be recognized, even if it imperiled his safety. For now, at least, he remained confident that he was isolated enough to still be invisible to those who might do him harm.

"Your dad must be thrilled you're home."

So he was alive. Falk's heart beat faster, and his face flushed.

"Just got in, actually. Hadn't even had time to see him."

"Then I guess you've heard the news."

"The news?"

Holman looked at the floor, shuffling his feet back toward the counter.

"It's nothing much, really, though I'd expect he'll be wanting to tell you 'bout it."

"Sure. Soon as I get over there." Wherever *there* was. He hoped Mr. Holman would mention a location without him having to ask.

"You been treating yourself okay? Living abroad, your father says. Doing work for the government?"

It was a little too close for comfort.

"He's been telling you about all that, has he?"

"Oh, yeah. Mentions all your letters from Europe. Diplomacy or something?"

"Yeah. Something like that."

Mr. Holman laughed, loosening up again.

"You sound just like him. Same way he always describes it, so maybe we'll think there's more to it. More secretive kind of work. But don't worry. I won't ask anything more."

"Right. Well, you know how parents are. Especially my dad."

"Says you still aren't married, though. Just haven't found the right girl."

Falk gulped. It was too uncanny, the man's intuitive knowledge. They'd been apart for two decades, and all that time his father had been weaving a history out of nothing, yet had nearly divined the complete picture. Like one of those forensic sculptors who could reconstruct an entire face from a few fragments of a skull. As a boy, Falk had always assumed that the old man had tuned out his family completely, thinking only of himself and his thirst. Yet he must have been paying some attention. It was instead the son who had withdrawn completely from the field.

"I stopped by the old trailer," Falk said.

Mr. Holman looked puzzled a moment, and then the light of recognition dawned.

"Your dad's old place, you mean. I'd forgotten you lived there, too, it's been so long. Had to give it up when he moved out to the nursing home, of course. But it's better for him there. Gets all his meals. Hell, I expect half his fishing buddies must be there by now. Give me a few more years and who knows?" Then he laughed a little too loud. "But he'll tell you all about it, I expect."

"Right. I'm sure of it."

There was only one nursing home on the island, and it was less than half a mile from their old house, just off the highway. The bell jingled as another person came in through the door, a tourist asking when the day's catch would be available for sale. Falk seized the opportunity to begin his retreat.

"See you later, Mr. Holman."

"Come back and see us, Revere."

But he realized he had no way to get there unless he wanted to ride seven miles on the bike. So he waited awkwardly by the door while Mr. Holman told the tourist to come back later, when the boats were unloading at the dockside scales.

"By the way, Mr. Holman, hate to ask a favor of you, but my rental car's acting up this morning, and I had to catch a ride into town. Do you think maybe I could . . . ?"

"Absolutely, son. Take my truck. She's right outside."

He tossed Falk the keys.

"Don't need her 'til four."

And by the way he said it, Falk wondered if Mr. Holman had ever believed a word of the tall tales about the glamorous overseas career of Revere Falk.

He climbed in and turned the key, and of course the sound of the engine was like the roar of a small factory, the muffler shot to hell by salt air and hard winters. No wonder everyone here over the age of fifty shouted, after a lifetime of talking over this kind of noise. The throb of the engine worked its way up his spine like Morse code, tapping out a message from all those predawn mornings of his past, chill hours when he had blown on his hands until the engine warmed during their ride down to the harbor.

Falk pulled out of the lot and headed back into town, then turned north on Highway 15. So this was it, he supposed, his stomach feeling light and fluttery, the blood rushing to his fingertips. A meeting for the ages. But what in the hell would he say?

He accelerated, engine grumbling. As he headed north he was so raptly attuned to the unfolding sights that he didn't even notice the dark blue Ford that tucked in behind him just as he was leaving the town.

The Ford soon dropped back, keeping a healthy distance but never quite losing touch.

CHAPTER THIRTY-TWO

JUST KNOWING THAT the old man was alive lightened Falk's burden, if only by taking his mind off Gitmo.

Part of him had always figured that by the time he worked up the nerve to return he would find only a headstone. Instead, his father was at this very moment only a few miles up Highway 15, perhaps cackling among old friends in a game room, checking the cards in his hand while awaiting the next deal. Sober, no less.

It was the unspoken implications of Bob Holman's news that were troubling, as if he had been tiptoeing around the edge of something catastrophic. Falk supposed it was possible his father was hooked up to tubes and monitors, with a glazed stare that would comprehend nothing, his son long forgotten.

He pulled into the parking lot beneath a canopy of young trees. The Blue Cove Nursing Home was a one-story brick building with only thirty beds, nonprofit and nothing fancy. Falk presumed that some sort of government money was paying the tab.

He approached a receptionist behind a long counter. At first glance the young woman reminded him of his sister, whom he had last seen when he was eleven and she was eighteen. He gave his father's name, and the woman typed it into a computer while eyeing a blinking screen. When she looked back up, the resemblance was gone and she seemed like any other young woman with dark hair and brown eyes.

"Your name?"

A twinge of doubt. What if the networks started broadcasting his name in this afternoon's newscasts?

"Revere Falk. I'm his son."

"Oh." She brightened. "I wasn't aware he had any . . . well, *anyone*."

So his dad hadn't continued weaving his little fictions here, apparently. Falk wondered if there would be any photos in the room. She pointed him down a hallway to the right.

"If he's not awake, just ask a nurse to help. Or you can always just wait in the room."

"Thanks."

The hall smelled like medicine and half-finished breakfasts, unwashed bedpans and antiseptic cleaners. A wheezing cough came from one doorway, a moan from another. A television seemed to be turned to top volume in every room. The air was stuffy here, as if the heat was on. All these old bones, so easily chilled. By the time he found the room he was back to the precipice of dread.

The door was ajar, so he knocked lightly, and heard sheets stir. An old voice croaked.

"Yes?"

Falk ducked inside and saw a face, vaguely familiar but winnowed to its essentials, skin translucent. He recognized the eyes first—china blue and a little watery—and as he moved closer they bloomed with recognition. Color rose in the old man's cheeks, and the difference was dramatic, as if someone had just boosted his energy by fifty thousand watts.

"Dad?"

The man actually smiled, and a tear formed at the corner of each eye. Or was his father just trying to clear the filmy haze from his field of vision?

"Son? Revere?"

There was a catch in Falk's throat as he spoke again.

"Yeah, Dad. It's me."

He crossed the linoleum floor on rubber legs, approaching the aluminum rails of the bed. A breathing tube led to the man's nostrils, a second tube dripped clear liquid into his right arm from a suspended bag, and a third tube snaked from beneath the sheets into a plastic bag that was half filled with yellow fluid.

"Son," his father said, the voice more familiar now. "You must have heard, then."

"Haven't heard anything, actually. Just decided it was time. Past time, really."

"Well, I'll be damned, then. I'll be damned." That weak smile again. His father raised a bony white hand and tried to reach across to him, but couldn't quite clear the railing, so Falk met him halfway, clasping it near the wrist as they grasped awkwardly. The palm was warm, the back of the hand chilly. The skin seemed as brittle as rice paper, as if it might crumble under pressure. At the wrist Falk felt the tiny bounce of his father's pulse. He squeezed at the palm and his father squeezed back. Falk cleared his throat.

"Saw Bob Holman at the co-op. Borrowed his truck to get out here."

"What? Big fella like you don't own his own car? And to think of all the junk I've been telling 'em."

"Mr. Holman told me. Living in Europe. Working for the government. Actually you weren't that far off."

He nodded, as if of course that would be the case.

"You got children?"

"Not married. Like you figured."

"Where you living?"

"Washington."

Gitmo was too complicated to explain. Besides, he didn't want to say the word aloud, as if it might make him detectable on some radar.

"Government job?"

"Yeah. FBI." He had already said too much for his own good. But the old man had earned at least that much of the truth. "I'm a special agent, Dad. I speak Arabic, do a lot of interrogations. I'm pretty much in demand these days."

"Knew it." He beamed. "Damn well knew all that reading would pay off. You were too smart to keep going out on the water 'til you drowned."

If he only knew. But that was a story for later.

"I take it you're not doing much fishing anymore."

The old man wheezed, the laugh shortly turning to a cough, which he was able to master by bending slightly forward, subduing a rattle deep in his chest.

"Not in years." He was hoarse again. "You seen the boat?"

"Yesterday, when I got in. Grass is growing up through the hull."

He nodded, not surprised.

"She hasn't been out since '98. You were right to leave like that, you know, taking off when you did. I was a mess, no help to anybody. I just wish you'd told me later. Just an address, you know? A note to let me know you were okay."

"I know. I'm sorry."

"No. *I'm* sorry." Then his dad nodded again, an acceptance of the way things were, an absolution, done with a grace and dignity that had always resided in the man, but that Falk had forgotten after witnessing so many moments of rage or stupor.

"So where are Henry and Lucy?" Falk asked. It felt strange saying the names of his brother and sister, as if they were speaking of the long dead, or quoting some tale of ancient history. His father shook his head, and the tears came in earnest now, rolling slowly down the stretched cheeks.

"Don't know, son. All of 'em's gone. Your brother, your sister, your ma. Drove 'em all away, me and my drinking. You're the only one that's ever come back."

"It's okay, Dad. I'm not leaving again. Not for good anymore."

Falk reached across the railing and took hold of his hand again. The old man seemed to settle back against his pillow.

"I tried. I know you never thought I did, but I did try. Just never hard enough."

"I know, Dad. It's okay. All that's over now."

His father nodded, sinking deeper into the pillow, now that they were both absolved. A certain ease crept into his features. He squeezed Falk's hand, then relaxed his grip.

"So how long have you been in this place?"

"Oh. Three years, a little longer. They'd know for sure out front. Wasn't so bad for a while. But once I stopped walking, well . . . things haven't been too good lately, is all. And the weight, I'm practically down to nothing." Then he grinned inexplicably. "You know, when I was born, the doctor out here used to charge for his deliveries by the pound. My mother always used to complain about it, because she said I was an eight-pounder, so I was extra. Maybe if they charged by the pound here I could save the state some money?"

The laugh returned, and with it the slight wheeze. But he never took his eyes off Falk, and Falk was pretty sure he knew why.

"You're dying, aren't you?"

He nodded, no tears this time, the mariner facing the storm head on.

"Bob tell you that?"

"Didn't need to."

“Cancer. They say it’s moving pretty fast. They don’t figure it will be too much longer.”

“Excuse me, Mr. Falk.” They both looked up in answer to the nurse’s voice, but she had come for his dad, strolling into the room with a rustle of white cotton.

“Oh, you’ve got a visitor today! How nice. Sorry to interrupt, but it’s time for your bath and your medication.”

“This is my son, Revere. Works for the FBI, so watch yourself.”

Falk smiled, glad to have supplied him with one little boast for the day.

“I’ll come back later,” he said, as the nurse wheeled the bed from the room while an orderly towed the IV stands. Entering the hallway they looked like attendants to a barge headed slowly down a river.

“Make it tomorrow,” his father said. “I won’t be worth too much by the time they’re done with me.”

The nurse nodded knowingly from the opposite side of the bed, affirming the wisdom of his father’s advice.

“Okay, then,” he answered. But by that time the wheels of the bed were clattering down the hall.

Falk strolled numbly back to the reception desk, not quite convinced the moment was real. He glanced over his shoulder in time to see the bed disappear around the far corner. Then he swallowed hard, collecting himself. He was already wondering how he would pass the time until tomorrow morning, and he stopped at the desk to leave the name of his B&B in case they needed to reach him. The receptionist looked up, as if she’d almost forgotten something, and said, “Oh, and Mr. Falk, there’s a man here in the lobby to see you.”

“To see *me*?”

“Yes, sir, right over there.” She pointed shyly, as if it were impolite, keeping her hand below the counter, but Falk didn’t dare turn around. Maybe he should say he’d forgotten something and head straight back down the hallway. Climb out the window of his father’s empty room. Peel back yet another screen to dash off into the woods. Steal yet another boat to strike out for God knows where. Isle au Haut, maybe, or Swans Island. But what would be the point, now that they had him in their sights?

So instead he took a deep breath, turned, and saw the round face of Paco looking up from a magazine, smiling like a mischievous old friend.

CHAPTER THIRTY-THREE

We are both, as they say in your military, absent without leave, yes?"

"I can only speak for myself," Falk said. "But how did you know where to . . . ?"

"Please." Paco thrust out a hand like a traffic cop. "Don't ask me to reveal trade secrets. And let's order some food. It would be uncivilized to discuss these matters on an empty stomach."

They were seated in a corner booth at the Fisherman's Friend. Paco had insisted on buying lunch before "doing any business," as he put it. He had then climbed into his rented Ford and followed Bob Holman's noisy truck back into Stonington.

On the way Falk decided that Harry must have tipped the Cubans to his escape. So much for keeping a lid on gossip at the base. But how had Paco known he would come here? And if a Cuban in Miami could figure it out, then surely the Americans would.

They were sprawled across the booth's vinyl seats like two laborers on lunch hour when a waitress approached with pen and pad.

"Aren't fried clams supposed to be good?" Paco asked, chattering away as if he did this all the time. His mood was contagious, and Falk decided to enjoy it while he could.

"That or the lobster roll. Can't miss, either way."

"The clams, then." Paco snapped shut the menu.

"Make it two."

Unreal. First, a conversation with his dying father whom he hadn't seen in twenty years. Now a chatty lunch with the little Cuban who had turned his life inside out.

"It must have been nice growing up here."

"We didn't eat like this very often."

"I mean the forests, the coastline. It's very beautiful. But I guess the winters can be pretty bad."

"Sometimes it was pretty bad all year long."

Paco mulled that a moment.

"Is that why you lied to the Marine recruiter and told him you were an orphan?"

"Please. Don't ask me to reveal trade secrets."

Paco smiled. He seemed to be enjoying himself immensely.

"So what do you want from me?" Falk asked.

Paco first took a long sip of iced tea.

"I think that is a question we should both be asking, because we are in position to help each other."

"Help each other? My next stop might be Canada. After that, who knows? But if you're on the run, too, maybe you'd like to come along."

"No. No more running. I meant help so we can both stay. Do you remember our conversation on the boat? Giving a little to get a little?"

"Yes."

"That would be a good start. Except this time you would go first."

"I seem to recall going first last time. Maybe you could start it off by telling me a little more about who you're working for."

"Since yesterday? The day I came home to find a couple of spooks from Havana snooping around my apartment? Since then I have been working for myself. I am a Nation of One. But you're certainly welcome to apply for citizenship."

Somehow, Falk believed him. Maybe because Paco's concept of nationhood sounded all too familiar, not just with regard to himself but everyone he had been working with at Gitmo—an entire archipelago of entrepreneurs in business mostly for themselves; a struggle of agency versus agency, plotter against plotter, and may the best scoundrel win.

"Okay, then," he answered at last, biting into a fried clam. A juicy bouquet of brine and grease spurted sweetly onto his tongue. "I'll play along. Let's start with a week ago last Wednesday, with that Yemeni you wanted me to take care of, Adnan al-Hamdi."

Paco nodded.

"You're right," he said. "These clams are great. Go ahead, I'm listening."

Falk told his story of the past ten days, while Paco supplied intriguing details from his own perspective along the way. Once or twice it occurred to Falk that maybe Paco wasn't really on the run; maybe he was still working for the Cubans. But Falk didn't care anymore. It was a relief to get the story out in the open and off his chest. And by the time they had polished off the clams, some fries, and a couple of huge wedges of pie—Falk had coconut cream, Paco apple—he had come to a firm conclusion about their unlikely alliance.

"I've decided," he said, wiping his mouth with a napkin, "that we've both lost our minds."

"You may be right. But there is also the possibility that we have both come to our senses."

"I like your version better, but I'm not convinced."

"A very rational response. Which only goes to support my position."

At that point they had little choice but to laugh and pay the bill, Falk leaving the tip while Paco went to the register. He wasn't yet sure what to make of this, other than to be relieved that he now had an ally—or a partner in crime, as the case may be.

Confessionals completed, they left their vehicles in the parking lot and walked down to the wharf while discussing their next move. They set off on School Street, moving downhill into town. It was sunny, with a crisp blue sky and temperatures already in the high seventies, but Paco, a creature of the Caribbean, rubbed his bare arms as if to ward off a chill. Falk, on the other hand, was already comfortable here, a chameleon changing back from tropical turquoise to a cool northern blue.

"They'll find you—or us, I guess—within a couple of days, you know," Paco said. "Our people in Jamaica say that federal agents were all over the docks in some place called Port Antonio. They impounded a fishing boat with a Haitian registry, then started talking to cab-drivers and hoteliers."

"When was this?"

The news shook him up, although he supposed he shouldn't be surprised.

"Yesterday. Midafternoon."

"They must have found the Navy's boat over in Haiti. Poor old guy. I guess by now they'll have my cover name."

"Ned Morris of Manchester?"

"Thanks for that, by the way. How'd you know I'd need it?"

"I didn't. It just seemed like a worthy precaution, considering where you were and what you knew."

"So you've been in touch with Havana. What happened to the Nation of One?"

"Only with my boss. The one man I still trust. I called and left a message on a beeper in New Jersey, and he actually called back on an unsecured line. That should tell you all you need to know about how desperate he is. He'll protect me as long as he can."

"And how long will that be?"

"A day or two. Then the ones on the fringes will come looking for me."

"What will you do then?"

"My boss thinks I should turn myself in. 'Defect' would be the operative term. He thinks that's the one way to stop this mess that's brewing. Warn your people about the 'cabal,' as you called it. These people on both sides who are so eager to bring on a little scrap."

"Insane."

"It's what always happens when both sides are sure they will win."

"Then maybe we should both go to Canada. But we'll have to take your car. Take Holman's truck and we'll be deaf by the time we reach the border."

"Running isn't the answer," Paco said. "Between the two of us, we have the one thing everyone wants most."

"Information?"

"And not just about your Arab friend. About everybody who has become part of this, on both sides."

"According to my supposed friend Ted Bokamper, it's not having the information that's important, it's having it first and then spinning it the way you want."

"He's right. Which is why we have to act now. But we'll need a paper and pencil."

"For what?"

"To compose an e-mail. One for a large viewing audience. Or a small one, if you prefer. You will be the best judge of who can make the best use of it. But it has to be foolproof, with no holes, no gaps. As of right now we are the only ones who know everything, and that's our ticket out of this. Our means of international recognition for our Nation of Two."

"I've got a notebook at the B&B. We could work on it there."

"Sounds good to me."

Reaching the bottom of the hill, they turned right on Main Street along the waterfront. By now the tourist traffic was picking up, and Paco seemed to be enjoying himself, peeking in shop windows and smiling at passersby. Halfway down the block Falk stopped, and put out a hand to stop his companion.

"They're here," he said. "Look."

A black Chevy Suburban was parked in front of the B&B.

"Now there's a giveaway," said Paco, all too familiar with the driving preferences of federal agents. "Look. A man on the porch, talking to the innkeeper."

"And the hell of it is they're almost certainly FBI, probably out of Bangor. Let's get our cars."

"You want some advice? Let the professional take over. I'm used to dealing with your people from the other side. Do as I tell you and we'll make it out of here."

Another insane twist of events. Letting the Cuban run the show so he could duck colleagues who had been trained the same way as Falk.

"Lead the way."

"The first thing we need to do is get you off the street. We might not even make it back to the cars before they start cruising. For all we know they already have a description of your truck."

They turned steeply back uphill, Paco in better shape than Falk would have guessed. One of the first places they passed was the town's barnlike Opera House. A narrow alley ran down the right side, just wide enough for a car.

"Go down there and wait," Paco said, glancing around. "Stay behind the back of the building. I'll bring the car down the alley to get you. If it doesn't look good, take off, and do what you can. But we'll need a fallback."

"The library," Falk said without hesitating.

"On Main Street?"

"Not in Stonington. In Deer Isle, six miles north on 15."

"Good. Out of town completely. We'll make a real pro of you yet. But one question. How would you get there?"

"I'm local. I'll find a way."

It was good enough for Paco, who nodded and took off up the hill. Falk headed down the alley, but his luck almost immediately ran out. No sooner had he rounded the corner at the end of the building than a stage door opened, and three laughing teens in black jeans and T-shirts poured into the small lot. They heaved boxes onto the bed of a pickup, then one of them propped open the stage door and shouted, "Okay, load her up."

It was obvious they would be there a while, and one was already giving Falk a funny look, as if wondering why a grown man was lurking here in the middle of the day. If they saw him get into the Ford they'd have a description of the car, and perhaps also its driver, so Falk walked back the way he'd come. With any luck he would catch Paco driving down the hill.

But he had barely turned around when the hood of the black Suburban nosed into view at the end of the alley. He ducked quickly behind a Dumpster, then watched the big vehicle creep uphill. Paco was right. If Falk had stayed on the streets a minute longer they'd have caught him. The driver was a woman, meaning the man they'd seen at the B&B was probably making the rounds on foot. He wondered if they had reinforcements, or local help. Whatever the case, Falk didn't dare go uphill now. Nor was he letting the kids behind the Opera House get another look at him.

He took off downhill and then turned left in order to avoid Main Street. He was on a driveway that led to a row of B&Bs. Maybe by cutting across a few lots he could work his way to Highway 15, then hitch a ride. No, he'd be a sitting duck. Better to stop somewhere first and calm down, plan his next move. Although if the agent on foot was going door-to-door, he'd still be trapped.

A woman's voice called out from behind.

"Revere? Revere Falk?"

Shit. It was over.

Bracing himself to run, he turned to see the old classmate he'd recognized the night before at dinner, the one with three kids and a few extra pounds, and now her name came to him like a benediction.

"Jenny? Jenny Kinlaw?"

"I'll be damned. You do remember. I thought you were eyeing me last night, but with Jeffrey running wild I never had time to come say hi."

"It's been a long time." He glanced past her, feeling the need to get out of sight.

"Tell me about it. But you look great. Where you living now?"

"Washington."

"Ooh. Sounds important."

"Not really. What about you?" He had to get moving. An idea popped into his head.

"I'm right up the hill here, behind my mom's B&B. Was just on my way home. Two more hours of freedom before day care lets out."

"Jenny, I know this will sound weird all of a sudden like this, but I'm in kind of a bind. My car's in the shop and I'm supposed to be meeting someone out at the library in Deer Isle in about five minutes, and was wondering . . ."

"If I could give you a ride? Sure." Something in her eager tone suggested she was taking this as a come-on, but in any event it had worked. Her red pickup was just down the lane, and he climbed in with a sigh of relief, while hoping he wouldn't have to duck under the dashboard if the Suburban passed.

"So, are you married?" Jenny asked as they turned north on Highway 15.

"No. Guess I don't have to ask you that, huh?"

"Well, you do now. Divorced two months now."

"Oh. Sorry."

"Don't be. Steve was a rat."

"Okay."

"I put the kids to bed around nine, if you want to come by later."

"Sure." Anything for a ride, as long as he could last another four miles. Maybe by then they'd be engaged. But she seemed to sense his nervousness, and perhaps she attributed it to her forwardness. Whatever the case, she steered the conversation back to small talk, and filled him in on the fortunes and misfortunes of classmates he hadn't seen in twenty years. When she ran out of names, she zeroed back in on Falk.

"I was thinking it was kind of funny to be meeting somebody at the library, but you always were kind of into books, huh?"

"Guess so."

"So are you gay, then?"

"What?"

"Are you gay?"

"Uh, no."

"Oh. Good. Then come on by sometime before you leave town."

Mercifully they had just pulled into the small parking lot by the white frame library.

"I'll do that," he said, offering his manliest smile as he unlatched the door. "And thanks for the ride."

"Anytime after nine."

"Got it."

There was no sign of Paco's Ford, which made Falk a little anxious. But when he stepped inside his emotions gave way to nostalgia.

What bowled him over most was the smell, the same musty blend of cloth bindings and old paper, and the oaken shelves and big reading table to the side where he had spent so many quiet hours of refuge. Then there was the silence, with its own hermetic quality, especially if you sat by the back window, watching the play of sunlight on the water in the tidal cove. Some things had changed. The old clock with its loud ticking was gone, replaced by a big gray wall model that hummed. There was now an Internet kiosk, and a table displaying the latest acquisitions. Most were titles from the best-seller list.

"Can I help you?"

Here was another change. The librarian was a trim woman who looked to be in her forties. No relation, he supposed, to Miss Clarkson, stern but gentle, who had always let him stay as long as he liked, as if quietly aware of all the hell breaking loose just up the road.

"No, thank you. I'm meeting someone for a little research."

"Well, just let me know."

"Thanks."

Paco's car pulled up outside a few minutes later, with no one following. He looked worried until he came through the door and saw Falk. Then he broke into a huge grin and nodded to the librarian.

"So you made it," he whispered, respecting the sanctity of the place.

"Barely. Got lucky. Where to next?"

"The nearest Internet café, I guess. Send our message, then wait for the dust to settle."

Falk asked the librarian if she knew of any likely spots.

"That's a tough one. Blue Hill, maybe? Bangor for sure, but that's a ways. Of course, you could always use this one." She gestured toward the kiosk. Falk felt like an idiot.

"Could we send an e-mail?"

"Long as you have a server account."

"Let's get to work."

For the next hour they sat at the big oak table laboring over a few sheets of notebook paper provided by the librarian, writing with the stubby yellow pencils you find in libraries everywhere. Somewhere beneath the table, Falk knew, were his initials, scratched into place with just such a pencil a quarter century ago. He wished he had time for a peek, but maybe by now someone had sanded them away. Better, perhaps, to just pretend they were still down there.

The work went quickly, and they made a pretty fair team. Once they had settled on the main points and overall thrust, they moved to the computer keyboard and Falk began to type. He began with a brief history of his work as an unofficial double agent for Endler—Falk owned the info, therefore Falk applied his own spin; if nothing else he was a quick learner—and their epistle continued with Falk's version of the recent doings at Gitmo involving Fowler, Bo, Endler, and Van Meter. He spared no evidence of Ludwig's murder and left no misdeed unrecorded. Supplementing all this were Paco's findings, which dovetailed nicely. They then offered a joint conclusion that rogue elements of U.S. and Cuban intelligence seemed determined to bring about a confrontation by misusing the above findings.

For the memo's pièce de résistance (at least, as far as the Bureau's interests were concerned), they detailed the plans of Cuban Directorate of Intelligence operative Gonzalo Rubiero, code name "Paco," to defect to the United States, effective immediately, in exchange for citizenship and confidential relocation. Falk then briefly explained his own means of escape from Guantánamo by saying that the actions of the above conspirators had left him no choice.

It was no masterpiece, but it certainly packed a wallop.

"Anything you want to add?" he asked Paco. After all this time, he couldn't yet get used to the idea of calling the man Gonzalo.

"Looks finished to me."

"It's as good as we're going to do with this much time. Now the question is who we send it to. My boss, or his superiors? Maybe the director himself?"

"The way I see it," Paco said, "it's like choosing between fried clams and the lobster roll. You can't miss, either way. But if you are hungry enough, why not have them all?"

Good advice. Falk typed in the names for all three. But when it came time to send it on its way, he hesitated.

"What's wrong?" Paco asked.

"I was just remembering who we're dealing with. Thinking about what they've already done to the few people who've gotten in their way. We need some backup."

He clicked back to the "cc" line and plugged in an e-mail address for a reporter he had dealt with in the Washington bureau of the *New York Times.* To be on the safe side, he also sent a copy to a reporter from the *Washington Post.* Nothing like the heat of competition to ensure critical mass. He didn't exactly mind that the Bureau would see those addresses, either.

Then he took a deep breath, clicked on the Send button, and sat back in the chair. They watched the blue line streak across the screen, a flare fired in distress from their leaking little raft. Now it was only a question of who would reach them first, their rescuers or their pursuers.

"What now?" Paco asked.

"I thought we might get some coffee. We can come back in an hour and check for replies."

"Sounds like a plan."

Falk slapped his palms on his thighs and stood, a little stiff after the intense session at the keyboard. He supposed he was still weary from the long cruise across rough seas.

"Oh, my," the librarian exclaimed, glancing out a window, "this is as busy as we've been all week."

Two more customers had just emerged from a familiar black Suburban. One, a woman in a navy skirt and white blouse, peered through the window of Paco's Ford. The other, a man in a polo and khakis—Falk knew the uniform well—was already coming up the steps.

"I guess this means no coffee," Paco said.

"I'm sure they'll have some at the office in Bangor." Falk sighed as the door opened, bringing with it the noise of the highway and the cry of a seagull. "Welcome to your new life, Paco. Hope it's what you really wanted."

EPILOGUE

THE STORY NEVER MADE the papers. Too many denials and too few confirmations.

There was also the matter of the so-called Gitmo spy ring to divert the media's attention. Two more military interpreters were arrested in the week following Falk's escape, and even though all but a few minor charges were eventually dropped, it captured the public's attention for weeks.

But four months later Falk and Gonzalo were still free men, which Falk supposed was victory enough for their Nation of Two.

Gonzalo's debriefing took up most of that time, leading to yet another flurry of deportations from Cuban interest sections in Washington and New York. The Bureau then relocated Gonzalo under a new name. Just as well, since Falk would always think of him as Paco. Falk asked around about possible whereabouts, but no one would admit to knowing anything, although one agent dropped strong hints that it was out west, perhaps near Scottsdale. Apparently a woman had joined him, and Falk wondered if it might be the mysterious Elena until someone offered the tidbit that she was Venezuelan.

Falk still had his job, at least in name, even if the Bureau had stripped him of his security clearance and stuck him behind a desk in the Hoover Building where he could be watched at all hours.

There were casualties, of course.

One was Adnan, swallowed into the belly of a transport plane the day after Falk reached Navassa Island. The best Falk had been able to determine, based on covert communications with Tyndall and a few others sympathetic to his predicament, Adnan had vanished into a Yemeni dungeon for a lifetime of either torment or neglect, hidden away as one of those minor national embarrassments who could do harm only if allowed back into the light of day.

Whenever Falk thought of Adnan now—an almost daily occurrence—he remembered the propaganda poster taped up in the interrogation booth, the stylized photo of the grieving mother wishing her son would come home.

Falk's father died three weeks after their reunion, without getting to see his son a second time. The debriefers told Falk they were too busy to spare him, although he was able to phone a few times. They did let him out for the funeral. It took only a day to settle the estate. Someone appraised the lot the trailer was on, and by the time the funeral home had totted up the charges both parties agreed to call it even if Falk signed over the deed. His father was buried on a hill with a view of the island's old granite quarry, where he had worked his first job when he was young and single and hadn't yet put out to sea.

But that was in late August. Now it was a Wednesday in early December, and as Falk sat at his desk in Washington opening mail, another name from among the wounded leaped out at him from a return address atop the pile:

"Doris Ludwig, Buxton, MI."

He carefully tore open the envelope, as if the fragile remnants of her grief might spill out and shatter on the desk. Her handwriting was neat and plain, the earnest penmanship of someone taking care not to ask for too much.

Dear Mr. Falk,

After all this time, it pains me to say that I have been unable to get anyone to answer my many questions about my husband's death at Guantánamo. I was hoping to enlist your help, since you were the investigator who called me last August. A Lieutenant Carrington from the Judge Advocate General's office tells me that you are no longer assigned to the case, and he repeated their earlier conclusion that Earl's misfortune, as he called it, has officially been ruled a "death by misadventure" due to a boating accident in an unauthorized craft.

But after speaking with you, and also with Ed Sample at my husband's bank, I am not satisfied that the Army has adequately looked into matters. May I ask if you are satisfied with their findings? I don't remember your words exactly, but you said something like, "I'll stay on top of it." So I guess that is what I'm asking you to do now. My e-mail address is below, in case you wish to respond in that manner.

Yours truly,

Doris Ludwig

P.S.—This is NOT about money. The Army has been more than generous in that respect. But at this point I no longer know who else to turn to.

So they'd paid her off, but not enough to buy her silence. Well, good for you, Doris, even if there was little Falk could do in his current position. That much had been clear only two days ago, when Bokamper had broken a long silence to phone and suggest a meeting. They had burned each other pretty badly, but Bo sounded interested in starting over, or at least coming to terms. So, they settled on a bar in Georgetown—no starched tablecloths this time—and agreed on 9 p.m.

Bo, who had never arrived on time and probably never would, walked in with his usual swagger.

"How's your gal?"

"We're hanging in there," Falk said. "She asks about you all the time, of course."

"I'll bet. But I'm glad to hear you're still together. I guess she proved me wrong."

She hadn't, actually. Pam and he still wrote every week, but the passionate tone of their earliest letters had cooled. Falk supposed distance was partly to blame. She was now stationed at Fort Bragg, just far enough to make a weekend drive impractical. But Falk suspected that Bo's earlier hunch was closer to the heart of the problem. Once she learned of his past, she seemed to step back a little, as if trying to decide if this sort of man could ever fit comfortably with her own ambitions. They had twice planned to meet for a weekend, but both times a last-minute assignment came up. At her end, not his. Falk hadn't given up, but he was beginning to wonder if maybe she wanted him to.

"Never got to tell you how impressed I was with the way you made it out of there," Bo said. "I mean, I knew you were a sailor, but Jesus, a tropical storm?"

"Tropical depression. Downgraded almost the minute I put in. No need to make it a bigger deal than it was."

"Whatever you say, Captain Ahab."

"Besides, Endler is the real escape artist. I hear he's getting all sorts of credit now for having averted a major embarrassment."

Endler's two main coconspirators hadn't come out of the affair too shabbily, either. One, a deputy secretary of state, probably got the worst of it, receiving an early retirement with a nice pension. The other, a ranking civilian at the Defense Intelligence Agency with a tendency for bombast, had been more problematic, until some bright light came up with the idea of turning him loose on the United Nations as the next U.S. ambassador. Confirmation was pending.

"What can I say?" Bo shrugged. "Another reason the Doc's so great to work for."

"I might agree, to a point, if he hadn't set that slimeball Van Meter free."

"Van Meter's not out of the woods yet. You watch. He'll get active time and a dishonorable discharge."

"But not on a murder charge."

"Not without the whole mess coming out in a court-martial. You take what you can get."

"Meaning he'll do a year or two, then join some security firm that will let him go shoot Iraqis for three times what the Army would have paid."

"It's a growth industry. Maybe you should get your résumé out."

"I've considered it. At least the Arabic's still marketable."

They talked a while longer. Drank a few beers. Falk was genuinely interested in hearing about the wife and kids, and Bo seemed genuinely interested in telling him.

But not until they paid the tab did Bo finally broach the question that had hovered between them throughout the conversation.

"So what are we now, Falk? Friends, maybe?"

"Why don't we leave it at comrades in arms? You proved that much, I guess, back at the marina."

"I can live with that for now."

"Yeah, but can you still sleep at night?"

"Hey, you know me."

"All too well."

Bo must have taken the remark in the best possible light, because he smiled. Or maybe not, because he then launched into a short lecture that Falk later figured was the message he had intended to deliver all along.

"Something like this never really dies, you know."

"Something like what?" Did he mean friendship?

"This whole mess down in Cuba. After a while people will stop talking about it, but that won't mean it's dead. It'll just be in remission. Like a tumor. Do something to stir it up and it'll be as malignant as ever."

"Are you warning me?"

"The warning's for everybody. Me included. So just lie low. Let it rest. 'Cause it's just not worth it. Start poking around again and you might wake up one morning in your very own Gitmo, one of those places without a name where no one knows the latitude, the longitude, or even the time of day."

Bo was smiling, as if to say this was all hyperbole, or some kind of a joke. Falk didn't see the humor, and said nothing.

"C'mon, man, you don't think I'm serious, do you? It's not like I'd ever help them pull off something like that."

"Maybe you wouldn't need to."

"Like I said. You're the one who controls your future. Just don't give them an excuse to make it otherwise. Is that too much to ask, one friend to another?"

Bo smiled again, then held out his big mitt for a farewell shake. Falk gave a halfhearted wave and walked out of the bar without looking back.

And now, with Doris Ludwig's letter staring up from the desk, he finally saw her plea for help for what it really was—an opportunity to either poke at the tumor or leave it in remission, perhaps for good.

Falk drafted six different replies, striving each time for that delicate balance between compassion and passing the buck. In one he even implied that perhaps something hadn't been on the up-and-up about the investigation, and urged her to keep digging.

Then he imagined her flying out to Washington, using her kids' Christmas money so she could spend a few days traipsing down the marble corridors of Congress, shunted into undersized and overcrowded anterooms with earnest young staffers who would nod and take notes and promise action, while striking that delicate balance between compassion and passing the buck. Then they would forget her name and face by the time they had downed their afternoon lattes.

It was with that despairing image in mind that he logged on to the Internet, clicked over to the server for his personal e-mail account and called up the menu for the "Sent" basket. And there it was, still alive, even if buried beneath four months of other correspondence, less like a tumor than a piece of unexploded ordnance. He supposed Paco wouldn't mind if he fired this bombshell of theirs on one last flight of fancy, so he clicked on the Forward prompt and typed in Doris Ludwig's e-mail address. Then he added a brief preface:

Dear Mrs. Ludwig,

These are the facts as I know them. As you will note from the original date and the listed recipients, the relevant authorities have already been notified. You are welcome to pursue further action, but I can tell you from personal experience that your efforts will be likely only to produce further grief for you and those you love. But that decision is yours, and yours alone. At the very least you are entitled to know these things.

Sincerely,
Revere Falk

After hitting the Send button he finally relaxed, wishing for a moment that Paco had been there to enjoy it with him.

Then he decided he had better get to work on that résumé.

ACKNOWLEDGMENTS

MANY THANKS to Torin Nelson, Mark Jacobson, and numerous others who would rather not to be identified by name, for offering helpful insights on the workings of interrogations at Guantánamo, and also for their observations on the strange atmospherics of the place. And without the tireless work of the American Civil Liberties Union in prying loose hundreds of Camp Delta documents through the Freedom of Information Act, I would have missed out on many valuable insights.

Thanks also to Lt. Col. Pamela Hart, the Army public affairs officer in charge during my trip to Guantánamo in the summer of 2003 for the *Baltimore Sun*, as well as to the many officers and enlisted personnel who agreed to speak with me then. Although Pentagon rules greatly limited my access and freedom of movement, the soldiers who assisted me were at all times as courteous and professional.

Several employees of the FBI, who shall remain nameless at their request, were invaluable in educating me on the workings of Cuban intelligence agents in the United States.

The descriptions of all things nautical in this book would have been hopelessly at sea without the help of my dad, Bill Fesperman, who could outsail Revere Falk. Thanks also to my good friend Chip Pearsall for insights from his Coast Guard days.

And, for those who were wondering, yes, those "OPSEC Corner" excerpts from Camp Delta's weekly newspaper, *The Wire*, are authentic.